The Storyteller's
Granddaughter

Also by Margaret Redfern and available from Honno

Flint

The Storyteller's Granddaughter

by

Margaret Redfern

HONNO MODERN FICTION

First published by Honno

'Ailsa Craig', Heol y Cawl, Dinas Powys, Wales, CF64 4AH

1 2 3 4 5 6 7 8 9 10

ISBN 978-1909983-01-4

Published with the financial support of the Welsh Books Council.

Cover design: Rebecca Ingleby
Text design: Elaine Sharples
Printed in Wales by Gomer Press

In memory of:

Annette: 1943 – 2010
Dave: 1958 – 2011
Graham: 1940 – 2013
Nigel: 1949 – 2014

And to both of you, of course

Acknowledgements

- to the writers of books that have delighted, instructed and inspired me

- to the Internet and its fabulous electronic book-hoard

- to the staff of Lincoln Central Library for their generous help

- to all at Honno for their patience, help and guidance

- to the Woad Centre, East Dereham, Norfolk, for a splendid workshop

- to the people of Antalya, Konya and Beyşehir for their many kindnesses to a stranger

Hereford: November 1326

1

This sorwe is more
Than mannis muth may telle
(Anon, 13thC)

This is how it was. This is what he could never forget. This was his remembering. *Blackest night, and him choking, choking. His eyes squeezed tight shut but still he couldn't shut out the Devil's face, blood clotted, bulging eyes blood red, and the devil himself lamenting and howling. My bowels, my bowels. Entrails wrenched from the living body writhing like bloodied snakes. Oh the stench, the stench and the she-wolf devouring them, cramming them into her open maw and the faces, grinning and leering, bawling their glee, and the screaming coming from that mask of a face…no man could make such moaning.*

Voices out of the suffocating black…

'Shut it, you.'

'What's to do? Is it murder?'

'It's my sleep he's murdering. Get 'im out of 'ere.'

She's not a wolf – she's a devil.

'I'll clout thee if tha doesna shut it.'

I saw her. I saw the devil feasting on flesh.

Hard knuckles on head bone.

Rough hands in hard hold over mouth. Gagging, gagging.

'For dear God's sake, he'll have us all killed. These days, there's daggers in men's smiles.'

'*Qu'est ce qui se passe?*'

'Nowt's 'appened. Nightmare is all.'

'Sweet Mary, that's all we need – that yappy little Frenchie'll 'ave us all locked up.'

'Or worse.'

'Do something, Tom. You're 'is father. Sort your brat out.'

'*Dit donc, bandes de bittes, qu'arrive?*'

'It's nowt – guts' ache is all. Stuffed 'is face at the feast and now 'is belly's suffering, little swine.'

And that other voice. A boy's voice, low, calm.

'Safe now. Safe.'

Hand stroking hair, wiping away sweat, smoothing away fear.

Safe now. Sleep.

That was his remembering. That was what he couldn't forget.

Anatolia: late summer 1336

2

What do they do with the old full moons?
They cut them up into pieces,
crumble them and make stars.
(Nasreddin Hoca, 13thC)

Every winter they dreamed of returning to the summer pasture. They were warm enough in this place where the ancient people used to live. They used the shaped stones to make the winter quarters sound. Their hearths were warm against winter storms. Their animals were well housed and there was food enough, for man and beast alike. But they longed for the time when the snow melted from the mountains, and the rivers rushed through gorges swollen with meltwater. They talked of it, while the rain beat down and white-capped waves tore at the shore. They crammed together in the smoky, steamy winter houses and the old ones told stories of past times, of the great warriors, of things that happened long before the girl was born, long before she and Nene came to live with the wanderers, the *yürük*.

There was a time long ago when the little tribe had belonged to the great tribe of the *sarıkeçilis,* but there was a quarrel between two friends, friends who had grown up together as brothers, who had fought together and hunted together and herded together. They swore to be loyal to each other beyond death. But when they grew to be young men they loved the same girl and one spilt the blood of the other and so had to leave the tribe. That was the law. Besides, had he stayed he would himself have been killed. So he left, taking his fought-for bride, and brothers and mother, and a share of the animals, and so began their tribe.

The girl thought she had just a memory of him when he was an old, old man, and his wife was a wizened face atop a scrawny body with wisps of hair – grey as smoke – twisted into skinny plaits. The women said she was beautiful when she was a young girl but the girl found it hard to believe. But that was when she was very young.

When the night was quiet and it was just her and Nene in the dim firelight, the old woman told the young one the story of her own long life, and how she met the girl's grandfather, and what happened in that magic year. And the story of the girl's mother, and the girl's story, and how they came to live with the tribe. All this she told in the quiet nights, and all the nights blurred into one, and all the winters.

Spring returned and the high valleys bloomed scarlet with anemone and poppy and pale purple with crocus, and white daisies with yellow eyes waved through grass that was lush and fresh. Then they left the mosquito-ridden coast lands, winding up and up the gorge through the corridors of rock and in the shadow of rock, through pine-scented air, higher and higher. Below them was the glistening river, brown as a horse and as strong, pulling and sucking at the trunks and bending the boughs of trees. Ahead of them was the tight flock of sheep – fat long tails and rumps waggling – hemmed in by black, curly-haired goats, with the shepherds and sturdy dogs pushing them on.

The donkeys were loaded with belongings: bedding and *kilims* and the *saç* for baking bread and the stout beams for the loom for carpet weaving and the spindles used for spinning goat hair and sheep's wool into yarn. There were the cauldrons used for cooking, the ewers and wooden bowls and copper bowls, the samovars and the big brass serving trays. There were the wooden chests for storing cloth, and the leather containers for water and others for butter making. There were the chickens in wicker carriers and the last sacks of corn. What the donkeys couldn't carry, the women carried on their backs, together with the babies – the toddlers too when they were tired out with the climb, as the girl was carried when she was a child. The men rode the fleet, sturdy mountain horses that were descended, so they said, from the ancient horses of the great plateau far from here.

All of it, clanking and jingling and creaking and hooves sharp on rock and bleating and barking and braying and squawking and shouting and chattering and laughter because all were happy to be on their way back to the *yayla*, to the summer camp, though they were quiet later in the day because the way was hard and steep and they carried heavy burdens and the little ones fretted because they were weary.

Every year they made their camp in the same flat stretch of land sheltered by craggy mountain sides that were backed by range after range, all blurring into blue.

They placed the tents carefully, like the swift ships the girl had once seen in Silifke harbour, in rows, sailing the grassy plateau. Some families lived in tents that were like upturned boats, with ribs of wood covered in black felt, but she and Nene lived in a black tent with its poles proud against the sky and wooden battens tethering it to the ground. They made their hearth and the platforms at opposite ends for the beds and stores; they spread *kilims* and cushions where they would gaze at the green and gold summer world through the framework of the black tent.

Here too, straggling up one side of the valley walls, were the ruins of another world, another time. Springs bubbled from the ground and gushed over pebbles and there were the cut and shaped stones ready to use if they had need of them. They used fluted pillars, end on end, to dam the stream for the grazing flock. The girl used to look at them, those old stones lichen-blurred with words she could not read when she was young. There were marble figures draped in marble cloth, all of them taller than she was. Paved streets and blocks of carved stone bleached by the sun lay half buried in undergrowth; whole streets of stone and stones that were once houses were tumbled now in heaps and cicadas sang loudest here, as if they were the souls of the dead. Who had lived here? If this was their summer dwelling, it was a place of miracles. If she climbed the steep-stepped half-circle in the ruins, right to the highest, loftiest, top-most point, on a clear day she could see the glittering blue of the sea far below. She liked sitting there, so high up with the mountain peaks travelling across the land and the lines of the tents lying at anchor below her.

When summer ended in the mountains, the tribe left, winding back down the mountain pass, down through the gorge to the coast where summer still stayed, to prepare their winter quarters once again. One year, winter ambushed them and frost and biting wind drove them back down the mountain. The girl loved that time, and the whole silent world of the high valleys, and the icy chill of morning and the frozen ground and mist hanging heavy and their breath spilling more mist.

But the summer months were as precious. At night, the sky was crammed with stars. 'As the roof of our tent covers our own little world so the roof of the sky covers the whole world,' Nene told her, 'and we are all part of that greater whole. All – men, women, children, fish and fowl and creeping things and creatures that go on four legs – all have their own stories. Stories within stories, never-ending, as infinite as these stars we gaze on.'

When the whole camp was silent and sleeping, she and Nene would sit outside under the sky blanket and stargaze.

'If you listen, you might hear the stars singing,' Nene told her. When she was very young, she would sit very still and very quiet and she thought then it was true and she could hear them, faint and far away, like the hardly heard singing of precious metal.

Once when she was a child she asked Nene, 'Where does the fat old moon go?'

'They cut it into little pieces, child, and make it into stars.'

The girl believed her. She was Nene, her grandmother, and the wisest woman in the whole world. Her eyes were grey as the grey-eyed goddess; the girl's eyes were deep brown flecked with gold and she wished she had Nene's eyes and that way she had of looking into your very soul. Nene said she had her grandfather's eyes and sometimes she would gaze into them and sigh and pinch the girl's cheek.

The girl had lived with her grandmother for as long as she had memory. It was Nene who taught her the names of the stars in the vast sky, and how to travel by their direction. She taught her the uses of plants for medicine, and the best way of making fire. She taught her how to track the wild animals, silently, scarcely breathing, making herself invisible. She taught her the ways of the seasons and the routes that were passable in summer but not in winter. She taught her to read the strange marks on the stones and to speak the strange language of the merchant men who travelled across their land from sea to sea and to far distant lands because who knew, she said, when the girl might need to converse in another's tongue?

It was Nene who insisted she was taught to ride bareback and to out-ride any mother's son because who knew, said Nene, when she might need to ride like the wind? The girl could out-shoot them, too, stringing and drawing the curved bow and loosing the arrow with speed and accuracy so they teased her and called her 'Çiçek's daughter', though that was not her mother's name, until she tossed her head and dared them to out-shoot her, dared them to race against her. They named her after the Lady Çiçek of the old stories, who out-rode and out-shot and out-wrestled all the warriors until the hero Bamsi Beyrek of the grey horse came and she was in turn out-raced and his arrow split her own and she was out-wrestled by him and became his promised wife, but he was captured and kept

❀ 11 ❀

prisoner for years before he escaped and returned to her. The girl wondered if there would ever be a Bamsi Beyrek for her, who would match her skill and be her equal. She was very young then.

So many things she learned as the seasons passed and she grew older and Nene grew old, though never to her, not old like the old chief's wispy-haired wife. It was that summer when she saw it, the summer when the moon and the stars shifted and slipped, and the world tumbled. It was as if the pole of the tent cracked and split.

They were toiling up the rocky gorge. Nene stopped to catch for breath and slipped suddenly on the rocks and was slithering away over the edge of the gorge. The girl grabbed at her arm and her fingers closed round bone as frail as a lark's wing. It was easy to haul the old woman back to safety.

'Well done, child,' Nene said quietly, because she was a quiet woman. The girl had never heard her raise her voice. It was then she saw her grandmother's dark face was wrinkled like a walnut. Always a small woman, she had withered into a bundle of skin-wrapped bone. Only her eyes were luminous and mysterious as the morning mist.

And then one night when the fat old moon was cut and crumbled and made into stars she died as quietly as she had lived.

Earlier that evening they had sat under the star blanket.

'Child,' Nene said out of darkness, out of silence, 'I want you to go to your grandfather's country. I want you to find him.'

The girl stayed still as she had been taught, whatever happened, whatever she heard or saw. That had been the hardest lesson and a long time learning because she was by nature impulsive and her face was a mirror of her moods and thoughts. Now she knew the value of the lesson. At last she asked, 'Leave you, Nene?'

'Leaving,' she said. 'What is that? It means nothing. While the heart remembers, there is no leaving.'

'What if he's dead, Nene?'

'He is not dead. I know it.'

The girl believed her. Those grey eyes saw what others could not.

Nene fumbled at her neck, pulling at a leather thong until she held up something between her fingers that gleamed pale in the night. The girl recognised it, remembered the first time Nene had shown it to her. 'This is old,' she had said. 'Very old. Who knows how old? See?' It was a tiny axe of polished jade from the far countries, a miracle of workmanship. The blade was honed and the carefully wrought hole in the gleaming shaft was threaded with leather. 'Your grandfather came by it on his travels. He said the people of the far countries value the jade stone for its many powers and gave it to me as a token of his love. I have kept it with me all these years wondering if he might some day return. It was not to be.' And she had sighed and replaced the tiny axe in the pouch and the pouch inside the neck of her blue tunic, nestling between her breasts and next to her heart.

Now she held it up in the starlight. 'I give it to you, daughter of my daughter,' she said. 'You are more precious to me than any carved jade or gold or jewels. I want you to go to your grandfather's country. Take this with you and it will protect you. Give it to him and he will know you are truly his grandchild.' She fixed those grey eyes on the girl's face. 'Do not stay here to be taken by your father's family and wedded to some sheep-brained oaf. Do you promise?'

What could she do but promise? She took the token of love so skilfully worked, so ancient, so safely kept, and she promised. And that night the old grandmother died as quietly as she had lived with no more than a sigh to say her soul was freed.

The girl sat with her all through that night at the dark of the moon. She watched the stars wheel through the vastness of the firmament. She watched rosy dawn stretch fingers across the morning sky and touch the mountaintops. She watched spiders' webs shimmering in early morning mist, glittering with dewdrop jewels. There was time enough to tell the tribe. For now, this forlorn body belonged to her alone. The stars shifted and slipped, and the world tumbled. Nene, grandmother, teacher, guide, home, lodestar, was dead, and the girl had promised to leave all that was left of their life together to journey to a strange, cold land in search of an old man of whom she knew only stories.

When Nene had thought the girl was old enough to understand, she told how she had stolen her granddaughter away after the mother, her own daughter, had died. The girl's father wasn't a bad man; stubborn and mule-headed, yes, and without the wit to use what sense God had given him. But not a bad man. It was the place where he lived that was bad. The house was carved out of the rock itself and the air had poison in it. It was this that killed the girl's mother when she was too young to die and the girl not a year old. No one would believe that this was true. We have always lived in these cave houses, they said, as our parents and grandparents did. Our people found safety here. You are a foolish woman to believe such things, some said. Others, that it was grief for her daughter that had crazed her mind.

'So I came at night and stole you away to save your life, even if I was too late to save my daughter from her painful death. Such pain she suffered. Nobody told me she was sick with the cave sickness. They kept it from me. But they forgot how news travels in our world. I was living then in my cousin's home. My father and mother were dead and my cousin took me in, but it was not an act of kindness. He was not a kind man. I was more servant than cousin. If I had taken you to that home, he would have sent you back. It didn't matter to him that my daughter was dead.'

It would have saved so much trouble if she had died sooner. Is that what the cousin said or was it what the girl imagined he said and not what Nene told her?

'He said he was lucky to find her any husband at all, let alone a good Christian husband like Pavlo, and that was true enough. That was because I was not married. I had no man, and your mother had no father. My father and then my cousin gave us a home and not many would have done so. My cousin was a rich merchant, like his father, like my father, so he could offer a good bride price and would have found me a willing man but I refused. When Pavlo offered for your mother, she did not refuse. I think she was pleased to leave my cousin's home. It was not a happy one.

'But when your mother died so young – much too young and so painfully – I took you far away from that place. I walked and walked until I could walk no further and I wondered then if I had done right after all, or if it was just another way to die. And then these good people found us and cared for us and we made our home with them.'

A small tribe with no more than nine yurts who gave life back to a woman no longer young and to a girl child; two Christians seeking shelter amongst the children of Mohammed. They were welcomed for their own sakes as much as for Nene's skill in medicine. 'To be of our household there is no need to come from the same blood,' said the old chief. 'Ours is a household of the heart. Whoever is of our heart is of our household.' That was the Sufi faith.

Of course, the family found them. News travels in the merchant world. That's how fortunes are made. But they were content to let it be. 'Until I am dead,' Nene said. 'That is the agreement we made. When I am dead they will come to claim you.'

But that day had seemed far off and the girl forgot it. And now Nene was dead. The girl wanted to bury her in the earth of the ancient basilica on the mountainside. It seemed fitting; the basilica was marked with the Christian cross and she was Christian after all, though happy to follow the Sufi way of life. 'All is one,' she said. 'All is one.' There was part of a carved angel that the girl took to mark the grave – the head and shoulders and two curving wings, one broken, but an angel for all that. In spite of rain that had fallen earlier in the week, the ground was baked stony hard by the summer sun, so they could barely dig deep enough. The girl had them lift a huge weighty slab of carved stone. She had seen such slabs covering the graves of the ancient ones and wanted to honour her grandmother in the old way. This one had a beaded carved edge and a Greek cross enclosed in a circle in the middle of the slab. It was well made, a craftsman's hand for sure, and warm from the sun; if anyone had taken the girl's heart in their hands they would have found it cold stone.

'Don't weep for me, don't say, Alas what a pity!
'The grave is but a veil before the gathering in Paradise.
'You have seen the setting, now see the rising…'

The Father Chief spoke the words of the great Sufi poet-philosopher, Jalal al Din Rumi, the Mevlana. The women mourned but her eyes were dry. Be still, Nene had taught her and so she was still, with the passion of grief locked inside her and pondering, pondering on the promise she had made.

A day later the horsemen arrived, cantering down the mountainside and into the broad valley of the summer dwelling. It was a day when the sky was spinning clouds like women twirling spindles to make yarn from fleece. Most of the men were away with the flocks because this was the end of summer and new pasture was needed. The chief was sleeping the afternoon sleep of the very old. The watchdogs that had been left behind were yelping and barking at their approach. They were huge, shaggy animals with spiked collars and the men's horses were prancing and shying and shaking their heads nervously. The men halted, keeping a safe distance from the circling dogs. The women gathered outside the yurts, leaving their weaving and spinning and stretching and tossing from arm to arm the thin dough that would be baked so quickly on a shield of metal laid over the fire. The children clung to their skirts. The girl stayed in the shadow of the black tent. Were these the uncles come to claim her already?

They were young men and foreign, dressed in the manner of the merchants from Venezia but neatly bearded like the tribesmen. One spoke in bad Turkish.

'Peace be with you. Good day to you. Last time we passed this way we bought yoghurt and cheese. We'd welcome the chance of trading for more.'

He was handsome, dark haired and dark eyed, on a grey horse like Bamsi Beyrek. His flesh clung to his cheekbones, his nose was arched, his jaw firm. He looked noble. He could have passed for a *yürük* chieftain except that he couldn't speak their language. Not well. His speech was riddled with strange sounds and only half intelligible and the women held the ends of their head-shawls to their mouths, hiding their mirth. The girl recognised him. He had come more than a year ago in the early summer, cantering down the valley side just as he had done now. Nene had bid her stay in the black tent. Who knew who these strangers might be? Slave traders or her father's kinsmen or robbers who preyed on merchants? Nene had gone out to greet them and the girl had watched through the framework of the black tent. She had thought him very handsome. Now he was here again.

The women huddled together, and she listened to their talk. They were debating the profit and loss of bartering with these barely remembered strangers, and their own men two days' ride away. That first visit, the strangers had brought soap, good soap from their own country, made in small pieces and packed in small boxes. Turkish soap was made from tallow and, while it served its purpose, the soap that these foreigners brought was far preferable.

'There was an old lady, the grandmother with grey eyes,' the dark man said suddenly. 'She gave us medicine for the summer sickness. One of our men is ill. She promised us more medicine when we returned this way. We hoped to ask for her help.'

Merih, the chief's daughter said, gravely, 'Our Anatolian sister is newly dead.'

'I am sorry for your loss. She was a great lady. I admired her very much.'

It wasn't the dark-haired man on the prancing grey horse who spoke but a quiet man, a brown man – brown hair, brown eyes, brown skin on a quiet brown horse. Beside the other, he seemed dull and plain, slight in build but his voice was soft as the threads of silk carpets, and had music wefted through it. He spoke in careful Turkish, though the lift and fall of his voice betrayed his foreignness. Was he the same companion of the other visit? The girl did not remember him.

'It is the will of Allah,' said Merih.

'May she be remembered forever.'

It was the accepted response, but she felt he meant it and her eyes burned. Nene, her grandmother, was a great lady.

The man spoke again. 'I would like to remember her name.'

'Sophia. Her name was Sophia.'

'Sophia,' he repeated, and he didn't comment on the strangeness of the Greek name of a woman who lived amongst the Sufi *yürük*. Instead, his head lifted and he was gazing straight at the yurt, into the shadows where the girl was hiding, and she had the strangest feeling that he saw her, though she knew he could not. She was invisible in the dappled shadows. And she remembered him then; Nene had brought the men to the open flap of the yurt. She had gestured to the girl to remove herself into the shadowy interior but the brown man had already seen her, his eyes steady and considering and she had looked back at him, challenging stare for stare, until Nene had gestured again and she had withdrawn. The dark man, the handsome one, had not noticed her at all and it irked her. Was she so invisible to him? His eyes were grey. Not clear grey like Nene's but smoky, like hearth fires, and his lashes were thick and long like a girl's. Beautiful eyes.

'Will you share your name with us, sir?'

'Of course. I am Dafydd ap Heddwyn ap Rhickert.' The names rolled proudly from his tongue though it was clear to him they made little sense to the women. A smile flickered and went. 'Mostly they call me Dai – easier on the tongue, isn't it? And my friend here goes by the name of Thomas Archer.'

The dark man dipped his head in greeting. So he was Thomas Archer. Or went by the name of Thomas Archer, the brown man said, and that was strange when he had announced his own name in that proud way. Thomas Archer, she repeated, and the name sounded strange on her tongue.

Time to puzzle later because the dogs were called to heel and two men dismounted, holding the reins to keep the horses quiet before one of the women led them to the corral where two of their sturdy mountain ponies had been left behind. The grey and the brown were turned loose with them, and the girl saw the brown whicker softly in greeting to the chestnut mare that was her favourite.

The chief was coming out from his yurt with the meagre retinue of elders, the old men who had stayed behind. They sat with their guests on one of the *kilims* woven in the tribal motif in the shade of tall walnut trees already heavy with green fruit while the women served bowls of cool, tangy yoghurt mixed with clear, sweet water from the bubbling springs. There were little biscuits sweetened with dried grapes and almonds that were Nene's favourite and fat figs ripe and bursting and warm from the sun and dribbled with mountain honey. The two young men were guests, and so they were welcomed, and were asked the questions all travellers were asked. Where have you come from? Where are you going?

Their merchant train was encamped at one of the *hans* on the Karaman road; they were bound for Attaleia, travelling from the far countries. It was late summer, and time they reached the coast before autumn gales made sailing impossible, except they had to halt until their companion was recovered. Where then were they bound?

'Venezia.'

Venezia, a name only though Nene had spoken of Venezia, the miraculous city that floated on water. And of Genoa, its great rival, and how merchants travelled from those prosperous cities across the sea to this broad land, crossing it from *han* to *han*, the resting places built by the Selçuk, each a camel's day journey apart, though the Selçuk were vanquished now and the land ruled by the Beyliks, each with his own province and some his own mint to cast the coins that said he was a powerful ruler. The coins were worthless down on the coast land, unless they came from the mint of their own Bey. It was one of the reasons they bartered goods; strange coins were no use to them up here in the high valley.

Merih's daughter, Gül, came into the tent to find her. The two girls were about the same age and Gül looked curiously at the girl's dark head bent over a basket of herbs.

'Why are you hiding away? Why don't you come and see the strangers? It's not often we get visitors as handsome as these two.'

The girl shook her head. She stood up with a small-stoppered earthen bottle in her hands. 'This is good for sickness. They will need to add six drops of this to fresh water. On no account use stale water. Make that clear to these strangers. They do not value fresh water as we do. Three cups a day, perhaps for three or four days. It's difficult to know without seeing him.'

'Why not come and tell them yourself?' The look she slanted at the girl was sly, teasing. The girl shook her head again and Gül sighed at her stubbornness.

'Your loss, then,' she said and took the bottle from the girl and walked back to the group of men, hips swaying, pleased to be the centre of attention. The girl stayed behind in the shelter of the tent. She didn't know why she had refused. Not shyness, not embarrassment, nothing as simple as that. She watched as Gül relayed the instructions, saw the brown man shake his head and those around him shaking theirs in agreement. Then Gül was swaying back to the tent, all too aware that her rounded haunches displayed tempting plumpness.

'You have to come. They say they need to talk to you. It's all guesswork, otherwise.'

The girl nodded and silently followed Gül across the space to the group of elders and the two guests. She stood before them, hands folded, head bent. Out of the corner of her eye she observed the dark man with the smoky, long-lashed grey eyes. He was watching her, eyebrows raised.

'She is very young.'

'That may be so,' said the Chief, 'but she has been well taught by her grandmother. We have every confidence in Sophia's child.

'Come, girl; hear what our guests have to say concerning their friend who is ill. It may be you need to add to your medicine.'

The brown man leaned forward. His gaze had not left her and she found it disturbing. His eyes were dark brown, almost black; they were the eyes of one who would look into your soul but his face was taut as a tent rope. A hard man, hardened by life. Not a man to be treated lightly. Deliberately, she distanced herself, became still, an empty vessel, as her grandmother had taught her.

'Of course, Father of our tribe. It shall be as you will.'

It was the brown man who talked, describing fever, a swollen throat, a wracking cough, sickness. Well, the sickness she had dealt with. The fever? She considered. What was it Nene had prescribed? Nene had followed the teachings of Ibn Sina, that greatest of great men of philosophy and medicine who the foreigners called Avicenna. What was it Nene had used for sickness of the lungs? Of course, the seeds of the plant they gathered every year at the ruins of the old monastery on the high crag. She could not remember its name but it was the one that was used for the incense in the Christian churches and was also the best for reducing inflammation and fever and clearing the lungs. Quietly, as Nene would have done, she explained how to burn the substance so that the vapours could be inhaled and breathing relieved and fever reduced. The brown man listened in that still way he had and the dark man – how pleased he was, how grateful. Her lashes fluttered over her lowered lids. It was enough to have served him, to have been of use. She would have left them then except that the

Father Chief indicated that she stay; it was an honour and she could not refuse. She sat silently listening to them.

The dark man was talking again.

'Dai here must go to Flanders. That's where our employer lives – Heinrijc Mertens, a rich merchant of Ieper whose business we are engaged on. But we'll not be going to England, that's for sure.' England: that strange, cold, far-off land that was her grandfather's country. She had sworn to Nene that she would travel there. The dark man laughed though there was no merriment in it. 'We haven't seen England for many a year and our companions are none too keen to see it again. But my friend here is homesick for the poverty-stricken little country he calls home.'

The brown man said nothing and his face gave nothing away. If he was homesick for his country he gave no sign. He had the gift of stillness and it disturbed her. The chief bartered cheese and yoghurt for soap – the last few boxes, he was told, saved specially for this tribe – and a parcel of bright patterned silk cloth they were carrying from the far countries, and she could see how much he was enjoying himself playing merchants' games with these two young men. He was like one of the small lizards, all wizened skin and bright dark eyes that shifted this way and that. When he was excited, spittle flecked the sides of his mouth and he flicked it away with his tongue. He was doing that now, gloating over his treasures.

Then the men were leave-taking, though they were pressed to stay and eat with the tribe and the brown man cast a hungry look towards the bubbling pot. They had some distance to travel, they said, and their friends were waiting for them. And they were away up the valley side, the brown man on a brown horse and the dark, handsome man astride the grey, away and gone out of her life.

3

Such is the ordinance of the Mighty One,
the all-knowing. It is he that has created for you
the stars, so that they may guide you in the
darkness of the land and sea.
(Quran: 6:95-96)

When the sun was sitting just on the rim of the mountains the chief summoned her to his great tent. It was one of the yurts like an upturned boat and inside was dark. He watched the girl as she walked towards him in that light, graceful way she had. Such a small girl, skinny as well, but fearless and with a surprising strength of arm for a girl of such small size. He'd heard them teasing her, calling her 'Çiçek's daughter', and there was much truth in that. Strength of mind, too. Stubborn. Once she'd set her mind to something, she didn't let go. Like that grave she'd had them make for her grandmother, with its lid of carved stone so heavy it took all their strength to lift it into place. Not that any of the old men had the strength of their youth. Not now. These were the autumn years and he had no regrets. A good life he'd had. But the girl! What would her life be now that the grandmother was dead? Not a sound out of her, not a tear. She had done well today, explaining to the visitors what medicine they must take; so very like her grandmother. He told her so.

She sat very still in front of him though her heart was beating fast. Through the opening she could see the round red ball of the sun sliding behind the mountains and the glow from it turned the valley to fire. For a moment, it seemed as if Nene's funeral mound was ablaze.

'We regret the death of Sophia our friend,' he said, as if he, too, had the same thought. He looked uncomfortable, his eyes flickering this way and that, and she wondered what next. 'Now that you have no kin…' He stopped and she waited. 'Now that you have no kin—'

'You are my kin,' she said. She kept her voice even and low. 'The tribe is all I know, all I have ever known.'

'It is not possible. We made a promise that you would be returned to your family when your grandmother died. A promise must be kept. Word will be sent to your uncles tomorrow. No doubt they will come for you at once – perhaps they will be here in three or four days' time. You will be cared for.'

Cared for. She did not want to be cared for by her uncles. She did not want to be returned to the rock home that had killed her mother. She said nothing.

'No doubt they will find a husband for you.'

'Nene did not want me to be married to any one of them.' The old man thought how like her grandmother she was. Not grey eyed and golden haired, as the old woman had been in her young days, but with that same remoteness, as if they looked into another world. A strange girl, so stubborn and self-possessed for one so young. And she needed to be.

'So she told me. But a promise is a promise. They will be here in three or four days' time.' His eyes flickered towards her and away. He looked beyond her, through the tent opening at the darkening sky. 'You are Sophia's child, and Sophia, our *Anadolu Bacı*, was dear to us all. You are as dear to me as my own daughter, both because you are Sophia's child and for your own sake. I do not want to go against her wishes but I cannot ask our men to defy your family. We are no longer warriors. We are peaceful now. We have forgotten how to make war.'

'I would not ask it of you.' she spoke as formally as he did. 'Father of our tribe, you are wise and careful for our people. I would not wish harm to come to any one of them.'

He nodded, accepting her obedience. His next words were unexpected, like stumbling on an unseen stub of root. 'Your grandmother will be much missed,' he said. 'Not only by us. The travellers who came, the two men who had need of her medicine; they also valued your grandmother.' A pause. A heart's beat. 'You also know how to make medicine from plants, Sophia's child. She taught you well.' Another pause. 'You also will be much missed.'

Her eyes narrowed. She knew then what his purpose was, and what was hers. She kissed his hand and lifted his hand to her brow, in their custom, and left him. In the short time she had been with him, the sun had dipped behind the mountains and darkness had come. The yurts were black shapes in a blacker land. How empty was their yurt now that Nene was no longer there. Nene's soul was gone but this was no time for grieving.

She sent away the women who came to beg her to eat the evening meal with them. She was tired, she said, and longed to sleep but when the last one had left she sat down on the embroidered cushions and patterned *kilims* and unplaited her long hair so that it fell over her shoulders and past her waist and spread over the cushion on which she was sitting. Kazan, her friend from childhood, had made a song in praise of her hair just last winter. Not black, like the yürük women, but dark brown, burnished like bronze, copper like the flanks of a fleet chestnut horse, gold flecked, shining like sun on the great flowing river. He sang it outside their winter house one bright morning but Nene had laughed and sent him away. She remembered this while she unplaited strand after strand. She remembered too the feel of Nene's hands gentle in her hair because this had always been Nene's task.

She took Nene's precious scissors, their inlaid blades always kept sharp and shining, and snipped and snipped until her hair was only to her shoulders, like the dark hair of the handsome young merchant, and the fallen hair lay in great coils on the *kilim*. Her hands didn't tremble but afterwards, when she felt the lightness of her head, and saw the copper-bronze-gold coils lying lifeless, she mourned for her lost self. She gathered up every strand and burned them in the hearth and watched them flare up and die into ashes.

She bound a length of thin cotton cloth about her breasts, thankful for once that she was small and slight and the little apple shapes were easily flattened. She pulled her plain blue *kaftan* over her *gömlek* and *şalvar*. Always blue because it was a lucky colour, Nene said, and kept away the evil spirits. The girl could not remember either of them wearing anything other than shades of blue, though only last year Nene had given her a beautiful *kaftan* patterned in blues and crimson and it grieved her to leave it behind. She fastened the warm *ferace* about her. No head covering that marked her out as a girl. Now she was a boy, in boy's clothing, with boy's hair and not yet years enough for chin hair. She secured a sharp-bladed knife in her belt. She put the jade amulet into a leather pouch and hung the pouch about her neck. She packed a satchel with food and skins of water and Nene's scissors and a comb skilfully made from bone that had belonged to Nene's mother, and her mother before that, and the little gold ring with its carved amethyst stone that she had found one day when she and Nene were gathering herbs and plants at the old monastery. She slung the satchel over her shoulder and fastened a quiver of arrows to the belt at her waist. She took up her curved bow and looked outside. All was quiet. A shadow in the shadows, she moved through the camp. The dogs watched her but didn't stir. They knew her too well.

Two of the horses had been left behind. The girl paused, eyeing them thoughtfully. One raised its head. It was the chestnut mare with the blaze of white on her nose, her favourite, the one she rode when she had the chance. They were corralled for safe keeping from the wolves and wild boar. Better not be on foot at night in the mountains.

And without a horse she had no hope of catching up with the two men and their caravan. She hoped she would not be named a thief for taking the mare. She clicked her fingers and called the mare by name: Rüzgar. The mare came trustingly, hoping for titbits. The girl whispered pet names to her and wound her hand through the pale mane and led the little mare out of the corral and up the mountainside. Once they were clear of the camp, the girl mounted bareback, easily, as she had been taught. The night sky was bright with stars. She gazed up at them, seeking out the familiar patterns that would guide her safely through the night. It was Nene who taught her the names of the stars in the vast sky, and how to travel by their direction.

And that was how she left her home of seventeen summers, secretly, silently, not daring to take her leave of anyone. It was better for them not to know.

It was easy for the mare to follow the familiar track that led up to the top of the gorge, even in the dark, though her flared nostrils and white eyes showed her fear. The girl looked back once to where the black yurts were just visible in the glimmer of fire from the hearths. The comforting noises of chickens and goats and dogs settling for the night rose up from the valley, familiar and loved and utterly lost to her, as Nene was lost. Oh my dearest one, my Nene, my wisest of grandmothers, grey-eyed Sophia, I shall miss you every day of my life. Leaving you is so very hard.

'Leaving,' she said. 'What is that? It means nothing. While the heart remembers, there is no leaving.'

It was as clear as if Nene had been standing beside her, as if the words were spoken aloud. The girl turned away and headed for the road that led to Karaman.

4

Love for the lovely shining maid will not
Be brought out from its nest...
(Dafydd ap Gwilym, 14thC)

Edgar was worse. The fever was not abating and the belly cramps had him doubled up in agony all through the night. He'd just dropped into sleep when he was woken up again by the morning call to prayer. No rest for the poor boy. No choice but to wait until he recovered even if that meant missing the last sailing of the season. Twm wasn't happy; Edgar was a chance-come-by traveller who had no claim on them whereas Heinrijc Mertens, their employer, would be anxious for their safe return. But Dai insisted they couldn't abandon the boyo, not now when he was ill. In the end he had his way but it was a disagreement, see, and he didn't like disagreements on the road. It was bad for the men, the cameleteers and muleteers. That was the way to a bundle of problems. He knew his guide from the last journey; knew him for a trustworthy man, dark as bog oak and eyes keen as a kestrel's but good in a tight corner. There was an edginess about them all this journey; a quickness to see a slight where none was meant and a quickness to argue, and that rubbed off on the animals so they were rarely placid and often restive. But the men had a fondness for Edgar. He'd not been with them long, for sure, but he was a well-natured boy who never fired up no matter how Blue teased him about his dainty ways. Indeed, Edgar's coming had made for better relations all round. Never a word about how he came to be wandering in these parts but then nobody asked questions like that. Never did. Best keep quiet, these days.

The *hancı* wasn't very happy about it – not at first. When he realised it was nothing catching, nothing plaguey, he said they could stay for the usual three days at no cost but had to move on after that or look to payment. A relief it was to be inside the high walls of the *han* and safe from robbers, with the comfort of a sound building and fresh water and bathing. The animals were stabled in the court with all the others – camels, mules, horses, dogs. At least they were looked after and a man on call at every *han* if a shoe was loose or a horse went lame or needed doctoring. You just had to get used to the noise and the stench. He'd known worse. Far worse.

Dai had pushed them on to reach this *han* because it was only half a day's ride from the nomad camp and the wise woman they'd met early last summer. If anyone could help them, it would be her. The physician at the *han* had done his best but he shook his head and sighed and pouted as if Edgar had no tomorrow. Well, that wasn't so. Edgar had tomorrow and tomorrow and tomorrow. A life of tomorrows. He'd make sure of that.

In truth, he was worried for Edgar's sake but – confess it now – he'd a wish to visit the nomads again. Would she be there, the girl seen in the shadows of the yurt over a year ago in the early summer months? Just a glimpse before the old woman sent her away but so slender, with that heart-aching curve of cheek and tumbling hair and golden eyes. He couldn't tear his gaze away though her eyes reproached him for staring like a moon-struck clod. Such glowing beauty that there was no forgetting her, though nothing could come of wishing. That ragtag group of boyos came before any girl's beauty.

Thomas Archer was happy enough to journey with him and visit his bad Turkish on these people. Thomas Archer. He said it was his name but Dai knew better than that. He had good cause. But that was the name he went by, and if that was his wish so be it. The men called him 'Tom', short names being easier to shout across a wide land, see, especially if there was trouble brewing. In Dai's mind, it was always 'Twm', the Welsh way, though Tom wasn't Welsh. Indeed he wasn't.

He hadn't recognised Dai. And why should he? Years it was since that strange meeting, and a few lifetimes ago for both of them. And then Twm Archer had been taken on by Heinrijc Mertens. Happenchance but as if it was meant to be. He'd brought his own man with him, Giles – from the West Country. Near the Marches, judging from his accent, but the English side; in his twenties, most likely, wiry and tough and kept himself to himself. He knew no more of Giles than when the man first joined them and they'd been travelling the trade route for months now, longer than he cared to remember, and Twm was right: he'd a longing in him to be home. Poverty stricken for sure, and rain-drenched, and bog-ridden, and beaten to its knees – the English Edwards had seen to that – but home for all that.

Fifty and more years since the second war had left Cymru in ruins, its last prince murdered, his brother Dafydd dragged through the streets of Shrewsbury then that brutal killing of him, at Edward's decree. The first Edward; a ruthless king, his *taid* had told him. It was his soldiers that had ravaged Cymer Abbey. The children – Dafydd's sons and daughters and Llewelyn's only daughter, Gwenllian, a babe-in-arms but the Princess of Wales for all that – all vanished, spirited away. There were rumours, of course; taken to England, to this castle, that nunnery, but *Taid* said better turn a deaf ear and keep a still tongue. Careless talk cost lives these days when the Welsh were little better than slaves in their own country. Times had changed and they were ruled by the English Edward who had ringed Wales with his great castles and towns where the Welsh were not allowed to live; out at the curfew, that was the order, but with Edward's cruel twist they were not allowed to trade anywhere except within the town walls. Come the morning curfew, back they had to trudge. Living was hard. Then Edward died on the banks of a loch in Scotland and the second Edward was king. That prince born at Caernarfon, the Prince of Wales promised by King Edward the first: a false prince, *Taid* said, nothing Welsh about him except the place where he was born. What was it the Irish said? 'Sure, if you're born in a stable it doesn't make you a horse' – but that had a heretical ring to it and these days it was enough to light the faggots under you. So many killed, so many burned alive, *Duw a'n helpo*.

All the burning and blood spilt and torture and dreadful deeds were done in the second Edward's name but it was the powerful and ruthless Despensers, father and son, who ruled the roost. The son was made Lord of Glamorgan and he was hungry for whatever he could lay his hands on. He'd do anything, anything, and by the foulest means. Dai's father said the common joke was that any sheep or cattle lost had 'gone to Caerffili' – a black joke because Hugh Despenser was notorious for confiscating any sheep or cattle found roaming on his land. That was a joke in itself; sheep and cattle were the least of it. Under his rule, human life counted for nothing. There'd come a hope when Rhys ap Llewelyn Bren led the uprising. Dai had been a young boy when his father joined Rhys's rebels. That was the last the family had seen of him. The revolt was crushed. Llewelyn Bren was Hugh Despenser's prisoner. No proper trial – *wel*, nothing new there – but savagely hanged, drawn and quartered at Cardiff castle and all his lands seized.

At home the horror had begun, and no man of the household to provide except for *Taid* who was old and feeble now – and himself, a mere boy, and all those mouths to feed with whatever he could find in those years of famine: his mother, his two brothers and three sisters and aunts and uncles, *Taid's* other woman he had kept, though his wedded wife was long dead, and her children and children's children…all through those nightmare years of rain and harvests ruined, cattle dead of murain, grain spoilt by mould, fields rotting, stomachs groaning with hunger then starvation and death…all those years ago and he still didn't want to remember. And all the while the wars going on: Isabella and Mortimer waging war against the King and the Despensers; her triumph and the desperate end of Hugh Despenser. That was when Dai was at Hereford castle. He'd been witness at that execution. An evil, ruthless man, true, but no man deserved such suffering. The stuff of nightmares. Then the King's death – murdered, though that was never proved, and he was buried with all pomp. Another reign of terror under Isabella and Mortimer, but by then Dai had escaped it all. That was when he'd taken ship, first for Flanders, away from that stinking cesspit. There was nothing to stay for: Wales was finished and England given over to vicious thugs on the payroll of the rich and powerful. His own bandit companions in the Welsh hills...? Poor men trying to stay alive, even if they were thieves and robbers, and protected by ordinary folk trying to stay alive.

He'd never been back, though Isabella's son, the third Edward, had despatched Mortimer – an honourable execution for a dishonourable man – and imprisoned his she-wolf mother in a castle that was comfortable, sumptuous even, with her minstrels and huntsmen and grooms, and luxuries poor folk couldn't even dream of, if rumour told true; but imprisonment for all that.

No, he'd never been back. But now...now he'd barter all the spices and silks and gold and silver and amber and pearls and grain and horses of this land, and its great plains and high mountains and fertile coast – all of it – for one glimpse of the Mawddach, for one moment of the long-wished-for speech that was sweet to his ear.

Dai *bach*, what are you thinking, man? There's no home and no family waiting for you. Best keep your wits about you and get these poor buggers to a safe haven. They're all the family you have now – these, and Heinrijc Mertens, that strange peacock of a man with a heart as big as *Taid*'s, though that's not what you'd be thinking from seeing him in his fine robes and well-fed plumpness and fluttery hands.

It was a hard ride to the summer pasture, further than he remembered. Always so, isn't it? But they found it easy enough by the shape of the valley and the ancient wrecked city on the further side with its line of broken pillars and the highest point tower-like against a sky that was fleecy with clouds. Hen scrattins. That's what Blue called them. Hen scrattins, these fluffy light clouds, though Blue never could say why. Just another of his outlandish sayings.

They came down the valley on a track that was brown earth this time of year. Bright green it was when they were there early in that summer a year ago, and full of flowers. A beautiful sight. He had misgivings when he realised their men were away, and there were only women and children, though they were hardy enough, that's for sure, and those great dogs loose. But the old chief and the old men were there to make them welcome and offer food and drink. Figs and honey, that God-given combination. Would fig trees grow in the old country? Would they grow in Flanders? He'd miss their smooth, fresh plumpness. Dried, they were light and easy to carry and kept hunger at bay. He could have done with a few dried figs in his satchel in the old days. He'd a mind to take a young tree or two back with him. And the biscuits! He wished he could have asked the women for the recipe, taken it back for Heinrijc, but he and Twm were there to barter goods and beg the medicine. Because of that, they let the old man make a good bargain and get the best of the deal. It pleased him well enough, the old boy.

The wise woman was dead. And such a woman. Honoured she would have been in the old country, and here she was, a woman living with the nomads and useful because she knew the art of turning plants into medicine. But, fair now, they claimed her as one of their own, this Christian, as one of the *Anadolu Bacıları*, That's what they were called, the Anatolian Sisters. Dai had heard talk of them before now. And the girl? She was there in the shadow of the tent. She thought she was invisible but he saw her. He felt her presence. Her sorrow became his own. This grey-eyed old woman who knew so much – her grandmother, then. Sophia. A strange name amongst the tent dwellers. Her name meant 'wisdom'. A good name for a wise woman.

And then the impossible made possible: she was there with them, talking with them, with him, but unaware of him as she was unaware of her glowing beauty. Her hair: not dark after all but streaked with bronze and copper and gold, rich as those metals and gleaming in the afternoon sun. And her eyes, when she raised them, were gold flecked. Her voice was soft and clear and precise in her instructions. No, not a thought for him. But for Thomas Archer, now, there was different. Time enough she had for him, however she kept her eyes downcast and no outward sign that she cared anything for him. The wonder of it was he'd taken no notice of the girl. 'Pretty enough,' he'd agreed, when Dai dared trust himself enough to say anything about her. 'Too skinny for my taste. I just hope the chief was right and she was well taught by her grandmother, or it's been a day's journey for nothing and Edgar sick as a cat.'

'What will happen now to the girl, I wonder, with her grandmother dead?'

Twm had shrugged. 'Perhaps there's some man in the tribe who's claimed her as bride. Who knows?'

Maybe it was as Twm said. Maybe she was spoken for. It was not Dai's problem. He couldn't – mustn't – think of her. He had his band of misfits to guide to some haven, if not home. Not one of them could go home – didn't dare go home. All had their own secret that was kept hidden, never shared whatever was suspected. Yet that memory of the girl with gold-copper-bronze streaked hair, her strange gold-flecked eyes, her body lithe and supple as her mind... Dai *bach*, keep your wits about you now.

The medicine they brought back was doing Edgar good. It was worth the day's journey, though he had worried about leaving Edgar in Blue's care. True, young Rémi had a head on his shoulders but Blue...a law to himself he was. A big man, tall and broad with a belly on him, and his head and shoulders were high above the rest of them and towering over young Rémi. It was the dye that marked him out, though – the blue-black staining that looked like bruising on fingers and nails and arms and face. There was a blue-black sheen on the straggled ends of his wiry beard, like a magpie's coat, though the fresh growth was rusty as old iron. His nails were blackest of all. Easy to tell he'd been a woad man at some time, though no one asked when or where or why he'd quit. And those cures he brought with him from the outlandish country he called home! The Fens, he called it, where sea and land were one and the ague was a constant illness. Blue swore the way to break Edgar's fever was to roll a live spider in butter and get him to swallow it. He'd made Blue promise not to try it. To wait until they came back from the camp with medicine from the wise woman. Should he ever have let the man travel with them? Twm was against it, of course, but how to refuse a man in need? Besides, in spite of the bluster and loud talk and hard drinking there was a loneliness about the big man that clutched at Dai's heart. He knew what loneliness was.

Edgar's fever broke in the small hours. He slept sound then till daybreak. He woke hungry and demanding to break his fast, as much as Edgar ever demanded anything. He whispered for food and drink, bless the boy, as if words were a sin. And maybe, for him, they were. *Wel*, there you go. Everybody has corners where secrets are hidden. He blessed the old woman, wherever her soul might be, and began to hope they could be on the move, if not next daybreak, then surely the morning after.

5

Until you've grown your own beard
Don't ridicule smooth chins
(Mevlana Jalal al Din Rumi, 1207-1273)

It was luck that had brought her to the merchants' camp. Not as far as the *han* at Karaman but at the edge of the flat plateau on a bluff of land that overlooked a steep valley with the wide sky swirling and the camels and donkeys and horses and dogs making noises that sounded so familiar but belonged to strangers. There were bright coloured pavilions set apart from the black tents, and a bright standard placed in front of the largest pavilion, fluttering in the breeze. Camels were grouped in *katars*; she could see at least ten and that meant over seventy camels. The pack mules and horses and dogs were close by. She could not see the grey horse or the brown horse but that was not surprising. This was a bigger merchant camp than she had expected, a prize for robbers, and she could not understand why they had not taken refuge in one of the *hans*. The glorious smell of food cooking wafted up to her, caught in the air together with the sounds and smells of animals, and her stomach grumbled with hunger.

It was evening and the sun was slanting long shadows. She had travelled through the black night, she and the mare shivering both when they heard the wild creatures roaming and snuffling and hunting. She had petted the animal, leaning forward to whisper soft

❀ 36 ❀

words into the flickering ears, stroking her neck, subduing her own fear so as not to alarm the mare who was nervous enough already. She remembered the stories told to children who wouldn't sleep, stories of three-headed dogs with huge pricked, pointed ears and great drooling mouths and flaring nostrils that sniffed out naughty children. Stories of the leopards that prowled this land and preyed on wakeful children; leopards with glittering eyes and dappled skin so that they were always hidden in the shadows, silently stalking until the moment they pounced on their prey with their snarling mouths and sharp teeth and curved claws. Nene had told her that was long ago. Perhaps there might still be such beasts but no-one in her memory had caught so much as a glimpse of a whisker, not the tip of an ear, not the top of a tail in this part of the country. Not even a flicker of a shadowed body or the gleam of eyes in the dark. Nene was the wisest of all women and Nene's soul was a new star high above her, watching over her. Even so, the night had been long and the shadows full of peril and the road uneven and stony and pitted with cracks and holes.

When daybreak came she was close to the ruins of the old monastery nesting high on its ridge above the road. She had been here before, with Nene. It was the place where they came to harvest the berries of the plant that made the medicine she had given the strangers.

At the bottom of the great rock were the houses of people she knew, where Greeks and Turks had lived alongside each other time out of mind and coaxed a living from the land. Fruit trees grew here, and olives, and corn. Nene said it used to be monastery land and was where the pilgrims came before making the steep climb to the monastery and the shrine of Tarasis of Blessed Memory, but that was long ago and the place was ruined and empty now of pilgrims though the saint's shrine was still there. She had seen it. She had walked there in the early morning with Nene and they had watched the sun rise over the crag and seen the tower of the ancient church silhouetted against a pinky lemon sky. Behind and below them was the valley of the Gök Su and, beyond that, Mahras Dağı and blue mountains ranging peak on peak further than the eye could see. A tangle of undergrowth lay thickly over the remains of walls built with the huge tawny stones of the old people.

A door opened in one of the small houses and a woman came out. She was yawning, sleepy-eyed, her mouth an 'oh' of yawns and her hair still loose about her shoulders. She was carrying a tall pitcher, walking over to the cistern the girl knew was close to the houses, piped down from the many springs up there on the crags. It was Maria. The girl knew her well from the visits she and her grandmother had made, year after year, to this ruined monastery on its great crag. Maria caught sight of the stranger on the chestnut mare and froze into stillness. One horse, one rider and that only a youth but you never knew these days where the danger came from. The girl guessed the thoughts that ran through the woman's head. An enemy or just a wayfarer?

A mischievous impulse seized the girl despite her fatigue.

'Greetings, woman of the house.'

'Greetings, young stranger. You are welcome.'

'I thank you. I am tired and hungry. I have ridden through the night.'

'Then you must break your fast with us, and maybe sleep a while, if your business is not pressing.'

'That would be welcome indeed.' The both spoke in the familiar polite phrases always used between householder and traveller. The woman stood stiffly, waiting for the youth say more about himself. He didn't.

'Let me draw the water for you,' he said instead and slid off the chestnut mare.

The mare nuzzled close and mouthed the girl's tunic. The terrors of the night were past and the mare could smell water. The girl held her hand out for the pitcher.

'There's no need for that, young sir.'

'But I would like to help, Maria.'

The woman stared warily at the youth. 'You know my name.'

'As well as I know my own.'

'And what is your name, young sir?'

'They call me Sophia's Child.'

The woman stared at her, at the cropped hair, at the slight youth before her.

'Who are you?' she asked, and now her voice was fraught with fear.

'Maria, it's me. It's Sophia's child.' She laughed, rumpled her hair with one hand. 'Yes, I know – I've cut off my hair. But truly it is me.'

'Sophia's child?' The woman's gaze took in the weary horse, the equally weary rider. 'Here alone so early in the day? Do I believe you? What are you about?' She was angry because of her alarm, still disbelieving.

'Truly, it is me. I am sorry, Maria, I would not vex you for the world. But it's good to know you really did take me for a young man.'

'Where is Sophia?'

'My grandmother is dead. She died four days ago. I have left the tribe because... There are reasons.' The girl swallowed on the hardness in her throat and she was suddenly the young child again, her grandmother's shadow, following her up the steep track to the old monastery, eating and drinking in Maria's house, playing games with the children, so careful of the youngest, the boy with one arm...

Always a practical woman, Maria nodded, accepting, recognising the girl's fatigue and distress. This was the woman who had cut off the arm of her youngest child to save his life when he had been savaged by a wild boar. 'You need food and a warm fire. Later tell us your news.'

'May God bless you, Maria.'

Maria surged towards the house, the water forgotten for now. She would send one of her children. Now, there was this weary young girl to take care of. Inside, a young boy was stirring a pot with his good hand. He was bright-faced with round pink cheeks and shining eyes. The right sleeve of his tunic was flaccid, empty, the sleeve dangling. Later he would pin it out of the way. There was no self-pity in him. Life was good and he was alive and he had his formidable mother to thank for that.

'See, Rehan, we have a hungry visitor.'

'He's here in good time, mother. Mmm. This smells good.' He looked again at the slim youth who had stepped into the house. 'Çiçek, welcome. What are you doing here so early? Where is your grandmother? Why have you cut your hair?'

The girl laughed. 'Dear Rehan, I think you'd see past any disguise. Give me a bowl of your porridge and I'll answer all your questions.'

And then there was the whole family eager with questions and exclamations and a heaped bowl before her and flat bread and figs and cheese and after that sleep with the knowledge that the mare was looked after and a promise to wake her in two hours' time.

She had slept but in her sleeping there were dreams of memories. She and Nene climbing up the steep slopes, up to the caves where Nene said the earliest monastery had been. It was a playing ground for a young girl, a honeycomb of rooms painted deep red with a church underground, white-plastered with a red line of paint as ornamentation. Outside was another huge ruined church where she had found her amethyst ring. Nene had shown her the way the old building had been remade, reused, with carved stones bolstering the old walls. It was a mystery. Who had lived here? Why had they left? Who had come back to re-inhabit the old buildings? Here was the Door Beautiful. That was how she always thought of it, the great door to the church, with its archangels, Gabriel and Michael, guarding the entrance, and the lion and the ox and the flying eagle and the angel and the tree that grows by the river of life. It was a miracle of carving, even now in its ruined state.

In her dreams she walked along the colonnaded terrace with the steep-sided valley on one side and the high crags on the other. Here was the shrine of the great Tarasis of Blessed Memory with its huge figures to either side and intertwining vines and a space in the stones where there was a partridge with an angel. What did it all mean?

In her dreams she had moved through the quiet morning towards the old church, roofless now but its walls still reaching to roof height. It was always cool inside, dark and cavernous. The three aisles stretched ahead of her to the central tower. Beyond that lay the high altar. Here was peace and safety. Beyond the church were more caves and springs and the shrubs they had come to find and harvest.

She had woken when the early afternoon sun slanted through the window opening on to her face. She stretched and wondered if she was too late and they were long gone, the dark man and the brown, but Maria had thought not. A comrade who had a sickness? Of course they would stay another day. Of course she would catch up with them. They kissed her and gave her parcels of food and wished her well.

'And come back to us, Çiçek.' Rehan's smile was broad and beaming. 'You must come back and tell us the story of your great adventure,' he said. 'Go with God.'

She and the mare made their way back to the road and hurried on, tiny as ants trailing across this broad land. The road led uphill and out of the trees to the top of the pass where it dipped again down to the clear high land of the plateau. That used to be forested as well, Nene had told her, but the trees were taken by the Selçuk for the new towns, for the mosques and *medreses* and hospitals and houses and *hamams* and buildings like the *han* she was heading for, before the Selçuk too were overthrown. Always that was the way of it, Nene had told her; army after army over years and years and years, conquering, settling, building, and then the wars and crops failing, animals scattered – worse, dead – homes destroyed, families separated; death and despair and suffering. This was how it was, Nene had told her, except that there would always be people like their small tribe, people who cared for each other, helped each other to survive. People like Maria and her family. These were the people who drank the delicious water of life, who loved their neighbours as themselves. These were the true believers. And the two men, the strangers, the dark man and the brown man, they cared enough about their friend to make the journey to find her grandmother, to seek out the draughts that would cure him. These must be men she could trust. She prayed it was so.

And here they were. Here was their camp. It was well protected. She knew she was watched as the mare picked her way across the rocky bluff towards it, little rocks and earth skittering from under her hooves and the pungent scent of thyme where it was trampled.

A group of women clustered round the fire and cooking pots. One of them was turning from the cooking pot, one hand holding the spoon still poised over it and her other hand holding something, herbs maybe, ready to add to the pot. She straightened up and shaded her eyes with the herby hand. A huddle of turbaned men was sitting in the shade of an awning outside the biggest tent, the one with the standard. A young boy was standing behind them, a small dark boy with curly brown hair and wary eyes under slanting brows. He saw her before the men. Strange, how clearly the eye sees details, tiny details that the mind does not acknowledge until later. He had been serving them with drinks, still held the copper tray and the setting sun glanced off the metal. She reached the edge of the camp at the same moment two of the men came to their feet, goblets in hand. Merchants, certainly, and rich, too, by their dress and turbans. She shouted a greeting, keeping her voice low, trying to sound like a boy, like her friend Kazan.

She must have looked the part, dishevelled and grubby, astride the panting horse. They returned her greeting – Turkish then, but not nomad. Nor like the two strangers, the dark man and the brown. Where had she come from, they asked her. Was she travelling alone, and so young? Where was she going? Always the questions to be asked and answered; that was the custom. She had her story ready, how she longed to travel to the great sea and had left her home and would be willing to work her way in a great merchant train like this one. She looked about her for the dark man and the brown but there was no sign of them. Perhaps they had their own place? She was about to ask about them but the men were nodding, unsmiling; they exchanged long looks with each other. One beckoned her forward, towards the great coloured pavilion.

'Come. Meet our master. You need to speak with him. Let one of the boys look after your horse.'

Their master? She had thought they were the masters, so rich and fine were their clothes. But they were servants. Perhaps now she would meet Thomas Archer and the brown man with the long, musical name. She turned to follow them and that was when she saw the boy watching her from under long lashes and as she met his gaze he did something very strange. He glanced to right and left. No one had noticed him. He tapped a finger against his lower lip, his mouth open. Then the finger was wagged across a mouth now tight shut. It was but a moment, and then his head was bent again to take empty goblets.

She was taken inside, into the dim coolness of the great tent. It was spread with wonderful carpets and cushions woven in tribal patterns she did not recognise. There was a great beaten copper *tepsi* on a carved wooden stand and, beside it, copper urns engraved and inlaid with silver. Beyond, a curtain screened off an inner part of the tent. A man emerged.

'What is it?' The high-pitched voice was querulous.

'Sir, we have a visitor. A young boy anxious to travel the world.'

'Indeed? Well, let him come forward.'

She saw a solid, square, swarthy man. Not tall but wide and plump, with a thick fleshy neck like an ox and buttocks like an ox and the sheen of good living on his face, and a mouth that was loose-lipped and sensual. Strange that such a man should have nothing but a high piping voice, like a gelding. *This is not a man to trust.* Nene's voice was clear in her head. *Take care what you are about, child.*

'Well, boy. So you want to see the world? And so much of it to see.' He asked the same questions. Where had she come from? Where was she going? Was she travelling alone? Was she a runaway?

The last question was short and sharp and he fixed her with a look so piercing that she shivered. She wondered what he saw. A thin young boy, she hoped, not very tall but holding himself straight and still.

'Not a runaway, sir. I am an orphan. My mother died only days ago and I never knew my father. I have no other family.' Not quite the truth but near enough.

'Hm.' His gaze did not shift from her. She forced herself to stay still, as Nene had taught her. Then he called aloud, high pitched, startling her, before she realized it was to someone else invisible behind the partition. A slim youth emerged, yawning and rubbing his eyes and clearly just awake.

'What is your wish, Vecdet?'

'We have a visitor, my dear. Here he is. Bring Signor Latticio.'

'Is the Signor still here?'

'He is, dear boy. Now bring him to me.'

The youth was scowling, petulant, pouting.

'Where shall I find him?'

'How should I know? Bring him to me – now.' Spoken so gently, so lightly, so threateningly. The youth left.

'Signor Latticio, he is one of our customers. A Venetian. He is honouring us with a visit, a meeting to discuss terms. I would like him to meet you.'

A Venetian! Not, then, the men she had expected to meet. This was not their camp after all. But perhaps here was the chance to take ship for the west, for the land of the merchants, and from there to her grandfather's cold country?

❀ 44 ❀

The folds of the door were swept aside and a tall, spare man stepped inside. He was dressed in rich robes of crimson threaded through with gold. A man used to command, she decided. Impatient, not pleased with this summons.

'What now, Vecdet? I was on the point of leaving.'

'A visitor, Signor Latticio. An unexpected visitor, and all alone.'

'What of it?'

'An entrancing visitor.'

But they were not speaking in Turkish. Her heart skipped with excitement. She recognised some of the words – not all. It was the language of the merchants that Nene had made her learn because who knew when there might be a need for it? And that need was now. Her mouth was opening to say yes, I can understand, I can speak your language, I can be useful. And then she shut her mouth tight and made her face blank because of what she was hearing.

'A grubby boy.'

'But a pretty boy. And such beguiling eyes! Clean him up and he'll sell for a good sum of money. Boys like this fetch a good price these days. They make the best slaves. That's what buyers are saying.'

'If you say so. You are, after all, the one who knows.' The way he spoke implied more than the words themselves. The girl shivered.

'Says he's an orphan. Could be a runaway.'

'Even better.'

'And he's brought himself here – a bit of a gift, you might say.'

'Never refuse a gift, heh? I'll leave you to deal with it, Vecdet. You know all there is to know about young boys and how profitable they might be. No violence, though – no marks on him, please. We've enough marked merchandise as it is.'

'I thought a drink, perhaps. The boy is weary and hot. Cool syrup should be very welcome. And afterwards, why, he will sleep.' He was nodding and smiling, his loose-lipped mouth glistening and cruel. The girl shivered again.

The signor smiled. 'As you say, Vecdet. You deal with it. Now it is time I left. I must be in Karaman before nightfall.' And he left them, left the tent, passing by so close his robes brushed against her. It was as if she were invisible. He had been consulted, he had agreed, and now she was no longer his concern. She was nothing to him but potential profit.

Vecdet was oozing charm, licking his fat lips, his skin glistening. He was sure of his prey.

'Come boy. Sit here. Such a pretty boy.' He leaned over her, pressing her shoulder to sit her down on the *kilims* and cushions and she smelt the sour smell of sweat on him. A serving man brought fruits and syrup and the Turk invited her to eat, drink. She must be hungry, she must be thirsty, she must be tired. Later, she would wash and then rest until the evening meal. She raised the glass to her lips, for glass it was, rare to the nomads, gilded and enamelled, a thing of beauty. She thought again about the dark boy risking all, his hands to his lips warning her against eating, drinking. She paused, admired the glass, traced the Arabic inscription with one finger.

'What does it say?'

'Drink and be filled with delight.'

She felt the shock of laughter bubble up and quelled it. Instead, she fumbled and the glass dropped from her fingers. The syrup spilled out staining a red cushion darker red. She grovelled with embarrassment. 'Is it broken?'

Vecdet picked up the glass. 'Not even chipped.' His high, piping voice was even but his face was as dark red as the cushion.

'I am so sorry…I am not used to such precious…I am sorry…'

'It is no matter, boy. It is no problem. Another shall be brought.' And the Turk Vecdet clapped his hands for the servant to take away the empty glass and she wondered how she could avoid drinking when the servant returned because now she was sure it was drugged.

But another man entered; this one was tall and muscular with a great sword in his belt. His nose had been hooked like a falcon's but was flattened, broken in some fight, maybe. A thick, seamed ridge stretched from the corner of his left eye down to his jawline. He looked hard as hardest rock. Vecdet pursed his lips, annoyed, and spoke sharply and the man bowed and apologised but there was a problem in the women's quarter and Vecdet Bey was needed urgently. If he could come now? There was not a moment to be lost.

The Turk made his excuses to her. 'I must leave you. I shall be a moment – no longer. Ah – here is your drink.'

He lingered, waiting for her to sip. She held the glass carefully. 'I shall be happy to wait for you in such comfort. You are very kind. Please do not let me keep you from your business.' And she raised eyes that held, she hoped, only innocent trust. He must have been convinced because he nodded, satisfied.

'If you require anything, my men are outside the tent and will attend you.'

Yes, she thought, pouring the drink on to the ground, ready, waiting and armed outside the tent. No escape that way. And there would be moments only before he returned. Her heart was pounding. She hurried to the curtained area. Empty. As she expected, it was a sleeping area furnished with a divan and heaped with carpets and cushions. Beyond it was the felt wall of the tent. She took her sharp knife and tried slitting it. It was tough, tougher than she had expected. She kept the fabric taut with one hand and tried again. This time the knife point sliced through and down. The noise it made seemed very loud and she paused. Impossible not to be heard but there was no rush of guards, no shouted warnings. She slit further, just enough to slide through, leaving satchel and bow and quiver and warm cloak behind. She stepped warily through the gap.

She was in luck. In one direction was the awning, the men's backs towards her. Open ground lay behind the tent and there was an outcrop of rocks a stone's throw away and beyond that the vast plateau. It was too exposed. They would spot her the moment she ran for cover. Where, then? There was no time to hesitate. He would be back in moments – there he was now. She heard his heavy footfall and his loud voice and the swish of the tent as he drew back its folds. His voice was sharp and angry and at first she thought he had already discovered that she was missing but not yet. Not yet.

And even as she hesitated, eyeing up the rocks and the camp, she felt a tug on her arm. It was the dark-eyed, curly-haired boy who had tried to warn her.

His name was Nikolaos but they called him Niko. He had lived in a remote Greek village until he was captured for the slave market. He was not quite nine years old. His sister, Agathi, was taken with him. She was fifteen, a pretty girl with silver blonde hair and soft brown eyes. She was kept in the women's quarters with the other female slaves. They were two of a cargo of forty slaves bound for Attaleia and from there to the market in Candia. Maybe further, to Venezia, the great city floating on water. It all depended on market prices, and they fluctuated as much as the exchange rate between Turkish *akçes* and the Byzantine gold *hyperpyron*. Besides, the city states of Italy were bringing their new silver and gold coins, their *florins* and *ducats*. Still, the slave trade was big business, as big as trade in horses and grain. Silks and spices were only a small part of the brisk trade in imports and exports between west and east, and not where the best profit was to be had. This caravan carried slaves and horses and bales of tough ox hide and opulent furs stripped from strange animals.

The slaves were a mixed bunch: Russian, Tartar, Turkish, Greek. Some Niko knew better than others. There was boy about four years old who no longer cried but didn't know his name or where he came from. They looked after him as best they could. That first night, his terrified screaming had kept them all awake and the guards threatened him with clenched fist, and angry oaths until one of the women took him in with her. He slept with her still. A harsh woman but oddly gentle with the child. Niko had heard her singing soft lullabies to him. Maria and Catarina were Russian, both eighteen, both 'in sound health', as the sales pitch had it. Maria was shorter, stockier; Catarina taller, almost beautiful and would fetch a better price. Women slaves were always more expensive than males, in Candia and Venezia. Greek Christians could fetch a high price as well. Niko and Agathi were Greek Christian.

Niko had listened intently to the men's talk, careful not to betray his interest. Virgins sold for more. He noted that. His sister was safe, then, from one point of view, at least until the market. Before then, he must have a plan of escape.

Hatice was the woman who had taken the child under her care. She had a gash across her forehead that would scar. She had never been beautiful – hers was a strong face with thick black brows and angular jaw – but it was pitiful to see the red, puckered flesh still raw from the blow. She had fought back when she was captured. She still fought back. She never seemed to learn that it was a waste of energy. Better to play dumb, be the idiot, afraid, compliant. You found out more that way and they forgot to watch you all the time. Look at the riot she'd caused just this afternoon, bringing that donkey Vecdet huffing and puffing to the women's tent.

Asperto wasn't so lucky, poor devil. He was one of the Tartars who'd escaped some months ago and stayed free for over a day and a night before they caught him. He was smashed over the head, a brutal blow. It was after that he had the falling down sickness. There were those who shouted 'possession', and swore he was bedevilled, but when he was well he was the same kind Asperto, though quieter now, as if life had been crushed out of him. Niko reckoned it was the blow to the head that had brought on the sickness and there were others who agreed with him. One of the slaves – a big, pale Russian whose name never came easily to Niko's tongue – said he'd seen the same happen in his village. They'd got used to Asperto by now, falling and writhing and frothing at the mouth, and simply waited until he was calm again. They kept it quiet from the guards as much as they could. The falling sickness meant falling profits and if Asperto wasn't going to fetch a good price, Vecdet would cut his losses and Asperto's throat.

None of them could hope for ransom.

Niko had seen the horse and its rider long before the men. He watched their progress across the bluff from under his lashes. He'd learnt how to keep a look out and keep his mind on his work at the same time. Several vicious blows had taught him that. Had he no sense at all? A youth, slim, not very tall but whose chestnut brown hair and gold-flecked brown eyes made him marketable. A pretty boy, riding alone straight into the net. They wouldn't want to mark him. Drugs, then. Niko had managed to catch his eye and mime 'don't eat or drink', but he wasn't sure he'd been understood.

And then the youth was led into the great pavilion and his horse taken by one of the men – a nice little chestnut mare, another bonus. Niko thought that was that, and the next time he'd see him would be in the male slaves' quarters, dozy with dope, but then there was Hatice's riot and everybody was focused on that, grinning and making bets on who she'd bite and how many strokes she'd get. They didn't hear the sharp sound of ripping felt. He edged back, moved cautiously around the pavilion. The boy was standing there, uncertain, and that donkey Vecdet was already mouthing off outside the tent. Niko hoped he wouldn't be missed. He had his excuses ready, just in case, but all the same... He tugged urgently on the youth's sleeve.

It was the dark-eyed, curly-haired boy who had tried to warn her. He had his finger to his mouth again. No noise. He gestured towards the huddle of tents and she pulled back. He urged her on. 'Stay behind the second tent. I'll come to you.' It was a breath of sound and then he was gone, back towards the awning and the men. Could she trust him, this young boy-slave? She would have to. She crept silently towards the first tent, carefully avoiding the pegs and taut ropes. Behind her came the first shouts of alarm and Vecdet snarling at the guards. Then she was at the second tent, huddled behind it, senses alert, body poised for flight but the pounding feet of pursuers was fading not growing. Moments later, the boy dropped down beside her.

'They think you've headed for the plateau. Come this way. There's not much time.'

He went ahead of her, skirting the tents, heading into the camp rather than away. She followed blindly, expecting any moment to hear the shout that she was spotted but there was nothing. The bluff ended suddenly in a steep slope. They slithered down it, slipping and sliding and clinging to rocks and the tangle of thyme and brushwood with thorny branches that tore at their hands, until they came to a narrow ledge. Below them was a band of stunted trees, and the sounds of a river rushing through.

The boy pointed. 'We have to go down there and into the trees.'

'They'll find me.'

He shook his head. 'No. There is a safe place but quickly. We must be quick.'

At the bottom, they slipped between the trees and waded into the water and followed the river. Above them, the last of the sunlight danced on the rim of the bluff. Down here, it was already dark and dank and the racing river water was icy cold, buffeting at their legs.

'Dogs can't track through water,' said this enterprising small boy. His face was serious and intent. 'A little way along there is a waterfall. A big waterfall.'

She could hear it, a loud roaring in her ears, a confusion of sound and movement and silver water gushing over the mountainside ahead of them.

The boy gestured her on. They scrabbled over rocks slippery with green slime, across the tumbling river until they were under the waterfall itself, its spray soaking them. To the girl, it seemed a dead end but the boy grinned, suddenly a child again. His back to the rock face, he eased behind the waterfall along a treacherously narrow ledge. He beckoned her to follow him. The falling water was a screen of grey mist tumbling before her eyes. There was an opening in the rocks…not a cave, less than that, but a cleft that gave some shelter from the constant roar of the falls, and from searching eyes. The boy turned and faced her.

'You'll be safe here. They don't know about this. I'll come back later tonight. I have to go before they miss me.'

He smiled crookedly and was gone. She settled herself against the dripping stone and waited.

Niko was breathless when he reached the men's quarters and wriggled under the goatskin wall into the dark tent. Asperto was on the lookout for him. He was a tall man, angular and bony now that he was losing flesh, as they all were with little enough to eat. His skin was the deep brown of oiled olive wood but he had a shock of thick white hair and a straggling white beard. He said he preferred to be clean shaven but it wasn't allowed. His face creased into folds, like a camel's, and his eyelashes were long like a camel's. He had thick dark eyebrows and a mouth that seemed full of white teeth when he smiled. An ugly face but a nice face, thought Nico, and a kind man. Before the falling down sickness he had been strong and full of plans to escape. Now, he shrugged his shoulders and accepted that his life would be short and bitter. He liked this resourceful young boy, and the way he was determined to save his pretty sister.

'You're soaked – and shivering. Come on, let's get you into dry clothes.'

'Where is everybody?'

'Sent out – seems there's work to do. Thought it might be a good idea to play sick – give me a good excuse to stay here and wait for you.'

'Have they missed me?' They were speaking in flat, quiet voices; whispers carried but not these deadened low tones.

'Big Aziz asked where you were but they were too busy searching for the new boy. Seems he's vanished into thin air.'

He slanted a glance down at the boy, naked now, and all skinny gooseflesh. 'Here – let me.' He rubbed warmth back into the boy with a rough blanket until his skin was glowing.

'What happened to the mare?'

'Still here. The boy won't get far on foot. Cloak's still here as well, and his bow and quiver and satchel. Vecdet's got those.'

Niko pulled a tunic over his head, shabby rough cloth but dry. 'You never know. If he can vanish into thin air, as you say, maybe he can vanish the mare as well. Pouff! Like that.'

'Better to leave the mare and vanish himself as far away as possible,' Asperto said. 'The mare is valuable – worth more than a boy slave – and too well protected where she's stabled.'

Niko considered that. 'You're probably right,' he agreed. 'What happened to Hatice?'

'She's all right. Beaten, of course, and the tents are to be well guarded tonight. Both of them. Best not try to see your sister tonight.' Asperto spat angrily. 'That Vecdet, he's a bad man.'

There was movement at the entrance to the tent. Both man and boy stiffened, waiting. It was Big Aziz, stooping his hulk, a lit torch in one hand which cast sinister shadows across his seamed and battered face.

'So you've recovered. Where's that boy? He's wanted.'

'Here with me.' Asperto's arm was clamped around the boy's skinny shoulders. He pulled him into view.

'And where were you?'

Niko whimpered, little animal sounds of distress, pressing closer to Asperto's side.

'Stop snivelling. And you, stop making a girl out of him. Answer me.'

Niko's lower lip was thrust out and trembling. Tears were gathering in his eyes, the long lashes fluttering.

'Please, *beyefendi*, I was frightened. First there was Hatice and then that boy who came... I was frightened. So I hid.'

'You hid?' Aziz's eyes narrowed.

'With the donkeys.'

'With the donkeys!' He was scornful, sneering. 'A growing boy and you hid with the donkeys! That bitch Hatice has more guts than you.'

'I'm sorry...' the desolate little voice trailed off.

'No wonder we couldn't find you, hey? A donkey amongst the donkeys. And you, you useless hulk.' He turned to Asperto. 'You're both needed. Outside. There's work to be done.'

'Now? In the dark?' Niko quavered.

It wasn't the usual routine. Usually, by dark, they were confined for the night.

'Yes, in the dark, you pathetic wretch. We're leaving at first light, after the dawn call to prayer.'

'I thought we were staying here for a few days yet.'

'Stop whining. First light, we leave. There's work to do before you get any sleep or supper.'

Niko wiped a hand across his nose and snuffled loudly.

'What about that boy who came?'

'What about that boy who came?' Aziz mimicked. 'Nothing about that boy who came. There's no time to waste on one poxy boy. Come on, move yourselves.'

He waited for them to move in front of him to the entrance. Niko braced himself for the sudden sharp cuff to the side of his head. He knew it would happen: that was Aziz's way. One day, he'd find a way of getting his own back for all the taunts and threats and blows that came his way.

Later, much later, they were sent back to the tent. Supper was meagre: that morning's bread but it was already hard, and rancid, crumbling goats' cheese cut from the big goatskin-wrapped rounds. But they were hungry. They were kept hungry.

'Short rations again,' someone grumbled.

'Yes,' Asperto agreed, briefly, then that warm smile lit up his face. 'Hunger is a treasure which is preserved with God,' he said gravely, 'who gives it to his special friends.'

'I suppose that's another of those famous quotations,' Russian Ivan said, unimpressed. He sniffed at the cheese and pulled a face.

'The Mevlana Jalal al Din Rumi.' Asperto bent his head respectfully as he pronounced the name of the great Sufi mystic.

'Well, I'd rather not be a special friend and then I'd not go hungry,' Niko muttered. He heard the men tutting in disapproval of such ungodliness but Asperto laughed. *That Niko, so young, so sharp, like bitter lemons.*

Short rations or not, Niko surreptitiously slid some bread and a lump of the cheese into the folds of his tunic. He was so tired he could hardly keep his eyes open but he had a promise to keep. He made himself focus on the men's talk. There was Hatice's latest folly to be talked over, and the useless search for the stranger, and Vecdet's bad temper until the messenger had arrived. News of a deal to be made at the next *han*, they were saying, that was the reason for the sudden departure.

Niko nodded. Slaves they may be but there were ways and means of sifting out information. He thought of the youth shivering in the dripping dark cleft behind the waterfall. He would be cold and hungry and he, Niko, had promised to return. He still didn't know what had made him risk his life like that. Something about the way horse and rider had ridden along the bluff, so innocent and so carefree. Something about the way the youth had held himself, so valiant and courageous. And the hiding place! He had determined this was how he and Agathi would escape. A lucky chance, the *han* being full so they were camping here instead. And finding the hidden place – that had been a chance in a million. Too good to miss.

He always grabbed the chance to reconnoitre and this was a gift of a hiding place. And now what had happened? That fool Hatice had caused a riot so there was no way he could rescue Agathi tonight. And then he'd handed over the hiding place to the stranger. And now they were to leave at first light, after the call to prayer, and he'd promised the stranger he'd return tonight.

She had given him up. Of course he wouldn't come back. How could he? Perilous, to escape like that from the guards, and in the dark such a dangerous route. And why risk it all for a stranger? Even so, she couldn't stop herself from hoping. She was shivering violently, short hair plastered to her scalp, clothes sodden, hugging herself in a vain effort to keep warm. Time stretched out. So much empty time and darkness and wetness. So dark, she could barely see her hand in front of her face, except that the ever-falling water was translucent in the night, itself reflecting a strange light. She stared into it. The world was shrunk to this narrow cleft behind the luminous falling water, yet it felt immense and frightening and she was very small and lost and lonely and sad. Her world, the lovely safe world of the summer dwelling, was gone beyond imagining.

The waterfall drowned out all other noise so that when he did arrive it took her by surprise. She didn't even hear the scrabbling of his feet on the rock. For long moments, she couldn't breathe with the shock of it.

Niko swung round the edge of the not-quite-cave and stopped there, listening.

'I'm here,' he said into the darkness.

'You've come back.'

'I said I would.'

'I didn't know...'

'I always keep my promise. I've brought you some bread and cheese. It's not fit to give to a dog but there's nothing else. One of the women caused a riot and they've put us all on short rations.'

He was next to her by now, a dim shape in the darkness, pushing the food into her hands. She took it gratefully.

'Plenty to drink, anyway.' It was a feeble joke but she heard the boy chuckle. 'Are they still searching for me?'

'Not now. Listen,' he said, 'there's news. Seems there's business to be had at the next *han* so we're leaving early in the morning, as soon as morning prayer is done. You were lucky – a messenger arrived while they were still looking for you. The donkey was hee-hawing so much about the chance of a good sale that he gave up on you.'

'The donkey?'

'That fat belly, Vecdet.'

It was her turn to laugh. It suited the man. Yes, he was a donkey and he did have a fat belly.

'You'll have to stay here until we go. Don't risk leaving this place. We'll come down to get water before we leave.'

'I'm very cold.'

'You must be. I was freezing when I got back and you've been here for hours. I couldn't get your cloak and things – Vecdet's got them – but I've brought a bit of blanket. It's hidden at the entrance to the waterfall under some rocks.' He considered. 'Let's go outside for a while, get you warmer and drier. But you must be back here before dawn.'

They negotiated the slippery ledge and recovered the meagre cloth that was the blanket and sat huddled together under its rough warmth where the rocks were out of reach of the incessant spray and the dark night covered them with safety.

'Why not go now? Why don't you come with me?'

'Too many guards and dogs,' he said briefly. 'And I can't go. My sister was taken as well and I can't leave without her.'

'Who are you?'

'Niko,' he said simply. 'They call me Niko. You?'

She hesitated. She had many names but all of them female. She did not want to lie to this brave boy who had risked all to save her. It was only fair to tell him the truth.

'It is our custom to be named after our grandparents. I am called after my grandmother. I am Sophia.'

Silence.

'Sophia?'

'Yes.'

'Your grandmother's name?'

'It's one of my names. There are others.'

'You're a girl.'

It wasn't a question but she answered as if it were. 'Yes.'

Silence. She wondered what he was thinking.

'You are as brave as any boy. As any man.' It was generous praise. She blushed in the darkness. 'I wish my sister was brave but she cries all the time. It's very hard to make a plan to escape when she won't help.'

He suddenly sounded very young, like the boy-child he was before he was captured.

'You're very clever,' she said. 'I didn't have a plan, not really. I had to escape before my uncles came for me.' That was last night, she realised. Only last night that she and the chestnut mare had left the summer camp and travelled through the dark land together. And because of this boy she had escaped again.

They huddled together there in the dark, exchanging stories in flat, quiet voices that wouldn't carry in the stillness of the night; the bare details only but the young girl and the younger boy interpreted each other's silences, unspoken truths, crippling fear, terrible sense of loss. His parents had been killed in the raid, he told her. He'd seen it, seen the sweep of sword, the spurt of blood. It still gave him bad dreams. Others had been taken from their village, all young – some younger than him – but they had been sold or given as gifts as they travelled the trade route. Now there was only Agathi and himself left from their village.

There were moments when they laughed quietly together, and sighed over their troubles, and laughed and sighed again. But empty time no longer stretched ahead of them. Soon it would be dawn.

'You'll maybe hear us leaving, maybe not, but wait until the sun is well risen.'

'Will you be safe?'

'No need to worry about me.'

'I'll come back for you.'

Niko shook his head. 'Better not.'

'I'll come back for you,' she said again. 'I'll come back for you and your sister. And I keep my promises too.'

Morning was grey and chill, sun sullen behind swirling mist. The sweet mountain summer was over. She had stayed outside until the sky lightened and she could hear in the distance sounds of men about their business in the half-light, their voices accentuated by the stillness and emptiness of this vast land. She had shed the rough blanket and carefully hid it from sight before she edged her way back to the cleft to wait. Sure enough, as Niko had said, a troupe of men and horses and mules and camels came down to the river. There must be a track, she thought; she and Niko had taken the steepest, quickest route. There was a moment of terror when one man dared to stand under the force of the water. He was naked, clothed only in the silver shafts of water. His eyes were closed and his mouth open, drinking in the gushing water. His body was brown and muscular, with pale patches where his clothes had protected him from the summer sun. His scrotum and penis dangled, flaccid and white like dead things in the cold water. After that first fleeting glimpse, she had shut her eyes and pressed tighter into the darkness of the cleft. She heard his friends call to him, laughing and jeering, and then they left. By then, she was so numbed with cold and fear that she had ceased to shiver and lay curled in a sodden heap on the rocky ground.

She waited...waited...crept out of the cleft and along the treacherous ledge to the edge of the waterfall. She listened. Nothing but the roaring of water. She went further, out into the woodland and listened again. Nothing. No voices of men; no bleating or braying or bellowing or snorting or coughing of animals. No smells of cooking only the faintly sweet-sour stink of animals. She uncovered the blanket again from its hiding place and huddled into its not-quite-dry warmth. Gradually, her shivering ceased. Soon it would be time to wade the river, climb up to the bluff, unless she found and followed the track. That was easy. She could see where the ground was churned up by trampling hooves and feet at the edge of the river, and where the track wound up through the rocks. Above her, the sky was heavy with mist creeping along the edges of the bluff. Her wet clothes clung to her skin and hung in sodden folds. Not a hope of drying them. Blue dye had seeped out, as it always did, no matter how many washings, and it tinged her skin with blue. Blue for luck, she thought. Well, she was alive and free so that was luck, wasn't it?

And they were gone. More luck. There was barely a trace of the camp; crusted pats of shit where the animals had been; flattened spikes of grass and thyme; the burnt out ashes of a fire. But she was hungry and tired and cold and there was no chestnut mare to carry her. No bow and quiver of arrows. No warm *ferace*. She felt for the jade axe in its pouch round her neck, clutching it tight to her. Protection, Nene had said, and now she needed protection even more than before. She still had her dagger, concealed in her belt. But there was no satchel, no provisions, nor Nene's precious scissors. And there was far to go before she could hope to track down the strangers' camp. Far to go. The first rain was falling as she struck out to rejoin the road to Karaman in its shallow bowl in the great central plateau ringed by high mountains.

leper: spring: 1334

6

I knew you straightway my friend, though we were all but ten years distant from our last – our first – meeting. We were striplings then. I was training to be a squire. You were a skinny, mucky, stinking pot boy not fit to kiss my boots and there you were, whispering comfort in that thick, dark night of terror, telling me I was safe, telling me to sleep.

It wasn't comfort that silenced me. I suppose you imagined it was. No, it was the shame of it, the shame. I was older than you. I was learning to be a warrior for Queen Isabella and the country that had been torn apart by that fool husband of hers. Then that day of terror that made me sick to my stomach. You weren't there to see it. How could you know? My father made me stand close to watch the execution of the King's Favourite. Who was fool and who was king? Despenser was a ruthless, cruel man and now he was caught, imprisoned. How we hated him. They said he'd tried to starve to death to save himself from grisly execution and he looked like a skeleton, like a death's head. He was stripped of his clothing and set up backwards on a horse and whipped through the streets and everywhere strident pipes and trumpets and the howls of a mob rabid with hate. He deserved all that. Yes, that was deserved. But then they cut him, they scratched holy words into his sinful flesh. Somebody crushed a crown of nettles down over his head. And he was screaming and howling, screaming and howling.

And after that. After that. He was raised high, high on the highest gallows I've ever seen. So high my head was dizzied. And after that.

After that. Taken down and then oh then the digging into a man's vitals and the drawing out of his innermost parts, yards and yards of gut and the burning of them in front of his eyes and him still living and screaming screaming screaming. Horrid sounds. Horrid sounds that no man should ever make. And his man's parts sliced off and burnt before his eyes and the crowd screaming with merriment and the man's ghastly howling echoing in my head. I couldn't get it out of my head. And the woman, his wife, his queen, the harlot with the man Mortimer at her side... How could she sit there watching and feasting and celebrating? It seemed to me she was supping his very innards, gloating over the bloodiness, slurping content. 'She-wolf.' That's what they called her, but spoken quiet, never loud for fear of her. Ravenous and dangerous 'She-wolf'.

And then you, unwashed pot-boy in a place where you had no business to be, wanting to bring me comfort. What comfort did you bring me? I was a laughing stock, a joke, the coward son of a knight-at-arms. I had disgraced my father and my name. I was outcast. Dishonour was hung around my neck and my father sent me from his sight. Oh yes, I was found a place at a convenient distance with a friend of my father's where I could learn the art of knighthood but they all knew and made mock of me behind my back. My father grieved at my disgrace. I was – always had been – the son who fainted at the sight of blood; the son who trembled to spear a wild pig; the son who screamed frantic fear in the night. Unbearable dishonour. And so I crept away, leaving at night, like a thief stealing away, like a leper, an untouchable. I crept away and found my own fortune.

And then we meet all but ten years later. But you do not recognise me.

Anatolia: late summer 1336

7

D...dronken, dronken,
Dronken, dronken, ydronken;
Dronken is Tabart,
Dronken is Tabart ate wyne,
Hay!
(Anon, 14ᵗʰC)

The call to prayer, early dawn like any other, woke him from fitful sleep. A dull day of mist and rain and the threat of more to come; not promising and time they were on the long journey to the coast. Could be it was fairer ahead, in the great bowl of the plateau where rainfall was scant. Edgar said he was well enough to travel, if they took it in easy stages, so all seemed set fair.

Well now, that wasn't to be. For one thing, the camels were fractious. They were the one-humped type, a sturdy breed. Not up to carrying as much as the two-hump but the goods they were taking back to Venezia were not weighty and the one-humps were good in this big country so that's what they'd settled on and not regretted it. Trouble was, they were nervy beasts, difficult to handle, and this misty morning they were not cooperative. 'Got the hump,' he said, and Rémi grinned at the silly joke. The thread-like scars above his mouth stretched white, a permanent reminder of what had been. How he loved this gallant child, Dai thought, and ruffled the boy's dark straight hair; his constant shadow since he'd found him begging for morsels of food on the streets of Ieper – how long ago, now? Six years? No one should ever go hungry. Always cheerful, he was never a moment's bother, not like some he could name.

'Let's be thankful they've only the one hump, hey?'

Rémi grinned again and set about cajoling the lofty animals to kneel. Maybe they were bothered by the noise and fret because the court was full of caravans preparing to leave. It took time to settle them, to load bundles, and Blue was missing. It was Blue's job to supervise the getting ready in the morning. Already, the courtyard was full of activity and the great doors of the *han* were open; caravans were already setting out, packs weighted on the camels and the camels flanked by donkeys and mules and dogs and the cameleteers twitching whips and shouting instructions and encouragement. Late risers would be scurrying into clothes inside the dim rooms of the great hall of the *han* or hunched in the latrines. In the courtyard the *mescit* still had its worshippers, though the Muslims who had risen early for the call to prayer were the first to pack up, the first to leave; Christians were bleary eyed, late to bed after sitting late over talk and cups.

That was what Blue had done – sat late over his cups. They'd come to tell him Blue was drunk. Not just drunk but reeling drunk and slurring that stupid song. *All stand still. All stand still. Let thy body go. Drunk drunk drunk…*

'Leave him behind shall we?' Twm said.

'No. Can't do that.' But he thought about it, thought how simple it would be to leave Blue behind and ride out from the *han*. This wasn't the first time, it wouldn't be the last. He'd had them in trouble before with his drunkenness. Of course, he ended as he always did, hurling abuse. Mercifully, that dialect of his was so broad that very little of what he said was understood by the staid, sober Muslims.

'Yer the wust coward that ever pissed,' he was ranting. Dai could hear him from across the courtyard. 'Turd in thi' teeth. Shit for brains. Lying arsehole. Stinking dog breath…'

Blue managed to land the first blow before Dai got to him, full in the face of the outraged man he was insulting so roundly. A big man he was, head and shoulders above Dai and with a belly on him. It took three of them to manhandle him, and him belching and farting and threatening seven hells all the way across the courtyard to the sleeping quarters where, of course, he'd woken the early-to-beds with his uproar and they had been bent on revenge. That was when Dai sighed with resignation and applied pressure just below the ear, a trick learnt in the old days, and Blue collapsed mid-word. Silenced but not silent. All night long his snores reverberated throughout the building.

And here he was, still drunk, giggling like a girl, face bursting shiny red under the bruise-blue stains and reddened eyes unfocused.

And behind him, of course, an irate merchant. Dai recognised the man from a meeting earlier in the season.

'That liar, that braggart, that thug. Is he yours?'

'He's mine. What's to do?'

'He's broken heads, that's what's to do. Your man there…'

Blue smirked and waved and chortled the next line of the song.

'*Dronken is Tabart…*'

'…smashed the skulls of two of my best men.'

'…*at wine…*' Blue carolled.

'No doubt they were in their cups too.'

'The wust cowards that ever pissed.' A reverberating belch.

'Who's to say?' The merchant was blustering, gagging in his outrage. 'I'm two men short now. What have you to say to that?'

'*Hay!*'

'I'm a man short. And seems I've the worst of the bargain.'

'Turd in thi' teeth.'

'It is not a joking matter.'

'Did I say it was?' He sighed, contemplated the angry man in front of him. 'What is it you want, sir?'

'I want compensation.'

'For what?'

'Two men, two days' pay.'

He sighed, nodded, sighed again, declined to bargain. 'That seems reasonable.' They agreed terms, shook hands, *akçes* were handed over. The merchant was mollified, reconciled to good terms.

'You are a good man to do business with. But that man of yours!'

'Yes?'

'My advice – get rid of him. No good. Always drunk.'

Dai smiled. 'But I follow your great Mevlana's advice.'

'What do you mean?'

'What was it he said? "Come, come, come again, even if you have broken your vows a thousand times." How can I refuse when the Mevlana himself says this?'

'You are a good man.'

No I'm not, he thought; if I were a good man it wouldn't be Blue's throat I'm wanting to slit.

Later, of course, when he'd sobered up, Blue'd be as penitent as he always was, weeping, making promises he would never keep. 'A were well on wi' drinkin'. A'm reet sorry, that A'm Dai. Nivver agaan. Nivver agaan.' Now, he was staggering about the court trying to load the mules though there were men in the service of the *han* whose job it was to do just that. It was Edgar who led him like a child, Edgar who was the butt of Blue's jokes and jibes, Edgar who was truly a good man. Not yet fit enough to travel but swearing he was well enough.

'O' course yer be. A new man, ent ya, altar boy? A knew yer wouldn't lig i' bed this morn.' Blue cuffed Edgar's head but lightly because despite the joking and jibing the big man had a fondness for quiet pale Edgar. 'And 'im as was deäd comed out,' he slurred and Dai turned away to smile because he recognised in the broad speech the story of Lazarus and his rising from the dead. He silently blessed the wise woman again but in the middle of the blessing he paused. He looked again at Blue, closely now. Too pleased he was with the boy's return to health. Too pleased with himself, more like.

'Blue, what have you done?'

'What yer meän? A've done nowt.' But his eyes shifted away from Dai's.

'I know you, Blue. You've been up to something.'

'Nowt as matters.'

Dai waited. Blue slanted a bleary-eyed sideways glance at him. Edgar shifted uncomfortably and pulled at the neck of his shift. Dai caught a glimpse of a thin leather thong. He reached out and pulled at it. A small bag came into view.

'What's this?'

Edgar blushed. 'It's done no harm, Dai, and it pleased Blue.' He opened the bag. Inside were three live spiders and a few specks that were dead flies.

'What is this?'

'That's 'ow we done it at hoäme. My dad told me, and his dad told him afore that, and our fore-elders all said as it was best to do to break a fever.' He was belligerent, loudly certain he was in the right of it. Dai sighed.

'Tell me, Blue.'

'Well, stands to reason, doän't it? Fever's all shivery, use a shivery spider to draw it out. And look at 'im standing straight up this morn.'

'It was the wise woman's simples that helped him, Blue. You must know that.'

'How can yer tell? How dust know it wan't the shivery spiders?' He spat, suddenly, vigorously. 'Best is a live spider rolled i' butter and swallered, like A said. But the boy weren't up to it and yer said A wan't to try. And A didn't. A promised yer that A wouldn't and A kep' mi promise.'

'So you did,' Dai said softly. 'You cared about him, Blue. That was maybe the real medicine.'

Blue's eyes filled suddenly and unexpectedly.

'Dai lad, A 'ad to do summat when yer were went. He were like to die afore you come back. A 'ad to do summat. A wrapped 'im in indigo to cool 'is fever then A thought on the shivery spiders. He's nobbut a bairn, Dai. It's what mi fayther did and it nivver did none of us no harm. A haven't done no harm.' His blackened nails scratched at his armpits releasing a rank stench of sweat and stale ale.

'No, you haven't.' Dai agreed but quietly, touched by the man's worry for the boy. 'Maybe you did him good after all, Blue. Now, get your body under cold water and do all of us some good.'

'You're too soft on that oaf, Dafydd. He'll have us all strung up by our wrists before he's done.' Thomas Archer glared at Blue's retreating back.

'He means no harm, Twm.'

'He might not mean harm but it's harm done, all the same.'

Dai sighed; he wasn't in the mood for another argument with Twm Archer.

'All right, all right, I can see you won't listen to reason. You're an obstinate man, Dafydd.'

'So I've been told, and often enough. Mam used to say I took after *Taid* – my grandfather.'

'Now there's a combination: a stubborn man of conscience.' Twm was angry. 'Worried her into her grave, did you?'

Dai gave him a hard look. 'Something like that.' His voice was curt, warning Twm Archer to say no more, but it was the bleakness in the look that silenced the dark man.

It was late in the day when they left the *han*. All day the sun struggled to be seen through mist and rain and now it was low in the sky beneath heavy swags of cloud, shooting pale light and shadows by turn along the land. As they were leaving, another large caravan was arriving, with camels and mules and a string of horses. His own dependable brown stallion snorted, nostrils flaring, then whickered and one of the horses in the string neighed in answer and sidled sideways. A chestnut with a pale mane and white blaze down her nose. Dai frowned. Surely he'd seen the horse before?

He recognised faces, though he did not know their names. There was that squat, greasy ox of a man he'd seen before at the market. Slave dealers. That was one commodity he would not deal in. He knew too well what it was like to be tied hand and soul to a cruel master. Slaves might turn a good profit but not for him and, God be thanked, not for the man he worked for. The Mevlana himself had condemned slavery. There was a glimpse of a skinny curly-haired little boy darting to catch some nothing, and a stream of abuse that followed him. He turned his head and Dai caught a flash of dark bruising down the side of his face. A babe of no more than four summers – too young, surely, to be a slave – was stumbling along, clinging to the hand of a gaunt, strong-faced woman with a lividly scarred forehead. By her side was a young girl, pale as the day's sun, her beauty all but extinguished by fatigue and fear and hopelessness. No, slaving was not for him. On their way to Attaleia, no doubt, and after that, if trade was poor, across the seas to Candia.

8

I wonder, is anyone here
A stranger so forlorn as I?
(Yunus Emre, 14thC)

Darkness again and the walls of the *han* sheer and stark in front of her. No windows. Never windows. The *han*s were built for protection as well as comfort. The huge gateway reared up in front of her, its portals elaborately carved, twisting and twining in a rhythmic, ornamental dance of stone. At the heart of it were the stars, Nene had told her, always leaping from one star to another in an infinite pattern. Continual linking paths, continual return to the centre of all things. *And so it is for poor weak mortals. Remember this, child.*

The doors were closing against the threatening night but not before she'd caught a glimpse of Vecdet and the huge scarred guard. Business. That's why they'd left so early. As luck would have it, this was the *han* they were headed for. They were talking with the *hancı* who gave admittance and their voices floated back to where she was hidden behind the grand portal of the *han*.

'A slave,' she caught, 'escaped.'

'We'll look out for him, never worry sir. Slim, brown hair, shabby blue clothes, travelling alone – shouldn't be hard to spot.'

A murmur she couldn't catch and the *hancı's* voice raised.

'No loyalty, these slaves. Not to be trusted.'

Better not beg for admittance, then. Better to accept another night of cold and an empty stomach. The family at Alahan was far away. Niko was somewhere inside the *han*. The sky had cleared with the rising wind and its great arc was crammed with star clusters that pressed down on her as she gazed into the vastness of eternity. The high mountains were black against the sky; there was the huge mass of Karadağ, the black mountain, rearing up as it suddenly did out of the plain. It was not yet frosted with white but further to the north-east was Argaeus glimmering white with the snow that never left it. The *han* was not far from the town that the Karamanoğlu had made their capital, their chief place, and from where they had decreed, only ten years ago, that Turkish was the official language. Christian Turks lived there though a mosque had been built on the ruins of their church. But the town gates would be closed by now and if she were given admittance there was no way of knowing that she would be safe. No, better by far the cold night and an empty stomach and keep the freedom so hard won. She bedded down with the sheep that ran outside the *han*, reared to provide provisions for the travellers. It was comforting to be close to their warm bodies, feel their warm breath, hear their steady munching. An easy target for prowlers in the night, man and beast, and it was the luckless sheep boy's job to protect them, him and the pack of dogs that ran with him. Both he and the dogs had gazed at her for long moments then accepted her presence without question.

She knew of this *han*. She'd never been to it, but Nene had told her of it. This was the place where Nene had first seen the man who was her grandfather. It was long ago, when the Osmanlı tribes were first raiding the coast towns. Nene had told her of it. She thought of it now, dreamed of the telling, slept while she dreamed.

I was young then – not so young, as far as my father was concerned; he still hoped for a bride-price. I was proud, disdainful even, and the young men dared not offer for me. It made my father angry. But I was young, with a young girl's dreams. I wanted a hero to sweep me off my

❀ 75 ❀

feet. Someone courageous and strong. Handsome, of course. He had to be handsome. You dream of Bamsi Beyrek – of course I know you do, child. How could I not? For me, there was the pick of our Greek heroes. Our history is heavy with heroes.

It was spring. We were returning from a visit to our kin in Cappadocia, father, mamma, me, my young brother. We stayed the night in the han. And there he was. Not handsome, girl, don't think that. Not handsome. Not even tall and strong. At first sight, not a hero either, but I know now that's what he was, in his own way. What was it, then, that tore my heart and soul? Who can tell, girl? When you feel this, then you will feel love and you will give your heart and soul and life for your beloved. Let it not be for the sheep-brained oafs! Never for them! Listen to me, girl.

He was telling stories in the courtyard. That is what he was: a tale teller. He had gathered about him so many, all religions and races. Christian and Muslim alike, and Jew, merchants from the east and west lands, they all gathered to hear him. He had a way of drawing you in, taking you with him into another world. We all love to hear stories. That is what he said. It makes children of us all and we forget to fight. Sharing tales and laughter is what makes peace amongst us. So wise, your grandfather. I stayed on the outside of the gathering, listening greedily to his words. His voice…oh…it was beguiling. Maybe I fell in love with his voice first, girl. Who knows? Our eyes met. Just once, fleetingly, but it was enough. Where was disdain now? Where was pride? They are nothing where love is.

I could hardly sleep for thinking of him, and when I did sleep I dreamed of him. Before the first call to prayer I crept out into the courtyard. The new day was soft with mountain mist that would clear soon after sunrise. Early as I was, he was already there. He was playing on a small pipe fashioned from a swan's bone. A haunting sound and a haunting melody though clumsily played. I'm no musician, he told me. This swan pipe was my brother's. My brother could make it sing like no other. From our first meeting, there was no pretence between us. Your grandfather spoke only the truth. How he was searching for his brother, had been searching for years, hearing scraps of news, meeting travellers who had heard his brother's wonderful music, recollections of hearing he was in this town, in that village, in one country, in another. He had the gift of languages and this made it easy for him to talk with strangers – I would say touched with Pentecostal fire but that would be blasphemy, eh child? He said it was useful to speak with all those he met but music was the true path to the soul. It was not his gift; that belonged to his brother.

He was here now because he had met Yunus Emre, our great poet so sadly dead now. That was in Kayseri. Yes, Yunus Emre remembered Ned – that was the brother's name – and the frail, grey-haired man who travelled with him. Two great musicians, though the older man could no longer play. One of his hands was crippled by a past injury and was now swollen with painful joints. That was three years ago. Where were they heading? Yunus Emre couldn't remember. They had all three travelled for a while together. They had played, sung, spoken poetry. Your grandfather felt so close, so close to finding them, his brother and the older man…and then nothing. Nothing. It was as if the earth had swallowed them.

He told me that first morning he would leave me if he had news of his brother. He never pretended otherwise, girl. He was an honest man who loved me as an honest man loves. That morning before dawn I shall never forget, never regret. Our souls met and recognised each other.

Great love is a gift not given to everyone. Such a man. I was blessed. To be in that place, at that time was God's plan. We should have travelled a week earlier but my mother had been feverish – not the cave sickness. Later I learnt from the servants that she had been with child but she had miscarried. We did not talk of such matters in my father's house.

Of course, I said nothing of our meeting; not to my father, certainly, and not to my mother. She would surely have told my father. But I

● 77 ●

always wondered if she suspected something. Love shines in the face, child, like the bright sun. There is no concealing it. My father never took much note of me, unless it suited him, and for once I was grateful. When we left the han later that morning, I knew he would follow.

The call to prayer roused her though she had been drifting between sleeping and waking for a long time, feeling the dew that had settled clammily on her eyes and cheeks and mouth. Now it was time to stir, to move, to follow the road to Konya and from there to the great lakes and from there? Attaleia, where she would find a ship to take her to the cold lands.

She had given up any hope of catching up with Thomas Archer and the brown man with the long, rhythmic name and their caravan. Perhaps she might, just might, meet up with them in Attaleia but by then she would not be useful to them. She wasn't even useful to herself this morning; she was dizzy with cold and fatigue and hunger. It was difficult to focus on the road, and the caravans following her, and there were swirls of mist obscuring everything. She heard the great caravan long before it loomed up and passed her, grey shapes in a sun-blocked land, hooves churning the road into a mass of wet sand and mud, whistles and shouts from the muleteers, curses too, and cracking whips. She had sidestepped into the shelter of a rock outcrop and shrank into it, invisible, feeling sharp prickly shrubs crushed against her. She watched the caravan unseen. She recognised fat Vecdet's outline. There was no sign of the Venetian lord. She looked and looked for Niko but there was no sign of him either amongst the rest of the slaves, roped together now and marching in a solemn column. She wondered where he was. She caught a glimpse of a slim, fragile-seeming girl with pale plaits hanging below her head shawl. It must be his sister, Agathi. Where the sister was, there he would be. 'Wait for me, Niko,' Kazan murmured. 'Wait for me. Stay alive. I'll find you.'

9

Who are you trying to run from?
Yourself? That's impossible.
(Mevlana Jalal al Din Rumi, 1207 – 1273)

There'd been no hope of reaching the next *han* by sunset. They knew that. No hope, either, of travelling with another caravan, as they often did for safety. Too late in setting off. Then one of the mules shed its load and they had to stop again to repack and refasten ropes. Blue hung his head in shame because it was his drunken fumbling that was the cause, not the muleteer's fault at all. Twm glared at him, his lips a tight line, but he said nothing. Uneasy they all were. Well known it was, this stretch of the road, for robbers and bandits. They had taken over a town high in the mountains, see, and launched raids from their stronghold.

There was an ancient citadel close by, not far from where the roads divided, one leading straight across the plain to Konya; the other winding down through the valleys and gorges towards Süleymanşeyhir and the lake. They were still undecided which route to take: Twm was in favour of the shorter route through the valleys but the guide, now, he was wanting to take the longer, straighter route to Konya then another straight road well-serviced with *han*s. Safer it was, he said, and his men agreed with him. They were fair to quarrelling over it and, what with Blue still sulking and Edgar swearing he was fit when he wasn't, there was trouble brewing right enough. Well, for tonight there was no need for deciding. The small caravan wound its way up the bare hill to the citadel. All was ruins now, except for the walls soundly rebuilt and a few of the buildings good enough to repair and use. There was a good, high, stone building, easy to defend. Dai knew the chief there, had stayed there before. Men shouted down from the walls, wanting to know who they were, where they were bound, the usual security. Then there was silence and a new figure joined those on the walls, his stooped gait betraying his age; his voice was rasping and hoarse.

'Dai – is that you? You're welcome, dear boy, welcome, you and your friends.' And then the opening of the gates and wiry arms reaching up to clasp him and exclamations. 'Where have you been? How long is it since you came to see us? Too long!' His three sons stood by him, two of them towering over him, the third slim and slight, all with dark, hooded eyes like their father and hair that was as dark as their father's had been when he was a young man, wild with curls hanging loose to their shoulders. A clutch of young boys hovered near them, all with the same dark eyes, dark hair. 'My grandsons,' Kara Kemal said. 'See how they've grown!'

Three years' growth it was; the youngest a babe-in-arms he was then and now a plump toddler trailing after his brothers. The women held back under the shadow of the arched colonnade, their heads shawled and faces half-hidden, shy where the *yürük* women were bold. 'We are quite a family now, don't you agree, my friend?' Kara Kemal was complacent with satisfaction. 'What more can an old man desire than the comfort of his home and his family?' His eyes glittered under their heavy lids. 'Now I have only to find a good wife for my Mehmi, my youngest. Better to be home than travelling the roads, hey? Time you were settling down with a brood of your own, hey?'

Dai laughed. 'That's what you said last time. And the answer's still the same: time enough.'

'There's never time enough, boy. Find yourself a wife!'

The eyes still glittered but moisture had gathered there. Dai reached out a hand and grasped the older man's arm. No words spoken, none needed; Kara Kemal's first wife, the mother of his sons, had been a good woman. Kemal had told him so though Dai had never known her. Kemal had married again late in life; he had adored his beautiful young wife, had never ceased to wonder at his good fortune in winning her. He had laughed at himself, quoting from the Masnavi, the book of the teachings of Jalal al Din Rumi, the Mevlana, the Sufi mystic revered by Kemal. Always there was a quotation, a lesson to be learned from the great teacher, he said, and that time he had recalled the story of the man whose hair was half grey who came hurrying to a barber who was a friend of his:

'"Pluck out the white hairs from my beard, for I have selected a young bride." Remember this, my friend?' Dai remembered the story and remembered how Kemal had spluttered with laughter in the telling, holding his young wife by her slim hand, his eyes softened with love for her. 'Remember how the barber cut off the man's beard and laid it before him? "Do you part them for the task is beyond me."' He shook with laughter. '"The task is beyond me,"' he repeated. 'This one says there is no need to separate the white from the dark. She tells me it is a sign of wisdom. I am become a wise man in my old age, Dai, my friend!'

'Wise in the choice of a wife, that is certain,' he had responded. Dai had met her but once; he remembered a beautiful, gentle creature years younger than her husband and devoted to him. She had died one hot summer. Out of sorts one day, feverish the next, dead two days after that. And Kara Kemal a ghost of a man he'd been, haunting his own household. Good it was to see him bright and spry again.

'How long can you stay? No longer than a night? But it's not safe – the bandits are on the move again. There's little we can do to stop them. The best we can do is make our home safe against them. You must stay longer – stay until a big caravan passes this way.' The words spilled out of him and the sons shook their heads, laughing. He had always been one for the words before he became a ghost.

'There's a caravan on our heels, Kemal,' Dai said, drily.

'Then wait for it, wait for it.'

'It's a slaver.'

'Ah, my friend, still the same as you ever were, aching to make this world a better place.'

'You and your conscience, Dai,' muttered Twm.

Dai grinned. 'That's what they said about *Taid*, my grandfather. Besides, Kemal, I'm only following your Mevlana's teaching – he didn't hold with slaves, did he now? Reckoned we were all free from birth, didn't he now? No, friend, we'll make our own way. We must leave tomorrow. Time we were heading for the port and the Venezia fleet. I promised Heinrijc Mertens we'd be home this year end.'

'Well, a promise is a promise and if it must be tonight only, come in, come in – welcome. We shall make a feast in your honour.'

Tomorrow they must leave, Dai said, but he was worried. Far enough it had been for Edgar to travel that day. As it was, he was wan-faced and feeble by the time they reached the ruined citadel and glad to rest his bones. Best place for him, for sure. Kara Kemal couldn't do enough for him. 'He's your friend,' Kara Kemal said again and again. 'Any friend of yours we honour for your sake, Dai my friend.' When he greeted Blue, his head tilted on one side in the way Dai remembered from his first meeting, mischief glittering in his dark eyes as he noted the blue-black stains on the man's hands and arms and face and measured the height of the Fenlander. He himself barely reached as high as Blue's broad chest. 'And now you bring me a blue man-mountain, my friend. Well, all are welcome for your sake – and maybe for theirs. Who knows except Allah the great, the all-compassionate?' His hands went out to the big man's fleshy paws to welcome him into his home. His gaze moved on to Rémi, stroking and soothing a skittish mule. 'You still have the boy with you, then. And how he's grown. He's a credit to you, my friend.'

Rémi's thin face split into a grin, pleased to be remembered, pleased to be praised for his master's sake.

'And these?'

'Twm Archer and Edgar and Giles, Twm's man. Heinrijc Mertens thought I should have more protection; Twm's a fighting man. Giles combines his duties of servant with those of a very competent man-at-arms. Heinrijc was in the right of it, as he always is. It's grateful I've been for Twm's company this journey, and for Giles's.'

Tom lifted an eyebrow in that quizzical, questioning way he had and between them lay memories of dangers past and passed by.

'He's a handsome man!' Kara Kemal chuckled. 'They are both handsome men, Edgar and this Tom Archer: one so dark, the other so fair. My women folk think so as well.' Behind him in the shadows the women were whispering and giggling in the way women do when handsome strangers arrive unexpectedly. 'Go and tell your mistress we have guests,' he called to them. 'Make some refreshment for our visitors instead of making such cackling. You're nothing but hens, the lot of you!' But he was smiling, well pleased. 'And this golden haired one with the so-blue eyes? This is Edgar?'

Edgar's face was flushed with embarrassment.

'Edgar was chance-found on our way and glad we are for his company.'

'More strays, my friend?' the old man murmured. 'Still the same as you ever were. Come, come – the old mother will be glad of your company. She'd a fondness for you, remember? She's not so busy about everybody's business now. All that nagging and chittering – she's too old for that now. And the thing is, I miss it. Isn't that a strange thing?' He was leading them into the courtyard Dai remembered, surrounded by pillars and arches and shadowy rooms within. 'Mother!' Kemal shouted. 'We have visitors. See who is come! Will you remember this stranger?'

Another thing almost forgotten: shouting his news. Never talk quietly if you could shout, that was Kara Kemal. Dai wondered if that was why his voice was hoarse and rasping or if it was only age creeping up on him.

The mother was three years older and three years frailer, her flesh shrunk on her bones and her eyes hooded and whitened, but her wits were as sharp as ever. 'About time you came to see us again, my son.' That was what she had always called him, ever since that first meeting so many years ago now. She stroked the thick Flemish cloth Dai heaped into her hands, crooning over its warmth.

And then the evening meal, though it was clear they hadn't provisions enough for themselves, let alone a whole company, but it was impossible to say anything, make any protest. That was to dishonour the whole tribe and their hospitality. He'd learnt that lesson many years ago now. It was one of the reasons he loved this country. Hadn't his own grandfather taught him to share, to make sacrifices so that others should benefit whatever the cost? And such a cost.

They must sacrifice a kid, Kara Kemal insisted. This was a celebration, a reunion. Dai sent one of the muleteers to unpack a sack of rice. Their offering, he insisted, given in gratitude for hospitality and friendship, and Kemal didn't refuse. Another packet followed, of sugar, and another of olives, and gladly given. No one should ever go hungry. They sat late over the meal, round the great platter of rice and meat spiced with cardamom and cinnamon and pepper, dipping in their right hands to take dainty mouthfuls. Even Blue took less than his share, recognising the hunger of their hosts. And Edgar – Edgar ate sparingly, true, but he ate, a sign that he was on the way to recovering. There was a dish of *aruzza*, the rice and sugar a trembling mass drowned in melting butter. Kara Kemal's delight betrayed how rarely such a dish was served. 'Come, eat,' he said again and again, pressing on them another morsel, just another...

There was music and storytelling. Mehmi, the youngest son, was a gifted storyteller and once had dreams of being apprenticed to a famous storyteller who lived in Akşehir. Not only that, this was where the great joker Nasreddin Hoca was buried. No more than fifty years since his death, his stories were told everywhere there was a gathering, and there were old men still living who claimed they had known him and who were always asked, 'Is this what he said? Truly?' and they would nod and swear it was so, however outrageous and incredible the tale, and say, 'That Hoca, that Nasreddin, he was a wise man, a wise fool. Listen to him; be sure you listen to him.' This night was no exception.

Mehmi began:

'One day Nasreddin Hoca got on his donkey the wrong way, facing towards the tail. "Hoca," the people said, "You are sitting on your donkey backwards!" "No," he replied. "It's not that I am sitting on the donkey backwards…"'

'…the donkey's facing the wrong way,' everyone chorused, and laughed. They knew this story but always there were stories they had never heard before. Some said the Hoca was telling them from his grave.

Mehmi continued:

'The Hoca was going to the mosque with his mullahs. He was riding his donkey backwards…'

'The same donkey?' someone shouted.

'The same donkey, Omar. The mullahs asked, "Why are you riding on the donkey backwards? Isn't that very uncomfortable?" "No," he replied, "if I sat facing forwards, you would be behind me. If you went in front of me, I would be behind you. Either way, I would not be facing you. This is the logical way."'

He waited for the laughter to die down.

'One of Hoca's friends wanted to borrow his donkey – the same donkey – for a day, to go to the mill, but Hoca told him it wasn't there that day. Just as he finished speaking the donkey started braying in the shed. "Your donkey is in the shed. I am disappointed in you. You won't let an old friend like me borrow your donkey just for a day!" "Oh," he replied, "you are a strange man! You don't believe your old friend and me a respectable old man as well; instead you believe the donkey."'

He held up a hand before the applause started, a mischievous grin on his dark face. He looked in that moment so very like the child he had been that Kara Kemal felt his eyes brim with tears.

'Hoca had no money and it was getting worse day after day. He cut down on everything he could, including the food he gave to his donkey. The donkey didn't seem any the worse for it so he kept on cutting down on the food he gave to the donkey.' They were quiet. This story they hadn't heard before. 'One day the donkey died. Hoca was very sad. "What a shame," he said, "just as it was getting used to hunger, it died."'

Laughter broke out and some stamped their feet and others tapped their drinking cups. More than one glance flashed towards Kara Kemal: they were always having to cut back on food, trying not to complain of hunger, and now these visitors had provided them with a feast. It was a subtle compliment – and Kemal enjoyed the joke as much as any of them. 'Another,' they shouted. 'The letter, Mehmi, tell the letter!'

Mehmi cleared his throat and picked up the stumpy pot he liked to drink from. He made a play of peering inside it, tipping it upside down and shaking out the last drops of wine until one of the men heaved himself to his feet and poured more wine from the jug and that too was emptied so that one of the wives was sent running to fill it. Mehmi waited until she returned. All the women and children were there, the children sleepy now, heads drooping, the youngest sucking his thumb. Years later, he would remember this night when the visitors came and they feasted and his uncle Mehmi the Storyteller held them spellbound.

'A man brought a letter to the Hoca: "Hoca could you read this letter?" Hoca looked at the letter, which was all in Arabic. He couldn't read it and gave it back to man. "Take this to someone else,

I can't read it," said the Hoca. "But why not? You are wearing the turban of a learned man yet you can't read a letter…" The Hoca took off his turban and placed it in front of the man. "If it is the skill of a turban, put it on and…"' Mehmi trailed off, waiting, smiling.

'…read your letter yourself!' His audience roared and clapped. Kara Kemal smiled, but if anyone had been watching him they would have seen sadness in his smile. But all eyes were on his youngest son.

It had seemed certain that Mehmi would go to Akşehir but the times were troubled and then, just when it seemed there was peace again, the bandits started their marauding and he had been needed here with the family and so it had come to nothing. But he played and sang for the family and it seemed that was audience enough. After the Hoca tales he balanced the tanbur in one hand, its long neck leaning against his shoulder, his right hand whispering the strings. He began to sing the story of Karoğlu.

'A hero's son doesn't mix with wine drinkers.
'A hero's son doesn't waste time in music…'

His face when he played was absorbed, transported to a different place from the room in which they were and Dai wondered if a wife and children would be enough for this hero's son who had not, after all, wasted his time in music.

'Let the white horse come
'Let it go free
'And let go of your grief
'Set that free as well…'

All around him were silent, listening like children. Dai's small troupe as well: Blue's face filled with wonder, Edgar's face transfigured, Rémi's glowing with the magic of it all, Giles bleary-eyed and softened, somehow, his ruddy face relaxed. Twm…Twm was intent, wholly absorbed, drinking in the words. The song, the words, had a meaning for all of these lost souls. For himself too, truth be told.

> '*Let go of your grief*
> '*Set that free as well…*'

He had heard *Taid* talk of another storyteller who, he claimed, he had rescued from drowning in the thundering Mawddach waterfall. A young boy he was then, the storyteller, travelling with his brother to escape the cruel King Edward of England at the end of the first war with Wales. And the brother; a strange one, a gifted musician who played as well as the great *pencerdd,* Ieuan ap y Gof, who was his guide and teacher; and this though both brothers were *Sais* born and the older spoke, if he spoke at all, in a garbled tongue. Neither brother had married, as far as his grandfather knew. Married to their art, more like, like this young Mehmi. Dai wondered who Kara Kemal would choose as bride, and if the son would be dutiful enough to marry her.

Later still the talk turned to their journey.

'Bandits, you say?' said Twm. He was more relaxed than Dai had ever seen him, leaning back against the cushioned dais, fingering the carved stem of the drinking cup. So beautiful his dark face with its high cheekbones and the proud lift to his head. Little wonder the girl had eyes for no one but Thomas Archer.

'For some time now. Since the last snow melted. Which route are you taking?'

'It's shorter through the valleys.'

Kara Kemal nodded. 'Not such a straight road but, as you say, the shorter way. I have friends who would gladly give you shelter.' He was frowning, pulling at his lower lip.

'But?' Dai prompted him.

'A dangerous route these days. My advice…if you want my advice, my friend?'

'You know I do.'

'Stick to the Konya road. There are more *hans* along the routes to Konya, and more travellers. Safety in numbers, dear boy, safety in numbers. If you are determined to leave tomorrow and will not wait to travel with this caravan you say is following behind you, better not take the road less travelled.'

Dai flicked a glance to where the guide and muleteers were sitting; he saw the relief on the Amir's face and wondered if he would have slipped away in the night had Twm insisted on the other route.

'Is it really so dangerous?' Tom asked, his eyebrows lifting.

'These are troubled times, and troubled times ahead. The bandits are roaming the land without any restraint. They're very fond of robbing merchants.' Kemal paused, his hand hovering over the almost empty dish of *aruzza*, then sighed, replete. 'Not another mouthful,' he murmured. Then, almost in the same breath, 'The Osmanlıs have taken Nicomedia. Have you heard that?'

'Not a thing – but we've been away for months now. Isn't that the tribe that besieged Brusa some years ago?'

'That's the one – they came out of nowhere. A puling, straggling horde, then. No one paid them any heed yet they starved the city into surrender. And Nicaea, remember, only five years ago? It took them twelve years of siege but they did it.'

'Are they planning to take over the whole Karası *beylik*?' Twm was amused, disbelieving, but Kara Kemal didn't laugh.

'It seems that way. After that, who knows? They may decide to come further east. The Karamans have made deals with them so they must consider them a threat.'

'But the Karamans have the strongest *beylik* in all Anatolia.'

'That may have been so but there's talk of marriage with the Osmanlıs.'

Dai frowned. 'You really think there'll be trouble, Kemal?'

The old man nodded. 'Yes, I do. There's something about them. Such a small tribe to make such gains. And they are getting stronger.'

'They have nearly a hundred fortresses, they say,' said the eldest son, 'and Orhan, the leader now, visits them all the time, making sure they're kept in good repair.'

'If they can control the sea roads, the Venetians and Genoese will have to dance to their piping.'

'I see what you mean – unless Venezia and Genoa go to war against them. Of course, war against a common enemy may end the feuding and fighting between those two city states.'

'Is that likely?' Kara Kemal's voice was dry with disbelief.

'Is any of it likely?' said Twm. 'You'll be talking next of the Osmanlıs taking Constantinople.'

Kara Kemal laughed. 'Enough, my friends. This is a night for rejoicing. Tell me, what became of that strange friend of yours, the young man from Tangiers who had such plans to travel the world? You were travelling with him the first time we met, remember, as his interpreter?'

Dai smiled, remembering. 'Abd Allāh Muhammad, yes.'

'That's the one. Everyone called him Ibn Battuta, didn't they? What news of him? Did you stay with him long? Did he return home or did he travel on to the Far Lands, as he said he would?'

Dai lifted his hands. 'So many questions! Let me see: as far as I know, he is still travelling. I left him at Nicaea. In fact, we were there not long after the Osmanlıs had taken the city. They were building a new mosque.'

'Then you know far more than we do, my son.'

'You're a dark horse, Dafydd.'

Dai laughed. 'It was horses that kept us there for over forty days. One of them was sick. Ibn Battuta refused to wait any longer and left with a few of his companions and slaves but me – well – it was nearing the year end and I was wanting to get back to Heinrijc Mertens. I knew the Venetian fleet would be sailing soon from Constantinople...' he shrugged. 'We parted company.'

'So he'd be without his interpreter?'

'Yes.'

And that hadn't pleased him at all, Dai remembered. 'Sometimes I hear stories of his travels from merchants who have met him. India? I am sure of it. How could he not arrive there with his baggage and companions and slaves?'

'Dai my friend, I think you did not entirely approve of him.'

'I liked him well enough. He was a man of courage and vision.' He paused, considered, and a memory came to him of when they were in Manisa, shortly before they arrived in Nicaea, and two of the slaves tried to escape – one of the slaves his own. Yes, Battuta had given him a slave, probably one of the many gifts given to the traveller by the people he visited. Battuta took it for granted there would be slaves. Everyone did. These two took the horses to water and made off for a town on the coast where the Genoese had – still had – a trading station. They were stopped and brought back, punished, resumed their life of slavery. It was one of the reasons he had decided it was time to go his own way. Battuta had made him a gift of his slave when they parted company and his first act had been to free the man. And the man had stayed with him, refused to leave. Madness! They'd sailed together on the Venetian fleet and he was with Heinrijc Mertens yet, a freed man who chose to enslave himself of his own free will.

Dai became aware that they were looking at him, waiting. Such a tale was not fit for a feast and he was a poor tale teller at the best of times. He laughed. 'Did you hear about the time Battuta visited Birgi and saw the black stone that had fallen from the sky? No? It was like this…'

Mist still clung to the circle of mountaintops the next morning but below them the great plain was clear, a cool dry wind whispering in the old stones of the building. Dai and Kara Kemal walked around the repaired walls, the old man proud in showing the improvements made since Dai's last visit. There were sections of wall that had been rebuilt using stones from the ruins that lay outside the gates of the courtyard; columns and carved stone that told their own tales of other times, other builders. Always there was a past, thought Dai, here and in his own country. Would they never be rid of it? Never be free of it? No future, it seemed, only the past.

They climbed the steps to the ramparts. Any crumbled stone had been cleared and made good. 'My sons' work,' Kemal boasted. 'We're safe here from any bandits and no-goods, hey?' They looked down on the activity in the courtyard. Blue was at the furthest end of the courtyard, huddled with the three brothers in a conference that filled Dai with misgiving. What mischief was the man into now when he should be readying them for the day's journey? Twm was directing the muleteers. Blue's job. Maybe Twm was remembering the collapsed bundles on the mule yesterday. Was it only yesterday? Giles was carrying out panniers, his arm muscles bulging, an enigma of a man, even now; spare of speech, skin that would never turn brown in the sun but was reddened and weather-beaten; close-cropped hair that hinted at indeterminate ginger; eyes that were neither brown nor green. A man from the Marches, that country that was neither Wales nor England. Edgar was directly below them, his hair tangled with gold curls and no sign of the tonsure that had marked him out for what he was and that he had covered with his hood until recently. The children were with him, drawn to him despite his quiet ways. Dai could see him smiling his pale smile, still weak as a day old kitten though he swore otherwise. The day before had worn him out, no mistaking, but he was better for the night's rest and female fussing. Rémi was with him, both young men as joyful in the games as the children. And had they played games when they were young? Dai wondered. Not much of a chance for either of them, from what he knew of Rémi and what he guessed of Edgar.

'He has a good soul, that one,' Kara Kemal said abruptly. 'Where did you find him?'

'More like he found us, Kemal.' Dai laughed, remembering. 'Tangling with the merchants in Aleppo and it wasn't the better part of the deal he was getting. He heard Blue blustering in that unspeakable language of his. Seems our Edgar comes from that part of the country.'

'Oh?'

'We don't ask questions of each other, Kemal. Best not.'

'So you take each other on trust?'

Dai nodded.

'That could be dangerous in these times, my friend.'

'Could be. It's worked out so far.'

'"Men's bodies are like pitchers with closed mouths; beware till you see what is inside them",' Kemal quoted.

'Then I'll be wise and look at the contents and let the inner meaning guide me,' Dai said carelessly. Kemal shook his head. 'Always an answer – and from the same teachings of our Rumi's *Masnavi*.'

Dai grinned. 'Of course. He is my teacher's teacher.'

'And when did you learn to speak with a flattering tongue?' Kemal asked.

On the road below spirals of dust resolved themselves into a long caravan. The rumble of trampling hooves and men's voices and whistling grew louder, and the squeaking and grating of harness and jangling of metal rose up to the two men. They watched from their safe nest. Mules plodding, heads down and a long procession of stately camels, all laden with heavy bales of furs and hides; a string of horses that would fetch a good price; an army of men riding as guards, one cantering back up the line – a messenger, probably. At the end of the caravan, trailing behind in the dust kicked up by the animals, came a lengthy column of men, women, children roped together. One of the women carried a very young child, no more than a *dwt*, thought Dai, but no doubt heavy enough for carrying a day's distance. Early morning and they walked wearily. They wouldn't fetch as good a price as the horses – couldn't expect to be looked after as well as the horses, either.

'They're early on the road.'

'Yes.'

'Ah. The caravan you would not wait for. Perhaps this is fate, my friend.' Kemal was mischievous. He recognised the tone in the one clipped word; *a stubborn man when he'd a mind to be, this quiet brown man.* Kemal leaned further forward over the rampart, squinting into the pale sunlight. 'Now there's a sight I thought never to see again.' He leaned further, so far that Dai gripped him by the arm, pulling him back.

'Wanting a closer view than you reckoned on, is it?' he grunted.

'No closer than need be, if that's who I think it is.'

'Vecdet. Yes, it's him.'

'Then you do well to keep clear of him. He's a bad man.'

'"The pitcher that holds deadly poison?"'

'As the good Rumi says.'

'Better travel alone than in company with that man.'

'You will take care, dear son?'

'Of course, my father.'

'And that one?' He nodded towards Blue, stretching now and flexing his muscles. Loud shouts and laughter and hands slapping his back and pinching his shoulder muscles. 'What kind of pitcher is he?'

'He has his moments.' Dai hesitated. 'There's no malice in the man, see. He's been good for Edgar – taken him under his wing, isn't it.'

They walked on. Beyond them, beyond the rock-strewn stretch of flat land, mountains reared up into the mist, their tops hidden. Dai was suddenly gripped by longing for his own mountains, and the glittering sea and wild riverlets tumbling down the mountainsides through land that was sodden and peaty, and somewhere above him buzzards hanging on the winds mewing their mournful cry and kites flashing red in sunlight as they soared and dipped. He shook his head, cleared the image from his mind, though memories were coming more and more frequently these days. He had to stay focused; there was work to be done, a day's travelling ahead of them.

'My friend…' Kara Kemal was saying. He sounded hesitant, stopped, fumbled for words.

'Say what you have in mind. What troubles you?'

'There's one wishes you ill, my friend.'

'So you were seeing that, were you? There's nothing gets past you, does it now?'

'You know? And you are not worried?'

'I am curious. There is no reason for any of these men to be holding a grudge against me.'

'Maybe it comes out of the past.'

'Maybe it does. But our past has no place here. We've all left our pasts behind.' Even as he spoke Dai knew it wasn't true; the past littered their way, forcing itself into the future as these scattered stones told of other, older lives.

'For your sake, I hope you are right. But take care, my friend, or perhaps one morning you will wake to find the past rising up and staring you in the face.'

'Better that than knifing me in the back.'

'So you do know there is danger.'

'Maybe.'

Kara Kemal nodded, his turbaned head bobbing against the sun-whitened stones. His eyes were hooded, impossible to read. 'I shall offer prayers for you.'

'Better to offer them for my troubled companion.'

'That as well. Come, if you must go, it is time you were on your way.'

They had circuited the walls and climbed down the re-made steps into the courtyard. Dai was on the last step when Kemal said from behind him, 'That wife I talked of – I think you've chosen her already?'

Dai waited until he had stepped down into the courtyard. 'You see too much, my friend.'

'"A true lover is proved such by his pain of heart."'

Dai grunted. 'Pain of the heart now, is it? And I'm thinking that it's nothing more than an ache in the guts from last night's eating.'

'Ah, my son, words, only words: "When we fall in love we are ashamed of our words."'

'Father Kemal, you tie me in knots with your quotations.' Dai's gaze was fixed on Twm and the horses. 'Is it so obvious?' he asked at last.

'Only to me, my son. "Love unexplained is clearer than explanation by the tongue." Who is she?'

'I don't know. Truly. I think she is the granddaughter of a wise old Greek woman who died only days ago. They were living with a *yürük* tribe that summers up in the mountains near the Göksu.

'The *Sarıkeçili*. Well, they used to be of that tribe. I think they go now by the name of *Karakeçili*.' He was poised on the last step, smiling. 'So, my son, what now? You have offered for her?'

'No.'

'No?'

'No.' Dai sighed, laughed at the expression on the old man's face, sighed again. 'I've hardly even spoken with her. Besides, she's probably promised to one of the men. And I have these to look out for.' He swept a hand to take in the courtyard, and the scattered group. 'It is not to be, my father.'

'My son, who are you to decide what is and what is not to be? Only Allah the all-compassionate, the all-knowing decides.'

'Well, I'm here and she's there. Allah has decided.'

The old man chuckled. 'Perhaps,' he said. 'There is always room for faith,' but Dai had already turned away and the old man had spoken quietly.

Twm and Rémi and the muleteers had already assembled their small caravan: ten mules, twenty camels, their horses, a cluster of dogs, no more than that. They carried lightweight, precious goods: fine silks of great beauty and richness and wonderful colour; precious stones – rubies, this time, and pearls and amber; pepper, of course, and saffron and sesame and ginger; high-quality goats' wool made into hats of the material called *bonnet* that was so popular in France and England just now – Heinrijc Mertens prided himself on being fashionable. The spun gold and gold thread so loved by the Venetians would be bought in Attaleia, together with silver and gold plates and spoons and trays and pots; Those, and their bedding, clothes, provisions, water were the most cumbersome bundles. And always there were the oddities Mertens loved; these were not for trade but for himself. His collection, he called it. Dai had a few items close hidden that he knew would please the old man.

Blue was nowhere to be seen and Twm was fretting, fearing the worst. 'Never here when he's supposed to be, Dafydd,' he grumbled. He was the only one of them who called Dai by his given name. A morning for ghosts it was to tap him on the shoulder, Dai thought, if ghosts could tap, for there was a note in Twm's voice that was just like his youngest brother's voice. *'He's not here, Dafydd. He promised he would be. He promised.'* He was about to mouth the same words of comfort he had used to his own dear, dead brother when Kemal's three sons came into view with Blue in their midst.

'It's another howry drear daäy,' he greeted them but he was smiling, well pleased with himself. The youngest, slightest of the brothers, Mehmi-the-poet, clapped him on the shoulder and all three were laughing, loud in their praise. Repairs to the walls that they had thought would take hours of heavy labour had been accomplished in a blink, a snap of the fingers, with the help of this man-mountain.

'Don't let it be another three years, my friend. Who knows? We may all be Osmanlı slaves by next year.' Kara Kemal was mournful. 'I may not be here to welcome you,' he added quietly.

'Your voice…' Dai muttered.

'*Tabii.* Harsh, isn't it? Not good. The physician says it's not good.'

'You know this?'

'What's to know? It is. I must accept it. But come again soon, my son, if you wish to see me on this good earth.'

'I shall pray for you.' Though little praying he did these days. 'Take care, my father.'

There was fresh flatbread baked in the early hours of the morning to take with them, rolled into warm bundles and wrapped in cloth. 'Little enough to send you on your way, my son,' Kara Kemal said with regret.

'Bread is God's gift. And your blessing is more than enough, my father.'

'That you gladly have. May Allah go with you and bring you your heart's desire.' He paused, added, 'May Allah protect you.' His gaze took in the assembled group. 'All of you,' he amended. His gaze lingered on Edgar, passed on to Twm, to the rest of the group. 'May you all find the peace you seek.'

Edgar's pale face flushed red. Tom frowned in puzzlement at the enigmatic words. The old man chuckled. 'What was it Jalal al Din Rumi said? Who are you trying to run from? Yourself? That's impossible.' He smiled. 'Go in peace, all of you.' He watched them from the wall ramparts until the small caravan was no more than a smudge on the horizon.

10

Seek not water, only show you are thirsty
That water may spring up all around you
(Mevlana Jalal al Din Rumi, 1207-1273)

He was still there when the sun was shimmering pale through clouds driven apart by the wind from the plains. He was there when a slight figure stumbled into view. Kemal peered from his high perch; a young man, though he seemed old at first – hunched as he was and with that shuffling gait. Shabby tunic and *şalvar*, no cloak, no bundle or satchel – nothing to keep out the chill at night. Alone and, judging from the way he was looking about him – look at the way he was eyeing these old buildings, turning to gaze down the road he had travelled – worried about pursuit. A strange young man to be travelling these dangerous roads alone. Beyond him, the straight way twisted between hills. Kara Kemal stared, rubbed his eyes, narrowed them, squinted into the pallid sun and cursed his old age. A scuff of brown dust was hanging in the air. He tilted his head, listening. He saw the youth turn also, saw his body stiffen. Kemal turned and shouted down into the courtyard. 'Aksay! Here now!'

Aksay, his eldest son, best with arrow and sword.

'Come up here with me. See? There's a stranger on the road who needs our help. Go and bring him here to me.'

'You think it's safe, father? You know the tricks these bandits play.'

'No trick. This one needs our help. See – he's fallen, and not for the first time today, I'm sure. Go quickly. It seems unwelcome visitors are on their way. Take Mehmi with you but don't frighten our guest.'

Already his men were moving towards the steps and lookouts; the weapons were kept ready at all times and these men of his knew how to use them.

'Think there'll be trouble?'

'Maybe – maybe not, if Allah is merciful.'

He watched from the ramparts, saw his sons ride out bareback on their quick-paced horses, saw the slight figure straighten and fumble at his waist, saw the flash of sun on dagger. His sons reined in, Mehmi leaning down to the youth. He would be speaking words of welcome and warning. He was gesturing towards the dust cloud, grown bigger now; a distant thrum was audible. He gestured up towards the citadel where his father was watching. A long waiting moment before the dagger was thrust back into the stranger's belt and Mehmi's hand went out again, this time grasping the youth's arm, helping him mount behind him on the horse. The stranger stumbled, had to be helped. Aksay waited, horse and rider alert and motionless as the youth was hoisted up. Kemal saw the figure sag forward as if too weary to support himself, then both riders were wheeling, galloping up the hill towards the citadel, little eddies of dust and sand thrown up behind them. Kara Kemal watched them race up the hill, his hands gripping the edge of the stone parapet. The thrum of hooves on the road grew louder, rhythmic. He sighed with relief as the two horses swept through the entrance and he heard the heavy gates crash to behind his sons. The band of horsemen – how many? Eight? Ten? More than that, surely – barely paused in their stampede along the dusty track. They raced past the citadel intent on other prey. Twelve of them at least. There was a flash of red trouser, of gold tassels on the pommels of saddles, of gleaming helmets…then they were past. Kemal watched their dust cloud into the distance. Had the horsemen turned for the valley road or were they continuing on the Konya road? If so, they would surely catch up with Dai and his people. Impossible to say from this distance. The dust cloud was too great and life was too precarious. Kemal edged down the steps, grimacing at the aches and pains of old age. He moved towards his sons and their unexpected guest.

'Welcome, traveller,' he said. The boy looked down at him from his pillion place, face expressionless. His eyes were flecked with gold, almond-shaped and long-lashed. Intelligence was there but dulled with fatigue and, try as he would to conceal it, suspicion and anxiety. No wonder. A lone traveller – and on foot – had reason to be afraid.

Mehmi dismounted in that quick, careless way he had and held a hand out to the stranger, catching him as the boy's legs buckled under him. 'Steady there,' he laughed. 'See, father, we have Blue's little brother come to visit us!' True, the boy's neck and wrists were stained pale blue. He'd travelled in wet clothes, then, that had certainly dried on him. Kemal frowned his son into silence; time enough for jokes later.

'No need to be afraid of us,' he said, quietly. 'You are safe here. You are thirsty and hungry and tired, I think, and welcome to eat and drink with us, to bathe and rest before you continue on your way.'

The golden eyes regarded him steadily, measuringly. When the boy spoke, his voice was low and husky. 'The last stranger to offer me shelter and food and drink would have made a slave of me.'

'We shall not do that.' Kemal paused. 'A caravan passed by here earlier today. I recognised the man who led it.'

The golden eyes flickered. The slim body stiffened.

'A slave trader. A well-fed man. His name is Vecdet.'

The boy held himself poised, his hand creeping again to the dagger at his waist.

'If he is the stranger you mean, you are lucky to escape him.'

'Yes.'

'Not without some loss, I think.'

'My chestnut mare, my curved bow and full quiver, my satchel. My warm cloak.'

'Loss indeed – but what does it compare to your life?'

'Nothing.'

'It is as Allah wills. And Allah has sent you in our way. Come, this chittering is no good when you are tired and hungry. Merih!' he shouted. 'Where is that wife of yours, Aksay?' He was walking them towards the arched way.

'Waiting until she knows it's safe to be about,' Aksay said, calmly. 'The alarm was given, remember.'

'Well, it's safe enough now so… Merih! Fatima! Come – we have a hungry guest to feed.' He shook his head as the women appeared from the shadowy interior. 'Hurry now, this one has a hungry mouth. Thirsty, too – bring water.' To the boy, he said, 'We are lucky here. We have fine fresh spring water that never dries up, not even in the hottest summer nor the coldest winter. Here – taste for yourself.' Merih came up to them bearing a pitcher and bowls. She poured a brimming bowl and handed it to the boy. 'Fresh and cold and delicious. The finest water hereabouts – well, we think so anyway.' He took the bowl held out to him and drank from it, watching the boy over the rim. He smiled. 'We like to share our good fortune.' The boy gave a little sigh and sipped cautiously then gulped down the water and returned the bowl to the waiting woman with a bow of his head and a word of thanks.

'We have just said a sad goodbye to friends who rested the night with us. I would have kept them longer but no, Dai was determined they must travel on. They are travelling to Attaleia to find a ship to take them home.'

'Dai?'

'Hm. Yes.'

'That is a strange name. Is he a brown man on a brown horse?'

'I believe he is.'

'Was there another? A dark man on a grey horse?'

'There was indeed.'

'I am searching for them.'

'Perhaps we can help you find them.'

'*Beyefendi*, I hope so.'

The slight figure sagged again, was held by Mehmi.

'Come, stranger, you must rest. Eat. No one should go hungry.' He nodded to himself. 'That is what my friend Dai is so fond of saying. No one should go hungry. Well, come then. What little we have we will share with you.'

How she had covered the miles she had no idea. The road was a blur of scrub and sand and distant mountains that wavered in front of her eyes. A range of hills reared up, an outcrop that was typical of this country. It was here the road divided, one way leading down through the valleys; the other was the straighter road to Konya. This was the way the caravan had taken. Here were the hoof marks of horses and the smaller marks of the mules; blurred imprints of the wide, two-toed, padded foot of the camels; footprints, some bare footed and dragging in the dust and sand that told of exhaustion. Niko, she thought. His sister. Or that strange, angry woman whose outburst had unknowingly saved the girl's life. And here was another set of prints mingling with the first, leading down from the outcrop of rock. She could see the outline of buildings high up on the outcrop: ruins or lived in? It was impossible to tell. The sun was shining from under cloud cover and dazzling her eyes. Was there a figure up there on the ruins or was it her imagination seeing threats where none existed? But the vibration she felt was not imagination. There were horsemen galloping fast towards her along the length of the road. She looked about her for cover, started to head for the rocky slope. But there were two more horsemen galloping at speed towards her from the ruins. Not deserted, then, and too late, too late to hide. She felt for the dagger in her belt but what chance did she have, exhausted and weak with hunger, against two men, and they on horseback? And beyond them came the thrum of galloping hooves.

The two riders reached her; they were bareback, their thighs and knees gripping tight to the horses' flanks and the horses were wheeling and rearing until their riders soothed them into quiet. They were two men, one younger than the other and brothers, by their likeness. Both had long, curling dark hair bouncing on their shoulders and high cheekbones and dark bright eyes. One was reaching out his hand, pointing towards the distant horsemen, urging her to mount behind him, it seemed, though his voice came from a great nothingness. The other sat still on his mount, his bow readied. Better to take the hand that was offered. She reached up, felt her hand gripped hard and when she lurched against the horse its rider swept her up behind him in a strong grasp and both men urged their horses up the slope to the ruins that were not ruins but a fortified citadel. They rode in through the big gates and she heard the sound of them close behind her. Rescue – or capture? If capture, escape was cut off. The men halted their horses in a wide courtyard surrounded by shadowy arches. An old man was slowly descending the steps from the ramparts. She waited. He came up to them, the two riders and she, mounted behind one of them, captive.

'Welcome traveller,' he said.

How could she know if they were honest? But she was helped down from the horse and held upright because her legs, her wretched, traitorous legs, were collapsing under her and a terrible faintness threatened to overwhelm her. She was given water that was sipped first by the elder with the far-seeing eyes as if to show there was no cause for anxiety. And she was so thirsty how could she not drink? Then the astonishing news that he knew of the brown man and the dark man. That they had been his guests overnight. If that were so, perhaps it was not too late? Perhaps she could catch up with them – if these people were honest and intended letting her go?

She was led into a cool, shady room. A woman brought a bowl of water and washed her feet and hands. She was offered hot broth, steaming and fragrant: it was mountain broth, redolent with herbs, very like that made by the women of the tribe but with subtle differences. There was fresh bread, still warm from the baking. Cheese: 'My eldest son's wife makes very good cheese.' It was good; sheep's cheese, not plentiful but white, tangy and fresh. She felt herself reviving with every mouthful. 'Here – take more – you are still hungry.' She glanced up at her host from under her lashes: he was smiling at her, but not in the leering manner of Vecdet. There was kindness in his eyes. Unexpectedly he leaned across and patted her arm. 'See – a little colour in your cheeks. Another bowl of hot broth? No? But there is plenty. A little more. A very little.'

'Indeed, sir, no. No more. Thank you; I have eaten well.' She sat back, dipping her fingers into the bowl of water at her side. The woman Merih hurried forward with a wiping cloth.

'There is nothing like hunger to season the meal.'

'Truly, sir, hunger or no hunger, I have eaten well.' With food in her stomach and rest it was almost humiliating how much braver she felt.

'Then you shall take more with you when you leave us.'

'Then you do intend letting me leave?'

The old man chuckled. 'You still think I shall make you my prisoner? I would keep you as my guest, if I could, but you wish to find our friends. Now if only Dai had agreed to stay another day, you would not be chasing after him. If you had arrived yesterday you could have feasted with us. Today,' he shrugged, 'we have only simple fare to offer our guest.'

'I am accustomed to simple fare and this was excellently made. Your son's wife makes excellent cheese. Whoever makes the broth that was also excellent.'

'Thank you.' He smiled. 'I am a fortunate man to have such a family to care for me in my old age.'

'Indeed – and they are fortunate to have such a father.' She waited a moment. 'Your guests – which road did they take?'

'Konya. They intend going only as far as the next *han* – a half day's journey. There is a young man with them recovering from a fever. A long day's journey is still too much for him, though he is much recovered.'

A flicker of a smile crossed her face. 'That is good to hear.'

'You know this young man also?'

'No. No, I don't. I have never met him.' She fumbled for words; lying to this courteous old man was very difficult. 'In truth, your friends would not know me.'

The old man tched tched, his tongue clicking against his teeth. 'My apologies; as Dai is always telling me, best ask no questions these days.'

'I owe you an explanation.'

'You owe me nothing – thanks to Allah, maybe, for bringing you to our home, Kazan.' She had given him the name of her friend. 'And my thanks also to Allah,' he continued, 'who has given me the honour of helping a body and soul in need.'

'You are very kind.'

'But come – something, perhaps, you can tell me. How did you outwit the loathsome slaver, that Vecdet? This I would love to hear.'

She laughed then. His face was that of a mischievous child, a child longing to hear a story. He looked very like the son who had hoisted her behind him on to his horse and who had made that joke about the blue dye on her neck and face; the blue brother come to visit. And so she told him of the mistake she had made, riding into the camp; how the boy slave had warned her; how she escaped through the felt walls of the tent; how the boy slave had saved her and of her hiding place behind the waterfall. How he had come to her at night to bring her food and hope of escape.

'That is a remarkable boy.'

'He is! Bright and sharp like pine needles and lemons yet brave and caring. He refuses to leave his sister, though I believe he could have escaped a thousand times without her – and yet he is only a young boy. I have promised to rescue him.' Her eyes, gazing into the old man's face, were wide, gold-flecked, angry. 'Niko said there was a very young child who had been taken. Scarcely four summers old.'

'Dai does not have slaves. He says no one should be enslaved to another.'

'He is right. It is a terrible thing, to take a man's freedom – a woman's – a child's.'

'This is strange to you, I think?'

'I have known only kindness in my life though, it is true I have run away from my tribe, but not because they were cruel. You must not think that.'

'Adventure, maybe?'

'I have sworn that I will go in search of my grandfather, who I never knew and who never knew me.'

'That is a great undertaking. You know where to find him?'

'My grandmother told me to go the cold country, to England. That is where I shall find him. That is what she said and she was never wrong.'

'Your grandmother?'

'She made me swear, before she died. She is buried these days past.' The husky low voice became huskier. 'I miss my grandmother. She was a great lady.'

The old man became still, his mind seeing into the mystery of life. Too late she remembered that he would have heard of Nene from his guests. Had they spoken of her granddaughter, the girl who had given them medecine?

'Then thanks indeed to Allah who has brought you to my hearth. Dai is the very man you need. Oh, he is the man you need. To rescue the young boy and to find your grandfather – and who knows? Your heart's desire? There is always room for faith, yes? Always room for faith. You must be sure to tell Dai so, when you see him. You must tell him I said so. Are you rested? Are you ready to go on? Yes? Then you should catch up with them at the *han* this nightfall, if Allah wills it so. Mehmi!'

The flood of words left her breathless. What had caused it? The mention of her grandmother, surely, but not an insignificant granddaughter. The old man had given no sign that he knew her for an imposter.

Mehmi-the-handsome hurried into the room. His eyes were bright, curious.

'Mehmi, I have a dangerous task for you.'

'Whatever you wish, father.'

'You are to take this young traveller to join our friends. There may be danger. Those horsemen – did you see which road they took?'

'I think they followed the Konya road, father.'

'Hm. That is a complication.'

'Nothing Dai can't deal with, father, if that is what worries you. He knows how to deal with bandits.' The dark eyes flashed and he grinned, a young man's grin. 'After all, he used to be one himself, he told me. He knows how they think.'

'Tch tch, enough, boy.' A pause. 'Did he indeed tell you so?'

'Last time he was here. Are we to go two-up?'

'No. That would be dangerous. You may need the speed to escape danger. Take an extra mount. And a bow and quiver for you, young friend. Can you use it?'

'Yes. I was accounted the best archer amongst all the young men,' she said with simple pride.

'Were you indeed!' He grunted with laughter. 'Then Mehmi will be safe with you.'

And then they were out in the courtyard surrounded by the brothers and their wives and the young children shouting with excitement. A satchel of food and skins of water; the precious curved bow and quiver of good arrows; a shining-coated piebald mare for her to ride.

And then there was the old man carrying another bright-woven satchel and with the tanbur on his back. He held it out to his son.

'What is this, father?'

'Go with them, my son. Go with Allah's blessing and with mine.'

'Father, I have promised to stay here with you. You need me here.'

'My song bird, I would not clip your wings. You were meant to fly. To sing. It was wrong of me to seek to keep you here. It is wrong to make a slave of any man, woman or child. And never should a songbird be caged. Your words and songs are needed in this dark world, as Yunus Emre's are needed. As the great Mevlana's are needed. As the wise fool Nasreddin Hoca's are needed. As the words of the great Allah and his prophet Mohammed are needed. We mortals need to be reminded of our foolishness and to seek for bliss.'

The young man Mehmi wept. He embraced his father.

'No mother to weep over you boy – that is Allah's blessing. If she had begged me to keep you here, I do not know that I could have parted from you.' He turned to the young boy astride the piebald mare. 'This mare, her name is Yıldız.'

'Star,' she murmured, and thought how close Nene's soul must be to her.

'When you see Dai, tell him this mare is his bride-gift. Remember to tell him that, young friend. This mare, this star, Yıldız, is his bride-gift.'

'*And there's always room for faith,*' she remembered.

'Indeed there is. You should remember that as well, with such a great adventure ahead of you.'

Always room for faith; it was what her grandmother would have said. She hugged it to her. There was already proof that this was true: the tribe and the chief of her tribe; Niko; Maria and her family; now this Kara Kemal who had helped her on her way. Always room for faith. The Vecdets of this world, what were they compared to those people? To Nene?

They left the ruined citadel, sweeping out through the gates and down the hillside and along the straight road to Konya. Both were slim, slightly built, no weight for their horses and they made good time, hooves pounding on the dusty, sandy track. Time enough to arrive at the *han* before the gates were shut for the night.

The old man watched them leave. He knew he would never see his youngest son again, not in this life.

They were well on their way, the *han* not so far, from Dai's memory of it. Edgar was lively enough and Blue still preening himself over his man-mountain task of the morning. And why shouldn't he? Dai thought. He'd done well, had the boyo. There was sun on their faces and the *han* ahead of them. They were rested from their stay with Kemal and his family. Yet he felt uneasy. He wasn't the only one, he could tell. The guide and the men were twitchy, looking about them, back over their shoulders, as if they expected to be attacked at any moment. Kemal's stories of bandits, maybe... Maybe not. Twm drew alongside him.

'Our blue boy was the man of the morning, then,' he said.

'Thoughts out of my head, Twm *bach*.'

'We'll give thanks for a new leaf turning, then.'

'We'll give thanks for small mercies, Twm.'

'You don't reckon it'll last, then?'

Dai didn't bother to answer; Blue was Blue. There'd be other drunken nights and other brawls.

'You're a strange one, Dai. Do you really mean to take our blue friend back to Ieper?'

It was an olive branch after their wrangling over Blue. He accepted it gratefully. 'Of course. He's a man after Heinrijc Mertens' own heart. There'll be a place for him, though I've an idea he's yearning to be back in his own country.'

'What will you do, after this trip?'

'You've said it yourself; it's *hiraeth* I have for that poverty-stricken little country I call home.'

'Are you really going back?'

'Really.' He laughed. 'Don't look so amazed. I must go back. Make sure there truly are none of my family left alive. After that…who knows? Heinrijc Mertens has treated me like a son, and I owe him the duty of a son.'

'Is it all duty? Do you ever follow your own heart, Dafydd?'

'Do I have a heart, Twm?'

'Sometimes, my friend, I think you are all heart.'

Dai grunted. No answer to that one. He was thinking it was time to stop, soon time for their Muslim men's call to prayer. Better to stop early, here in a place like this, rare enough on the plateau – easily defended if need be, see. Rémi was kneeling on the ground, his forehead touching the earth like a good Musselman himself. He tilted his head, laid an ear to the ground, straightened and looked up at Dai, alarm on his face.

'Trouble, Rémi?' The boy had acute hearing, as if to make up for his lack of speech. Rémi nodded. He pointed back along the way they had come, held up both hands, all his fingers and both thumbs. He laid his ear to the ground again. Dai knelt with him. He could feel it, the slightest of vibrations that warned of approaching horsemen. A number of them, it seemed. Dai thought a moment, rapped out orders. Edgar to look after the animals – God save him, the cameleteers were better used to fighting than he was.

'Rémi, that iron wire we traded in Bursa – the length I kept back. It's in my satchel. Quick now.' The boy raced off.'

Blue? Keep him ready behind that ridge, hidden from view. 'Keep your backside down, Blue! It's a target from here!'

'Two targets.' Twm scowled at the big man's efforts to conceal his bulky buttocks. 'Kara Kemal's bandits?' He tilted his head held high, listening to the thrum heard now in the air.

'Seems likely.'

'Preparing a welcome for them, are we?' He looked down at the thin wire Rémi had thrust into Dai's hands.

'Bandits' trick, Twm, learned from bandit friends in the wild hills of my poverty-stricken little country. We'll need Rémi one end of it – right, Rémi? After that, you keep clear. Understand?' His hand forced the boy's face up to him. 'You keep clear,' he repeated. 'I can't waste time worrying about you. Edgar will need help with the animals. They must be kept safe, and their packs. Can't say the same for our visitors. This will cripple their horses and there's a pity.'

'All heart, Dafydd,' Twm's voice was dry. 'Think we can keep the caravan safe?'

'Oh, we should do that, *bach*. Let's be at it now. Get your archers where you want them.'

The thin wire was stretched across the road from stunted tree to stunted rock; a good place to choose, this, in case of need, he thought again. Kemal would tell him to give thanks to Allah. And so he did. And thanks to the God of his childhood, and all the austere saints of his poverty-stricken little land. If faith was needed, it was now; and there was always room for faith, Kemal said. Well, maybe so. The cameleteers and muleteers were grim but ready and that was a gift in itself. He'd known hired men slope off in the face of danger. And who could blame them? Hired men, not their fight, not their risk.

'We are tired of these bandits marauding when they will,' Amir the guide told him. 'It is time we made a stand against them. Honest men cannot travel the roads these days.'

Himself and Twm the only trained men, though Giles was as good as a trained man. Well, so be it. They waited, watching the dust cloud whirl closer and closer.

11

Be seen as you are
Or be as you are seen
(Mevlana Jalal al Din Rumi, 1207–1273)

They had travelled through the afternoon over the brown land. It was late and the sun sinking when Mehmi reined and held up his hand. 'Listen,' he said. She tilted her head, felt rather than heard the soft shuffle of hooves on the dusty track, a faint jingle of harness. A slow-moving group but not a caravan. A party of horsemen moving slowly towards them.

'Are you really skilled with a bow or was that boasting?'

'It was not!'

'That's good to know but let's get off the road – see if they pass us by. They're coming very slowly.' They wheeled their horses and cantered towards a narrow band of trees. From there, they watched the procession of limping men and stumbling horses and men bent over bloody wounds. Some of the horses were burdened with bodies that lay stiff and still over the saddles. Others were led, themselves halting and lamed.

'No need for your shooting skills today.' Mehmi said. 'I recognise those men. Looks like they met up with Dai.'

'What do you mean?'

'These are the bandits who have roamed freely over the land for too long now. You were in their path, remember? Father was worried that they would catch up with Dai's caravan and it looks like they did and had the worst of it. I hope… When they've passed, let's hurry on and see.'

His mouth closed tight and she thought, yes, the caravan of the brown man and the black man. It was attacked. And her heart beat faster. They waited until the last of the sorry horses and disconsolate men had passed them by, then they quietly urged their horses on. They came to a narrow part of the road where there were rocks and trees on either side, forming a shallow gorge. 'Here – see?' Mehmi exclaimed. The earth was trampled and there were dark stains that she knew must be blood. No sign of the caravan. They rode on, closer now, surely, to the *han,* and the sun sinking lower and lower.

And then there it was ahead of them, its walls rising high and clear above the plateau and its portal open. Ahead of them, travelling from the opposite direction, an important-looking caravan was arriving. The string of camels stretched away in a distant cloud of sandy dust, silhouetted against the setting sun. The nearest they could see were high-loaded with goods covered over with bright camel cloths. Some were ridden but mostly the cameleteers trudged alongside, weary and dusty at the end of another long day. A pack of hounds kept pace; a mounted armed guard flanked them all, the air bristling with their spears and, in their midst, the glimpse of a turbaned head and rich robes of the merchant.

'Let's hurry,' said Mehmi, 'or we'll be waiting for hours for this lot to get inside. And it's almost time for the Evening Call.' They urged on their tired mounts, came to the gateway, even as the muezzin call rang out: Come to prayer. Come to prayer. Allah is Most Great. *Allahu Akbar.*

Mehmi guided them through the huge iron-bound gateway, through the passageway to the guard posts where they were halted by the *han* guards.

'Two of us,' Mehmi told the gateman. 'We are hoping to meet friends here.'

'Oh yes – and who might they be?'

'A small caravan that arrived earlier this afternoon. We think they were attacked on the road. Maybe you know his name: Dai the Welshman?'

'What kind of name is that?'

A second man leaned across. 'I know the man you mean. They came in not an hour ago. Seems they had a set-to with our local bandits.'

'I'm wondering who came off worse. The tribe passed us a while back on the road. They looked well beaten.'

'*Belki*. These folk are nursing wounds as well.' He looked beyond them to where the first of the new arrivals was crowding through the gateway. 'You'd best come in, quick as you can. This must be the big caravan we're expecting. They sent on a rider to warn us to make ready for them. Go through – the attendant will see to your horses and tell you where to find your friends. Go through.' He waved them on into the din and smells of the great courtyard, open to the sky and seeming lighter now after the gloom of the entrance.

The girl looked about her with interest. She had never been inside a *han* before. It was exactly as Nene had described it, teeming with animals and people and noise and smells and activity. So much happening all at once, it was enough to dizzy her. The *mecdit* was the quiet centre with its cooling, chuckling fountain of fresh water spouting into basins. There were some still rolling up prayer mats after the sunset call but the general activity of the end-of-day was already once again under way. Around the whole vast space of the courtyard was an arched colonnade, some nine pillars in all. On the left were the stables and smithy and laundry and storage space for the goods the caravaneers brought with them. Sweating attendants with strong shoulders and bulging biceps were rapidly unloading the pack horses and mules and kneeling camels of their casks and bundles and sacks of hides and furs and salt, alum, sugar, cloth, spices, gems, silver, gold...all the wealth of the trade routes heaped into the storage space carefully allotted to each caravan so that there would be no mistakes the next morning. On the right was the *hamam* complex with dusty, drooping men lined up outside it and spruce men with shining clean faces walking out, upright and rejuvenated. Next to that the kitchens with their huge earthen tandoor ovens. One was open and the burning red hotness of its inside was visible. A kitchen boy was nimbly removing flat breads and preparing to load more against the insides of the oven walls. Great cauldrons were steaming, full of fragrantly spiced rice. On the third side was a portico and beyond, in the shadows, were the lodging rooms. At this hour, it was especially hectic with arriving caravans and the bustle of animals being unloaded by the *han* staff in a practised routine and grooms to stable and rub down and feed the beasts. There were men and their servants to accommodate, as well as the few women travellers and maidservants. Voices mingled in a babble of languages: Genoese, Venetian, Turkish, Arabic, Hebrew, Greek, French, strange dialects that only those speaking and those listening could understand. Already, merchants were greeting each other, preparing the way for deals to be made before the next day's journey. Rangy hounds were lying with heads on paws in shady corners, too exhausted to snap and growl at each other.

Mehmi dismounted, held up a hand to her but she slid off the piebald without taking it. She caressed the horse's nose and patted her sweaty flank; not her lovely chestnut mare but a good horse for all that, patient and untiring. A star. They handed the tired horses to a waiting groom. They were assured that the animals would be well cared for, well looked after, they must come and see for themselves after they had rested and bathed and eaten. The attendant pointed across the courtyard to where Blue and Rémi were helping the *han* staff to unload the mules and camels and stable them for the night, out-of-doors in the courtyard because the early autumn nights were still warm enough. The animals were restive, fractious after the fraught afternoon but calming under the soft sounds Rémi murmured to them.

The girl felt her stomach clench with nerves. Now that she was actually here, had caught up with the dark man and the brown, the whole idea seemed preposterous. How could she show herself, here, in this man's world? True, there were women but few and all accompanied by their menfolk, all retreating with their servants into the female quarters. She tugged at Mehmi's sleeve.

'What is it, little blue brother?'

'They have no idea who I am,' she said urgently. 'I…I was away with the men when they came to the camp. They don't know the old woman was my grandmother.' She couldn't meet his eyes, was aware his gaze had narrowed, sharpened.

'You don't want them to know,' he guessed.

'No. I can't say why. I just don't. I mean no harm. Please…' She was hardly aware of the pleading in her voice, nor of the way her fingers clutched his sleeve. He stared intently into her face; whatever he saw there seemed to satisfy him. He shrugged. 'If you want to make a mystery of it, it's your affair.' His mouth curled, amusement she realised. 'And Dai would say best ask no questions. It seems all of you have shady pasts. I'm the only one with nothing to hide.'

'Thank you,' she breathed. They came up to Blue.

'Greetings, Blue. I've brought you a little brother.' Mehmi said cheerfully. The big man turned, wiping glistening beads of sweat from his forehead. He straightened, easing his back with the other hand, recognised the dark eyed, dark haired young man and grinned. Beside him, Rémi's face split in a wide smile, the snail-trail white scars stretching with the smile.

'Greätings to yer an' all. Weer's yer sprung from, singing-boy? And what's yow mean, yer's browt mi' little brother?'

Mehmi's eyebrows quirked upwards. 'This is going to be difficult,' he murmured to the girl.'

'Why? What did he say?'

'That's the problem – the boy has no power of speech and I don't understand what the big man says. He talks a strange language. He helped us dismantle a wall this morning – it would have taken us hours but he did it in two shakes of a dog's tail – but the only talking we did was sign-language.' He grinned up at the big man, pointed to the girl standing beside him.

'Here's another blue-dyed soul. See for yourself.'

She stared up at the huge man, saw the dark blue stains on his straggling beard and the blackened fingers and nails and dark bruising that was not indigo dye at all and congealed blood on his face and arms, realised then what Mehmi meant. This was a dyer – or had been a dyer not that long ago. He stared back, taking in the blue stains where flesh showed at her neck and wrists.

'Well lawks-a-massy-me! Who's this blue boy, then?'

Mehmi understood that. 'Another waif and stray.'

'Weer's yer fun 'im, then?' He saw the baffled look on their faces and laughed. 'No use gawming at me. It's Dai yer be wanting, A reckon. He's inside sorting out weer we're goin' to put oor 'eäds.' A jerk of the head towards the portico. 'We've 'ad a right set-to wi' them baändits yer fayther talked on. We giv'em a good wapping but we didn't come off unscaäthed.'

Mehmi clutched at the name he recognised. 'Dai?'

'Aye. Inside. Mebbe.' He scratched at his beard. 'A'll 'ave to remble these beästs afore we et but A'll tek you to 'im. Coöme on.' He used his big hand to wave them on with him into the shadows of the high-arched inner courtyard. 'Is Dai aboot?' he yelled over the din of voices. Edgar turned his head.

'Not here. Gone to see about the meal. It's Friday,' he said, by way of explanation.

'So it is. Fish daäy,' he told them, 'and altar-boy here weän't et meät on a fish day. A'm not right fussy, meself, theëse daäys, and theer's no God's man aboot to tell A'm bound fer hell. A knows that anyroad. A et what belly-timber A can get. Coöme on, ya two.'

Blue led them back into the courtyard. The new-arrived caravan was streaming through the high gates into the huge courtyard and the air was full of the shouts and calls of the muleteers and cameleteers and the calmer directions of the *han* staff, used to the commotion, even the arrival of a large caravan like this one. They mounted the platforms ready to unburden the beasts. The mules were snorting and stamping and braying, sensing fodder and water. Steam was rising off the flanks of the animals; they'd come a distance that day. The camels were bellowing and limping at every step. It was the end of a long day.

The kitchens were busy. Dai was outside the entrance talking in his slow, careful Turkish with one of the cooks, a small dark man with his long beard in two plaits tied behind him and a cloth turban wrapped tightly round his head. He was rubbing at his chin where the strands of the beard parted, nodding solemnly. His hands and arms were marked with the faded red and puckered skin of old scalds and burns. Beyond them, the shadowy vaulted rooms of the kitchens glowed with the fires from the great hearths. There was a glimpse of huge blackened cauldrons crouching on the embers of the fires, hissing and bubbling and steaming, teasing all who passed by with tantalizing, mouth-watering, belly-rumbling aromas of spices and herbs and meat and vegetables and *fasulye*.

'There's good then,' they heard Dai say. 'Plenty even without meat. Pilav with butter. Beans, fresh and dried, cooked in olive oil and spices. Now there's riches. Smells good. We're ready for it, I can tell you.' He swung round at the sound of Blue's voice. His face was flushed with the heat of the nearby tandoor ovens. 'Blue! Are those beasts stabled and the goods lodged?'

'All'un saäfe, Dai.'

'Well done. You be going now to the bathhouse. Take Rémi with you. That's a big caravan coming in – there'll be no chance for you once those men start crowding in.'

'A'll do that, gladly, but look, A've brought yer foölks.'

Dai focused on the two behind the big man. He raised his eyebrows at the sight of them.

'Thowt that would gi' yer summat to think on.' Blue was gratified. He went whistling away, first to collect Rémi then to the bathhouse in another effort to scrub and pumice the dye out of his skin and nails and ease the aches and pains from his battered body.

'Mehmi! Welcome! But what are you doing here?'

'Father sent me. He says I'm to go with you, if you'll have me. You can't be more astonished than I am. To give me leave to go like that...' His voice shook. He stopped, recovered. 'And here is someone who has been searching for you. He arrived at our gates just in time for us to keep him safe from the bandits. See – a little blue brother for our painted man.'

His hands on her shoulders pressured her forward so that she was standing in front of the brown man.

'This is Kazan. He comes from the *Karakeçili* tribe you visited. He was away with the men but he wants to travel with you. He's had enough adventures on the road these past few days to keep us entertained to the end of the journey.'

She braced herself for the dark eyes focused on her, searching like sunlight over the great plateau, seeking out all that was hidden. He was suddenly very still, very silent. He was studying her closely and she held her breath, feeling herself exposed before him, as if he knew her secret.

'*Wel*, Kazan, you are welcome also. You both have adventures to tell, it seems but later, after we have eaten. For now, Mehmi, if you would find the *han* physician I'd be grateful. He's tending to Tom Archer and stitching up our guide's son. Giles is with him. Find out what is happening, how serious their wounds are. Tell him I'll be there as soon as I can. We had a run-in with Kemal's bandits but it's later we tell our stories, isn't it?'

Mehmi hurried away towards the archway where the *han* physician had his room. She was left alone with the brown man.

'So, you thought to come with us?'

'Yes. If you'll have me.'

He was frowning, pulling at his lower lip. Now that the gaiety of his greeting was gone, he looked tired and under the flushed brown skin there was bruising down the side of his face visible even under dark stubble.

'I am skilled with a bow and arrow. I can track and hunt. I am the best of my tribe. If you meet with more bandits, I can be useful.' She looked up at him then, fixing her eyes defiantly on his. 'Mehmi and his father said you asked no questions.'

'That's true.'

'You think I have something to hide?'

'I'm certain you have plenty to hide.'

'You are right,' she said, 'but Mehmi said you all have secrets. There is nothing for which I have need for shame. I have a good reason for wishing to make this journey. To travel with you to Attaleia and then across the sea to the cold lands to find my grandfather. That is what I wish.'

'*Wel*, not so much to wish for now, is it?'

'And I want to rescue the boy who saved me from Fat Vecdet the slave trader.'

'By yourself? Or is it that we are to help you in this rescue?'

She glared at him. 'Kara Kemal did not mock me. He gave me a bow and a quiver of good arrows and a horse because mine was stolen when I was captured—'

'Captured?' His voice sharpened.

'Yes, that is what I said; by that fat man, that donkey Vecdet, and the boy Niko helped me escape. I have sworn to rescue him.'

'I see.' The brown man was thoughtful. 'These are adventures indeed.'

'The mare – the piebald – is for you. Her name is Yıldız and she is indeed a star. She is a gift from Kara Kemal. I am to tell you she is a bride-gift and that there is always room for faith.'

'Did he say so? Well! This is a day of wonders, Kazan, and it's the better off I am for a gift-horse, though the old man can ill afford to part with any of his beasts, and the better off for two new companions. A singer-poet and a champion archer and a star of a horse.' He was smiling, though his dark eyes glittered, but the relief that flooded through her vanished at his next words.

'Come. With all those adventures you must be tired and hungry – and as much in need of the bathhouse as our big friend Blue.'

The bathhouse. Here were new dangers that she had not thought about. What a fool she was, thinking herself so clever, so well disguised.

Dai frowned, watching the crowd of dusty tired men.

'The latrines are over there as well – the latrines for the men.' He paused. 'Maybe we should go dirty tonight. What do you think, Kazan? It will soon be time for the evening meal and I am hungry. So must you be. Are you content to sleep dirty tonight? Or must you be bathed and in clean clothes for Friday Prayers?'

He was smiling in a way that was kindly, waiting for her answer, because he *knew*. She realised that now. He knew, but he was giving her the choice of lies or truth and reminding her of what she had been foolish enough to ignore. Worse, it had never entered her head: the *hamam*, the latrines, the desperate need for fresh clothes, the question of where she would sleep amongst all these men and, of course, the Muslim Friday evening prayers and she a Greek Christian. She was a fool, a fool to think for one moment she could live the lie. A fool to think she could hide the truth from this man whose eyes searched out the deepest secrets. There was a long silence that lengthened and lengthened. It was she who broke it.

'You know.' It wasn't a question.

'Yes.'

'Mehmi did not.'

He was silent again then said, 'Mehmi did not see you at the summer dwelling,' and she nodded, accepting it.

'What now?'

'I'm still waiting for you to tell me. Dirty to bed? *Wel*, you could wash your face and hands or…'

'Yes?'

'We could go late, together.'

Her face flushed crimson, bright as the springtime poppies, remembering the man under the waterfall and his nakedness. Were all men made the same?

She saw dark colour rushing up the man's throat as well, into his brown cheeks. '*Wel* now, not exactly together. I was meaning we could ask the women for help. Soon the *hamam* will be closed to men and the women staff will take over. There are some travellers who are female. They, too, will wish to bathe. We can ask the *hamam* women for help.'

'They will despise me.'

'I think not.'

'You must despise me – think me a fool.'

'I think you have great courage and must have good reason for what you have done. No, you do not need to tell me. I keep many secrets.'

'Will you tell your men?'

'That's up to you.'

'You'll take me on trust?'

'As Kara Kemal would say, there's always room for faith.'

'He was right. He said you would help me to rescue Niko and find a ship that will take me to England. He said you were the very man I needed to help me.'

'Did he indeed? What else out of all these many words did the old man say?'

She blushed, remembering. 'That you could help me to my heart's desire.'

'*Wel* now, that might be more difficult. Let's deal first with the little matters of rescuing your slave and getting you to England – and before that, and most important, bathed and fed. Come. It's wishing us away from here they are. They need to set out the evening meal. Butter rice tonight and *fasulye*. I like that very much. Isn't it remarkable, that they can feed such a company night after night and so well? And we pay for nothing. Now there's good, isn't it?'

He was walking her towards the physician's room. 'I must see that Rashid is well enough – our guide's son, a good boy and sorely wounded. His father is anxious. And there's Twm Archer with a knife wound in his arm. You remember him? He came with me to the camp. Mehmi has not returned and...ah! Here he is. *Wel*, Mehmi?'

'Rashid's wound is grave but the physician has cleaned it and bound it with salve. If there is no fever, he should be well. He's sleeping now. The physician says come later. Thomas's wound is not serious. A flesh wound only. But he is very angry. He says he should have expected the blow.'

Dai sighed. 'Always he is like this after a set-to. He will recover his spirits, and better if left alone a while. Rashid, though...you say he's sleeping?'

Mehmi pulled a face. 'Part sleep, part the darkness that comes with pain. His father is with him.'

Dai pondered. 'I would like to see him, all the same, and his father. Then Kazan and I need to bathe. Ask Edgar to call all the men together for supper. And where is Rémi? I have need of him.'

'He's gone with Blue to the *hamam*.'

'So he has. Well, no matter. I hope he's left his good set of clothes behind. Come, Kazan.'

He led her first into the physician's room, a quiet place with an arched and vaulted roof like all the rooms in this great *han* but here were herbs strung from hooks and stoppered glass jars of potent mixtures. The physician was a tall, lean man, seeming all the leaner for his white robe and long beard. He was an Arab from the countries further east and knew his craft well.

'A grave wound, yes, but the boy is young and strong. If there is no fever and no inflammation he should do well enough.' A physician's answer, always hedged with 'if' and 'but'. 'The wound was clean when he was brought here. Was that your doing?'

'Yes. My patron knew a physician – famous he was in his town of Ieper and he was trained in the ways of the east and in battle. He always said a wound must be kept clean, isn't it now.'

'Indeed. That was well done.'

'My man said he's sleeping now?'

'Yes, though somewhat restless. That's only to be expected.'

'Is his father with him?'

'Yes – though I wish the man would take some rest, some food and drink. That would do him more good than sitting by the boy.'

'I'll have words with him.'

Heavy fabric divided the apothecary's room from the treatment room and an area where there were two truckle beds. Rashid lay pale, his head bandaged and his face white and drawn. He muttered and murmured and turned restlessly. His father was hunched beside the bed, equally white, equally drawn.

'How is it now, Amir?'

'He is alive.'

'It's a pitiable sight. I would not have had this happen for the world.'

'You did all that was possible, master. The boy was determined to prove himself.'

'He was very brave, Amir. You should be proud of him.'

'And I am, master, I am.' The man's mouth worked. 'What should I tell his mother?'

'Wait and see, Amir. All will be well and all will be well and you will take him home for his mother to praise him and scold him as she did when he was only a *dwt*. But you – you must come now, leave him to sleep. You must have rest and food or you'll be no good to him when he wakes up. Isn't that right, Kazan?'

She nodded. 'Indeed it is. Dai is right in this. You must look after yourself if you are to take proper care of the boy. Look.' She rested a hand on the boy's forehead. 'His breathing is good and he has no fever. Later he will need you but now you should do as Dai says.

Food, drink, rest and then return.' She spoke with the same authority Nene had used and the man responded to it. He nodded slowly.

'Yet it doesn't seem right to leave the boy alone. If it's all the same with you, master, I'll come back and stay with him through the night.'

'Of course. And I'm thinking you must stay here with your boy tomorrow.'

'It's my job to take you safe back to Attaleia, master. I've sworn to do that.'

'Your son is of greater importance, Amir. He needs you. But don't worry now. We'll think about tomorrow when tomorrow comes. Go and have your supper. I'll stay here in your place.' He glanced towards the girl and saw her nod. Of course the man would not leave his son unattended.

'I can't let you do that, master.'

'Of course you can.'

But there was no need after all. Edgar came in quietly, smiling, apologising for his presence but he wondered if perhaps Amir would like to eat now, sit with his son later. Edgar? He would eat later. He wasn't hungry now. Tired but better for the *hamam*. If Dai didn't go now it would be too late…

The girl looked at the pale golden boy; this was her patient and he seemed to be healthy despite his pale skin. So quiet, so calm and with such blue eyes. And such a ridiculous head of yellow curls. She smiled at him and he returned her smile though abstractedly.

She followed Dai out into the courtyard. This quiet brown man, he was used to command, she thought, but mindful of his men. 'Will you let the father stay?'

'Of course he must. He'd be no good to us, worrying all the time about his son. Better if he stayed and we had a new guide. The journey is easy enough from here.'

His voice was matter of fact, business-like in the way of the merchants from the western countries but she had seen the flicker of concern in his eyes. He cared about the boy and his father, of that she was sure.

He led her into the great inner hall, its high vaulted roof vanishing into shadows. Windows were black slits against a sky already darkened. There were torches in sconces high on the stone walls that cast flickering light and shade and shadows that crawled along the ground. She shivered.

'Have you stayed before in a *han*?'

'Never. I have never before entered such a huge place. So many stones and so little sky and only one way in and out.'

He glanced down at her. 'It must be strange after your tent.'

'The *yurt* is for summer. In winter we live in houses, but not like this.' She shivered again. This was how wild animals must feel, trapped in dark places. 'Yes, it is very strange.'

'We're in the dormitory – only the rich and important have their own rooms. The sleeping cubicles are narrow – space enough for two sleeping ledges. I'm sending Rémi to sleep with Blue. You,' he said as if it were of no importance, 'will sleep in my space.'

'With you?'

'Unless you prefer to sleep in the women's quarters?'

Always, it seemed, he gave her a choice that was no choice. 'With you,' she agreed.

'You're safest with me.' Again, his words were lightly spoken. He had been rummaging in a saddlebag woven in many colours, like a *kilim*. Now he thrust a bundle into her hands. 'Here – fresh clothes.'

She felt the fineness of good cotton beneath her fingers, caught the glow of crimson and blue patterned cloth so like the one left behind she caught her breath though these were the clothes of the merchants.

'But these are fine clothes.'

'Rémi's best. His clothes will best fit you. You're of a size. He'll be happy enough – I'll get him new clothes when we get to Attaleia. Don't argue. Come.'

They were in the courtyard again, in the dusk, heading for the *hamam*. Blue and Rémi came towards them shining clean.

'Scrubbed and polished, the pair of you! Kazan needs fresh clothes, Rémi. I am giving him yours. I'll get you new clothes in Attaleia.'

The boy nodded, not at all perturbed by the news.

'And you, Rémi, will sleep with Blue tonight. If he snores, it's my permission you have to throttle him.'

The boy chuckled and drew a finger across his throat. The girl protested: 'His clothes, his bed…I cannot.'

'Rémi does as I ask – isn't it, Rémi?' The boy nodded. He thrust his thumbs upwards. 'See – that is the archer's sign for all is well. Not to worry, now. He knows what I do is for a purpose.'

She was still frowning. The boy placed a thin hand on her arm. He nodded, raised his thumb, grinned at her so that the snail-trail scars above his upper lip stretched and glistened in the torchlight. She laughed, suddenly light-hearted. 'Thank you, Rémi. You are very kind to a stranger.'

'Now come, Kazan. You are in greater need of the *hamam* than even I.'

'Kazan the unclëan,' Blue agreed. Her cheeks reddened; it was true. She was rank with the sweat and dirt of the days' journeyings and the nights' rough sleeping. Even so, her chin lifted and her eyes flashed.

'You only say so because you come fresh from your bath. Your smell was rank enough when I first met you, blue man.'

'Grubby little fustilugs, baärely up to my kneecaps and brusting fer a fight.' But he was grinning.

It was as the brown man had said; the *hamam* was ready to close its doors to the men and already a huge, broad-shouldered woman had arrived, clearly the *hamam* female overseer. She glared at Dai and Kazan.

'You're the last,' she said. 'Lucky for you – you're almost too late.

Another few minutes and you'd have to have come back later tonight. Hurry along now.'

'*Hanımefendi*, we have a great favour to ask,' Dai said. He beckoned her to him, to where they were out of hearing of the rest, and started to explain. The woman's eyes rounded with astonishment and suspicion then she eyed the girl with a hard look.

'Not a boy? You ask me to believe this? What kind of *han* do you think we keep here? You foreigners, you're all the same, no sense of shame.'

The girl bent her head. 'It's all right,' she murmured to the man next to her. 'You go. You're tired and as dirty and dusty as I am and you fought off the bandits.'

The woman stared at them again, squinting and screwing up her eyes so that they all but disappeared into her broad, fleshy face.

'So you're the one who thrashed those thieves and robbers who've been tormenting us all this summer. Is it true then? This is a little maid and travelling as a boy amongst you great men? And she's been on her own these past days? The poor little rabbit. You go on, sir. You'll have to hurry. There's little enough time for a proper scrubbing and soaping let alone massaging and oiling those aching muscles of yours. That's a fine bruise showing on your cheekbone. Make sure Mehmet uses a cold cloth on that. Don't have a care about this little pigeon. We'll look after her and no one will be any the wiser. Come now, my little lamb, let's make you more comfortable. No sir, put away your coins. I want no pay for this. May Allah and his Prophet bless you.'

Dai hurried into the cool interior of the *hamam*. He grinned then winced at the bruising: rabbit? pigeon? little lamb? The woman looked formidable but her heart, now, was soft as melted butter. He was sure he could rely on her. And now there was the pleasure of marble slabs on which to relax, and flowing warm water, and the bath attendant to scrub and soap and massage. Nothing like this in his own land. Above him was the domed ceiling with its light holes hazed over with dusk and now should be the time to relax and dream. But not tonight. No dreaming tonight. The girl was here, against all expectations and he held her secret – for once, for the first time, a secret he wished he did not have to guard. A girl alone amongst a world of men needed a brother, not a would-be lover. Besides, she had no glances to spare for him.

'*My son, who are you to decide what is and what is not to be? Only Allah the all-compassionate, the all-knowing decides.*'

Well, I'm here and she's there. Allah has decided.

The old man chuckled. 'Perhaps,' he said. 'There is always room for faith.'

Old man, Kara Kemal, how did you know?

The bath attendant tapped him on the shoulder. Time to turn over. He blanked his mind.

There was no sign of her when he emerged from the *hamam*. The few female travellers still waiting were talking quietly amongst themselves. They turned their eyes demurely from him but he felt their sidelong glances and heard whispered comments and soft giggles. They'd doubtless take him for one of the Turks, with his brown skin and hair and the comfortable *şalvar* and *gömlek* and *kaftan* he'd put on. Bright yellow *gömlek* and blue patterned *kaftan* and deep red and green *şalvar*. Gaudy colours, tell the truth, but he liked the looseness of the *şalvar* and the softness of the fine cotton. He'd tied a dark blue cloth belt about the *kaftan*. The clothes had been a gift some years ago, from another generous soul like Kara Kemal. Not long after he'd parted company with Ibn Battuta, he remembered. He sat down on a bench outside the *hamam* and settled himself to wait for the girl. It was dark now. The pale half moon was drifting behind thin cloud and the stars glittered in an infinity of silence. For a moment he envied those great men of learning, those stargazers, whose lives were lived in the infinite, ineffable peace of the vast firmament. Had any one of them truly heard the inaudible, endless singing of the cosmos?

A burst of laughter came from a noisy group of Genoese. He

dragged himself back from the half-trance he'd fallen into. He grunted: silence above and cacophony below in the courtyard where animals and men were penned for the night. The animals were quiet enough, stabled and fed and thankful to rest themselves. The men it was who brayed and snorted and bellowed. They were gathered in groups around the great platters of food. Torches and lamps cast shadows, lit up faces that were laughing, intent, worried, pensive. Over there was a group of merchant men intent on business. Next to them, a bickering pair. In the shadows where they thought themselves unseen, a discreet flirtation. Someone was playing the *tanbur* softly, and he thought of their own new-come musician, Mehmi-the-youngest, the favourite, the well-beloved. What had it cost the old man to let him go, his son, his darling? Not long for this world – death had him by the throat, his hoarse throat. Odds were, he'd not see his son again, not in this life. Did the boy know? Dai doubted it. Not in the old man's nature, see, to give with one hand and take with the other. A two-handed man he was, like *Taid*. And shall I ever see him again? Not in this life. He closed his ears to the laughter and buzz of talk and fixed his eyes on the vast firmament wheeling and swinging and singing above him. *There's always room for faith.*

She thought he was asleep at first. She was relieved to see him sitting there, waiting for her, as if he felt no hunger, as if he had no men to look after. She'd wondered how she would find them in this huge, heaving mass of travellers. But there he was and it was as if she had always known him, this brown, enigmatic man. He opened his eyes and smiled at her.

'Good. Better? Ready to eat?'

She nodded. 'That woman – Fatima – she was so kind. She gave me a new cloth to bind myself.'

'Bind yourself?'

'Of course. I am very thin but not so thin, you see? I must bind myself to look like a boy.'

He understood. How could he not? He tried not to think of the body beneath the covering of clothes.

'You look nice,' she said shyly. 'Like a *yürük*.' He felt the blood rush up his throat and into his cheeks then he was laughing because she was patting and stroking the material of her tunic and preening like a courting peacock. 'Rémi's clothes are very beautiful. I think I look nice as well. Don't I?'

'Indeed you do.' He paused. 'Kazan,' he said deliberately.

At once she became still. 'I must be Kazan. For a little while. I cannot tell you why I feel this.'

'You don't have to.'

'You are very good.'

'Twm says I am a fool.' He introduced the name deliberately.

'Oh.'

'He is not badly hurt.'

'I am pleased to hear this. But the son, the young man, he is not so good.'

Dai grimaced. 'Not so good. It is in God's hands. And Allah's.'

'With all the gods,' she said, surprising him. 'It is what my grandfather used to say.'

A strange thing to say and dangerously heretical, in the western world. He shrugged. 'Twm should be with the men now. Let's go. Let's see if Twm recognises you.'

'What if he does not?'

'Then you are Kazan.'

'Yes.'

'Come – little rabbit.'

She laughed, a low chuckle. 'I am a little lamb, I think. She is a good woman.'

'Indeed she is. Little pigeon. Come on now, I'm hungry.'

'You are always hungry. It seems to me you were born with a hungry mouth.'

'That's truer than you know.'

'Oh?'

'Another time – maybe.'

He was silent, regretting his words. She thought, 'No one should go hungry. That is what he says. This man has known hardship but he says nothing. And that bruise is fierce but he has not gone to the physician for himself. What kind of man is this brown man? This quiet man with the all-seeing eyes? He knows my secret but he says he will say nothing.' She thought, 'I am in his power,' but she didn't feel fear. Instead, there was a strange sense of comfort.

They had found their group easily, already eating.

'We waited for you, Dai.'

'Blame this one, strutting like a peacock in Rémi's fine clothes.'

'I was not!'

'Looks better on yow than on 'im, Fustilugs.'

'And you look better for a good scrubbing, blue man.'

Rémi patted the empty place next to him. Dai pushed her into it. She was next to the big man.

'Nice dye, that,' he said. 'Good colour.'

She looked at him with gold-flecked eyes. 'A dyer knows these things.'

'That they do. It's magic, it is. Woad magic.'

'I have seen it, blue man.'

'Have yer now? Have yer seen that moment when the cloth comes out of the vat? Green and stinking and right there in front of yer eyes it turns blue? All manner of blue, like God 'imself was doing it.'

If she listened closely, she could understand some of his words; but it was his face she watched, his face that told her who he was, this big man with the big voice and big opinions. He was very like Yavuz the drunk, always loud and full of argument but inside himself he was delicate like spring blossom. Look at him now, tongue-tied and blushing because he had shown his soul and making silly coarse jokes to hide it from the world.

She looked around them all. There was Edgar, her patient, recovered now; she felt a quiet satisfaction and gave thanks to Nene whose skill had saved him. But so young and handsome and his eyes so blue, like the summer sea. He sat quietly listening to the talk but she knew he was not so quiet. His soul was troubled. Rémi-the-speechless, Rémi who obeyed his master without question, as a slave would, but this was no slave. Ah Rémi! A gentle soul. He had the patient face of an old man but he was only a young boy. How had he come by those snail-trail scars? Giles the fighting man, lean and tough. An enigma. Straightforward it seemed but who knew if it was so? He was loyal to his master, Thomas Archer, or so he called himself. Proud, beautiful, like the hero Bamsi Beyrek. She hardly dared look at him. Such beauty. His cheekbones and his brow, his bow-lipped mouth, his arched eyebrows and dark grey eyes like the smoke. His body – ah – was lithe and sleek and his skin had a sheen like the purest of silk. His arm was bandaged and he moved it stiffly as if it pained him. It was his fighting arm. He stretched out his left hand to take morsels of food, apologising as he did so because this was not the hand that should take food. A man of manners; a noble man.

There was the other, the boy who was wounded. Rashid. He was badly hurt. Before they came to the evening meal, she and the brown man had gone again to the physician's room. The boy was lying there, still and pale. His father had returned, sat close by. Guide and servant to the foreigners, father of this pale, frail boy: where did his loyalties lie? He respected the man who employed him; respected him for a man who took care of all who worked for him. He had promised to serve him, guide him safely back to Attaleia. Now his son needed him but a promise was a promise. Kazan the stranger, the newcomer, had passed a hand over his son's forehead.

'No heat.'

'Is that good, Kazan?'

'Yes. This man, this physician, he is good. He knows his craft.' The stranger had smiled at the father. 'It is well. Your son will live.

He is strong, like his father.'

And the man had felt comforted which was ridiculous because this was a young boy who knew nothing of the skills of medicine. Yet there had been something in that dark, gold-flecked stare and the way in which he stood beside the bed so confident, so sure that all would be well. Tears had streamed down the father's cheeks. The boy leant forward and kissed him on the forehead and it felt like a blessing.

Later. They had eaten hungrily; drunk thirstily. 'Clam,' Blue said. 'I'm that clam I could sup a gallon.'

'I was so hungry I could have died,' confessed Edgar.

Thomas Archer had eaten little. He was pale, his arm bandaged and supported in a sling. A dagger wound, he said, but not serious.

'He swears he's well enough,' Giles said, 'but he's lost an armful of blood and gained an armful of sutures.'

'Well, what of that?' Tom Archer said. He sounded bad tempered. 'It was nothing. A glancing wound. That young muleteer – the guide's son – he had it worse.'

'Rashid? True enough,' Dai said. 'He's going on well enough but we'll not be moving from here tomorrow.'

'Can't we put him on one of the horses?'

'Not if you want to keep Amir happy – his father and our guide, remember?'

'I suppose so.'

'Come now, Twm, you'll be better for a day's rest, isn't it now?'

'Don't you mollycoddle me. Giles's fussing is bad enough. He's like an old woman.'

The dark man was angry. She saw Dai and the man Giles exchange looks. Giles rolled his eyes. This she could tell, but the rapid to-and-fro of language was too difficult for her to follow. It was not the language of the merchants, nor the strange tongue of the blue man. She was perplexed, worried. He looked pale and she longed to smooth his head, ease his pain. She wondered if the physician had given him the opiate that brought sweet relief. The brown man was looking at her now.

'Don't worry,' he said, quietly. 'We're all tired and, tell the truth, bad-tempered now it's all over.'

'I do not understand what it is you say to each other.'

'That's the strange Norman English tongue – though Blue's tongue is stranger than most.' He said something to the big man that had him laughing. 'We're a mixed bunch. Twm and Edgar are English; young Rémi here is Flemish; Giles is from the Marches, the in-between country. I am from Wales. From Cymru.'

'I have heard of that country.'

'Have you now?' He was surprised.

'Nene. She talked of it.' The girl stopped, flushed. They were all listening. 'We all called her Nene. She was the grandmother of our tribe though she was not a *yürük*.'

Thomas Archer was scathing. 'And you say this grandmother had heard of Dai's poverty stricken little country? Can we believe this?'

'Why should you not believe? I do not tell lies, me.' She raised her chin, flashing him an angry look then away because she was forgetting he was wounded and tired and in pain and she was, after all, living a lie in her boy's disguise. 'Our Nene talked of Cymru,' she said more quietly. 'She had met a…traveller who had been there. He told her it was a land full of song makers and storytellers.' She looked at Dai. 'This is so, is it not?'

'It is so.' He sighed. 'Well, it was so. Our bards would sing the stories of our great days and great princes and great chiefs. The English kings have ended much of that. Now we are, truth to tell,' he slanted a glance at Twm Archer, 'a poverty stricken little country. Once, we had our own princes and our own laws given to us by Hywel Dda. Now, the Edwards have taken away our right to rule ourselves. We've lost…*wel*, more than enough.'

It was more than he usually said. He shrugged. 'I am a Welshman.

These things matter.'

Mehmi broke into the little silence. His poet's soul longed to hear more of the singers and storytellers but he felt also the unease of this man his father called 'son'. He said, 'I want to hear about your great adventure. The bandits passed us. They were a sorry sight and Kazan here did not need to show his prowess with a bow. What did you do? There must have been great deeds.'

The men laughed, relieved because the talk had turned into a different course. Dai flashed Mehmi a grateful look. 'Let Blue tell,' he said, mischievously.

'But no one can understand him!'

'Edgar can – Edgar, you tell what he says.'

The pale boy smiled. 'I'll try. Go on, Blue – though your story telling is far better than mine. It's a shame these infidels can't understand the good Fen language.'

It was unexpected, such a comment from quiet Edgar. Was it the girl's doing again?

Blue was grinning, pleased to be the teller of the tale though the telling was neither Blue's nor Edgar's but as if they rolled into one voice.

'It were close run,' he said. 'There they were, coming down on us and still Dai said hold. They'd plans to circle us but we forced 'em into the neck of the little valley we were in. No more than spoon-shaped but wi' trees and rocks. It were as good a place as any along that road. They came pounding up. We could hear the hoof beats, close and closer, and their horses panting and snorting. Close enough to see their sides steaming sweat. Then Dai gives the shout and his trick wi' the wire brought most of them down. Caps owt A've seen. Yer should of seen 'em slither and land arse-end-up. We stopped 'em brusting through. Then there were the archers. You had the men well in 'and, Tom Archer. Arrows? Air were thick wi' em.'

Rémi grunted, hoarse-voiced.

'Says he did his share,' said Blue. 'And so you did, little runt.

You'd one end of the wire and pulled it tight at the right time.' He ruffled the boy's hair, looked towards Edgar. 'And so did you, altar boy. Keeping them beasts quieted was hard work.'

Edgar flushed bright red.

'We had a spot of close fighting after and that's when Tom 'ere took it – and young Rashid. He was like to be killed except Giles wapped the bastard as was pounding him and laid 'im out.'

'All turned out well then,' said Giles. He'd bruises and scratching but nothing serious. He was well pleased. This was why he'd been taken on the journey – guard and keep safe, that was what Tom Archer had said. But that strange man Heinrijc Mertens! Why Tom had wanted to be in the man's employ, why he had wanted to go on this journey – well, that was no man's business. He was Tom's man and that was all that mattered. He'd been Tom's man for years now. A good master, in spite of the black moods that came on him, and he paid well so if he chose to travel in these God-forsaken places, so be it. Besides, they'd been to places he never thought existed and met strange people and stranger thoughts it would be better to pretend were never there, or he'd fear for his soul, if he still had a soul. He'd hoped he'd see the men whose heads were beneath their shoulders, or the men who had only one leg with a foot so big they used it as a shade from the sun. He'd seen such things once on a wonderful map full of terrors and wonders.

There'd not been a glimpse of either of them but it was a world of wonders all the same. Like these *hans* with their bathhouses and clean, fresh water and meals and rooming for hundreds and hundreds of beasts and men and all free for three days. There was nothing like that in England, only the rapacious lords running riot in the land, and filthy water and grubbing for food for such as him, and death to any who disobeyed or disbelieved. Better to be here, in this big, broad land, even amongst the Muslims. Better to be amongst Muslims who did not consign brothers to the fire.

As for the journey, it had been too quiet so far – a few run-ins but nothing to count. This was better, though Tom had come off worse for the encounter. That rush of riders and the moment when they hit the stretched wire: he'd never forget it. The slither and screams of the horses; the flubbering of flesh as they fell to the ground trapping their riders beneath them; the flailing of arrows in the air, his own as well because he was Tom's man; the riders behind crashing into those floundering and crashing in their turn. So simple a plan, so devilish. He wondered who this Dafydd the Welshman was, where he had come from, where he had learned his craft. He wasn't a lord's son, for sure. Then the close hand-to-hand fighting, and the Welshman with his falchion, a peasant sword if ever there was one but lethal with its axe-like, curve-edged blade designed for slashing and chopping. Merciless. That quiet, brown man suddenly become a lethal, merciless killer and not a sign of emotion on his face. A dangerous man.

'Thowt we'd nivver get here afore darklins,' said Blue. 'Thowt yer'd be a ghost walkin' afore that, altar boy.'

'Why does he call you that?' Kazan had nestled closer to Blue while he told his tale. Edgar was on her left side.

'Call me what?' Edgar picked nervously at a ravelled thread on his jerkin.

'Altar boy. An altar boy helps the papas, doesn't he? In the monasteries?'

His pale face flushed. She saw the colour creeping up from his throat into his face, into his hair. He burned.

'I am sorry,' she said, quickly. 'Dai says no questions. I should not have asked.'

Edgar breathed in heavily, breathed out again. His hands stilled. 'Why not?' he said, and his voice was hoarse. 'Why shouldn't you know? Everybody guesses at it anyway.' He looked around at them all, unexpectedly defiant, his face still flushed and his blue eyes bright. 'Why does he call me altar boy? Because I was one – until I ran away.'

No one moved or spoke. They looked away from him. No one told their secrets. It was the unwritten code: it was Dai's Law. The girl was unheeding.

'You ran away?' She was interested not shocked, settling herself more comfortably against Blue's bulk – *cwtching*, Dai would call it – preparing to listen. 'You did not want to be an altar boy so you escaped?'

'Yes.' He glanced down at her. 'Aren't you shocked by my wickedness?'

'No. Why should I be? I think it was very clever of you to escape from a life you did not want. How did you do it? And why were you there in the first place?' The golden eyes gleamed up at him, curious and bright like a falcon's except that this was no bird of prey. A golden-eyed kitten, maybe, or a child waiting for a bedtime story, curled up against the big man who made no protest but rather shifted to give the boy ease. And there he was, twitching again at his sleeve, smoothing a fold of cloth, a small peacock parading in Remi's best clothes. Edgar was surprised into laughter, startling the men because this was pale quiet Edgar who so rarely spoke let alone laughed aloud.

'What's to do, altar boy?' Blue asked, and Edgar laughed louder. He shook his head.

'Kazan here wants my story. Well, he shall have it.'

12

Edgar's story

'My home was in the flatlands of Lincolnshire. You know as much –
I'm the only one of you who can properly understand our friend
Blue here, though Dai is not far behind. My father owns two manors
and the land rights. Not great manors but a good enough living. I
am the youngest of three sons. My mother died in childbirth and my
father never cared very much for me because of this. I think perhaps
he blamed me for her death. He loved her very much. He didn't want
me about him when I was young.' Edgar shrugged. 'That was not
important. It was all one to me. I was happy enough with my books
and music and the archery practice and riding and hunting – the
usual life of the youngest son of an unimportant Lord of the Manor.
Besides, my brothers looked after me. They made me spears and
swords from the sedges and plaintains when I was little. It's a game
we used to play,' he explained. 'The plaintains have a knobby top
and we would have fights, hitting one against the other to see whose
top was knocked off first. Alfred fashioned me a wooden sword
when I was older and Eric used to make me spillcocks at Lenten.
They used to sneak out for the Feast Day of the Holy Innocents and
go with the village children begging for titbits and gifts of money.
When I was old enough they took me. We dressed up in old clothes
and smeared our faces with soot then walked from abbey to priory
and to our parish church and to the manor houses. Once, we went
to our father's door and laughed because even our servants did not
recognise us. Or maybe they did.'

'But the monastery, Edgar!' a husky little voice prompted him. 'This is very interesting and you shall tell me about your children's games another time but now,' determinedly, 'I want to hear about your escape.'

'And so you shall, little blue brother. When I was thirteen summers my father called me to him and told me my eldest brother would inherit the manors and lands, according to custom. My middle brother was to marry the daughter of our neighbour. His lands ran with ours, and we had known the girl since childhood. She was happy to marry my brother – no hardship, though it was to secure the land and property. As for me, it was my duty to atone for the death of my mother by entering a monastery. To begin with I would be a student and later I would take my vows. The monastery he had chosen was as far from our chief manor house as was possible. A Benedictine house but the choice – well – it says it all. Crowland, the abbey founded by St Guthlac. Of course, you don't know the story of Guthlac and the island of Crowland.

'Let me tell you,' he slanted a glance down at the boy who already had words of protest on his lips. 'Then you will better understand the rest.' The boy sighed and settled against Blue's bulk, face expectant. He paused, thinking how best to explain.

'Guthlac was a holy man of long ago who wanted to be in the most desolate place he could find and so he searched the Fens until he found the very spot he wanted. It was a dreary, dangerous land of bottomless black pools and deep marsh and in places there was raised land and it was here, on one of these small islands, that Guthlac lived. He and his companions dressed in skins and ate scraps of barley bread and drank a small cup of muddy water after sunset. They were very holy men.'

'Why does this make your holy men more holy?' the boy asked. 'They sound very sad and silly to me, without joy in their lives.'

Edgar nodded. 'So it seemed to me as well but it was heresy to say so.'

'Stop yer blethering, pipsqueak. Let the altar boy tell his taäle.'

Kazan poked his tongue out at the rebuke but subsided again.

'The Fens are well known for fever and ague – there's a need for shivery spiders, hey, Blue? But this was also a place where demons lived. Terrible demons with blubber lips and fiery mouths and scaly faces and beetle heads and sharp long teeth and long chins. They had black skins and humped shoulders and big bellies and cloven hoofs and long tails at their buttocks. And there were legions of them and they all attacked Guthlac and his companions. Biting and switching their filthy tails and nipping them by the nose and giving them cramps and rheums and shivering agues and burning fever and putting dirt in their meat and drink – oh these were evil demons. Guthlac and his companions prayed and sprinkled holy water but it wasn't enough. Guthlac was carried off to the very jaws of hell. And it was then St Bartholomew appeared to him in a vision and gave him a whip to beat off the devils.'

'This is a terrible story and a terrible place, Edgar. Are there really such demons in your country?'

'It is how it was told to me. Should I doubt the stories of our saints? He beat off the devils with the whip St Bartholomew gave him and founded a great monastery.'

'And your father sent you there?'

'That's the one my father chose. I think he liked the idea of demons attacking me.'

'A've heärd of yon boggards. A've heärd 'em howling on glistery nights.'

'But Guthlac lived a very long time ago, Edgar, did he not?' broke in Twm. 'I believe the land is much changed now.' His voice was as dry and disbelieving as only he could make it. Edgar's throat and cheeks flushed poppy-red, even in the torchlight.

'That is so.'

'Edgar, I think you do not want to tell your story.' Kazan was reproachful.

'And if he doesn't, it's his choice, isn't it now? Let Edgar be.'

'It's all right, Dai. I've promised you my story. It's just – well – I've not spoken of it till now. It doesn't come easy.' He was silent, considering.

'It's true what Tom says. Guthlac and the demons were a long time ago and since then the abbey has grown and the monks have worked hard to dig dykes and ditches to drain the land. It's planted now with apple trees and vines and oats and flax, and it's a pleasant enough place to be in the summer months. But there's no causeway, like the one that was built at Ramsey Abbey. There's no way to reach Crowland except by water. Then there's flooding in the winter months when the salt tides are high and driven by the bitter north-east winds and the fields and pastures and meadows are overflowed and drowned and returned to watery marshes and black pools and deep and boggy quagmires. Easy to believe, then, that there are still demons there in the Fens. Easy to imagine you can hear them howling on glistery nights, as Blue says.'

His audience shivered. Giles stirred the brazier so that flames and bright sparks shot skywards and they all moved closer to its light and warmth. 'Go on, Edgar.'

'It wasn't a peaceful place. Always, there was always conflict with the people who lived thereabouts – and with the other abbeys. Always there were quarrels and violence and litigation. Who was responsible for what drainage? Whose boundaries ended where? Who had the rights to graze cattle and sheep and when? Who had the right to cut turves and cut down wood and alders? Quarrel after quarrel after quarrel; dispute after dispute, sometimes settled in favour of Crowland, sometimes in favour of Spalding or Peterborough or the landowners.' He chuckled suddenly and unexpectedly. 'It was only last year that Thomas Wake of Deeping had his men mow the rushes on the Crowland meadows and they made off with them together with hay and turves and cattle. And there was no fair last year because of Thomas Wake. When the

Father Abbot took it to court, Thomas of Deeping said there'd been falsification of the documents that gave the land rights and I suspect he was in the right of it. Holy men can be as corrupted as any mortal. Anyway, while it was trundling through the courts, there was plenty of night-time damage done – setting fire to turves, moving the landmarks, levelling one another's trees. As far as I know, it's still going on. I don't think it will ever stop.

'And there was I in the thick of it, where I'd had no wish to be in the first place. How the days dragged, every day the same, every night scrambling into robes for Matins and Laud and dawn creeping in with Prime and those readings in the cloister every day until I thought my head would split.'

'A knaw summat about that,' Blue broke in. 'We'd an owd priest when A were a lad who droned on like an 'umble bee in a jug. A could nivver 'ear nowt what he said.'

'Stop yer blethering, blue man,' Kazan said in a quaint imitation of his voice so that they all laughed.

'Go on Edgar,' Giles said. They were all listening intently.

Edgar sighed. 'There was no escaping: Terce, Sext, None, Vespers, Compline, bed and start again. Demons. Demons in my head and in my bed, night after night until I thought I would go mad. The novice master despaired of me. I swore I would fly from the place. I pleaded with them to let me go but they saw me as unclean, filled with devils. Besides, my father had paid a great deal of money to have me schooled there. Money talks louder than God. That autumn, great mists rose up from the sodden land and days would pass without our being able to see more than a hand's breadth in front of us. That's how I felt my life was – drifting through mist day after day until the day I died. I was already in purgatory.'

Edgar was silent and so were they, imagining his life in that desolate place; a life he had not chosen. He glanced round at their serious faces. 'You should see them at table,' he said suddenly. 'No speaking – that's the rule – but they have sign language down to a craft. Look, it's like this. You want bread? Brown bread? Make your thumb and two forefingers round as a compass and touch your cowl with your sleeve. Butter? Draw your two right upper fingers to and fro on your left palm. Yes, like that! Do you want cheese with that? Hold your right hand flat-ways in the palm of your left…'

'What about a drink, altar boy?'

'Blow on your right forefinger and put it on your nether lip.'

'How about a hot drink?'

'Side of the right forefinger into your mouth. Keep it fast and closed.'

'Ale, Edgar!'

'Make the sign of drink and draw your hand from your ear downward.'

'A glass?'

'Sign of a cup with the sign of red wine…like this…'

'Fish, altar boy. It's Fish Friday, after all, innit?'

He wagged his hand like a fish's tail swimming.

'Salt!'

'Mustard!'

'Water!'

They joked and laughed and signed for what they wanted. Edgar seemed a man reborn, laughing and demonstrating and Dai wondered at him. Was this truly pale Edgar? Edgar the silent, the biddable? Some miracle had taken place here, this evening. Dai's gaze moved to the girl, her cheeks flushed, laughing with the rest, delicately signing for bread. His gaze moved on, fixed on Rémi. He was wide-eyed, his fingers flying as he gestured for salt, bread, ale… He was for the first time in his life one of the men, Dai thought, where the only language was this signed language. He realised the girl was as intent on Rémi as he was, then she shifted her gaze to his, and smiled, and deliberately leaned across to the boy to gesture for water.

It was a little while before someone said, 'What happened then?' and Edgar resumed his story.

'You can't fight against your father and the authorities of the monastery. They have too much power. I swore I would take the first means of flight. I swore I would not abide in the abbey. I wept. I shed bitter tears. I demanded my clothes, my everyday clothes. Of course, I was refused. I was punished. They were adamant. And so I left. I ran away.

'It was springtime. That is a joyous time in the flat lands. The birds return and the marsh greens over and the sky is a great blue arc – as blue as the lightest, bluest woad. Blue knows. A party of young squires came on pilgrimage. We were a place of pilgrimage, did I say? St Guthlac's shrine was a marvel of marble and precious metal and jewels. We used to get folk coming and praying for a miracle. But these young men – how I envied them! I was of an age by then – eighteen summers. I'd been five long years in the abbey and it was time I made my vows but I resisted. These young men, they made reverence, that's true, but then they were free to go riding and hawking. The local men rowed them about in the marsh boats so they could set up the fowls that live there in abundance. And there was fishing and hawking of a different kind. I heard them talk of it – which girls from the villages were ripe for tumbling, which had to be persuaded. I heard them talk of fresh lips and smooth skin and rounded breasts with perky nipples and hot quims until I was ready to faint with longing.' He looked round at their astonished faces. 'Well, it's true – I was – I am a man with a man's longings and they were not to be satisfied by fumbling the choir boys as others did!'

An intake of breath. This was something they had not dreamed on; holy men were holy men. Then Blue guffawed. 'Eh, altar boy,' he roared, 'we'll set yer right – woän't we?' He was grinning wide-mouthed, yellowed teeth showing. 'Fust place we coöme to, we'll set yer right. We'll mek a man of yer, waäit an' seä – right bors?'

'That we will,' Giles smirked, 'and no choir boys – unless anyone here has a taste for 'em?' He looked around the table, one eyebrow raised. There was loud laughter, even from Mehmi.

The girl knew she was blushing. Her face felt as hot and red as the tandoor ovens. Nene had told her how men talked together. She had listened to the old stories, heard the lilt of love poetry, but that had been about love and longing for a beautiful woman. This? This was different. No love; only raw lust. Were all men the same?

'Hey Fustilugs,' she heard, 'we'll tek you wi' us an' all. Look, lads, he's all a-glimmer. 'Appen 'e's one fer t' choir boys? Looks like one 'issen, doän't 'e, wench-faced recklin?'

'Virgin more like,' Giles said. 'That so, Kazan?'

'Leave the boy alone, now,' Dai said. 'Let Edgar finish his story. We've yet to hear how you escaped, Edgar.'

'Eh, yer right, Dai. Go on, lad, tell us the rest on it.'

'It was quite easy in the end,' Edgar said. 'One of the men had a son who was my particular friend. Ivar, his name was. It was he who helped me to escape.'

'Did you climb over the abbey wall?'

'That would have been no use. There were no roads, remember. I needed a boat and a guide and Ivar brought me both, and clothes to wear and what pennies he could steal from his family. One night after Compline I crept out of the dormitory and through the abbey grounds to where Ivar was waiting by the water gate. That was the abbey sewer and the stench of it is in my nostrils still. The great monastery, and the water around it, and the strange bridge we have there, timber built and three-cornered, straddling the two great rivers of the Nene and the Welland; all so silent. We went under the bridge and there we were, floating down to freedom. The moon was full – not the best night for an escape – but the mist rose up from the marsh and we sailed into it. It lifted and fell, lifted and fell and swayed and twined itself around us and pressed itself against the side of the boat as if the water wraiths had come to keep us company – or drag us down to their homes under the water. We neither of us spoke. It was all silent except for the dip and swish of the boat and the rippling sound of water, with Ivar using the oar to keep us in the channel. And the sounds of the night birds whistling and hooting and sometimes there was a rush of wings through the mist. When the mist lifted the moon shone through, pale; it was like looking through the great veil at the greatest mystery of all.

'We sailed down the waters to the sea and the sun rose. The whole of that watery land was like a great burnished mirror. Where did water end and sky begin? It was peaceful. I felt at peace.' He smiled, remembering, his eyes blue and far-seeing, gold curls a nimbus round his head.

He was beautiful, Kazan thought, this Edgar. 'What then?' she breathed.

'Why, then we came to the coast and I found a ship bound for Flanders willing to take me as ship's boy.'

'What of Ivar?'

'He went back home. I wanted him to come with me but he said he belonged to the land. He was a fen man like his father and his father before that.'

'But you went as ship's boy…'

'Yes. I am not a good sailor. They didn't get a good bargain out of me. It was rough seas all the way and I was sick most of the time. I even began to wonder if the abbey life was not the best one after all. But it was not for me. Now don't you think me wicked? I was a gift to God and I've run away from Him.'

The question was spoken to all but it was at Kazan that Edgar was looking, and for Kazan's answer that he waited.

'There was wickedness, certainly, but not of your doing. Your father did not make of you a gift; he did not want you with him, and you should give to God only what you most love, what you most desire, or the gift is worthless.' The golden eyes were gleaming bright. 'Great wrong was done by your father, and by the monks who would not listen to you. There are more ways of serving God than that of life in a monastery. That is what Nene used to say. *Each to his own. Find gladness in your living*. That is what she said. It is in gladness that you worship and honour the life God gave you and for which you are intended.'

'Do you really believe this, Kazan?'

'Indeed I do. Have I not run away myself from a life I did not want? Me, I do not feel guilty. It was not a life of my choosing and I do not believe it was of God's choosing. Would God wish me to be unhappy? Now I give thanks to the good God who sent me to you.' She yawned suddenly, putting a hand in front of her mouth. 'But what happened then, when your ship arrived in harbour?'

'Another evening, another story, Kazan. Come, you are falling asleep where you are.' Dai's voice.

'But this Blue is very comfortable. He makes a good pillow.'

'Come Kazan – or should I carry you?'

'Indeed you will not. Goodnight, all of you, and I thank you, Edgar, for your story. It was well told. I would like to see these marsh wraiths but the demons…no!' She shuddered. 'Those I do not like. Yes, Dai *bey*, I am coming.'

13

All day parched with burning love
All night a restless sense of separation
(Mevlana Jalal al Din Rumi, 1207–1273)

She had never in her life slept close to any man, not father nor brother. When she went hunting with the young men she slept separately with the women. And now she must share the sleeping space with this stranger, this brown man with the soul-seeing eyes. She followed him from the courtyard into the huge chamber along which lay the shadowy sleeping alcoves. He paused at one. The ledges were covered well enough with a straw mattress. Coarse-woven wool blankets were folded ready. 'Ours,' Dai said. 'We find they come in handy, and warm enough though they're not the best quality.' He handed one to her. 'Don't mind the men,' he said suddenly. 'It's good-hearted they are for all their coarse talk.'

She felt herself blushing again. 'I know that. Thank you for…for ending their talk.'

He nodded. 'I'll give you room to make yourself comfortable. I'll be back in a few minutes.'

He left her alone in the dim shadowiness. It was so different from the tent – different from the winter quarters. She had never been inside such a huge building, never imagined sleeping in one. She felt trapped, suffocated. She spread the cover over the thin mattress then pulled off her soft skin boots. She hesitated, pulled the beautiful crimson and blue patterned jerkin over her head and lay down in her borrowed breeches and undershirt and wrapped the rest of the blanket round her. Outside in the corridor torches in wall sconces cast feeble light and longer shadows; within the sleeping alcove were dark shadows. It was much later when one shadow separated itself from the rest; the brown man had returned. She heard rustling as the man arranged his own bedding, stripped off his own outer clothing. She heard him ease himself on to the mattress; sigh with relief as he rested his body.

She lay in silence, listening as his breathing became regular, deeper. Not the light inhalation of Nene, no little sighs or murmurings; instead, this deep, regular drawing in of breath and its exhalation. If she stretched out her hand she would touch him. In… out…in…out… She wondered if it was possible for her to sleep with her nerves stretched taut as the ropes of the black tents. In…out… in…out…her own breathing was falling into the same rhythm. In… out…in…out… The girl had no sense of sleep overwhelming her.

He left her alone in the sleeping alcove. She needed space and time and there was little enough of that in the great hall of the *han* even without his presence. He walked through its dimness, past the alcoves where tired men stretched out their bodies, out into the courtyard, dark now and quiet. There was the snorting and coughing of animals; the trickle and splash of water sounding louder in the night, the usual mutter of voices and stifled laughter of the late-to-beds. Blue was not among them tonight; he'd been as good as his word. Wasn't it always so, once his word was given? The sky was clear and a bright sickle of moon hung high above him.

So this was what was meant by 'exquisite agony'. He'd heard it said that professional torturers knew their skills so well they could inflict pain passing all endurance yet death did not come. He'd known pain enough in his own life, of body, soul and heart, but not like this. Not this piercing agony of heart and soul. She was here, the marvellous maid, the shining, bright-as-dawn girl – fashioned of gold and bronze and copper, more lovely than the Mawddach, her cheeks curved as perfectly as the white sickled moon above him. Even in her wretched filthiness he had known her at once, the girl he had thought to be miles away in the nomad camp. Kara Kemal, how right you were. *My son, who are you to decide what is and what is not to be? Only Allah the all-compassionate, the all-knowing decides.*

And his own answer: *Well, I'm here and she's there. Allah has decided.*

There is always room for faith. Kemal's answer to everything

What had driven her from her home with the *yürük*? From all that was familiar and loved? True, her grandmother was dead and she said it was her grandfather she was seeking – a Sais *taid*! But if it were only that, only the quest, the father chief would not have let her leave alone, disguised as a boy with her glorious shining hair cropped short. She needed protection and comfort; he would do his best to keep her from harm. Lead her to her heart's desire? Not him, that was for sure. *Breuddwyd gwrach.* Nothing but old woman's dreaming. What was he to her, plain, brown man that he was without the gift of words or music with which to woo her? A free man yes, as all Welsh were free, in spite of England's rule, but a woeful Welshman outside the land of Wales. If he tried to speak the words in his heart, they came out crooked. He'd have no sleep tonight. She would lie close to him and if he stretched out a hand he would touch her, so close to him she was; yet he must be far apart. There must be not one sign from him of this agony of love and desire for the shining maid.

'Dafydd?'

'Twm.' He answered as quietly as the dark man had spoken his name.

'Not abed, then?'

'Nor you. Is the wound paining you?'

'It's well enough – well enough to travel tomorrow. We're running out of time, Dafydd. We'll arrive too late – we'll miss the fleet.'

'Time enough. Konya next day's end, then it's an easy road to Suleymanşehir and down to Attaleia.'

The fountain trickled water into the silence between them.

'I'm sorry I was churlish tonight.'

'So you were.'

'You're angry with me.'

'No. No reason. You're angry enough with yourself and it's true – I was close to mollycoddling you like a broody hen.'

'You mean for the best. I am angry with myself. If I hadn't taken so long to strike he'd never have caught me out like that. Still, best left. Couldn't you sleep?'

'I'm giving Kazan time to settle. Not used to buildings, let alone a great place like this. No starlight.'

'You should have let him sleep with Blue – his snores would have lulled the boy to sleep fast enough.'

Dai laughed. 'Thought I'd spare the boy that, first night at least.'

'He's a strange one – with a knack for loosening tongues. Could be dangerous.'

'You always say that. But Edgar was the better for it, wouldn't you say?'

'True. Another one for Heinrijc Mertens, I suppose.'

'Not this one. To England in search of a grandfather.'

'Moonshine. And you'll go with him, I suppose?'

'It's on my way home, isn't it now?'

'I hope you know what you're doing.'

'So do I. In deep water I am this time.'

'Sometimes, Dafydd, I don't understand you.'

'Sometimes, Twm, I don't understand myself. Nor you – or why it is you stay with me. I've reason again and again to be grateful to you. Mertens made a good choice. I'm sorry for your wound.'

'Aye well, no matter.'

Silence again. Twm seemed in no hurry to leave him. Not looking forward to a night of pain, Dai thought suddenly, and keeping himself quiet so as not to disturb the place.

'Look at us all crowded in here,' Twm said suddenly. 'Christians, Muslims, Jews, like hens in a coop. There was a time not long since when we'd spill each other's blood as freely as we now trade goods. And what were we doing in those Holy Wars but warring one against the other for profit? Kings, princes, noblemen, holy men…what's to choose amongst them? It's the poor devil of a commoner that suffers. Not even any value as a prisoner – no ransom for a poor man though his blood is freely spilled for his masters.'

'Trading goods is better,' Dai said. 'There's been blood enough spilt. Those bandits today, probably wanting no more than bread to put in their *dwts'* mouths. They'd a hungry look about them.'

'I thought so too,' Twm said slowly. 'Tell the truth, that's what put me off my stroke. He seemed no more than a boy to me, at my sword's end, and fearful.'

'Kill or be killed, isn't it? It's a "wud" world, as Blue would say. It is that.'

'It's a violent world. We've lived through hard years, Dafydd – you, me, Giles, Blue. Edgar's too young to remember it all: the years of famine – civil war with nothing to choose between the second Edward or that she-wolf French wife of his. At least the first Edward kept peace in the country.'

'There's not a Welshman or a Scot who'd agree with you there.' Dai's voice was curter than he'd meant it to be. He didn't want to remember those times. He didn't want to fall into a dispute. Not tonight. He shrugged. 'We're better off here, aren't we now? Muslim, Jew and Christian, English and Welsh, with trading on our minds, not bloodletting, and good fellowship besides. Even the Venetians and Genoese have a truce.'

Silence again. Twm's face was averted, deep shadowed.

'Do you think there's any truth in what Kazan said?' he asked abruptly. 'Do any of us have the right to make our own choices? Find our own happiness?'

Dai took his time answering. 'There's a part I agree with,' he said, slowly. 'The world is changing, Twm; we are no longer bound to our masters, nor a fixed place in the world. War and famine has put paid to that, and wealth that comes from trade. Many good men question the priests and are treated with savage cruelty by these so-called holy men. The Pope in Avignon has made bonfires of too many. We have seen for ourselves that those who worship a different god are not all devils and blasphemers.' He sighed. 'But it's not always possible to choose, is it now? Sometimes there is duty, honour, call it what you will. Then it's patient you must be and wait for God to unravel it all.'

'But if there is no one to whom you owe allegiance?'

'Then Kazan is in the right of it. Best choose your own path, make your own happiness and honour the life given to you. But it's not all as Kazan says, is it now? It's honouring a promise made, isn't it, this journey he's after making?'

'He seems happy enough with his choice.'

'He has courage, that one. He'd sing his way to death.'

Twm raised an eyebrow. 'Sounds as if the boy's found favour with you.'

'Aye, well, best get to bed. See what the morning brings. Sleep well. If your wound pains you, rouse me. I still have some of the wise woman's medicine.'

'I'll be well enough.'

'Mollycoddling again? It was not my intention. Pain is pain and can be dealt with and better so than tossing and turning.'

'I know. I'm sorry. Goodnight.'

It was barely dawn when she was woken by a hand on her shoulder, a quiet voice close to her ear. Drowsiness was gone; her eyes were wide open and there was that tautness of nerves again, making her catch her breath.

'Did I startle you? I'm sorry. And sorry I am to wake you so early. A change of plan: Twm swears he's well enough to leave and there are two caravans bound for Konya leaving together straight after the Morning Prayer. Rashid as well. His father wants to take him to Konya for the Mevlana's blessing and healing, though the doctor advised him not to travel today.' He sighed. 'There's no fever and he slept well enough but it seems too soon for the boy to travel. But they wish it so, both father and son.' He sighed again, became practical. 'The latrines are quiet, if you go now. We haven't much time – go and get yourself ready. If you're quick enough, there'll be time for a bite of break-fast; if you dawdle, you'll leave without.'

He left the alcove, clearly expecting her to obey him.

By the time they were ready to leave, the rising sun was sending thin shafts of light through the narrow slits of windows of the *han,* settling on eyelids, lighting up dancing motes of dust, shifting patterns across the stone walls. If they couldn't make Konya by the end of the day, said Amir, there was a small *han* where they could stay. More of a rest place, really, the gift of a not-so-wealthy lady who was stricken by fever on this road to Konya and nowhere close to rest her weary body. It was his cousin's village that had taken her in, found a bed, summoned a physician, cared for her until she was well enough to travel. Of course they would not take a penny from her, not one of them, like the man in the Christians' Holy Book, a Samaritan who did as much for a traveller. How did a good Muslim like Amir know of this? The lady herself of course, a Christian returning to that cold country she came from. She had told them. She paid for a small *han* to be built just outside the village and the cousin was the *hancı* – a cousin by marriage to his youngest sister – and he would see them right. They could rest there, stay there the night if Dai wanted, and have an easy journey to Konya the next day.

Dai had never heard so many words from Amir all at the same time. The man was agonised, torn between an easy journey for his son and his own honour to deliver this caravan as swiftly as possible to Attaleia. A night spent in fitful sleep by his son's bedside hadn't helped. Dai nodded, agreed; better for the boy, wasn't it, to take it in easy stages? See how he was when they arrived at this *han*.

Edgar begged them to set Rashid up with him, bolstered with blankets and cushions, but Dai shook his head. It was Blue who roundly objected: 'Yer got mawks in yer heäd, altar boy. Yer reckon yer clink an' cleän but yer straight from liggin i' bed and likely as need tenting yersen afore the day's ower. E'll coöme along wi' me.' He added slyly, 'A'm good fer a piller, Fustilugs reckons.' The boy made no complaint though his teeth ground into his lower lip when he was lifted up into Blue's brawny arms. Then his head lolled against the man's broad chest, his face pale as a corpse, but a weak smile touched the corners of his mouth.

'He's right,' Rashid murmured. 'A good pillow. I'll do well enough. Tell father not to fret.'

Looking at them as they waited to fall in behind the two larger caravans, Dai sighed: Edgar the new-recovered; Rashid new-wounded and who should, by rights, not be moved at all today; Twm with his sword-arm bound up and resting in a sling, reins gathered up in his left hand; Blue as bruised and battered as Dai knew himself to be; Giles surreptitiously easing bruises and stinging flesh wounds; the muleteers and cameleteers moving cautiously, carefully – 'crambling', Blue said – and Amir for once not urging them on. Even the animals seemed subdued. Only Rémi seemed the same as ever. And a musician and a girl-boy added to their group. Easy pickings they would be for any scavenger that came their way today and his responsibility to see they came safe to journey's end, wherever that may be. Twm was looking his way and rolling his eyes in disbelief and suddenly he felt laughter gusting through him and saw Twm's face unexpectedly crease into hilarity. *All will be well and all will be well yet*, he thought.

It was a slow journey, made slower by the combined caravans, but, even so, it was their small caravan that lagged behind until Dai urged the other two to go on without them. He settled his mind to a night at the unknown *han* and the *hancı* who was cousin-in-marriage to Amir. A quiet day; windless and warm with the mountains at their backs and the great bowl of the high plateau ahead of them and that city of learning where Kara Kemal's revered Mevlana lay in his tomb.

'The Mevlana. Who is he?' Twm asked. Dai remembered what Ibn Battuta had told him: in early life he was a theologian and a professor. One day a sweetmeat seller came into the college-mosque with a tray of sweetmeats on his head and, having given him a piece, went out again. This was a rough, crude man but Jalal al Din left his lesson to follow the man and disappeared for some years. Then he came back but with a crazy mind, speaking nothing but Persian verses which no one understood. His disciples followed him and wrote down his words in the book now called *The Masnawi*. Love and acceptance, love and acceptance. That was the creed of the holy man, the Mevlana, Jalal al Din Rumi, even though his beloved, his Shams, was killed, murdered, by the very people who claimed to revere the Mevlana. Love and acceptance. That was everything.

Afterwards, Dai looked back on that day as a turning point in all their lives but he couldn't pin it down to any one thing. The day before should have been the pivot: the girl, of course, and the miracle of her coming; and Kara Kemal's choice to send with her his youngest son; then that short, vicious battle that had done as much to bond them each-to-each as it had to set them moaning and groaning this dawn, and had itself become a tale for the telling; Edgar's tale that had them all staring – 'gawming', as Blue would say – and set still tongues wagging; the signing that had given Rémi new life – look at him now, riding by Edgar's side, fingers flashing as he sign-talked, and pale Edgar flushed and chuckling and Rémi making those snorting noises that passed with him for laughter. There was as well a new respect shown to Edgar by Giles, and Blue crooning all the while they made ready: 'Who'd 'a thowt it, altar boy?' Then grinning and nudging Edgar so vigorously that the boy was sent constantly reeling. 'A'll 'ave ter find yer a new naäme, woän't A? Can't keäp on calling yer "altar boy" when yer not no longer, can A?'

Dropping into Dai's thoughts was the memory of the dark night and Twm's insistent questioning: do any of us have the right to make our own choices? Find our own happiness? *Taid* made his choice, he thought, but it wasn't for his own happiness. It was for mine. Has his choice given me happiness? And what of my own choices? Were any truly made freely? He shrugged the questions away from himself. Another day he would think about such matters, a day when he was alone and his mind was not moving as sluggish as water along a silted shoreline.

But today, this slow journey with the wounded boy and anxious father and any hope receding of reaching Attaleia before the Venetian fleet sailed, this was where all changed. He had expected the men to be fractious, quarrelsome, edgy as they had been for so much of the journey but they were all of them buoyant, in holiday mood, singing snatches of song whenever Mehmi played for them, or played for the invalid cradled in Blue's arms as the *tanbur* was cradled against Mehmi's shoulder. He was letting his horse pick its way with no hand on the rein; Blue was riding with the reins in one hand, the other secure about Rashid in his cradle of bedding, for all the world as if it were a *dwt* in his arms. Ambling, they all were, as if time no longer existed. As if they were with Rashid in his drowsy poppy-sleep. As if they were moving through a dreamland that shimmered in late summer sunshine where they would be healed of the most grievous wounds of body and heart and head and soul. Even Twm was rested, his skin less taut, the worry-line that so often creased his brow eased. He had trotted the grey horse alongside the girl's piebald, Kara Kemal's bride-gift, and there they were, talking together, Twm's head bowed, the girl's tilted up in that way she had.

That would please her, Dai thought, Twm's company. He wondered what language they were speaking; Kazan's halting Venetian or Twm's murdered Turkish? Whatever it was seemed to be not a problem. He pushed away all other thought.

They arrived at Amir's *han* just after mid-day. The cousin-in-marriage wrung his hand until Dai was sure it would drop from his wrist. They were welcome, welcome – to rest, to eat, to stay the night, if that was their wish. And the boy, Amir's son! A thousand pities to see him wounded and so pale but what a brave son, for sure! How proud Amir must be to have such a son!

Amidst the flow of talk, the fat little man summoned servants to take charge of the animals, his comely, plump wife to bring pitchers of water to wash off the dust of travelling, his dark-eyed daughters to bring fresh water to ease their thirst. He had them seated on plump cushions in the shade of the courtyard and great platters of rice and yoghurt and olives and fresh fruit in front of them, enough for everyone, everyone! As for the boy, a spoonful of broth would put fresh life in him. This wife of his, she would know best what to give him. She was a wonder, a marvel! What a lucky man to have such a wife! What a lucky man to have such daughters! Such a family! Amir was welcome, welcome, and his friends with him!

And the broth did do much to restore Rashid. A miracle, Amir's cousin-in-marriage claimed, his wife worked miracles! She was as clever as the cleverest apothecary. She was the best of wives, the best of mothers, the best of sisters, hey, Amir? Now let the boy rest awhile and he should be well enough for them to travel on to Konya. How far? Not even an afternoon's travelling! Soon they would be close enough to see Konya and its wonderful gardens and rippling streams; its many minarets and domes of the *medrese*, the learning places. It was but an hour distant – two hours maybe. Well, maybe a little more because they were travelling so slowly but no more than three. Four at the most!

Ah Konya! Did they know that the Ilkhanids had sacked other cities, destroyed them utterly, killed thousands of people in Erzurum, in Sivas, in Kayseri, but though the castle was slighted, there was no massacre in Konya? The great Mongol commander, the man of war, met with the Mevlana, the man of peace and love, during the siege of Konya. Love and peace won. The Lodge of the Mevlana was proclaimed so holy it must be inviolable. Had they heard of this?

Ah Konya! Not what it used to be now that the Karamans had made Laranda their chief city – and renamed it 'Karaman' after themselves, in a show of vanity – but Konya was the place of the sublime Mevlana's eternal rest! Amir did right to take his son to that holy place for blessing. A pity this was not the April month when the healing rains collected in the beautiful April Bowl given to the Mevlevi only ten years ago. A wonderful vessel of bronze skilfully inlaid with gold and silver motifs and inscriptions to the benefactor, the ruler Abu Sa'id Bahadur Khan. Never had he seen such a miracle of workmanship! Had they heard tell of it?

They had; Kara Kemal had told them of it but Dai hadn't the heart to tell this cousin-in-marriage, so full of goodwill and pleasure in their visit. A bursting bladder of a man he was, with short, thick arms that waved about like the trunk of that extraordinary creature Dai had seen once in the Far Countries. It was Mehmi who broke into the torrent to say that his father, too, had journeyed to Konya to see the great April Bowl just after it had been presented to the Lodge. His father also was a follower of the Mevlana.

'Is it so? Is it so? That is good,' beamed the cousin-in-marriage. 'He saw it with his very own eyes, as I did?' He had taken his wife when she was grieving over the loss of their youngest, a boy not yet three years old and his wife no longer young enough to bear another. Ah! A bitter time that was. He thought his wife would never cease grieving the death of the little one and so he had taken her to Konya to the Holy Men at the Mevlevi Lodge. He saw for himself, with his own eyes, these eyes looking at them even now, how the tip of the holy Mevlana's sash was dipped in the water and the water given to such supplicants as he and his wife to drink, or poured over them if they could not. And its powers were so great that all who were afflicted were healed; and those who were barren became fertile. See for themselves! See this youngest of his daughters! The miraculous gift of Allah and the Mevlana, born nine months after his wife had drunk the healing waters of the April Bowl, and grown now into this imp of mischief!

He swung his daughter up into his arms. Seven years old, and like to break hearts when she was older. A beauty, like his wife. Didn't they agree?

The dark-eyed, plump-cheeked little creature giggled and dimpled and patted her father's face with plump, dimpled hands. For sure she would be a beauty, Dai thought, a day-bright maid, and not a murmur of regret that this was not the sturdy son that all fathers longed for. He only rejoiced. Who would have guessed this beaming, garrulous fool of a fat man had suffered such a loss? Suffered still for the loss of his precious *dwt*, his son, his three-year-old? Dai wondered if the man berated himself because he had not been able to keep the boy alive. A bitter loss indeed to have any family – brothers, sisters, mother, grandfather – who you could not keep alive, though you begged and begged God's help and forgiveness and offered your own life in their place.

He became aware of Kazan's thoughtful stare fixed on his face, realised he had been lost in his own dark thoughts, that the cousin-in-marriage was talking on, talking of the Mevlana's mausoleum standing four-square in the Palace Gardens that themselves had been gifted by Sultan Alaeddin Keykubad to the Mevlana's father, with its great pyramid roof pointing a finger to the sky.

'My father says there is talk of building a new roof,' said Mehmi. 'Have you heard of this?'

There was talk of a dome as high as a Mevlevi's turban, a 'Dome of the Sky', to soar aloft as befitted such an exalted man, though he'd wanted nothing more than the dome of the true sky itself above him and his father. What would he think of all this splendour, this man who cared nothing for show? Look at his tomb, draped in costly covers embroidered with gold thread! And next to it his father's grave, the coffin standing up out of respect for the son. Did they know about that? Wasn't that a wonder? Wasn't that a marvel? Had Mehmi's father talked of it? And now they were dancing – dancing! – to the music of the *ney* and *rebab* and *tanbur* and *çalgı zilleri* and *def* and turning in circles when there had never been such a thing before. Ecstasy, they said, they achieved ecstasy and oneness with Allah. But the Mevlana, Jalal al Din Rumi, he had never done this. How could it be?

'I'd forgotten he talks more than a donkey drops turds,' Amir said later that afternoon.

'He's a good man, Amir.'

'He'd be a better man if he talked less.'

Dai laughed out loud. After a moment, Amir let his face relax into the beginnings of a smile. 'He's done well enough by my youngest sister. When the boy died, we feared for her reason. His one son lost to him and never a word of reproach.'

'He seems to me a man who counts his blessings.'

'Endlessly. No stopping him.' But he was smiling still then silent and Dai wondered what it was he didn't – wouldn't – say. At last he said, 'He looked after us well enough, for sure.'

'Very well – and Rashid is the better for it.'

'He is, isn't he?' The man sighed with relief. 'I'll be easier still when he's had the Mevlana's blessing.' He glanced sideways at the calm-faced brown man riding alongside him. 'You're a good man as well, master. There's not many masters who'd do as you've done.'

'And a non-believer at that,' Dai laughed. He was moved by Amir's praise but he wondered what it was the man had wanted to say.

They were ambling again through the warm afternoon. Even the animals snickered and brayed and barked softly and the soft pad of their feet on the dusty road was soothing. From behind them drifted mellow snatches of sound of the *oud;* echoes of sounds from a far-off world, it seemed. Edgar had insisted on taking his turn with Rashid and Mehmi was keeping pace with him. Twm came alongside him.

'Your Kazan is a strange one.'

'*My* Kazan?'

'You've chosen to make him your man – or boy, I should say.'

'Maybe.'

'He's some strange ideas.'

'Yes?'

'Dafydd, you know he has!'

'Well now, no I don't. What ideas are these?'

'You'd try the patience of all the saints that ever were – including all those obscure saints of your benighted country.'

'Well now, there's many of those never famed for their patience.' He chuckled. 'Come now, tell me. What has the little blue brother been telling you?'

Twm didn't laugh. 'I asked him about what he said. Freedom to choose. You know?'

Dai nodded.

'I told him what you'd said – that there was duty and honour that couldn't be shirked. Know what he said?'

Dai shook his head.

'That there was something in what you said but you'd got the wrong words.'

'There's nothing new, then. I suppose he gave you the right words?'

'Yes. Yes, he did.'

'Now who's trying the patience of all the saints?'

Twm smiled. 'That Nene he talks of – that's the grandmother we met, isn't it?'

'Yes.'

'What was her name?'

'Sophia.'

'Sophia. That's it. A Christian, Kazan said.'

'That's it.'

'Strange, that, isn't it? A Christian living amongst the *yürük*?'

'Maybe.'

'Seems this grandmother was as much a Sufi as a Christian, according to Kazan. It was all one to her. Love and tolerance – or love and forgiveness – the two most important beliefs for Christian and Sufi. That's what she said, according to Kazan.' He glanced sideways at Dai. 'And that's where Kazan says you got the wrong words.'

'Is it now?'

'"Not duty and honour," he said, "but love and tolerance."'

'Well, there's good now.'

'Don't go all Welsh on me.'

'But it's Welsh I am. A true Cymro.'

'Dafydd, sometimes you exasperate me beyond reason!'

Dai laughed but he relented. 'Did Kazan quote the Mevlana?'

'What do you mean?'

'There's a verse in the Mevlana's book, the *Masnavi*…' Dai heard the words ringing in his head as he had heard them the first time when he was in a black hell of despair and guilt and anguish: *Gel, gel, yine gel…*

Come, come, come again,
Whoever you may be,
Come again, even though
You may be a pagan or a fire worshipper.

Our Centre is not one of despair.
Come again, even if you may have
Violated your vows a hundred times.
Come again.

He translated the words aloud, fumbled them, tried again, wondered if Twm really was listening.

'I think he told me this,' Twm said, when Dai had finished. 'We had a few language problems.' He grimaced. 'All right, so my Turkish is not as good as yours.'

Dai said nothing.

'Dafydd! It's not as bad as that. We managed to understand each other. Kazan's Venetian isn't so good, either.'

'Good enough to put me right, isn't it now, telling you I'd the wrong words? He's a bright one. Don't you think so?'

'It's clear you think so.'

Dai didn't answer. How could Twm not see for himself that this was the marvellous maid, the gold-copper-bronze maid of the *yürük* summer camp?

Twm sighed. 'The words of the Mevlana, Dafydd – to have your sins forgiven again and again and again no matter whether you are… What was it? Pagan or fire worshipper?'

So he had been listening. 'Or Muslim or Christian or Jew. What would the Pope in Avignon make of that, now?'

'He'd have had him burnt at the stake,' Twm said with certainty.

Dai opened his mouth to agree but he didn't get the words out. From the back of the caravan came shouting. Loud shouting. Mehmi? Blue? Dai's head came up. He turned his brown horse, rose up in the saddle, trying to see beyond the swaying heads of the camels, their bulky loads, cursing himself for his carelessness. They were alone, weakened. Close to Konya, true, they could see it already, silhouetted against two breast-shaped mountains and, behind them, the sinking sun, but they were not safe. Not yet *safe*. A horse and its rider were galloping at full stretch across the level land of the plateau, the rider almost flattened on the horse's back. Its mane and tail were blown in the wind of its own making and its hooves were kicking up spurts of dust. *Away* from the caravan. A rider at full pelt cantering away from the caravan. Had a horse bolted? Who with?

14

Warrior on the prancing Arab horse
What warrior are you?
(Book of Dede Korkut, c. 9thC)

'What's happening?' Dai yelled across the wide flat spaces. It was then he realised there was laughter and cheering mixed in with the shouting, and the muleteers and cameleteers were joining in as well, and the late afternoon sun was glinting off the horse and rider, catching the white and dark chestnut patches of the piebald and the gold-copper-bronze of the rider's head: *Kazan*. The rider was Kazan. She suddenly dropped sideways in the saddle. Thrown, he thought, at that speed, and his breath caught in his throat, choking him, stifling words. But no. She was up again with a strung curved bow in her hands. In both hands. A horse cantering at that speed and the girl without a hand on the reins? And suddenly she had drawn the bow and loosed an arrow in less time than it took him to drag air gasping into his body. And another arrow, curving high in the air before it was rushing back earthwards. Then rider and horse were wheeling, racing back towards the caravan.

The ambling caravan had come to a stop, dogs circling anxiously, mules shifting nervously. The camels waited, motionless, incurious. 'Stay here,' Dai flung at Twm and rode past the halted caravan to the last riders: Blue nursing Edgar and Edgar nursing Rashid and Mehmi nursing the *tanbur* and Rémi dog like following Edgar. They were cheering and clapping their hands as Kazan and the mare called Star covered the final distance. Even Rashid was wide-awake and smiling. The girl reined in and Star reared up, front legs air-dancing before dropping down. Kazan leaned forward to rub the mare's head between pricked ears.

'See what a star she is!'

Dai heard the girl's praise for the mare. His gaze took in the laughing faces of the men, the girl's bright excitement, and he felt anger rise in him. Such anger that he had not felt for a long time. Where now were the high ideals of the Mevlana's love and tolerance? Vanished, swallowed in his rage.

It had begun in the dawdling, ambling afternoon. Five of them with as many languages but not one they could all understand. 'It's Pentecostal,' said Edgar.

'Eh, that's heretical, innit?'

'According to some it might seem so.'

Edgar nursing Rashid, determined to take his turn; Mehmi with his *tanbur* playing music to heal the wounded one; Blue lurking protectively; Rémi never far from Edgar now; Kazan, moving through her first day with these strangers. Strangers no longer after last night's story-telling and then, today, their cheerful acceptance of her as Kazan, the new boy, the little blue brother, Fustilugs, though she had no idea what Blue meant by that. Nothing flattering, that was for sure. And now this talking together in five languages but not one they could all understand. As for that strange conversation with the dark, handsome Thomas, she would think about that later, would unwrap each cherished word they had exchanged, would rejoice because he had sought her out. No. Kazan. She must remember it was Kazan he had spoken with.

'I only meant,' said Edgar, 'we are blessed with many tongues.' There was a hasty translation from one to the other.

'My father would tell the story of the man who gave money to four friends.'

'One of the Mevlana's stories?'

'Of course. What else?' Mehmi smiled at the joke but in his smile there was love and awed respect also for his father

'Tell us it then, music man.'

'A man gave money to four friends – a Persian, an Arab, a Turk, and a Greek. The Persian said, "Let's spend the money on *angur*," but the Arab wouldn't agree. "No," he said, "I want to spend the money on *inab*." "No," said the Turk, "that's not what I want. I want to spend the money on *üzüm*." The Greek shouted, "Stop all this nonsense! All this arguing! We're going to buy *istafil*." And they fell to fighting – all because they did not know each one of them was talking about grapes.'

The story went from one to the other, laughter following like waves breaking on the shore on a calm day.

'Knoäw what we should do?' said Blue. 'Once we're all off-loaded in Konya and we're fresh washed, we should go wenching.'

'All of us?' Mehmi asked.

'Well, not Rashid. Not that it wouldn't do him a deal of good, heh Rashid? But Edgar's gaäme, en't yer, rebel-boy?' He watched the red creep up Edgar's face, saw the brightness in his eyes. 'Yer'll be saying yer allelujahs to a right lovely shrine this night. Fustilugs, and Rémi too – caän't leave them behind, can we now?'

Kazan would have liked to go with them in this new guise of boy's freedom, seen the wonderful city, known more of how men spoke and acted when they were private together and no women present. But to go with them to a brothel? Her face was aflame.

'Konya is a holy city,' she said. 'How can such places be there?'

'Where men gather,' Mehmi said cynically, 'there will always be need of the blessing of a good woman.'

'Or moöre than one,' Blue sniggered and Mehmi laughed. They were in holiday mood, already anticipating the evening, already lusty with longing.

'Seven,' Blue said. 'One for eäch on us. A'm not shaäring. one,

two, three, four, five, six, seven – all Dai's men shall goä to 'eaven,'
he warbled.

'Look at our young friend!' Mehmi was laughing, teasing. 'Kazan,
the red-faced!' He reached over and clapped her vigorously on the
shoulder. 'Our Kazan here was set to rescue you all yesterday and
now look at him!'

'What? This wench-faced recklin? A thowt that fancy bow and
quiver yer's carrying were nowt but decoraätion.'

'Gifts from my father for Kazan, the keenest bowman, the swiftest
rider,' Mehmi teased.

'Coöme on, Fustilugs, show us what yer maäde on!'

She laughed, leaned forward to whisper love words to Yıldız the
star, her face alight with the mischief that had always been the signal
for Nene's words of caution. Then they were galloping fast, she and
the mare, and she was gripping tight with her knees, feeling the air
rushing past her and the mare's mane streaming bright in the sun
and then the sideways slip she'd taken so long to perfect and up
again balancing with the bow in her hands and a shaft ready to loose
and riding, riding fast but not as fast as the arrow hurtling through
the bright air and a second close behind then they were wheeling
and turning and galloping back across the flat land and she was
pulling on the reins so the mare reared up, dancing her forelegs in
the air.

'Now do you believe me? See what a star she is!'

She was panting and exultant and glowing and Dai felt his anger
raging through him. He saw again the moment she slipped sideways
in the saddle and felt again the terror that she would fall under the
pounding hooves of the mare, be dragged along the stony ground,
her body trampled, all that precious gold-copper-bronze beauty
destroyed.

'What is it you think you are doing, now? What idiot game?
Playing the hero, is it? Where's your sense, *boy*?' He bit out the word

'boy', white-faced with anger so that the men were open-mouthed with the shock of it. Quiet fury, yes, iron-willed when it suited him, but never this sharp, white anger.

'Nay, Dai lad, it were us as egged 'im on.'

'We were teasing him, Dai-bey, we're to blame.'

'We must share the blame, Dai.'

'It was Kazan's choice to play the fool.'

The girl had cringed under his anger but now she lifted her head, her chin up-lifted and her eyes sparking gold. 'Yes, it was my choice. They wanted to see me ride and shoot. That is nothing so bad.'

'We've no need of another wounded – or maimed – or worse.'

'There was no risk. I know what I am doing. And this little mare, she knows what I want from her. I told you, I am the best of all my tribe – the fastest rider, the best with a straight arrow.'

'Yer can shoöt well enough, that's fer sure, but can yer hit yer taärget?'

'Enough, Blue. You…' a jerk of his head towards the girl, 'ride with me.' He turned the brown stallion towards the head of the caravan, waving the men to continue.

Kazan rolled her eyes at the shamefaced men, poked out her tongue at Dai's back and followed sedately behind him, her colour high. Edgar hastily controlled a nervous snigger; Blue nodded to himself. So young Fustilugs didn't lack courage. He'd never have dared take on Dai, not like that. And 'ow was that for fancy riding and shooting? He'd not never seen the like. Nor had he never seen Dai in such a taking.

They came up to Twm. 'That was pretty riding, Kazan. Where did you learn tricks like that?'

'From the *yürük*,' she said shortly.

'Are they all as skilled as you, boy?'

She shot a smouldering glance at Dai. 'I am the best of my tribe.'

Twm raised an eyebrow, looking from the boy's angry red face to Dai, frowning and tight-lipped.

'Don't encourage him, Twm. It was a fool's trick and so I've told him.'

Angry words were burning his mouth. 'She – she – she,' he wanted to shout and was afraid he would in his anger. Better say nothing. Better ride along in silence until he could talk quiet. Already he was ashamed of his anger; sorry that it had destroyed her bright gladness and pride. She was alone in the world and only he to know her for what she was. He should have had more care of her. But that moment when he thought she had fallen!

She rode behind the two men, the brown man on the brown horse and the dark man on the grey. The wave of shock and anger was ebbing and shame was washing over her. Shame at the public humiliation before all the men but shame also because she had wanted to boast, to prove herself, to impress them with her skill. It was exactly what Nene had warned her against. She was a fool, as he had said, and now she had lost his goodwill. He had been kind and patient and willing to keep her secret with no questions asked and now she had repaid him like this. He wouldn't want her to stay, that was for sure. He had problems enough without her. He'd leave her behind in Konya and she would be alone again and there was Niko still to be rescued. The thought caused her stomach to clench and her eyes to burn tearless.

The sun was dipping further behind the mountains, casting long light over the walls and towers which in their turn cast long shadows over the land. A spider's web of roads led to Konya and the dusty cloud of a large caravan was visible on the Ereğli road but it was heading towards another gateway, one of many that led into the city because this was where the great trade routes crossed and roads led north and south and east and west; had done since time out of mind. Their own gateway was dead ahead and leading straight to the *bedestan* with its safe storage for precious goods, and its market places with separate areas for each trade and craft, and lodgings and *hamams* and mosques and *medreses*, all in the Turkish quarter. In the south of the city, behind its own high wall, was the Greek quarter. This was an ancient city, well used to travellers and merchants, and secure in the knowledge that the great Mevlana protected all, Turk and Christian alike. The city walls and its many towers had been breached and repaired and breached and repaired again and again; it was no longer the glittering capital of the Selçuk Empire and, truth to tell, parts of it were ruinous now that Laranda was made the chief place and renamed Karaman. But this city was still Konya, the burial place of the holy Jalal al Din Rumi, the Mevlana, and because of that it would forever outshine the new capital.

They were halted at the checkpoint; all caravans were required to register outside the city before they were allowed entry. The high walls and higher towers stretched away as far as the eye could see. Then they were in the gloom of the gateway, with the great double eagle of Konya carved in relief, and its stone vaulting high above them, and out again into the broad streets of the city, passing fine stone houses and fruit gardens and streams running through them, and houses less fine, sinking into ruin, and their gardens unkempt. But here as well were the learning schools, the *medrese,* some small with their courtyards open to the sky but there were other, grander buildings surmounted and enclosed by a huge dome. 'But that is very clever,' the cousin-in-marriage had told them, 'because the memory of the courtyard is kept by means of a skylight and perhaps a fountain and it protects all from the terrible winters of the plateau.' Soaring high above all the buildings, dizzyingly high until it seemed its tip would touch the sky itself, and so slender that it was a miracle it could stand upright, was the thin minaret, the *ince minaret*, the masterpiece of a master builder, now almost a hundred years old and still a marvel. There were two balconies for the *muezzin* but who dared climb so high?

They came to the *bedestan* and the place where they would lodge for the night. It was like the day before: the noise, the orderly confusion of travellers and townsmen and animals; the dismounting and handing over of animals to the servants used to handling larger caravans than this; their sleeping places and the offer of a servant to take them to the *hamam*; directions to the place where they would eat their evening meal. But here, as well, was a servant to take Dai and Rémi to the *bedestan* where they could secure the most valuable items they carried.

'Will you go with Rémi?' he said to Twm. 'I've things to do here.'

'You'd trust me with this?'

'Of course. But, look you, trust no one. Keep sharp eyes.'

Twm glanced across to where a despondent Kazan was fondling the piebald mare. 'You were very harsh, Dafydd.'

'I know.'

'He's young and impetuous. He's learned his lesson.'

'I know.'

'So what will you do?'

Dai sighed. What would he do? He hardly knew. It was his fault all the happiness of the day was destroyed. The men were subdued and there were anxious looks cast his way. And Kazan? If she chose to leave them now, where would she go? How could she survive, alone and unprotected?

'You go with Rémi,' he repeated. 'I'll deal with problems here.'

Twm still hesitated. 'You won't cast him off, will you, Dafydd?'

'I won't do that. But what's this, now? You've taken a liking to the boy?'

'Yes, I have. He's a strange one but – I don't know – there's something about him, Dafydd. The men feel it as well. All of them.'

Well, this was something, Dai thought, the cynical, suspicious Twm pleading for Kazan to stay. And for sure he was right, something stranger about the boy than he realised. 'I'll deal with it,' he said.

Twm was not content, that he knew, and Rémi was anxious but they left together taking the precious bundles, with Giles and Blue to guard them. Amir came up to him.

'A word, if you please, master.'

Dai nodded and they retreated to the side of the stable where the noise was less. Dai waited but Amir did not speak. He scratched his neck under the edge of his turban. Dai prompted him.

'Your boy is not worse for the journey, I hope?'

'He is well enough.'

'No fresh bleeding or fever?'

'Thanks be to Allah.'

'But he is tired out, of course, by the journey.' It was a statement, not a question. The man nodded.

'That is so, master.' Another silence. This time Dai waited.

'I have a cousin of a cousin here in Konya. I can take my son to him, Dai *bey*, if you are willing, and I can leave him there.'

'You have a cousin here?'

'A cousin of a cousin, Dai *bey*.'

'Do you have cousins in every part of this country?'

'Not in every part, master, but we are many.' He pulled a face. 'I have many sisters.'

'I see. Well, Amir, that seems a good plan but I have a better one.'

Amir waited; the brown man took his time.

'What I think you should do is stay here in Konya, Amir. Stay here until your son is recovered.'

'I cannot do that, master. We agreed terms and I have promised to take you safe to Attaleia.'

'Haven't you a cousin of a cousin who can take us to Attaleia in your place?'

'Certainly, sir. There is one who lives in Süleymanşehir.'

'That's sorted then. You stay here and your cousin of a cousin of a cousin takes us on to Attaleia. We can see ourselves to Süleymanşehir. The road is good. There'll be others travelling west, from this place and at this time of year. It's no more than two days' travel, isn't it?'

'It is possible in two days. Three is more comfortable.'

'We'll have to stir ourselves. Two days is better, isn't it now?'

'You are a good master.' The man's eyes were bleared with unshed tears. 'That is an honest man who leads the camels. Honest and dependable. He is honoured in his own city.'

'Sakoura?'

'He will take my place and guide your caravan to Suleymanşehir and to my cousin.'

Dai thought a moment. 'Amir, you come from Alaiye?'

'Yes, master.'

'Your wife, now, she'll be wanting to hear about you and your son?'

'She must wait, master, until we return.'

'But she will worry. Let me take news to her. Let me tell her how you are. How your son is.'

'There will be no time before the sailing.'

'Yes there is. It's almost in our way, if we take the road down to Manavgat. I'll send the men along the coast road to Attaleia and go alone. It's not even a day's journey to Alaiye, travelling alone. Let me do this. You have been a good guide, none better, and more than that. Without you and your son and your men, the bandits would have beaten us. I owe it to you. Let me give news to your wife that you and your son are well and safe here in Konya and will return before the winter.'

'I would be grateful, Dai *bey*.'

'There you are, then.'

'Master?'

'Yes?'

'I wonder, master, if you will let me do something for you in return. Let me take the boy with me this evening to my cousin's house.'

'The boy?' He knew, of course. There was only one boy Amir had in mind.

'Kazan, master.'

'Why do you wish this?'

'He is good with Rashid.'

'Yes.'

'And we will send him back bathed and rested.'

'Yes?'

'There will be no problems, no questions, no worries about the *hamam* or where he will sleep.'

Dai breathed in. 'No?'

'No, master. My cousin and his wife – she is a friend of my older sister, my *abla* – they know how to keep secrets.'

'I see.' Dai drew the words out. 'So, it seems, do you.'

How did this man know when the others did not?

Amir answered as if he had spoken the question aloud. 'I know that tribe of *yürük*. Sometimes we have traded with them. It was well known that a Christian woman and her grandchild were living with them, and the old woman was good with cures for many illnesses. I was sorry to hear of her death.' Amir shook his head. 'Last night, at first I didn't recognise the boy but when he laid his hand on my son's head, and kissed me, then I knew. It is what the grandmother would have done.'

'Yet you said nothing.'

'There was no reason. He is a good boy. The men like him very much even though he is young and impetuous – perhaps because of this. He has much courage.'

He. How careful Amir was. Kazan would be safe with the man, Dai was sure, and with the comfort of womenfolk for the night.

'Will you let me do this thing, Dai *bey*?'

'Willingly. Take Kazan with you and – take care of him.'

'Of course, master. I shall return him to you tomorrow morning early.'

Dai looked around for the girl. She was still with the mare, brushing the piebald's mane. He strolled across to her, saw the flash of anxiety in her face, quickly hidden behind a blankness that gave nothing away.

'Tonight you are to go with Amir and his son.'

She rested her head against the mare's flank. 'You wish me to leave,' she stated.

'You will stay the night with him and his family and make yourself useful looking after Rashid.'

'If that is your wish.'

'It is Amir's wish.' He paused. 'Amir knew your grandmother.' He added quietly, 'Don't worry,' as she turned startled eyes on him. 'Your secrets are safe with him. It is why he asked to take you with him. His cousin and his wife will make you comfortable – but don't be late in the morning.'

'I am to travel with you, then, tomorrow?'

'Of course.'

'I thought you would leave me here.'

'Why would I be doing such a thing?'

'But you were so angry and truly I am sorry. Nene said I am too impulsive and she was right. She was always right. She said pride comes before a fall.'

He sighed. 'I was too hasty. I should not have spoken so. It was my fault also.' He looked away from her, across the courtyard. 'I thought you had fallen,' he said, his voice curt because the words in his heart came out crooked. Oh this woeful Welshman outside his land of Wales! 'When you dipped down in the saddle. I thought the mare had thrown you.'

'That is why you were angry? I was a risk to you all?'

A hair's breadth of hesitation. 'Yes.'

'Are you still angry?'

'No – but no more tricks like that one, Kazan.'

'We are still friends?'

'Of course.'

'But I am to go with Amir and Rashid?'

'For tonight. To the home of his cousin – well, the cousin of a cousin – and the man's wife who is a friend of Amir's oldest sister.

❁ 179 ❁

Yes, I know,' as he saw her lips curve, 'so many cousins they rival the Karamanğlus themselves. But they will look after you. You will be safe with them.'

She was missed. 'Peaceful, innit,' said Blue, 'without Fustilugs yapping.' But he sniffed and coughed and scratched until Giles snapped at him to shut it or go elsewhere. The men of the hospice had taken them to the *hamam* then to the meal house. It was Konya hospitality, with many dishes followed by sweetmeats and fruit, but for once Dai had no interest and less appetite.

'Not even a mouthful of this one? It's delicious.' Twm held up a triangle of sweetmeat dripping with honey and rosewater and stuffed full of ground pistachios. There was another Dai liked, stuffed with ground almonds and sugar and musk, thrown in batter and fried then thrown in syrup and sprinkled with sugar. But not tonight. Tonight he had no appetite.

'Missing the boy, Dafydd?' Twm popped the triangle in his mouth and chewed thoughtfully. 'Mmm. Good. Not like you to miss out on a feed, Dafydd.'

'All mouth and stomach, you mean?'

'All heart, maybe, hankering after a pair of golden eyes?' Twm raised one eyebrow in that way he had. He raised the other as he observed the blood creep up Dafydd's throat. He had meant it as a joke, a jibe; he had not expected a straight hit. Not Dafydd. This was a new and unsettling thought. This was something to be mulled over.

Now they were sitting in the flickering light and shadow cast by the torches, too tired to move and somehow melancholic. The holiday mood was gone. Mehmi sat apart from them in his own world, muttering under his breath and plucking softly at the strings of the *tanbur*; Rémi was making his nightly visit to the animals; Twm rested his arm, now out of its sling, rebound by an expert physician who praised the work of the *han* doctor. 'And your own health and strength, young sir?'

'No pain,' Twm said, but he was even more withdrawn than usual.

'The boy's gone with Amir, you say, Dafydd?'

'Amir asked for the boy.' Dai shrugged. 'He took it into his head that Kazan knew some medicine. Maybe he does. I don't know. He seems to keep Rashid calm. It will be good for him to be of use.'

'He is coming back, isn't he?' Edgar asked. 'He comes with us? He'll not stay behind with Amir and Rashid?'

They were all looking at him now, waiting for his answer as if it mattered to them.

'Tomorrow morning – an early start, I said.'

All of them sighed with relief.

'He's nobbut a bairn when all's said and done,' Blue said. 'He's a bit wild, but he's easy snaapped if 'e knows yer mean it. He were right down in the mouth after yer fettled 'im, Dai.'

'He'll get over it.'

'We'd promised him a night out, an' all. One, two, three, four, five, six, seven, all Dai's men shall goä to ' eaven,' he warbled.

'What's this then?'

'We were going wenching, like A says.'

'Were you now? Who was this "we"?'

'All on us! Yow, me, Giles, Thomas – do Thomas good to have a night out – rebel-boy, blue-boy and finger-boy.' He ticked them off on his fingers.

'And you'd promised this to Kazan? And he agreed?'

'He didn't exactly agree, did he, Blue?'

Blue laughed. 'Thowt as he'd go pop, he were that red 'i the faäce. A reckon that's why he went galloping off like he did – acting the man though he's nowt but a pip-squeak.'

'He's a crafty rider,' Giles said. 'That trick of shooting while galloping. I've seen that before. Tried it myself. Couldn't get the hang of it. Couldn't keep my balance.'

The strings of the *tanbur* reverberated more loudly. 'Kazan the keenest bowman, the swiftest rider,' Mehmi half sang, half spoke then, unexpectedly, 'my father took a liking to him.'

'We all have,' said Twm. 'Yes – even me. Laugh if you like. Impudent wretch that he is. Seems to have fallen from favour with you, though, Dafydd?' The one eyebrow lifted.

Dai was at his most impassive. 'He's well enough but there's to be no encouraging him in his tricks. He must ride steady with the rest of us.'

Giles laughed out loud. 'Ride steady? That one ride steady? He's like that flaming star the old men still talk of. You know the one I mean? Must do. The star with the fiery, flaming tail. Burned its way through the night skies for almost a year. Must be near enough thirty years ago.' He stopped, his ruddy face reddening even deeper as he realised they were all staring at him, Giles the laconic, the uncommunicative.

'I didn't know you were a poet, Giles, all these years we've travelled together. You'll be competition for Mehmi here.'

'Bright fiery star,' carolled Mehmi and twanged dischords on the strings. They were chuckling now, relaxing.

It was the girl again, Dai thought, and speaking of her. He said, 'That star – it was more than thirty years ago. Nearer thirty-five years. *Taid* – my grandfather – spoke of it.' He had been told of it, Dai could have said, by the storyteller saved from drowning when he was just a skinny brat, and who had returned years later, a grown man who had travelled the world searching for his lost brother. Was still searching for him. A never-ending story, *Taid* had said. Strange it was, now, to think the storyteller had seen the fiery star when he was here in this very place, in Konya. But he said nothing of this.

Dai was glad to get to bed, glad of the quiet, but he missed her, and the sound of her steady breathing, and that he could put out his hand, if he wished, and know that she was there in the darkness. He wondered if she was wakeful like him, or if she was cocooned in her blankets and sound sleeping.

Early morning and the *Imsak* Call to Prayer echoing and re-echoing around the city, the call from the nearest minaret taken up by the next and the next…and Blue's own call: 'Yer 'ere then, yer wench-faced blaggard. ' Bout time yer showed up. We've to fettle them beasts yet. Coöme on, Fustilugs, set to.'

And there she was, bright faced, with her hair gleaming gold-copper-bronze in the early morning sun.

Kazan was glad to be back with them. Amir and his family had been kind. His cousin and the wife who was a friend of his *abla* had shown no surprise at the appearance of this strange boy-girl. Indeed, the wife was more shocked and worried by the boy Rashid. She hurried around making him comfortable, putting him to bed, calling a physician to re-dress his wound, happy that it was clean and knitting together already, and there was no sign of fever. But he was pale and listless for all that, exhausted by the day's travel. Then she had bathed the girl herself, massaged her body with sweet-smelling oils, washed her hair and brushed it dry, sorrowing over its short length. 'I have sons,' she said, 'and I give thanks to Allah that is so but sometimes – like now – I think it would be very pleasant to have a daughter.'

Yes, she was a kind woman but the girl was relieved to be given her mat in a quiet place in the women's sleeping chamber, and to be alone to think about the day and the place where she was. She did not think of Thomas Archer but of her grandmother because this was the place where Nene and her lover, the storyteller, her grandfather, had met in secret. It was the place where her mother had been conceived.

He followed me to our home in Ihlara. It is where Christians have lived for many years. There is a deep gorge and at the bottom is the great Menderes River. I always thought it a beautiful place but that spring it was more beautiful than ever because he was there. He was well-liked, of course, because of his stories. We all love to hear stories. That is what he said. It makes children of us all and we forget to fight. Sharing tales and laughter is what makes peace amongst us. So wise, your grandfather. Then one day a neighbour returned from a pilgrimage to the tomb of the Mevlana in Konya. The Mevlana was not long dead and many still mourned him and came to see the holy place where he was buried. This man brought news of two strangers. One was a tall, thin, black-haired heron of a man who was without words; the other was small, grey-haired, with a wizened hand. It was the one without words who played music for the heart and soul. They were the guests of the qadi.

He knew who it was and he had to go, no question of that. I begged him to take me with him but he would not. He said I was too young, so much younger than he; that he was penniless, that his life was that of a wanderer on the earth. How could he expect me to travel with him, wherever he went? How could he expect me to share his hard life and harder bed? He loved me too much to see me suffer. I was used to a comfortable home, he said, and it's true my father was a wealthy man; not rich but wealthy enough. I told him my comfort was with him; my life was rich when I was with him. He would not give way though I knew he wanted to. This searching of his, he said, would destroy the love I had for him. I deserved better: a home of my own, a man who would love and honour me; children and grandchildren to fill my heart and my life. This is what he wished for me. But not with him. It could not be. He had sworn to search for his brother, however long the journey, wherever it led him, even to the end of his life.

He never said that I would be a burden. Perhaps he never thought it. I don't know, child. All I knew was that I loved him and there would never be any other man for me. I determined to find a way to be together for a while longer, to at least have memories to nourish me. Besides, if his brother truly was in Konya I wished to meet him, this strange dark man who played music for the heart and soul but who could not speak the simplest of words.

You must understand, child, that my father knew nothing about us, about our love, our meetings. He liked the storyteller well enough, had entertained him in our home, but to my father he was merely a wayfarer, a traveller who would soon be gone. I think perhaps my mother guessed but she said nothing. My father was not a kind man for all he professed to love God and his Son our Lord. My father had wanted a son and instead he was given a difficult daughter.

I plotted. I planned to go with your grandfather to Konya, whatever he said. I was headstrong – much like you, child. There was a girl-cousin who lived in Konya. She was betrothed and wedding preparations were underway. We would be guests at the wedding but I begged my mother to let me go to help, to be a companion to my cousin. She talked with my father and he agreed. I think he was pleased to be rid of me for a few weeks. Maybe he hoped the family would find me a husband where he had failed.

So I was packed off to my uncle and aunt. Agnes, my cousin, thought it romantic to help me escape the house to meet my foreigner. Lucky for me she was happy in her father's choice of husband. It was one of the houses with a long garden and orchards. It was easy to pretend to spend time there, where it was cool and shady in the heat of summer. Easy, as well, to pretend to be about the business of the wedding, with so many coming and going. Easy to meet.

It was the year of the comet, the great star trailing a fiery burning tail. Air and fire and, the learned ones said, it foretold death and plague and famine. It meant strong winds and earthquakes and clouds and rain. It meant wars and murder and massacre. It meant illness and pain for women who bore children, and miscarriages and difficult deliveries. It meant visions.

And it was at that time and in that place your mother was conceived. In that holy city under the night sky and its burning comet. Was it an omen? Perhaps. At the time I thought only of him, and the short time we had together, burning with our love as the comet burned above us.

As for the brother and the grey-haired man, they had gone. It was *true they had been there but two – maybe three – years before. There was no trace of them. They had left the hospitality of the* qadi *and travelled on. Perhaps north to the cold countries; perhaps east to Mecca. Nobody knew. There was one man, one of the Mevlevi, who remembered them and their music. Your grandfather took out the swan pipe and played. Not well – he was never a musician – but the man recognised the song. 'That is the song of Ieuan ap y Gof,' said your grandfather. But the man said, 'Listen! He played this also, your brother, and he wept while he played.' And he played haunting, lilting notes on the* ney, *the reed pipe, one of the instruments of the holy men. 'My song,' said your grandfather. 'That is the song he wrote for me and played for me before we parted.'*

I knew then for certain he would leave me. Before that, there had always been a little hope that he would stay, that he would give up his search. We shared a great love but the love he had for his brother ah! That was greater still. And it was right and proper in this place of the Mevlana. 'The way of our prophet is a way of love. If you want to live, die in love; die in love if you want to remain alive.'

He left in the last days of summer. There were more rumours, this time that the two had been seen travelling westwards. It seemed to me he followed the comet and those who foretold illness and pain and difficult deliveries were in the right of it. My cousin was married, my father and mother took me home. It was not long before my mother realised that I was with child. That was the long winter of my disgrace and the difficult birth of your mother.

Amir's choice of guide was Sakoura, the leader of the cameleteers. He was a whip-thin, black-skinned man with a quiet patience to rival Dai's. His legs were so skinny it was wonderful how they supported his body, Giles said; his hair was wiry black, and his full lips were blue-black, as if dyed in indigo, said Blue. He had been fascinated by the black man since the first day he'd joined the caravan. He marvelled over the man's pale palms and paler nails, over the

burnished darkness of his skin. 'And his blood as red as any of us.'
He'd seen it spilt that day when they were attacked by the bandits.
Sakoura had laughed, showing white teeth and the red inside of his
mouth. 'You are a blue man,' he said, 'but your blood is red too.'
And he had continued winding an indigo-dyed cloth around the
blade slash on his forearm.

Blue smiled at the sight. 'A've seen that done afore, in the country
weer men like you coöme from. Worked, too.'

'You have seen the magic of indigo, blue man. Truly it is magic.
This that I do now, this bandage of cloth dyed in indigo, will help
the wound heal faster than any other cure.'

'Aye,' Blue sighed. 'Magic it is.'

Now they rode out of the gateway that led to the Suleymanşehir
road and the two days' travelling before Suleymanşehir itself where
there would be another of Amir's endless supply of cousins to guide
them through the mountains and down to Attaleia. And tonight –
tonight – there was a small *han* where the *hancı* was known to Amir.
If all the *hans* were full then Yusuf would find them a safe place to
camp and food to eat and fodder for their animals. That was good
to know, said Dai. This stretch of the route was always busy,
especially at this time of year, and even though there were more *hans*
than usual they were mostly small and soon filled.

Soon they were winding up into the mountains and Konya lay like
a dream behind them in its great fertile bowl high up in this central
plain of Anatolia. From the Greek Quarter came the distant sound
of bells tolling for the Sabbath, yet another sign of the tolerance of
the Sufi because the Muslims held the ringing of bells in abhorrence.
'The angels will not enter any house where bells are rung,' they said.
Not even Edgar had protested at travelling on the Sabbath. They had
been double blessed, he said, first by a Christian priest who had slept
in the same lodgings then by the Sufi *imam* at the tomb of the
Mevlana because all had agreed they could not leave Konya without
paying their respects. Curiosity, said Twm, but he stood silent before

the great tomb with its rich covers and high headdress, and he was silent for a long time after they left.

There had been unseasonal frost that morning, melted now. Above them the sky was clear and the sun was warm but it was 'back end', as Blue said. The summer had gone and winter would soon arrive, and the snow and ice that would freeze the land until spring returned.

Amir had predicted right: the larger *hans* were full but Yusuf found them a place to camp outside the walls of his own *han* that was too small even to have a *hamam*. Another caravan was already encamped nearby. 'It's safe enough,' Yusuf said. 'Not like that Karaman road. You were lucky there. A shame about the boy. He's a good son.' He was as terse as Amir, as terse as the cousin-in-marriage had been voluble. 'Store your valuables with us. We'll set a guard tonight. With your own men, and those of that other caravan, you'll be safe enough. They've dogs enough to guard a fortress.'

There were no clouds; only the clear night sky and its stars blinking and a thin hanging moon that would soon belly into a half crescent. It was chill enough to send their breath smoking into the air and they were glad of the fire they had made and were feeding with faggots sent out to them from the *han*. There was, as well, the promised meal and fodder for the animals.

'It's a fine night for us,' said Twm, 'and that's a blessing.' They didn't carry tents or coverings so it would be open-air sleeping. Might be another frost, come morning.

'We'll roll up snug all together,' Blue told Kazan. 'Yer've as much meät on yer as finger-boy there.' That was his new name for Rémi-the-signer. 'Not enough on yer to feed a crow.' He pinched her arm with his thick, hard fingers so that she yelped. 'Yer nobbut a recklin,' he told her.

'And what are you?' she flashed back.

'Eh, a fine flitch o' ham, A reckon,' he said, 'wi' haändsome trotters.' He looked ruefully down at the big hand on the skinny arm and they laughed together before her face clouded.

'Nene would say we had star-blanket for a cover,' the girl said. She spoke sadly. 'She said if we listened, maybe we would hear the stars singing.'

Mehmi was already cradling the *tanbur* against him. 'A star-blanket for cover and stars singing and the *tanbur* to keep them company, heh?' he said, and ran his hand over the strings so that they shivered and whispered. They drew closer to the fire, to the singer Mehmi, waiting to hear his songs. At first, it was songs to the Christian God because this was the Holy Day of the Christians and there was no church for them. 'But we are in the land of your prophets,' said Mehmi. 'We are on the road your St Paul travelled when he was preaching to the unbelievers.'

'Even though he was at first an unbeliever himself,' Twm said. 'That moment of revelation, how strange that must have been.' He chuckled. 'Well, Kazan, there's one who didn't choose for himself.'

'But he was shown his true life, Thomas Archer, and he was brave enough to live it.'

'On the road to Damascus he found his way. Yes, perhaps you are right, boy.' He was quiet after that, leaning his head on his hand, half-asleep seeming while Mehmi played.

He played a love song praising dark eyes and crimson lips that had them quietly yearning for what they did not have. Then he ran his hands over the strings. 'An old, old song from one of the old stories. Well, an old song made new,' he said. 'This is for our friend Kazan.' He bowed his head over the *tanbur*.

'*Warrior rising from your place*
'*What warrior are you?*
'*Warrior on the prancing Arab horse*
'*What warrior are you?*
'*Shame it is for a warrior to hide his name from another.*
'*What is your name warrior? Tell me!*'

She recognised it immediately: it came from the story of Salur Kazan, one of the great warriors of the Oğuz Turks of long ago, in the days when they had lived in tents and ridden the plains and fought tremendous battles. It was the time when Bamsi Beyrek of the Grey Horse had won the love of the Lady Çiçek. She dipped her head, wondering what Mehmi would sing next, wondering if he had guessed her secret.

> *'I am the hero Kazan, the falcon-like warrior.*
> *'I am the hero Kazan who rides a bright star.*
> *'I am the hero Kazan whose bright arrows fly fast.'*

This was new. The muleteers and cameleteers were nodding, smiling, casting glances at Dai to see how he would take it but he was smiling as well.

> *'I am the hero Kazan whose boasting words fly faster than arrows.'*

There was a roar of laughter and Kazan was laughing and indignant. Mehmi's last words were almost unheard.

> *'A weaver of words is Mehmi the Minstrel.'*

'Again, Mehmi! Sing it again!'
  'Oh Kazan, bright star, hero, warrior!'
  'Hey, Fustilugs, yer can ride and shoot but do yer ever hit yer target?'
  'My hero!'
  'Enough! Let the boy alone! Is that what you were working on, Mehmi?'
  'Of course. A worthy subject, don't you think?'
  'A victim, Mehmi.'
  'Then a worthy victim, Dai.' He laughed, and slanted his look

towards Kazan sitting near him. The girl gave him back look for look.

'It was well made and well sung,' she said, 'but not well enough to sing again.' Then she laughed, joyously, and they all laughed with her, and it was as if peace and harmony and love flowed about them.

Later. The fire was burning low and Edgar was piling faggots on it to build it up because the night was cold. Blue stopped him.

'Yer'll slocken that fire, cramming it like that. It's all of a heäp, like a bull turd. Yer needs to tent it. See?' He poked a sturdy branch under the heavy loading of faggots and watched as a flame ran through the burning embers and caught. 'A likes to sit by the lalley-low.' They had drunk from flagons of sweet red wine and it was not what they were used to. 'But it's English ale A'd be drinking,' slurred Blue. 'That's for me.'

'I thought anything for you, Blue,' scoffed Giles.

'Ah well now, that's where yer wrong, innit, bow-man. English ale, that's what A'm after. In an English tavern.'

'Why not go there?'

'Why not? Why not? Because theäy'd get me for sure. A can't go back theer.' He slurred the words. 'Theäy'd be after me.'

'Why is that, blue man?'

'Why's that? Why's that? Yer've heärd altar boy's story an' now it's mine yer after. That it, Fustilugs?'

'That is what I want to hear,' she said, leaning forward, patting his arm.

'It's not like altar boy's and A caän't not tell it like 'im. Yer'd think me a nowter.'

'He means you'd thing he was nothing,' Edgar explained.

'But no, it is your own story, your very own, and this I would like very much to hear.' She looked around at the dim shapes huddled by the new-blazing fire. 'That is what we all want.' She shot a mischievous glance at Dai. 'Isn't it now?'

A ripple of laughter flowed around the campfire at this bright boy and his gift for mimicry. There were, too, sidelong glances towards the Welshman but he was laughing and they were content that the sharp quarrel between Dai and the mischievous newcomer had ended in peace.

'Come on, Blue. Kazan is right, it is your story we are all wanting to hear.'

'Ah well.' The big man took another long swig from the flagon and wiped the back of his hand across his mouth. 'The flat lands, that's weer it starts. Near enough saäme flat lands as altar-boy 'ere.' He grinned. 'Rebel-boy. That's what A moän call yer now, innit?' He spoke into the shadows, to where Edgar was curled under a blanket beside the fire. 'Hey, rebel-boy, A'd be right glad to 'ave yer 'elp telling me story.' His grin widened until it seemed his cheeks would split. 'Then we woän't get no *uzum* muddled wi' *inab*, will we?' He winked at the girl then blushed fiery red because she darted close to him and kissed his cheek.

'You are a good man,' she said. 'I know this before you tell your story.'

'Aye, but will yer knaw it after?'

She chuckled. 'A sinner saved, perhaps. And it is true what you say, blue man: none of us except Edgar and Dai can understand all your words so the good Edgar must help in the telling.'

'I'm here, Kazan.' Edgar raised himself from the shadows and went to sit beside Blue. 'I'd be honoured to help in the telling of his story.'

Afterwards, no one was certain how they understood. Blue's broad dialect was leavened by Edgar's retelling and hasty translations into other languages but somehow the Fen man's voice was what all remembered.

15

Blue's Story

'I'm from the flat lands but north a bit of Crowland, where rebel-boy was a prisoner of Our Lord. My father was born a serf and I was born a serf's son. My mother didn't live long after my birth. I was a hulking great oaf even then, see, too big for a little body like hers. My father married again but she was a miserable woman. They'd brats, one after another, each as whining and quarrelsome and peevish as the last. Then the hard times came and my father died and they said I wasn't a serf no more. New law, see. I couldn't even inherit my father's serfdom. So then I was all on to find means to feed that woman and her brood. This was the fens and we were used to making land out of water but it was hard work, a hard life and made harder by bad summers and winters. Never known nowt like it. You remember that and all, Dai? Those bad summers and worse winters? Went on forever, it seemed, and no let up. There were those as dwined to death, what with no harvest and the cattle sick and dying and all – remember it, Dai? Well then, you've an idea how hard it was.

'I was working on one of the manor farms by then – for the son, not the father. He'd died that autumn, and not from starving, believe me. The son was strict as the father but a fairer soul. It was the father who had stripped my serfdom from me and cast me out. The son gave me the chance of work and life and if I were a dog's body, who was I to bother about that as long as there was food to put on the table for that hungry-mouthed lot? Even then she complained. Said as I was eating more than the rest of 'em put together, me with my big mouth and bigger stomach, that I was taking food from the mouths of babes. Well, that weren't true. I was half starved. It's hard work made harder when you're treated like a nowter.

'I did any job I was told to. Cutting and binding rushes, that were one job. There had to be eight score bundles to make one work. That's a lot of bundling, believe me. There was turving, log-gathering, wood-chopping, ditch-digging, working the bellows for Aaron-the-smith, carrying the hod for Peter-the-builder…didn't matter. All one to me and it still didn't put enough on the table so I used to go out on the marshes when I could, looking for eggs: ducks and coots and dabchicks. Heron eggs, if I were lucky, or water-crows. A few of us did it. You'd to be careful though, balancing on them stilts so as you didn't fall in the deep pools. I've known men drowned that way. And if you were caught – well – you weren't allowed to take anything from the fen except by favour of the lord of the manor. Not even a bundle of lesch. Lesch? Rushes and reeds and suchlike. Weren't supposed to sell them to strangers – that were the law. Everything were law-driven. Folk like me, we'd no rights, see, not even to what was God-given. I'd a few narrow squeaks, I can tell you. They knew as I were foraging but they had to catch me, see, and I knew where best to hide, even a hulk like me.

'Anyways, that's how it was and that's how I thought it was going to be until that day, the day that was the end of the old life and the beginning of the new.

'Like this it was, see.

'It was a howry winter's day, past the meanest Yule I've ever known. It was just when winter's at its bleakest and it seems spring's never going to come. It was all lowering grey skies and vicious rain that drenched you through to the skin. There was snow in the air. I could smell it. Before nightfall, I reckoned. I remember hoping it would hold off till we was home. I was low enough an' all. I were that miserable. Couldn't see an end to it, see – like rebel-boy here said. Seemed like I was already in hell. When the priests were spouting hell-fire I wanted to shout at 'em that they didn't know nothing. I could tell 'em about hell-fire and it wasn't nothing like what they were saying. It were freezing cold, for one thing, not burning hot. Cold words and colder looks, and she'd turned the brats against me. Hell's a cold hearth with no kind word.

'That day, then, we'd been chopping wood for the fires. The manor couldn't seem to get enough that winter, although we'd worked hard enough through summer and autumn, building a log pile high as Lincoln church, and that's high, Fustilugs. Lincoln's a grand sight, high on its high hill. You can see it from miles and miles away on a clear day.

'Anyways, we'd worked our way through a wagon load that day, and then the hayward said as we'd to take the load straight up to the manor, to the drying sheds out by the stables. Normal, like, we'd take a load to the farm, especially soaked through like they were. It took us some time and the snow was falling by the time we got to the manor gates. We were white over as well as drenched. We couldn't have got any wetter and every stitch we had on was clinging to us sodden. We stacked the load and the gaffer sent the rest of the lads off home. 'Not you,' he says to me. 'There's a load needed in the manor.' Seems they were running short, what with all the guests they'd had over the Yule and now there were more arrived. Hayward was friendly with one of the dairy lasses so he knew these things. 'You take a dry load up there and mind your manners, you big oaf.'

'I didn't mind. They said as anyone who took owt up to the manor kitchens always got a bite to eat – a hunk of bread and cheese or a bowl of broth – maybe a sup of ale. Better than what I'd get at home. Home. Wasn't a home. Just somewhere's I laid my head.

'Now, I hadn't never set foot in there. Wasn't my place. I worked outdoors, where I belonged. But off to the manor, he said, they need a great load of fuel there, and you're of a size to carry a heavy weight. So off I went. Bent double, I was, with the load. I went to the kitchens, of course, where they took half the load, and because they were busy as flies wi' blue arses they sent me through the screen to the hall. Leave it there, they said, ready by the fire. Don't touch nothing. As if I ever would, I thought. Not a word about a bite or a sup though I could smell meat roasting and spices and bread cakes and all till I thought my belly would cave in.

'So I went through the screen and into the great hall. I'd never seen owt so grand. It was proper dark by now. There were torches in the sconces and a huge fire was burning in the great hearth – huge enough to set my clothes steaming. No wonder they needed all them logs. It was one of those manors that had a proper modern hearth and chimney, see, not the old style in the middle of the hall. That's how I saw them. Wonderful things. Great swags of woven cloth hanging all down the walls with the firelight and the torchlight dancing over them. I can't tell you. I haven't the words. It was a miracle. It made me think again about my own dull life and the grind and hardship and here was such beauty I'd never thought to see. Never imagined. Other worlds woven in cloth, and in colours I'd never seen the like of. Blues and reds and greens and yellows and gold thread shining and every colour in between. I think, now, it were tapestries of the scriptures but then I wasn't right sure. Too used to church walls painted full of damnation, wasn't I?

'I went from one to another, just looking. And then I got bold, bolder than I should have, and touched them. Oh, that feel of soft cloth on my finger ends. Magic. I got right close to them and looked and looked and tried to remember every strand, every weft and warp so I could think about it after. See it in my head.

'I were so bound up looking and touching I didn't hear no one coming till there was a voice shouting, a bit high-pitched and shrill. It was the woman of the manor, with those skinny little hounds of hers about her skirts. She must have come down from the solar, but in those days I didn't know much about those things. She stood in the archway with the firelight and torchlight playing over her and she was like…well…it was like magic again. Was she a beauty? I don't know. I don't think so. I never took no notice. It was the robe she was wearing. I were used to drab and this were like bright flowers on a May morning. Bright red with a deep blue band round the bottom and some kind of sleeve that was green like apple trees in spring and it were all a'gleaming in the torchlight and firelight.

'"Who are you?" she said. "You're not one of the house servants. What are you doing here?"

'"I've brought wood for the fire, mistress," I said.

'"You're nowhere near the hearth. Come here where I can see you."

'She was a brave lass, I'll give her that, calling over a big oaf like me with nowt but yappy little dogs with her, but I didn't think of it like that. Not then. Then I was afeard she'd think I was up to no good and sure enough that's what she said.

'"What are you thieving? Hand over whatever it is you've taken."

'"I haven't took nowt," I wanted to say, but I couldn't get the words out of my mouth. I think I put my hand out to touch the robes she was wearing and that's when she started to scream for the men and them yappy little hounds were yelping and snapping at me and servants rushed in and men armed with swords and staves and I ran. Couldn't see how to tell them I weren't stealing nowt so I ran. They wouldn't never have listened to the likes of me. I was out of that hall and out of the manor and I can't tell you now how I did it. They were chasing after me. I was afeard they'd set the dogs on me. Not the dainty little hounds that I'd seen in the hall but the hunting pack. Now they were vicious. If they were turned loose and I was caught I hadn't a hope in hell, frozen or fiery. I couldn't go home – she'd have turned me in straight – and I didn't know anyone who'd give me shelter. My head was buzzing. I was a dead man, I thought. So I ran and kept on running. I knew a place where I could bide a while. It were in the marsh and I reckoned none of 'em would be too keen to risk setting a wrong foot there on a bitter winter's night. There was no sound of the pack and the chase got fainter and fainter. A cold, snowy night, see, so they gave up. Why bother for a nowter of a great oaf like me? Easier to catch me the next day – if I survived a freezing night out on the fen. That was their reckoning, I suppose.

'And of course they were right. I couldn't stay out there and live. Not on a night like that. And I couldn't stay on manor land. But I wasn't a serf no more. I was a free man. So I went. It was a hoary cold night, like I've said, and I'd have perished if it wasn't for the old man at the tavern in the next village. I knew him a bit and he knew what a tongue that woman had on her. He found me laid down in his doorway. "Best be out of the cold tonight, bor," he said, "and go your ways tomorrow." He didn't ask no questions. Just took me in and fed me hot broth and spiced ale that had a hot poker stuck in it – that were good – and dried my clothes and found me somewhere to sleep for the night. He were a saint, that man. But, "Best go your ways," he said, and that's what I did.

'I worked my way down to the south, to the sea. I had to go begging but there's nobody as thinks a big oaf like me is starving. So I had to help myself to a bit of this and a bit of that. I did honest work as well but there's little enough in winter. It was better when the spring came. And that's when I found the woad dyers. Stumbled into 'em accident-like though I suppose you could say as it were God's hand. I smelt 'em first off. The stench of the vats were awful. Fierce. It clung to you, to your clothes and skin and got up your nostrils till you couldn't smell nothing else. Steam and stench. There's days when woad men can't not see each other across the fermenting house because of the steam. And the stench of them men! Stink gets into your clothes, see, like I said. Set yourself anywhere near a warm blaze and the stink gets stronger. Weren't given house room, sometimes. They'd a place for themselves all together away from the rest – but then, they had to keep the heat steady, night and day. That's where the craft comes in and it's crafty they had to be, keeping the vat and keeping its secrets.

'Blue-black they were, worse than what I am. Pockmarked with it, they were. Horny nails like mine are now, black with dye. But it didn't matter, see. Nothing mattered except that moment when you lifted the cloth from the vat. Hot, it were. You'd to mind you weren't scalded. But lifting the cloth bright green and dripping and seeing it turn all shades of blue right there in front of your eyes. That was worth it all. That was something. All my life I'll remember seeing that. Something like a miracle, out of all that filth and stench and back-breaking work and then that. Makes you believe in summat, that does. Fresh batch, see, that's a deep black-blue. Then it weakens and it's more blue and green. Woad's used to make other colours too. Beautiful greens – that's woad mixed with yellow from weld or dyer's broom. Then there was all the scarlets and pinks and violets – that was woad mixed with madder or kermes. And the russets and tawnies and greys and the best blacks…got to keep the vat the right heat but, like I says, that's secret stuff, see, along with the mixing. Can't tell you nowt about that. A woad vat's like a man, see, that wants to eat and drink, else he dies. It's alive and you have to cherish it. Humour it, else it gets sulky and won't do its magic. There's some as calls it woman-like.

'I got work there. I was big and strong and could lift heavy loads. I wasn't much help with the weeding – too big, see – but when seed's been wanted I've knocked and flailed seed from straw. And I've carried full loads of woad balls many a time, carrying board set on my hat that I'd padded out wi' straw – helps take the weight, see – and the woad'd be dripping down my neck. We had horses to crush the plants once they'd been picked but there's been times when I've done that an' all, round and round and all of a sweat till you thought you were like to drop in no more time than a blink of an eye. I've always felt sorry for them horses. They went in spry and they came out wrecked, poor devils, liked drowned rats.

'Trouble is, they liked us to drink, see, as much ale as we could. We pissed into buckets and it was saved for the vat. Saved for fulling as well. Saved for anything and everything. They wanted our staäle so we drank their ale. I got a taste for it. You know how I am, Dai. I try but sometimes I can't help myself.

'Then I heard tell of the big dyers in the lands across the seas. Flanders and the like. We were just a small place. We sent our wool across to Flanders and they dyed it and sent it right back to us. Madness. What were wrong with our dyeing? I wanted to see what it was they did that beat us. I wanted to see those other worlds where the woad was rightly worshipped. I thought about it. That woman who'd married my dad, and her brats, I hoped as they'd enough to eat, but I wasn't a serf no more so I could go where I wanted.

'And I did. I took a ship for Flanders – worked my way across same as you, rebel-boy, but I've a stomach for the sea. Doesn't bother me none. Once I were there, I did anything I could to keep body and soul together. Couldn't get much out of the dyers, though – kept their secrets to themselves, they did – but I heard tell the best work was done in Venezia so I took ship there. Now there's a rare place they've made out of water. Beats owt we've done in the Fens. That's when I saw the churches and the paintings and altar cloths and the rich clobber that were worn, if you'd money, of course. Poor were like poor everywhere – nowt in their skips and nowt in their bellies.

'There were the traders, of course, place like Venezia, bringing back silks and damasks and fine cotton and brocade and the like, and one of them had a batch of indigo. Indigo! That's magic, that is, same as woad's magic. Isn't it, Sakoura? So I thought as I'd like to see it and got myself set on as a wharf man then begged myself a ride East and got set on the caravans. I tried to keep out of trouble but I've not been right successful that way. I've had to do a runner more times than I care to remember. Still, it got me places I never knew existed let alone thought as I'd ever see.

'Places where they made indigo. Balls of it – looks like some sort of metal but it's not. It's plants, same as woad, and nice and light and fit for carrying. They use it for making their paintings and books and such, in Venezia. Pay a packet for it. Does more than that, though – look at Sakoura here, with his indigo cloth wrapped around that wound of his, and it's healing real nice. I wanted Rashid to try that but I knew it weren't no good telling you. I swear it were as good as the shivery spiders for pulling down rebel-boy's fever – begging yer pardon, Kazan, and I'm sure as the wise-woman's potions did their work an' all. But I've seen women hold their bairns over an indigo vat to heal 'em of jaundice and bites and burns and fever – all manner of ailments. I've seen women in screeching hysterics calm down when they've been wrapped in indigo cloth. Aye, and the falling down sickness, helps with that an' all.

'I've a few bits of cloth to show for my travelling, some of it real old, lovely stuff. I'll show you tomorrow when it's light. There's one as I'd like you to see, rebel-boy – said as it were Abr'am sacrificing his son, the man as sold me it. That were in Egypt and I'm not sure how he came by it but I weren't asking. Abr'am's got pop-eyes – he looks daft – and you can see a scrawny sheep high up in a corner. Got its ribs showing. Not much of a sacrificial beast, I'd have thought. But it's real workmanship. I've a nice little bonnet, as well. Got it from your place, Sakoura, where the black men live. Indigo's nearly black an' all – wards off the evil eye, does that deep indigo. The way the patterning's been done on it sounds real simple but it's not so easy as it sounds… You tie screws of the cloth tight to stop it being stained. They let me try and I made a right mess, I can tell you. Mind you, these ham-fists of mine aren't fit for dainty work like that.

'Eh, I've seen wonderful things. When I met up with you I was coming from Baghdad – that's where the best indigo dye is. Baghdad Blue, it's called. Tell you secrets as I shouldn't, I've got some with me now, in my bag. I wanted to take the indigo back with me to Venezia, to them painters and such, maybe make something of myself after all. But then somehow the devil gets into my head and I can't think straight. I didn't come by it as honest as I should. I were on the run when I met up with you. You lot don't know this but if it weren't for Dai here I don't know where I'd have been. I were that in need of belly-timber I could have et a horse. You were camped, remember, for the midday Call. I crept up and stole a roll of flat bread. I were making off wi' it when Dai here catches up with me and says it would go down better with a bite of cheese and a sup of something. So I stayed. Not never been anyone kind to me like Dai here, putting up with me bad doings and never a cross word nor asking me owt about myself...

'Yes, it needs saying Dai boi. I won't be hushed – though I know as there were those of you as didn't want me with you and I don't blame you. I wouldn't want me neither. I swear to you on sweet Jesu's life, I'd not never take nowt from any one of you, not never, however sore tempted I was, or hard-pressed.

'Anyways, that's my story. A drunken nowter, like I said. Yes, tell 'em that, rebel-boy. A quarrelsome, drunken nowter and a runaway and a thief. I'll mog on tomorrow, if you don't want me here no longer.'

Blue looked round at them with that half-guilty, caught-out expression on his face. They were silent. He shrugged. 'A'll mog on, then, like I said.'

Kazan started to move towards him, felt her wrist gripped, clamping her to where she was. It was Dai. He slanted her a quick glance and an infinitesimal shake of his head. Then his eyes were fixed again on Blue, and Edgar who had helped tell his tale looking more an angel than ever, with his golden curls a nimbus in the light of the fire.

'That's not true,' said Edgar. 'Well, you're drunken often enough, that's for sure, and quarrelsome often enough. And yes, you're a runaway same as me, and runaways have to take what they can get, sometimes. But nothing? A nowter? How can you say that?' He stumbled over his words, searching for what he wanted to say, and she realised this was why Dai had held her back. It was Edgar whose words mattered most to this hulking, clumsy, too-often-drunk Fen man. 'You're a hero, that's what you are. And you've the soul of a poet, a mystic. You've a gentle soul.'

'His soul is coloured in the magic of the indigo.' Sakoura's voice came from the rim of darkness beyond the glowing embers of the fire. 'In my country, one who understands the mysteries of the blue as this man does is honoured by even the greatest of men.'

'Nay now,' said Blue and his big hand crept up to wipe his cheeks. The girl felt her own eyes brimming. Now the rest of the silent listeners were breaking into words, applauding the big man's courage and resourcefulness, amazed by what they had heard, that peeling off of the outer layers, like onion skin, so that the coarseness and belligerence and superstition and strange outlandish tongue, all the things that had grated on them for so many miles, all were peeled away to reveal the poetry of this man's inner soul. Like the indigo itself, hiding its secrets in stench and murk. Perhaps tomorrow he would annoy them all over again but tonight, tonight he was, as Edgar said, a hero, as much for what he had dared tell them as for the life he had lived. But the loneliness, she thought, how lonely he had been. A life of desolate loneliness, this man who had never been loved. This was the nearest he had come to a family, this little group of travellers thrust into each other's company and every single one a lonely soul hugging their own dark secrets to themselves. She wanted to cry for his loneliness, for the loneliness of them all.

'Well, Fustilugs,' he said at last, 'what does yer reckon to me now?'

'It is just as I said: you are a good man. Me, I knew it before your story but this I found of great interest and Edgar did very well in helping you with the telling.' She considered the big man. 'A man with a gentle soul must have a God-given name.'

He rubbed a thick finger up and down across the side of his nose. 'A doän't knoäw as anyone nivver called me by my naäme.' He was blushing. 'It's Oswald. A reckon as A've got used to Blue.'

'Then Blue it will be.' Her head dipped so that her face was hidden by the fall of hair. 'Nene always wore blue-dyed clothes.'

'Colours of a wise-woman.' Blue nodded his great tousled head. 'A'd like to have met her.'

'I wish it too.' It was true; Nene would have recognised at once this man's true nature. She drooped her head more, wanting to tell them all that this was her grandmother who she mourned, that she herself was not what they thought. She wondered, if she told her own story, and how she had deceived them, could they forgive her? *Be as you are or be as you are seen.* The moment was lost in the scramble for sleeping places and feeding the fire. She found herself curled up between Dai and Blue's bulk. 'In caäse yer frit in the night,' he teased.

'I am *yürük,*' she reminded him. 'I am used to star cover.' She made her voice sound sleepy but she was wide-awake and sad for herself and the big man lying near her and lay for a long time listening to the steady breathing and snores and muttering around her; somewhere, a camel coughed and a horse stamped its hoof. A dog barked and was answered by another. Closer, someone ground their teeth in sleep. There were rustlings and squeakings of invisible night creatures, a dark shape swooping. Far off, a wolf howled but kept its distance. She watched the pale, thin moon travel across the dark sky and traced the outlines of the star patterns that winked and blinked in the frosty night. Which one was Nene? They all seemed so far away, so cold and distant. At some point, a shadowy figure piled more faggots on the dying fire until warmth spilled out again; firm hands tucked the blankets about her more securely and the figure settled beside her again and she realised it was the brown man, the one who knew her secret but did not despise her; the one who had spoken with such anger but who had readily forgiven her. She must have slept after that.

16

Sorrows and pleasures of life vanish in time
Leaving behind only the good name one has gained
(Yunus Emre, 14ᵗʰC)

The fire was still glowing red embers when she was roused by the first Call to Prayer of the new day. Rémi materialised beside her, balancing a bowl of hot broth, steam rising from it into frosty air and mingling with her own ghost breath. He offered the bowl to her and she took it gratefully, shamed into realising that she was the only sluggard still rolled in blankets that were white and cracking with frost. Rémi shrugged and smiled and signed. 'No sleep,' she recognised. 'Dai says let you sleep now.' She wondered how he had known, if he had been as wakeful. She was comforted by his care for her. Yes, a kind man, as Blue said, despite those sharp words spoken to her alone. *All shall be well and all shall be well.* Nene's voice was close in her ear. Her heart lightened. *All shall be well.*

The earth, hardened by the hot summer, was sharpened by the first frost of winter but the way became marshy the closer they came to the great lake, and there was the sound of water running in stream beds. At times the animals squelched through mud, churning the surface of the road. They passed villages remade from more ancient villages, half-hidden amongst the undulating hills, and orchards where a few late apples were still hanging from almost leafless trees, and those leaves were already bronzed and yellowed by autumn and swirled along the road in front of them. Sometimes, the land dropped into forested ravines. Beyond the gentle hills, the mountains rose dream-like. The sun travelled before them, sinking lower and lower, flooding the sky red and orange and pink and staining the mountaintops.

'Not much further,' Thomas said. He had been riding alongside her for most of the afternoon but in a silence to match her own. 'See? Where the sun is reflecting on the water?' He pointed to a shining line away on his right. 'That is the lake and Suleymanşehir is on its shores. Wait until we come to the top of the last pass then you will see.'

Then there it was, a vast stretch of water high in this highest of plains ringed by mountains and the sun drowning itself in a glory of rippling, dazzling, crimson splendour. They came down to the lake level along a good stretch of old road, repaired and made new and leading to the walls and the main gateway. There was the tail end of a caravan moving through; then only their own. The road led into a broad street busy with the traffic of horses and camels and mules and oxen and carts. In the middle of the street, a welcome sight, a tall fountain trickled water from ledge to ledge to fall into a deep curved bowl at its base. The street was bordered by buildings, many two rooms high and, at the furthest end of the street, the imposing *bedestan,* domed, four-square, its deep recessed arches marching around it; next to it, the *cami* and *hamam* and stabling and lodgings, all of them shining still with newness because, said Sakoura, they were not yet forty years old. It was called Viranşehir – the desolate city – until the town was new built and the trade route brought prosperity. Then it became Suleymanşehir but some were now calling it Beyşehir. Inside that flat-roofed mosque, he said, was a forest of cedar pillars and, marvellous sight, under a star-patterned grille high in the roof, was a pool dug deep into the ground, stone-lined and filled with water so that the stars in the sky above danced on the surface of the water below. The wise ones, the men who studied the heavens, came here to observe and read the stars. There was talk, said Sakoura, of building a *medrese,* a teaching school, next to the *cami* like the ones in Konya. Like the ones in his own city. That would be a fine thing for this town. Learning was a great and wonderful thing, and books were the only way to true knowledge. In his city there were many books. 'Purity of writing is purity of the soul,' he said. 'It is putting God on paper and the heart can only be happy with the mention of God.' He breathed deeply. 'Mountain air made even fresher by the lake,' he said. 'This is a wonderful place. Some day, I would like to leave Attaleia's heat and dirt and noise and come here to listen to the men of learning, though my wife likes the busyness of the city and the chatter of her women friends.' He had a way of speaking that was calm and measured with many pauses to make sure he had been understood. His Turkish was good enough, he said, but his Arabic was better though it was not his own true language.

'It's a good plaäce right enough,' said Blue, 'but all the saäme A'd like to be back hoäme in the flat lands, even if we doän't have nowt like this fer comfort.'

Back home, thought Dai, that poverty stricken little country where the mountains were not so high and the lakes were not so vast but the air was as sweet and the rivers of home wound down to the shining sea and around him was the old language of his childhood. *Hiraeth,* he thought, stabs as painful as a dagger wound.

The stables and lodgings were beyond the *bedestan* and closer to the lake-shore. Here the bustle was at its height; here, the caravans were being unloaded and goods taken to safe storage in the *bedestan.* Small boys, dark haired and dark eyed, scampered between the tall legs of the camels and missed by inches the kick of tired mules, and begged coins in return for small services. 'You want fresh good water to drink?' 'You want me carry your bundles?'

Long, narrow, high-prowed fishing-boats were moored, side by side, by wooden jetties that were precariously balanced on stakes driven into the river bed. Fishermen were readying themselves for the night's work on the bobbing boats, fixing nets and spears and torches. Reeds clustered thickly, and thickets of stunted trees grew out of the lake itself. A rising chill wind blew down from the mountains through the reeds and leaves and ruffled the lake so that small waves lap-lapped the shoreline. Overhead, a flock of long-necked birds was silhouetted in arrow-shape across the darkening sky. The long line of mountains wrapped themselves around lake and town and over all was the glint and glimmer of fading red sunset. Yes, a good place to live quietly enough, though it was on the busy trade route. So very different from the summer pasture, she thought, it could have been another world. So far from home and the measured life of the *yürük* that was lost to her now. She felt she was drifting, like twigs blown on to the lake and tossed up and down on the waves.

'It looks deep,' Dai said suddenly, startling her because she had not supposed he was so close to her, 'but it isn't. There was a grand palace round the far shore with shipyards and mansions and mosques and gardens and a causeway across the lake that led to another palace. Much of it is ruined now. The palace in the lake is still lived in but the splendour has gone.'

'How do you know?'

He grinned suddenly, still gazing out over the lake. 'I was a guest some years back. Well, the guest of a guest. I was interpreter for a man from Tangiers, a traveller, and he wangled himself an invitation – more than that, he got the Sultan to cough up provisions and horses and an armed escort as far as Ladhiq.'

'Armed escort?'

'Bandit country,' he said briefly.

She was silent, wondering about his life; so adventurous, while hers had been set in the routine of summer and winter dwellings, and the travelling between them, and the little activities of every day. No wonder he had been so angered by her foolish boasting and posturing.

'What's troubling you?' he asked. He knew his voice was abrupt. 'Is it that you're tired? I know you didn't sleep – I wasn't for sleeping much myself, last night. Or is it you were thinking of your grandmother?'

His perception shouldn't have surprised her. Besides, there was a growing habit of honesty between them.

'Partly that. She seemed very far away last night.'

'And?'

He sounded impatient and behind them Blue's voice bellowed something unintelligible. This was no time to be standing idly by the lakeside, however beautiful. No time to tell him how she hated this deception the more she was accepted, the more these men revealed truths about themselves. No, this was not the time.

'It was nothing. Nothing of importance.'

'It was enough to keep you awake most of the night.'

'I'll sleep all the better tonight.'

A growing honesty; that was all.

He nodded. 'Come then – best get you sorted for the night.'

'Rembled,' she murmured absently, and saw the corners of his mouth lift.

'It's good Welsh you should be learning, not that heathen tongue of our blue man.' Blue's shout came again, more urgently. 'Seems it's me he's wanting, now, isn't it?' He turned. 'What now?' It was Edgar who reached him first.

'Amir's cousin is here. He recognised Sakoura and came looking for Amir and Rashid.'

'I'll come.'

There were the courtesies to be got through first; then the lamentations for ill fortune that threatened to go on and on. Amir would have stamped on it, Dai thought, and subdued a smirk. This cousin was genuine in his concern, no matter how wordy he was. As bad as that cousin-in-marriage at the *han*, and as afflicted. That was the word he used.

'How I wish we could welcome you as our guests, Dai-*bey*,' he was saying, 'but our house is afflicted. My wife is suffering, and her women. The physician is puzzled by their fever and sickness. They are, indeed, very ill.' He was all but wringing his hands, twisting the ornate rings that bedecked every finger. His robes and turban were of fine woven cloth: a prosperous cousin of a cousin.

'I am sorry for your troubles. Do not concern yourself with us. We'll do well enough with lodgings and stabling here.' The last thing they wanted, Dai thought, was sickness that might lay them all low.

'But Sakoura says I am to give you a guide to take you to Attaleia.'

'It was a thought only. We'll do very well with Sakoura. He's done well by us these last two days and he knows the road through the mountains as well as any man. That right, Sakoura?'

'I have travelled the route many times before.'

'You must stay with your household. I hope your wife and her women will soon be recovered. God's blessing on them.'

'And may God's blessing be on us as well,' Twm muttered in his ear. 'Let's hope it's nothing catching.'

'Probably some food or drink the women have taken. What's left to do?'

'Nothing. All's well. Sakoura knows the best lodgings and the best places to eat. He's well known hereabouts. Just as well – the place is heaving. Best if we take our turn in the *hamam* while we can. Lucky they built it double – no waiting around for the women to prink and preen. Now what are you looking after?'

'Where did the boy go?'

'I don't know – back to the others, like as not.' Twm frowned, his dark brows drawn together, the skin furrowing between them. 'I've never known you coddle anyone as you do this boy. Not even Rémi who used to be your favourite.' There was no response to the pricking words. 'What's to do, Dafydd? Something you should share?'

Dai shrugged. 'Too green behind the ears, isn't it now, for the boy to be loose in this place.'

'Too many opportunities for mischief, you mean.'

Dai sighed. 'Maybe so.'

It was clear he would say no more. Clear, too, that there was much to say.

The chestnut mare recognised Kazan straightaway. One of the stable hands was pulling at her halter, urging her towards a stall but the mare was jibbing. She whickered and tossed her head, yanking the man's arm so that he swore and cursed all animals and this one in particular. And its owner. Especially its owner. The man tugged hard on the leading rein. He was tired. It had been a busy afternoon and he wasn't in the mood to deal with fractious animals. Humans were bad enough, and the human who owned this mare was more beast than man. Kazan pushed her way through the crowded yard.

'That's a fine chestnut mare.' She put out a hand to stroke the blaze on the mare's nose, patted the shoulder nearest to her, felt the coat to be rough and dry. 'Not looked after as she should be. Who does she belong to?'

'Rich, fat man. Arrived this afternoon. Big caravan. Job finding room for them all.' He was sullen, reluctant to talk. He watched the mare's ears prick, saw her stop rolling her eyes till the white showed. She blew lovingly down the stranger's tunic. His voice was less curt. 'You've a way with horses, boy. Help me get this one into the stables.' They walked the horse together into the dimness of the long building. It was already crowded with packhorses and mules and camels and riding horses and the smell and sound of them clogged the air. She pitied the chestnut mare, used only to the open air and starry skies. Well, that she would have back again. She would not stay with fat Vecdet to be sold to the highest bidder.

'He's a cargo of slaves,' the man told her. 'I pity the poor devils these cold nights, and the ones to guard them. He'll lie in comfort but they'll have to camp out in the marsh meadows down by the lake.' He watched her again; she had taken a handful of hay and was smoothing down the mare's flanks. 'If you're interested in buying, you'll have a hard job to beat him down. I know him from past times. He's a hard man.' He looked past her, over her head. 'Here's that man of his. Great brute. Wouldn't want to get the wrong side of him.'

Her head came up sharply. Yes, it was him, the big man with the nose hooked like a falcon's but flattened, broken, and the great seamed scar from eye to jaw. A man hard as hardest rock.

'Neither would I,' she agreed. 'I'll leave you now.' She gave the mare a last caress. The stabler jeered at her cowardice but then he sobered, caught at her arm. 'Listen, boy. Take my advice. Don't tangle with this fat bastard. He's a bad man. Not on your own here, are you?'

'No, I'm not alone.'

'Best not be. He's not choosy who he takes as slave. It's bastards like that one that make us glad when winter comes and there's no caravans travelling.' He looked over his shoulder. 'Take my advice, stay close to your people.' He gave her a push. 'Go now, before that one gets here.'

She hurried out of the crowded stables into the crowded courtyard. Where was he? She was too small to see over the heads of the crowd. There was Blue, head and shoulders above the rest. Edgar's gold curls. She pushed her way towards them. And then there he was, walking with the handsome dark man, with Thomas, who had ridden by her side all afternoon though he had said barely a word. A troubled man. Not at all the hero she had thought him to be but a winsome man for all that.

Dai turned sharply as he felt the hand tugging at his sleeve. Pickpockets were rife in towns like this. He looked at her strained white face and eyes that were huge and dark.

'What's to do?'

'He's here,' she breathed. 'I've seen my chestnut mare and the man they call Big Aziz, with the scarred face.'

'Have you now?'

'The slaves are camped down by the lake.'

'What's this, Dafydd?'

'Vecdet is here. Kazan has a score to settle.'

'And you're just the man to help? Dafydd, the man's a brute and well protected.'

'Even well protected brutes can be cornered.'

Twm looked down at Kazan's white face. He sighed. 'So what score is it, boy?'

'He has my chestnut mare and my satchel with my belongings and my good curved bow and quiver. He wanted to make me his slave.'

Twm raised his dark eyebrows. 'Indeed. You knew this, Dafydd?'

'Yes.'

'But you escaped, boy?'

'With the help of one of his slaves, a boy called Niko, and I have sworn to rescue him and his sister.'

'Dafydd, you knew this?'

'Yes.'

'You should have told me.'

'It was not for me to be telling.'

Twm sighed. 'But you were planning to help Kazan here rescue his friends. You and your conscience, Dafydd!'

'I know.'

'Don't tell me – your grandfather was just the same.'

Dai rubbed his nose. He grinned. 'Well now, funny you should say that…'

'Isn't it? Was this rescue to be with or without our help?'

'With your help I was hoping it might be.'

The girl listened to them in alarm. She didn't want to be the cause of any rift between them and Thomas sounded furious. Small wonder, when Dai was so aggravatingly calm and non-committal and his voice had fallen into that sing-song that she knew now was the rhythm of his own language. She looked from one to the other, relieved when she saw Giles sauntering towards them. His quick glance took in the two men and the white-faced boy. He pursed his lips in a soundless whistle.

'Problem?' he said.

'No problem. Not what this one would call a problem, anyway. We're just going to liberate a horse and a couple of slaves from our friend Vecdet. That's all.'

'And a good curved bow and quiver and a satchel and warm *ferace*. That's what you said, isn't it, Kazan?'

She nodded, speechless. Giles considered, shrugged. 'There's nothing else to do tonight except sit around a fire and drink. Unless you've a story for us, Dai?'

'We could plan a rescue.'

'That too, Thomas.'

'You're as mad as he is.'

Giles considered. 'Not quite as mad.'

'My own man traduced by this Welsh bandit. Let's hope he has a plan that will work. I've no wish to be netted and gutted like the fish in this lake.'

Dai laughed outright. 'You're a good man in a hard place, Twm. It's not fighting I had in mind. It's a hard business man we're dealing with. A man without a conscience. How do you feel about bartering for a couple of slaves?'

'I suppose it has to be me? It's against your principles, isn't it?'

'You know it is. Besides, the man knows me and what I think about slavery.'

'So I'm to be the one to haggle.' He sighed. 'Very well. Bath first and discuss this over supper. Nobody is going anywhere tonight. This has to be thought through if we're not all to be food for the lake fish. Kazan, I begin to regret your company.'

'Take no notice, Kazan. He's as wild for this as Giles here.'

'But I don't want... You must not...'

'Listen to the boy, Twm, stuttering and stammering. Put him out of his misery, for the sake of Dewi Sant.'

❀ 214 ❀

Thomas' gaze fell on the boy's unhappy face. 'Be sure, Kazan, we have no love for Vecdet. We'll all be happy to do him down. If we can help you as well, so much the better. And it's clear it would please Dafydd here. Now, come on, time we were moving. We've a busy night ahead.'

It was like the first night over again; the asking, the granting, the careful taking of her into the female section of the baths, except that the women attendants here did not want to know her story; they were modest women who had seen too many strange and scandalous happenings when the caravans came in. There were few women bathers tonight and those were mostly one party travelling with husbands and fathers and absorbed in their own, safe lives; the stay-at-homes, the women of Süleymanşehir, had already visited the *hamam*, avoiding the busy hours when the caravans arrived. But she was scrubbed and oiled and clean when she sat down to supper, and back in her own new-clean, indigo-dyed *kaftan* and *gömlek* and *Şalvar.*

'A little blue brother agaän,' Blue greeted her. 'Fish night and it's not Friday, Fustilugs.'

She looked at the great fish on the platter, all bony scales and fins and sharp toothy heads and whiskers. 'What is this?'

'Lake fish. It's carp. Seems the lake is boiling with them. They jump out of the water and into the boats, they're so keen to be eaten.' Edgar was full of energy and foolish humour. 'Try it – it's good though there's not much flesh on it.'

That was true. More bones than meat. True, as well, that it was good. She wondered what Niko was eating, down there on the bitter-cold marshy lakeside.

It was an evening of talk and plans, everyone keen to contribute, everyone indignant when they heard the story of her capture and escape.

'You make a habit of escaping,' Giles joked. 'The bandits – and now you tell us from Vecdet himself.'

'Yer did all that all aloöne by yersen?'

'I was not alone – well, not all the time. There was Niko. And there was the good father of Mehmi.'

'Eh, young Fustilugs, weren't yer frit?'

Frightened? She stopped. She had intended denying her fear; would her friend Kazan have admitted to fear? Surely not. No boy or man admitted to fear. But there was such a constriction in her throat it was difficult to utter any words, let alone careless bravado. 'Yes,' she admitted, 'I was frightened.'

'So would we all have been, Kazan,' said Thomas. 'You are a brave boy.'

'Kazan the not-so-fearless-warrior,' murmured Mehmi but his voice was comforting, not mocking.

'But why did you leave your tribe?' Edgar innocently questioned. She drew a breath. Now was the time to confess but she thought again what they would think if they knew she was an imposter. Impossible, now, to say who she was, to expose how she was betraying their trust, but the lie lay heavy on her, a wearisome burden, even though a part of her whispered how reluctant she was to give up the freedom of this boy's guise; freedom and friendship with these men, and their admiration. But at least she could tell part of the truth, ease her conscience that way.

'I promised to find my grandfather who I never knew. He came from your country, Edgar, and yours, blue man, but when he was a young boy he went to your country, Dai. That is how I know of your country. He was a great storyteller who travelled the world searching for his lost brother. His name was Will. Will-the-Wordmaker.'

She was not prepared for their reaction.

'A've heard of him, A have, though not nivver fer many a year. Will-the-Wordmaker. Well, A nivver did.'

'He came to Swineshead Abbey in his old age. The Crowland monks spoke of him.'

'You speak as if he is dead.'

'As far as I know, he's alive and well though he'll be an old, old man by now.' Edgar's face was alight with what he knew. 'He made quite a stir when he told the monks that the last, true Princess of Wales was made a nun in Sempringham Abbey. That's not so far from Crowland. It's one of Saint Gilbert's abbeys. Our monks were full of it but no one ever knew for certain if there was truth in it, or if it was just another of his stories.' He turned to the Welshman. 'Did you ever hear of that, Dai?'

'No. Not a whisper. *Taid* – my grandfather – only said that Gwenllian, the infant daughter of our last prince, Llewelyn, was taken when she was a babe, no one knew where. There was talk of a nunnery but never a place. His brother Dafydd's sons and daughters were spirited away from our country at the same time. There was word the boys were kept close prisoner in Bristol castle, poor devils. *Y Groes Nawdd*, too, a splinter of the true cross, our most holy relic. Edward Longshanks took that from us as well.' His dark eyes darkened to blackness, remembering. 'But this storyteller, this Will, *Taid* spoke of him often. *Taid* rescued him from drowning – pulled him out of the Mawddach Falls when this Will was but a *dwt* and my *taid* a young man himself.'

'You all know of my grandfather? But this I cannot believe! It is impossible!'

'It is God's will,' Edgar-the-altar-boy said solemnly.

'There was a brother, as Kazan says. A music maker he was, as great as any of the Welsh bards though he was English born.' Dai paused. 'No – he was half Welsh, that was it. He couldn't speak but he could make music out of the air itself, *Taid* said. He was taught by Ieuan ap y Gof, one of our greatest bards, Mehmi.'

Mehmi smiled. 'I think…I truly believe…I remember my father speaking of this wonderful music maker. And a companion, I think, a small man with a wizened hand who used to be a music maker himself.'

'That's him. That's Ieuan ap y Gof. His hand was ruined in the first Welsh War. How does your father know of them?'

'They were in Konya. He saw them in Konya.'

'My grandfather heard of this but when he arrived in Konya it was too late; his brother and your music man had already left.'

They were silent, barely able to comprehend the forces moving about them, nor the time shifts, the much-longed-for meetings missed by a breath. And now this, their own meeting, and all with their own tales to tell of Will-the-Wordmaker.

'That yer grandad then, Fustilugs? The storyteller?'

Her eyes shone golden in the firelight. Her hair glinted gold-copper-bronze. *Is this what is meant by alchemy?* thought Dai. Here is mortal flesh, the base metal, turned to the pure gold of this girl's soul. 'That is my grandfather,' she said.

'No wonder you want to suck our stories out of our souls, boy,' Thomas said. 'It is in your blood.'

'We all love to hear stories. That is what he said, my grandfather. It makes children of us all, he said, and we forget to fight, and that is truth. Sharing tales and laughter is what makes peace amongst us.'

'He's right an' all, Fustilugs. A've not nivver met a man yet as doesn't love a good taäle.'

'And your story, and Edgar's, see how we loved listening to your stories,' she said eagerly. 'See how we shared in your adventures and your misfortunes.'

'And you are going to England to find him?' Twm persisted.

'That is what I have vowed to do. And now you have told me where to find him, in this abbey you speak of.'

'But yer've nivver not known him, Fustilugs. How's he going to know it's yow?'

'I have this token.' She scrabbled under her tunic and pulled out the tiny jade axe swinging from its leather thong.

Giles leant forward. 'I've seen these. They're from the far countries, far away in the east. They say the sun sleeps in that land until it's ready to rise the next day.'

'Do they say so?' Twm murmured, his one brow raised in disbelief.

'I only say what I've heard.'

'A've heärd as theer's men theer as has one greät foot as they uses fer a sunshaäde and there's others as 'ave long bird beäks and legs 'as end in claäws, just like a bird. A've heärd that.'

'I've seen none of this and I've travelled far enough.'

'I've heard there was a man who vanished into the Far Lands and he was not heard of or seen until many, many years had passed. When he returned to his family, they did not recognise him. And the tales he told! He was mazed... So I've heard,' said Edgar.

'I think it is the Venetian you mean – his name was Marco Polo,' said Dai. 'And his tales were true, though he said nothing of big-footed men nor bird-headed men. Heinrijc Mertens knew of him. This is a well-crafted piece of jade, Kazan.'

'They say this stone protects those who wear it,' she said. She slanted a mischievous glance at Twm. 'So I have heard.'

'Do they say so?' Twm said again, but he was smiling. 'Tell us more about your grandfather.'

'But I want to hear about him from you, Edgar, and you, blue man and you, Dai the Welshman, whose grandfather rescued mine from drowning in this river with the strange name.'

'Waterfall. It was the Mawddach waterfall.' He sighed. 'I've no gift for telling tales, Kazan. My Welsh tongue is tied if I try.'

She was disappointed. 'But you could tell me why he was there, in your country.'

'That I can do. He and his brother had come with Edward's army – that's the first Edward – to build his new-fashioned castles, but they ran away and made their way to Cymer Abbey, where the rivers meet and flow down to the sea. That is my *bro* – where I come from. They were looking for Ieuan ap y Gof, who had been Ned's music teacher.

'Ned?'

'That was the brother's name.'

'The brother who could not speak but who made beautiful music. I know.'

'They slipped and fell – it was winter and icy and only boys they were; hungry and weary boys. My grandfather and his friends were nearby, pulled them out, put them on a cart and took them to the monks at the abbey.'

'And there Ieuan ap y Gof was waiting for them.'

'You already know this story, is it?'

She shook her head. 'Only that they went to Wales and that was where they parted from each other. The brother stayed with the music man and my grandfather went back home to his mother and sisters and always regretted the choice he had made. He said he…' she frowned, trying to remember the strange words, 'he made the wrong choice and shut out the saint. And some years after there was a great flood in his country and all his family was drowned and he had nobody so he set out to find his brother. But he never did. It is a sad story.'

'It is sad that he has never seen his grandson,' said Edgar.

'But he was a storyteller,' said Blue. 'Everybody knew him and his stories. He maäde foölk laugh and cry with his stories. Like yer says, Fustilugs, everybody loves stories and they forget to fight when theer're listening. That's not sad. That's a miracle, that is.'

Mehmi smiled to himself at the big man's words; they would cheer him when he remembered his father's face at their parting and inspire him to sing and play as well as he could so that he would win for himself a reputation like this Will-the-Wordmaker.

She couldn't sleep. She was again by Dai's side, but this time she had seen Twm's raised eyebrows and knew what it signified. Secrets, she thought, were very difficult to live with. But when they were shared, what marvels happened. Like this of her grandfather. 'Nene,' she whispered, 'if only you had known about this brown man and his grandfather who saved mine.' She raised herself up on her elbow. She knew he wasn't asleep though he was lying very still with one arm behind his head. 'What else do you remember?' she asked.

'Nothing now. Later. Go to sleep, Kazan.'

'But…'

'Go to sleep. Tomorrow we must rescue your Niko, remember?'

No, she thought, I didn't remember. Here am I, warm and safe, and I had forgotten him because of the stories of my grandfather. She huddled into her guilt and was quiet but there was no chance of sleep or slumber.

17

Lullay lullay little child lollay lullow
into uncuth world icommen so ertou
(Anon, 14ᵗʰC)

Next morning, reeds shivered and rustled in a wind that blew from a swollen grey sky. 'That wind's snide this morning. It's the back end right enough and theer's some weather to coöme.' Blue was cheerful, chuckling with anticipation over the morning's plans. That fat-arsed, trouser-farting, brusting-bellied shithouse. Try to make Fustilugs a slave, would he? Take his clobber and his horse?

Vecdet's caravan was hurrying to leave. The tent in the marsh meadows was almost packed, mules burdened. Most of the slaves stood roped one to the other, shuddering in thin clothes in the cold morning air. There was no sign of Niko, nor the pale girl who was his sister. Others were hauling on the ropes, straining against the wind that whipped through the billowing fabric. Guards stood with whips at the ready.

Twm rode the short distance to the house they knew was Vecdet's lodging. It overlooked the lakeside and the slaves' tent. Edgar was with him, outwardly attentive and servile; inwardly, tense and alert.

'I wish to speak with your master.' Twm was aloof, arrogant, very much the noble man in fine clothes.

'What is your wish?'

'My wish is to speak with your master.'

The servant scurried away. Twm raised an eyebrow, watched the slaves struggle with the last stretches of the wind-blown, dew-laden felt of the tent. A corner snapped out of the hands of one man and into his face then it blew free and the guards cursed and threatened. The servant returned, Big Aziz with him. He looked formidable, a man as big as Blue and harder though his words were polite: his master had much to attend to this morning before they could leave. He regretted he could not spare time to entertain guests.

'I have not come to be entertained but to do business. Surely your master has time for business? It will not take long; a simple transaction only.'

That was a different matter; he would speak again with the master. Meanwhile, perhaps the young *efendi* would care to have his horse attended to? Twm nodded and dismounted. Edgar stood by the bridle until a slave came to take the horse.

Big Aziz came a second time. The master would see him for a short time.

Watching from a safe distance, they saw Twm and Edgar disappear into the shadowy entrance. Dai was impassive, expressionless but the girl knew he would be on edge until he saw his two men reappear. She remembered how she herself had disappeared into the great tent, but that had been herself alone and unprotected, and in a lonely place. Here was the middle of a busy town. Surely no harm could come to them here?

Inside the lodgings, Twm and Edgar were led into an upstairs room. It was light and airy, with windows covered with an ornately carved, fretted wooden screen. Through the fretting came glimpses of the lake and the shoreline and the huddle of miserable men and women and, somewhere amongst them, a young boy and his sister. There was a cushioned seating area and there sat Vecdet, a solid, square, swarthy man with a thick fleshy neck like an ox. His chins were resting on his chest and his belly resting on his thighs and his buttocks spreading over the cushions. His rich robes were warm against the cold. His loose-lipped mouth was pursed with annoyance and speculation.

'You wish to do business with me?' Strange that such a man should have nothing but a high piping voice, like a gelding.

'If you are the leader of this caravan, then yes, my business is with you.'

'For what reason?'

'I see you have slaves. I wish to purchase a young boy to serve me. You have a slave who would be appropriate?'

If Vecdet was surprised by the request, he did not show it. He gave every appearance of being pleased at the unexpected sale. Certainly he had a boy, a good boy, Christian Greek. Highly desirable, were the Greek slaves, and no doubt would bring a good price in Attaleia but perhaps they could make an equally good price now, he and the young master, between them? After all, they were men of business.

'Let me see him,' Twm said.

Vecdet clapped his hands, ordered the young Greek boy to be brought to them. But when the boy was presented it was seen that he had dark bruising down the side of his face and he nursed his right arm.

'A good boy, you say?' Twm raised an eyebrow. 'This one looks as though he might be rebellious. As for his condition…'

'A trifling matter,' he was assured. 'A zealous nature.'

'But I wish for obedience,' Twm said. 'A rebellious slave is not for me. What is your price? Too high.'

He bartered the man down. Still too high. Perhaps they could reach an agreement if he bought two slaves? The boy he needed now but he intended buying a young female slave in Attaleia. Perhaps Vecdet had a young female and they could negotiate a reasonable price for both? Two for the price of one, as it were? There was a young female, and a virgin, but there was no question of any 'two for one'. This was a slave who would fetch a good price in any market. Did the young master wish to view her?

The girl was brought, fair and pale and thin with downcast eyes. She submitted to the usual checks of healthy teeth and gums and unmarked flesh. 'A very useful female, whatever your needs,' Vecdet murmured.

'But so feeble – not well looked after at all. There's no saying how strong this pair is, nor how hard they can work before they are no use to me whatsoever. You're asking too high a price. I shall do better in Attaleia, and have more choice.'

It would have been almost pleasurable, Twm thought, if so much had not been at stake. It was clear the man longed to be rid of two who must be troublesome. There would be keen competition in Attaleia, Twm pointed out helpfully, and if Vecdet were to take them to Candia in this condition, well, odds on neither would make it. He was tempted to push the price lower but remembered Kazan's face and Dai's instructions: agree a price, send them to safety with Edgar, get out of there. Then, once on the street, in public view, and only then, negotiate the mare and Kazan's belongings. Even so, that would be trickier.

The watchers observed the small party that emerged on to the street. Edgar first, then the girl shivering by her brother's side: he short and sturdy-seeming, despite his thinness, with curly dark hair and slanting brows and sullen, watchful gaze; she taller, slender, pale as a crushed moth.

'Eyeäble,' murmured Blue, 'for all she's near lost wi' muck, poor soul.'

'Is that the boy?' Dai asked, quietly. She nodded.

'He's nobbut a bairn – more of a recklin than yow, Fustilugs.'

All she could hear was the cascading waterfall and Niko's young voice: 'I wish my sister was brave but she cries all the time. It's very hard to make a plan to escape when she won't help.' Was the bruised face and injured arm because of her, she wondered, because he had helped her escape? She could hardly breathe. Get them away, Dai had said, before you broach the matter of the mare and Kazan's belongings. Now, the matter of those belongings seemed trivial. Only let all go free and safe. Sure enough, they were walking away with Edgar towards their own lodgings. 'Where's Twm?'

'Business still to do. The fool should have come out by now.'

Aziz followed them out, watched the trio's progress along the street. His gaze shifted; it seemed he was staring straight at them, hidden though they were in the shadows of the busy *bedestan*. Blue shifted uneasily.

'A'd like to tek a ding at that un,' he murmured. 'A'd like to brust his noöse agaän fer him.'

'Stay peaceful, Blue. It hasn't come to fighting yet. He may not have seen us.'

'There's a matter of another of my slaves,' Twm was saying. 'I believe we have you to thank for his safe return to us.'

'Another slave?'

'A young boy. Kazan. He came across your camp some days ago. I believe he left behind a good chestnut mare, a satchel, a warm cloak – all stolen. A good bow, the curved style. Such things as this. You remember? No doubt he spun you a good tale but it seems you did not believe him and so he – er – left you somewhat abruptly. We caught up with him not long after. We wish to thank you for the safekeeping of our belongings and arrange their return.'

'I see.' Vecdet spoke slowly, thinking through what he had heard. 'There was a young boy but he was no slave, that one. He came and left of his own free will. The horse and bow he gave as a gift for our hospitality.'

Twm sighed. 'A slave, sir, and one with a ready tongue. He has a fair face, an innocent-seeming face; he took us in at first.'

But the fat man was pursing his lips, shaking his head and his chins shook with him. 'I am not so easily persuaded, young sir.' Aziz had come back into the room. He leaned down to speak softly.

Vecdet's loose lips rounded O in astonishment. He looked again at Twm. 'It seems we have met before. This one has an excellent memory. He remembers having seen you in the company of the Welshman who does not deal in slaves. He will have nothing to do with slaves. What do you take me for? Some fool? What is his intention?'

'His intention? Why, only to recover what is his, and the mare is his. As for me, I am not answerable to him.' Twm's nostrils flared; he was deliberately fastidious. 'He is not my master. Did you really think he was?' He laughed, dismissive, deprecating. 'No, sir: though it is true both of us answer to the same man, Monsignor Heinrijc Mertens of Ieper. The Welshman may have no liking for slaves but it is my right to do as I wish. The slave belongs to me.'

'Yes. Just the fool I took him for.' Vecdet smiled, satisfied. 'Well. So. You will have slaves despite him. Interesting. And now you expect me to hand over this – what did you call him? Kazan? This Kazan's belongings. But he left them behind. He had no further use for them. Therefore they are rightly mine. What do you say to this?'

'Only that you are known as a fair man who will see justice done.'

'Is that what they say?' Vecdet smiled at the flattery. 'You shall have the satchel. I have no use for it.' He was magnanimous.

'The satchel and its contents?'

'And its contents, for what they are worth. But the horse and the other things, they stay with me.'

'The horse belongs to Dafydd ap Rhickert. The boy stole it from him.'

'That may be but you must name your price. I shall not part otherwise.' Aziz stood threateningly just behind his master.

Twm raised an eyebrow. 'The satchel and its contents, sir,' he said firmly, 'you will return to us together with the cloak and the bow and quiver. It was our intention to reward you for your care but perhaps agreeing a price for the mare would be more agreeable to us both.'

Cat-and-mouse, thought Twm, but who is the mouse? Who is the cat? The effort of keeping his face expressionless was exhausting. Time, as well, to be out of this room before there was trouble. Dai had said get out of a private meeting before negotiating the difficult part; he was in the right of it, as ever. Twm could feel sweat beading his forehead. *Keep it peaceful, if you can.* Made sense enough. That brute of a man of his was itching for trouble. Brusting for a fight, as Blue would say. For the good Lord's sake, listen to him, falling into Dafydd's way of quoting the Fenman's outlandish sayings. Dafydd, he thought grimly, getting him into this. Cat-and-mouse? That was Dafydd's game, and never a doubt there who was cat, patient and prowling. *Keep your mind on it, Thomas!*

'A reward?' The man's little beady eyes glittered. 'And what had you in mind?'

Twm sighed. 'First, I would like to see the mare. If she is in the same condition as your slaves, perhaps she is not worth reward nor rescue.'

'Why doesn't your Welshman do this for himself?'

Twm shrugged. 'Leaves me to do the work, you mean? Doesn't believe in slaves but he drives us all hard.' He allowed annoyance to creep into his voice.

'Not such friends, then.'

'I never said we were. We work for the same man, that's all.' He turned to the door. 'Shall we go?'

Dai sighed once, quickly, but he didn't relax his stance. There they were, all three, emerging from the house: Twm, the bulky merchant, the huge bodyguard close behind. Edgar had quietly come back to Twm's side; he took the satchel and bow and quiver and gave the briefest of nods: the brother and sister were safe with Rémi, then. Twm slung the cloak over his shoulder. 'Blue,' he shouted, 'come here and make yourself useful.'

'Remember, no trouble, if we can avoid it,' Dai muttered.

'A'd like to tek a poäke at him but A'll remember, doän't you fret none, Dai bor.'

Blue strolled across the street to join the group. Aziz's eyes widened at the sight of a man as hefty as himself. He smiled, his mouth twisted because of the ridged scar. Blue sized him up and down. Neither man spoke, nor needed to. Brusting for a fight? Both of them, thought Tom, and desperately wanted to laugh. What a comedy this would be, were it not for the boy and the wretched slaves. They walked to the stables. There was the chestnut mare, instantly recognisable from Kazan's description, but with a dull coat and eye. The man with her was a lout, begrudging any care spent on the animals though every one was a lifesaver. More bartering and a price agreed, and gifts of spices and amber. Not Tom's wish but Dafydd had said avoid trouble, as far as possible, so a price was agreed for the chestnut mare and the deal was struck. The horses were brought, Tom's grey and the chestnut. Aziz watched Blue take the two horses in hand and lead them away from the stables, back towards their own lodging. He watched for a long time, long after they were out of sight.

'A good deal done,' said Tom. 'You are a fair man, as they told me. Will you drink with me to seal our bargain and our friendship, sir?' He hoped the answer would be no, but the fat man was genial, pleased with the outcome of the morning's business.

'Edgar, go ahead with Blue; make sure all our purchases are comfortably stowed,' Tom said. He looked pointedly at Aziz.

'Leave us, Aziz. Make sure we are ready to leave inside the hour. Come, Thomas Archer, we shall be comfortable in my lodgings.'

It was as they were walking away from the lakeside, back to the street that the commotion began. When all had been agreed, all deals completed, commotion. It began with running feet, shouts of alarm. Aziz was gone, moving quickly for a big man, but before he had gone far a servant raced up to them, gasping with news. It was a child, a young child. He'd been found in the river by two fishermen. No, not a hope of reviving him – he was dead, drowned. He must have wandered off in all the preparations for leaving. No one was looking out for him.

'Where is that wretch Hatice? Bring her here. She was responsible for him.' Vecdet's high-pitched voice was shriller than usual and his expression ugly. 'Someone must pay for this. Useless donkeys! Idiots!'

The woman was dragged to Vecdet. Her face was white, grief-stricken, terrified. 'Yes, I left him. Asperto was ill. I couldn't leave Asperto... I thought the boy was safe.'

'Asperto? Asperto? What is he worth to me? It was the boy you should have looked out for! Now he is dead. Dead. He at least had some value. How will you pay for this, you useless, worthless, troublesome woman?' The man's face was livid purple with fury, and the veins stood out on his forehead. The huddled slaves knew only too well what his fury meant, how it would end.

Asperto was flung at his feet, and the body of the dead child tumbled to the ground, limp; a small body with baby-fine wet hair plastered to its scalp. A child too young to remember his name, too young to be taken as a slave, no mother or father to mourn for him.

Hatice ran, as fast as a hawk could stoop, towards the tumbled corpse and the fallen man. She was seized and pulled back by the guards.

'Get her out of my sight. Get rid of her. Him too.' Gesturing to the ghost-pale, flaccid figure of Asperto. 'I've no use for such as these. They have burdened me for too long.'

'Wait!' The voice was abrupt, a voice of authority. Everyone stilled, movement stopped mid-action. Like one of the scenes from a mystery play, thought Tom and following rapidly on that thought: trust Dafydd. Everything settled, friendly, just as he said, and now he's stirring for trouble. *You and your conscience, Dafydd, will have us all killed.* He edged his sword hand closer to the scabbard, eased the hilt free, saw Giles close by, his hand resting on his own broad sword. Dai strode closer, bystanders making way for him.

'So there you are, Dafydd the Welshman. I thought you could not be far behind your man.'

'I'll take them.' He didn't waste time answering but pointed at the two slaves. 'These two – I'll take them.'

'How much?'

Dai snorted. 'You expect me to pay to take them off your hands?'

'Of course. They're worth money to me and, it seems, of some value to you.' Vecdet was sly, calculating.

'It's wanting to be rid of them, you say. I offer to do just that, save you the bother of disposing of unwanted baggage, isn't it, and it's valuable they are now, hey, *bach*? A broken man and a bashed-up woman who's not young nor fair-faced? And that's not to mention what they both eat.' He looked them up and down, the man slave and the woman. 'Not that they eat much, from the look of it. You don't waste money on food, do you now? You'll have to fatten them up before market, *efendi*, or there'll be no fat purses willing to buy.' The contempt was there in his voice for all to hear, and a crowd was gathering, drawn by the drama. Thomas and Giles edged closer to Dai; out of the corner of his eye, Thomas saw Sakoura and, with him, the men, the muleteers and cameleteers, pushing their way through the crowd, staves and swords in their hands.

'Take them then! Rob me! What else can I expect from the English? Take these worthless wretches.' Dai could hear the slow grinding of the man's teeth in that milling head of his.

'I am *Cymro* not *Sais*.' Lightly said, but the menace was there lurking at the edges of the brown voice, at the back of the brown eyes. 'We *Cymro* know how to value life. It shall not be said that this man and this woman are worthless. Here – take this.' He flung a bag of *akçe* at the Turk. 'Count it. Make sure the price is enough. Blue!' A switch to English, a jerk of the head to the big man. 'Take our new possessions – all our new possessions – back to the lodgings.'

Nobody moved. How much money had he thrown away?

'Well. Come on now, Blue *bach*, it's not all day we have to be standing here.' Then words spoken softly in the Fen man's own language. They galvanised the big man. He hoisted Asperto to his feet, hustled Hatice past Vecdet. She pulled back at Dai's side, a tall, gaunt woman with a livid scar on her forehead. Her mouth was working.

'The child,' she said.

'Ah yes, the child. A corpse, *efendim*, does it also have value? Shall I buy this dead boy from you as well? Name your price. Or is it enough that we shall give him a burial?' No emotion; only that ice-cold voice, cutting as the wind from the mountains.

'Take him and be done with it. The parents were glad to be rid of him. I shouldn't have taken him off their hands. He's been nothing but trouble – like that accursed woman. Take him.'

Dai nodded. He unfastened his cloak and swaddled the child in it, holding him as if he were still alive.

'Our business with you is finished, *efendim*.' He turned and walked away, leaving the man impotent and furious, aware of the sniggering crowd, the humiliation that had been heaped on him. His beady eyes followed the Welshman's progress, saw the slim boy who met him and his eyes narrowed.

18

Behold, thou art fair, my love;
behold, thou art fair;
Thou hast doves' eyes.
(Song of Solomon)

'And my curved bow and quiver of straight arrows as well.' An hour
ago Kazan would have crowed with pleasure but not now, not with
the child dead and the haggard woman grieving beside him, and the
man they called Asperto as white as a corpse himself. But there was
Niko, still watchful, still hardly believing what had happened.

'You've come back.'

'I said I would.'

'I didn't know…'

'I promised you I would come back for you,' she had said to him
when they all crowded back into the lodgings. 'I always keep my
promises.' The girl, his sister, Agathi, was close beside him, frail
and shivering and beautiful, even in her sorry state. Kazan was
ashamed of the flicker of irritation she felt at the admiration in the
men's eyes. Edgar was gazing at her as if he had seen all the glories
of the Kingdom of God, she thought, then shivered at the
blasphemy. Struck by love, she amended, like a sharp arrow swift
in flight and straight to its target. The girl was glancing at him from
under lowered lashes; quick little glances when she thought herself
unobserved. This was the beautiful stranger who had led her to

safety. His head was aureoled by golden curls and his eyes were blue as the Great Sea on a summer's day. *Our eyes met. Just once, fleetingly, but it was enough.* Nene's words were true. This was how love came.

Kazan sighed then twirled the warm cloak from her shoulders, from where Tom had dropped it only minutes before, and dropped it into Edgar's hands. 'Here, give her this. It is cold today.'

Agathi clutched the warm wool *ferace* to her with pale, slender hands. She gazed adoringly up at the young man who had wrapped it round her with no thought for the boy who had given it. Kazan walked away before the girl could whisper her thanks. Dai followed her, put a hand on her shoulder, bringing her to a halt.

'Satisfied?' His voice was terse, angry, but she could not be sorry.

'Mm.'

'It was good of you to give her your cloak.'

She shrugged. 'The cloak does not matter. It means nothing. I can get another.' Her fingers had tightened on the satchel. Dai nodded towards it.

'That does?'

She thought of what was inside; Nene's precious inlaid scissors, the carefully crafted ivory comb that had been handed down from mother to daughter to granddaughter. The amethyst ring. 'No, that is nothing. He is. He is what matters.' She nodded towards the boy Niko. He was so young; where had he found the courage and strength to look after himself let alone his sister, let alone the stranger he had befriended? She wanted to thank the brown man by her side but his cold anger choked the words in her throat.

'Best get them to the physician, Blue, then they look as if they need feeding. May as well stay here the day. We've a burial to attend to, and our newcomers.'

'The *hamam* before food, perhaps, Dafydd? And clean clothes?'

'Ever fastidious, Twm?'

'Ever food on your mind, Dafydd?'

They measured looks. Dai nodded. 'Perhaps you're right. What have we in the way of clothes?'

'Should I go with them to the physician?' Edgar, his face luminous with pent-up emotion. 'She is very frail.' His eyes lit on the pale slender girl and away, but that one look told Dai all he needed to know. Heaven help them all, the boy was smitten. Everything in his gentle nature was roused by her helplessness. Giles pulled a face. 'Our young rebel's caught,' he muttered to Twm. Twm sighed. Another four mouths to feed; another four lost souls. How many this journey? Blue, Edgar, Kazan, Mehmi and now four miserable slaves. Dafydd and his conscience! Heinrijc Mertens was a saint of a man if he countenanced this.

'What will you do with them, Dafydd?'

'Do with them? Nothing. As soon as they are fit they are free to go.' Dai glared at him. 'Are you worried about the money I paid for them? Don't be. That was my own. Heinrijc Merten's profits are safe and so is your commission.'

Twm sighed again. 'You know that's not what I meant.'

'Isn't it?'

'You are a difficult man, Dafydd.'

'And my conscience will kill us all. Yes, I know, you've said it all before.' He turned away. 'Rémi! Come here. Now.'

Tom glanced down at the young boy next to him. No elation here but tearless burning eyes. 'Don't fret, Kazan. Dafydd can be the very devil when he's minded.'

'Is it my fault? Did I ask too much?'

'Too much?' Tom laughed but it was a bitter sound. 'You wonder why he's so angry. It's because he couldn't save them all. Couldn't save the child. That conscience of his...' He stopped. Sighed. 'Cautions us all to be peaceable, negotiate, strike a bargain. And we do. We did. Then in he comes with that peasant sword of his all but drawn and ready to do battle with the devil himself.' He glanced down at the boy by his side, subdued for once. 'Well, that's Dafydd for you. He's a riddle. And so are you, Kazan.'

'Me?'

'You're no slave – no *yürük*, I'll swear – a champion rider and bowman yet you can cozen stories from our souls – and Dafydd's heart from out of its armour.'

'Indeed I do not. You are mistaken.'

'Am I? But do you wish us harm? That is what I wonder.'

'Wish you harm? No! How can you think so?'

'You may be a spy – an enemy amongst us. How do we know?'

'I am not.' She was indignant. 'You know about my grandfather and my journey to find him.'

'And that is all I know. What other secrets do you keep, Kazan?'

Her face blanked, expressionless. 'I have secrets, that is true, but so have you all. Dai knows my secrets.'

'Dafydd knows your secrets?'

'Why should he not?'

'He has said nothing.'

'He is a man of honour and I have a right to silence, as have you all.'

'As have we all…' He was baffled. 'That is true but…'

'You do not trust me. Well, I cannot help that. I can tell you only that I mean you no harm. I am in your debt. Your Dafydd' – she used the name the dark man gave him – 'has been my good friend and I would never do him harm.'

They were glaring at each other, she and the dark man, and she wished it were otherwise, and wished that it had been he who knew her secret. How could he ever trust her now?

'Well,' he said, 'so you are his friend. As I said, his good friend.' He paused. 'His very good friend.' His voice was heavy with meaning.

'In that you are wrong as well. As I said, he keeps my secrets.' She looked away. 'Perhaps, some day, I must tell you all.'

'Perhaps you could tell me now?'

She shook her head. 'I cannot. This is not a good time. Listen! He is calling for me.'

'Better hurry then, Kazan.'

She was troubled, and this should have been a joyous time, to have won Niko out of slavery from the loathsome Vecdet; and his sister, and the two who had been his friends, but there was the dead child, and Dai so cold and angry, and Thomas suspicious and all but accusing her of terrible things...

'Kazan, quickly. Stop dragging your steps. You are needed here. Go with Edgar to the physician. The boy's arm needs attention. The woman as well – see what he can do for that gash on her forehead. The man and the girl – make sure they are in good enough health. God willing, they need nothing more than warm clothes and food in their bellies and rest. Well, what are you waiting for?'

Nothing, she thought, but a soft word, but already he had gone. The woman Hatice tugged on her arm.

'This master of yours – he is a strange mix of care and harshness. He will treat us badly, do you think?'

She shook her head. 'No. He is a fair man. A good man.' She hesitated. 'He does not keep slaves.'

'No slaves?'

'He is an honourable man. He does not believe in a slave system – like the great Mevlana, remember?'

'I have heard them speak of this prophet but I know nothing of him.'

'He was the great man of these places. He is much revered. He has his shrine in Konya. He would not have slaves.'

'And your master thinks like this?'

'He does.'

'Then will he cast us off?'

'I do not know.'

'Then what will become of us? Asperto – he is ill with the falling sickness. He cannot work. He can fetch no price. Vecdet was ready to kill him, I know. If he does not believe in keeping slaves why has this man bought him? And paid good money?'

'I do not know.'

'And the young boy and his sister – still a virgin, thank the good God – what will he do with her? Is there no hope for her?'

'I do not know. I know only that he is a fair man, an honest man.'

'He is a dangerous man, that one.'

Kazan shrugged. 'Perhaps. But he will not leave you destitute and without protection. Of this I am sure. Now we must do as he says and go to the physician and after the *hamam* and then we shall find a way of giving the little boy a fitting burial.'

'But there is no church here and the little boy was Christian, as I am.'

'As I am also. Do not torment yourself, my friend. All will be well. You shall see. For now, comfort yourself and the girl in the *hamam*. Make yourself clean and fitting for the child's sake. Afterwards, it is your care to wash him and dress him for his burial.'

Hatice stared at her… 'You are the boy Niko rescued. You are very young to speak so wisely.'

She smiled sadly. 'Boy.' So Niko had not betrayed her secret, not even to his good friends. 'Niko is much younger than I, and braver than I could ever be. When he rescued me from that evil man I promised I would come back for him.'

She laid a hand gently on the boy's curly head. So quiet, so subdued. Had Vecdet broken his spirit entirely? Had his rescue come too late? She couldn't bear to think of it. 'Come, Niko. We must do as Dai has said and see the physician.'

It was late morning before they gathered together around the pitifully small wooden box one of the town carpenters had hastily made. Homage, he said, to the strangers who had shown such courage and goodness. Homage too to the small soul who had not deserved to die so young – who should never have been taken from his family. Shame on the mother and father who would part with such a child. Shame on the evil man who would treat him so.

Word had spread throughout the town: there was no need to find clothing; the townswomen were generous in their gifts so that Amir's cousin, belatedly arriving, was too late with his offers of help. The Imam himself had come to see the dead child. Gravely, he offered a small space in the garden of the mosque. 'Not Christian, I know, but your prophets are our prophets; your Jesus is one of our prophets. Allah will watch over one so young even if he was not born into our faith.' Yes, he said, they could place a cross, if that would give them comfort. He offered to speak holy words but in the end that was not needed because a caravan arrived, seeking shelter from the rain that was falling heavily now, and with the caravan was a Franciscan friar travelling with it for safety.

Kazan knew she would never forget that forlorn day. Rain was falling as the coffin was lowered into its grave; sharp, sleety rain that swept down from the mountains, rustling the reeds and raising an earthy, swampy smell from the muddy shoreline; obscuring rain that enveloped them all in its grey shroud. The unknown friar in his homespun brown habit bound by its white cord, his sandalled feet bare despite the cold, weary from his journey, devoutly speaking words of comfort and hope and Our Lord's love for the children of this earth that gave them a place in Heaven at His side; Hatice, composed now, clean and dignified, holding in her grief, her head covered in the indigo-dyed bonnet Blue had given to her. Help heal the wounds to her heart and her head, he said, and to 'Think nowt on it.' Who was the more astonished was not clear; the big, clumsy fen-man or the gaunt-faced, haggard woman. Asperto, clean-shaven, his white hair tamed, was wrapped in cloth of indigo – good for the falling sickness, both Sakoura and Blue reminded them, and no one was minded to scoff, not even Thomas Archer. Edgar, eyes glistening with new love, standing watchful by frail, pale, beautiful Agathi; Niko by her side, his arm soothed with salve and bound with clean linen; no break, said the physician, but savagely bruised, but the boy was young, the bruising would quickly fade. Ah, she thought, but what of the bruising of his soul and spirit? Thomas and Giles standing straight, like soldiers on guard. Dai, impassive, unreadable; a quiet, brown, kind man who they said was dangerous.

Mountains, lake, rocks, reeds, earth were lost in the obliterating rain. Rain lashed the buildings. It swept through the town until the streets themselves became rivers carrying all the debris of a busy town on a busy trade route. All day came the rattling and jiggling of boats and their rigging. There would be no sailing tonight for the men of the town. No travelling for the merchants and their caravans. There was nothing for it but for all to remain indoors. The rising wind moaned through doorways and windows and howled round corners. Inside their lodging, the wind gusted down the kitchen chimneys and the smoke from the fires billowed out into the rooms until the air was choking. When Blue came in through the outer door, the cloud shifted and lifted but didn't disperse.

'It's thick-wet out theer,' he said, shaking the rain from his cloak. 'Yer'll get yer death o' cold.'

'It's as well we didn't set out today,' Edgar said. 'There's no travelling in weather like this.'

'Even so,' Thomas said, 'it puts us back again.' He stared out moodily at the lashing rain. 'Wonder how long it'll keep this up?'

'The old men say it should blow itself out by morning, and they're usually in the right of it,' Dai said. 'If we start out early, travel the Seydişehir road, we can be well on the way to Manavgat by evening and then the coast road to Attaleia.'

'If it blows itself out,' Tom said.

'Where is Kazan? And the boy?'

'Stables,' Blue said. 'Rêmi's gone wi' them. Like A told him, yer'll get yer death o' coöld but he wasn't having nowt. Wants to see the chestnut, he says.'

'What state was it in?'

'Better than what them poor beings are in – and better stabling than what they've got an' all.'

'The "poor beings" cost you dear. What do you you plan for them, Dafydd?'

'Nothing. They are free to do as they wish.'

'You mean to leave them here?'

Dai sighed. 'What could those two do here? A man with the falling sickness and a half-crazed creature? They are free to choose but I hope they accept our protection down to the coast at least. Better weather, more choice, a Christian community to provide for them.'

'You're not taking them on to Ieper then?'

'Not these two. They belong here.'

'And the boy and his sister?'

'Ah, there's the problem, isn't it? The boy and his sister. What is to become of them?'

The chestnut mare was calmer, soothed by soft words and a voice she recognised and the rhythmic brushing as the girl set about restoring some of the glossiness of the chestnut coat.

'What is she called?' Niko asked. It was almost the first words he had volunteered. When the physician had probed his injured arm, he had gritted his teeth and only a sucked-in breath betrayed the pain it caused him. Now, his young face was already less care-worn. Food, and warmth, and the comfort of good people, she thought, made all the difference.

'Rüzgâr.' *The wind.*

'Rüzgâr,' he murmured and stretched up his good arm to stroke the white blaze down her nose.

'She is not mine, not really. She belongs to the tribe. It was wrong of me to take her.'

'But you had no choice. It was a matter of life or death to you.'

'Yes.' Life or death: Niko was right. She gave the mare a final pat and moved over to the piebald. 'This is Yıldız. She is not mine, either. She is a gift from Mehmi's father to Dai.'

● 241 ●

'Dai. That is the man called Dafydd. The man who bought Hatice and Asperto. Has he bought Agathi and me as well?'

'He bought your freedom, Niko, not you.'

Niko considered this. 'And you? Has he bought your freedom?'

'No, but I owe him my loyalty and my life.'

'Does he know who you are?'

She glanced to where Rémi was grooming the big brown horse Dai rode. He was crooning under his breath, absorbed in his task. 'Dai knows. The rest do not.'

'Why does he do this for you?'

'It is how he is. It is what he does for all of us. For Rémi. For Edgar and Blue who were both chance-met and who now travel with him. Besides, Dai and Thomas – the dark man who bargained for you – came to our summer camp in search of my grandmother but they came too late and she was new-dead. They spoke to me and I gave them medicines for Edgar, who was sick. Dai recognised me when we met again.'

'But not the dark man. Isn't that strange?'

She shook her head. 'Dai is a man who sees much that others do not.' She hesitated. 'I believe he is a good man, whatever his past has been.'

'His past? You know of this?'

She gave a jerk of head that meant no. 'He does not talk of it but sometimes I see him look into the past and it is unhappy for him.'

'I think you see much as well, Kazan.'

'I see that they hurt you. Was that because of me?'

Niko shrugged. 'Vecdet was angry with me when I said I had hidden myself with the donkeys when they were searching for you.' At last he grinned. 'I think he knew I called him "donkey" and I was making fun of him. He grabbed me by this arm and shook me and threw me across the floor. I crashed against that big chest he carries with him. That is how the bruising came but I don't remember very much.'

'Poor Niko.'

'It hurt then but it is much better now. Everything is better now, except the little one is dead and Hatice mourns for him.' Niko shrugged again with a child's pragmatic callousness. 'He would have died anyway. He was ill with a fever and would not eat.'

They were sitting side by side now on a heap of hay. Outside, the rain fell incessantly. 'It is like the waterfall,' Niko said. 'Remember?'

'Of course.'

They talked then, of what had happened to each of them after Niko had left her that night. Rémi joined them, peeling straws and plaiting them, listening to the talk and confessions of fear, smiling his snail-trail smile and snorting laughter when they laughed. Niko touched the pale scars with his fingertips.

'What are these, Rémi?'

'Dai.' The name was unmistakeable. Niko and Kazan exchanged looks. Rémi shook his head; he had no signs to convey what he wanted to say. 'Dai,' he repeated and gave his thumbs-up sign. He thought a moment. 'Good Dai,' he signed and grinned gummily.

They all ate together, every one of them, muleteers and cameleteers elbow to elbow with the rescued and rescuers alike, eating right-handed from the common platter of new-killed sheep, still new-tough. Brother Jerome was with them, his tonsure shining pink in the torchlight, the short finger-breadth fringing of hair shining silver-grey. A pink-and-grey little friar, thought Dai, rosy cheeked and cheerful. He leaned now towards Giles.

'It is you, my son. I thought so, though it has been many summers since we last met. And your brother? How is he? I've had no word of him since we fled the country with William Ockham.'

'He is dead, Father.'

'Dead? How?'

Giles fixed his gaze on his hands, clenched on the table.

'He did not escape?'

'From this life, yes. It is not a fit tale for this company nor this night, Father.'

'Before we part I would hear this tale.'

'As you wish, Father.'

Dai regarded the two, Brother Jerome sombre faced, Giles rigid. He felt a tugging on his sleeve, Rémi gurgling his words.

'Sure of this, boy?' A nod. 'Rémi would like you all to hear his story.' Dai shrugged. 'And I must needs tell it, though I've no gift for telling tales.'

19

Rémi's Story

'This is part my story as well because it concerns our master, Heinrijc Mertens. Without him, Rémi and me wouldn't be alive today. A good man he is, Heinrijc Mertens, isn't he now, Rémi?' The boy nodded vigorously. 'Well now, like this it was.'

He paused, gathering his words to keep pace with his thoughts, his memories. 'Ten years since, it was. I'd not been long in Flanders, and not long with the man who has since been my master.' Dai stopped again, rubbed the side of his nose in unfamiliar embarrassment. 'Tell the truth now, give you an idea of what manner of man he is, I was caught in his house, red-handed, stealing.' Dai smiled, remembering, hardly aware of his audience until Edgar prompted, 'Stealing, Dai?' There was doubt in his voice.

'Stealing,' Dai repeated. 'From his kitchens. As Twm would say, my mind was on my stomach and my wits had gone begging.'

'Starved were yer, Dai?'

Starved? Yes, he was always hungry in those days. Had been all his life. He'd taken a chance that winter's day. Freezing cold, and him penniless and in rags, the aroma of basting meat wafting from the window of the grand town house, so he'd sneaked into the old man's kitchens, snatched what he could, filled his mouth with half-cooked pastry that he hadn't time to swallow before he was seen and grabbed and hustled out. The old man had come to see what the commotion was. All rigged out in one of those velvet robes of his, all lavish embroidery, and those ridiculous shoes with curling toes.

Dai had gazed at him mouth-wide-open, the clogging pastry there for all to see.

'Yes, I was hungry so I stole food. They caught me and all Heinrijc Mertens said was, "You'd best sit yourself by the fire – you'll be more comfortable there." Ordered his man to cut me a slice of meat pie, bring broth. "No one should go hungry." He was fond of saying that, just like Kara Kemal.' He smiled across at Mehmi. 'Two of a kind they are, for all the differences in country and religion. He shamed me with his goodness.

'So when I came across Rémi here, begging in the streets, I knew just where to take him. A scrawny little *dwt*, you were, knee-high to a grasshopper, isn't it now? And in those days he'd an ugly little mug on him – that right, isn't it now?' The boy grinned and nodded and drew his forefinger over his top lip.

'He'd a harelip. Don't know if you've seen one – cleft lip, some say, but looks like nothing as much as a hare's lip turned up over its nostrils. Poor little devil was begging for scraps he could hardly eat. How he'd survived six winters I'll never know. Never did know. No family, no one of his own. A *dwt* of six years begging in the streets on an icy winter's day and no one to care.' Rémi murmured something they couldn't understand but his gesture was clear; he took Dai's broad, brown hand in his and kissed it. 'Enough of that, boy,' he said. 'It wasn't I who healed you – or had money to buy you healing.'

'But you cared,' Kazan said. 'That is Rémi's meaning. You did not walk by on the other side.' She saw the boy's intention, how he had heard the talk about his master and it had troubled him; he wanted them all to know that Dai was a good man. A man who cared for others.

'Well, that's as may be. But it was Heinrijc who knew best what to do.'

Heinrijc, he remembered, who hadn't turned a hair when his new protégé came back from his first commission with a ragged, ailing, ugly-mugged scrap of a *dwt*. 'I do not know how to heal him,' he'd said, 'but I am acquainted with one who has experience of these defects. Come, Dafydd-the-Welshman, let us see if Master Jehann Ieperman can perform for us a small miracle.' Dai shook himself back from the memory of the old man and the comfortable room with its blazing fire and the huddled child hardly daring to trust these strangers. Then, he could barely understand what was said to him and he had no speech.

'Heinrijc was friendly with a physician,' Dai continued, 'who'd made a name for himself in the Low Country. Jehan Ieperman. He was trained at the University of Paris and proud of it, though he didn't come from a wealthy family. Afterwards, what he'd learned in Paris he put into practice on the battle fields of Flanders. He worked in the hospital Del Belle in Ieper most of his life, caring for rich and poor alike, and that was where we took Rémi. A clever surgeon, skilled above all others. I watched him work on Rémi.'

'I cannot work on this child unless he stays still,' the surgeon had said in that precise voice of his. But nothing could keep the *dwt* from throwing himself about; in the end, holding him down by force was the only answer.

'See, Master Ieperman cut along the edge of the cleft, only as far as needed, to lift a flap of skin. The raw surface was underneath. Then he brought the edges together with – what was the word now?'

'Sutures?' murmured Brother Jerome.

'There you go. That's it. Sutures. Inside and outside the boy's mouth, close and neat. Then he took a long needle and passed it through both sides, keeping it well away from the sut – sutured wound.' Facts. Facts were easy to tell but… 'Truth to tell, turned my stomach, it did. If I hadn't promised the boy I'd stay close, I'd as soon been away from the sight. He was braver than I'd have been.'

Promised him? At sight of the strange room and the waiting table and the surgeon's instruments, the *dwt* had set up a strangled screaming and grabbed hold of Dai's arm with a grip that they could not release. So Dai had held the shuddering child and comforted him and then he had held him down by force until the surgeon had done his careful, brutal work.

'Then Master Ieperman wound a thread round the ends of the long needle and put some powder on it – red powder, I remember – then covered it with plaster of egg-white and oil of roses. Smell of roses always takes me back to that time.'

The child so thin and feeble, feeling the agony of it, his face a mess of stitching and raw flesh and his hands trying to pull at the needle so that Dai had still to hold him down, and the *dwt's* knees jerking up-down-up-down and those terrified, strangled noises coming from his throat until Master Ieperman quieted him with the poppy medicine that brings relief from pain. And that smell of roses in the air. Forever and ever it would be with him, and at that moment he had wondered whether he had done the child any good at all. Dai felt a hand touch his arm. He looked down. Rémi, bringing him back from the dark places: smiling, alive, re-made.

'When all was well-joined Master Ieperman removed the needle. And there was Rémi, good as new, smelling of roses.' Dai smiled at the boy but his face was serious. 'He suffered for it, did the boy, and bore it bravely.'

'It is indeed extraordinary craftsmanship,' said Jerome, 'but the good surgeon had the best of materials to work on.'

'This was true courage, Rémi.' Thomas was sombre. How could the boy have born such agony? And he so young? He was barely grown, even now.

'Has Master Ieperman written down his instructions for others to follow?' asked Brother Jerome.

'Now there's another remarkable thing about the man; he has written it down but not in Latin. It's in good, solid Flemish, for his own countrymen. Heinrijc Mertens told me Ieperman meant it for his son, who spoke no Latin, but it was the father's regret that the son did not follow in his footsteps. The son had no taste for war wounds and maimed and hacked limbs and bloody mess and carnage and who can blame him?'

'It must have been a disappointment for Master Ieperman.'

'Truth is now, the son's made a better merchant than ever he'd have been a surgeon. Sometimes it's better to choose your own life, isn't it now, Kazan, as the good grandmother said.'

'And what of the father?' asked Twm. 'What does he do now?'

'I expect he is dead. He was on the point of death when I left Ieper for Venezia. He was worn out, poor soul, with all he'd seen of death and suffering. Burnt out, you might say.' He was silent, remembering the gaunt face and hollow eyes of the old man. 'Heinrijc will miss his friend.' He ruffled Rémi's hair. 'And it's this one's second long journey. It's clever he is with numbers and counting. We found that out soon enough and Heinrijc put him to schooling. He was the best of his year. The Masters were astonished by him. Now he's here to keep me in order with the buying and selling – clean sheets to give to Master Mertens. Me, I've no head for numbers. I can count on my fingers and two thumbs but book-learning – well, not for me. Can't read nor write, neither, but Rémi now...'

'Burying your light under a barrel of bushels, Dafydd? You've a gift for languages.'

The brown skin reddened. 'I've picked up what I can. Self-preservation, it is. But Rémi here, I can't say he's worth his weight in gold. He's no more flesh on him than a Jenny Wren, has he now? Wouldn't weigh heavy enough. Or maybe it's his spirit that keeps him light.' He listened closely to the boy's garbled language. 'He says you must remember Kara Kemal's words: *there's always hope*. Even when it seems all hope has gone, there's always a thread.'

Brother Jerome said, 'Better to light one small candle than sit and curse the darkness. Isn't that so, my friends?'

'That is well said.' Sakoura spoke as quietly as ever. He was half-visible, his dark skin blending into the dark shadows of the room they sat in. 'Who knows what the future holds, except Allah himself

'– and your God,' he added with reverance. They caught the flash of white teeth. 'It should also be remembered that a good master makes all the difference.'

'That's well said, Sakoura. None better than Heinrijc Mertens.'

Sakoura glanced across at Rémi whose rapt gaze was still fixed on Dai.

'Do you say this because you have a good or a bad master, Sakoura?' asked Thomas.

'I have known both, sir, and so I know the difference.' He hesitated, dipped his head in deference. 'With your permission, masters, I would like to tell you my story.'

'Get yersen closer,' Blue said. 'Nobody can't hardly see you back there, with yer black skin an' all.'

The cameleteers and muleteers crowded closer as well; this was Sakoura who all knew well, promoted to guide and speaking out in front of these strangers, these infidels.

20

Sakoura's Story

'My country is the great kingdom of Mali far away across the burning lands of the desert. You will have heard of Mali, the fabled kingdom, the land of gold? Yes? Of course you have. All the world has heard tales of Mali and how all that is touched is turned to gold. But what is gold compared with salt? Salt is as good as gold – better! Salt keeps us alive. But that is another story.

'Not all have equal fortune in this great kingdom. My father was a court slave, and my mother, and I was born into slavery. My mother named me Sakoura after Mansa Sakoura who was also born a court slave and lived to become a great general and Mansa. "Mansa" means "King" in our country. When Mansa Sakoura was foully murdered, he was given a kingly burial, in spite of his slave origins.

'My master was a learned man. His home was in our great city of Timbuktu. It is a place of great learning with many schools. There is a great library that contains many scrolls, many books – the law, mathematics, astronomy, the written words of the holy men, all these. My master worked hard at his learning and he would let me help him, though it was forbidden for a slave to learn to read and write. I thought this was how my life would be, pecking at crumbs, but in one year my life changed.

'It happened in this way. You must know that I speak now of a time that is more than ten years distant. The Mansa then was Mansa Musa, a great ruler who made our country very wealthy. He was a devout Muslim and a man who insisted on the strictest honour. All who obey the laws are safe.

'Let me tell you how it was when I lived there. There was a white man, a traveller, who stole from the Mansa four thousand *mithquals* of gold. This is a great weight of gold. When Mansa Musa knew of it he was so angry with the white man he exiled him for four years to the country of the heathens. This is a country of cannibals and no one expected to see the white man again but he lived and at the end of his time of exile Mansa Musa sent him back to his own country. The heathen cannibals would not eat him, they said, because he was not ripe enough to eat. White flesh cannot be digested. Only black flesh and the choicest parts are the palms, and the breasts of females. This I know to be true. I have seen these cannibals visit the court and receive hospitality-gifts of female slaves. One was my own good friend who I hoped to take as my woman.

'On certain days the Mansa holds audience with his people. This is not within doors, as you do in your country, but in the open air. He sits on a platform under a tree and it is carpeted in silk and has beautiful cushions placed on it. Over it is a pavilion of beautiful silks. There are musicians and an escort of three hundred armed slaves. My father was one of these. The Mansa's wives sit with him, and his slave-girls, and all the women wear beautiful robes, and silver and gold headdresses. There are poets who wear the costumes of birds and who recite the noble deeds of our Mansas and young boy acrobats who turn wheels in the air. It is a sight of splendour such as you do not have in this country.

'The day of this audience Mansa Musa told his people that he must go on pilgrimage to Mecca. Many abased themselves before him and covered themselves in dust and ashes, as is the custom, and begged to be allowed to travel with him on his great journey.

'And so a great assembly accompanied him. When we travelled, our caravan stretched for many miles. Many miles, as if there were no beginning and no end. My master was one who begged to go, and

I was one of the slaves to accompany him. I shall not tell you of the journey, only to say it was very far and very hot. On the journey and when we arrived in the Holy City, Mansa Musa made so many gifts of gold no one there could believe such wealth existed. They say he gave so much gold it swamped your world as a tidal wave inundates the land.

'As for me, I saw wonderful things and it should have been a time of joy except that my master fell ill of a fever and died. I was given as a hospitality-gift to a white stranger who chained me and took me with him to Attaleia. Many of us were chained together, hands and feet and necks in cruel yokes, and marched many miles over the mountains and through the valleys to Attaleia. If one dropped dead, he was left to rot where he fell and his empty neck yoke reminded us of his fate and ours.

'When we arrived in Attaleia we were a sorry sight; all bones, no flesh except where it was festering in chains. We were jeered at in the market place. Worthless rubbish. Who would spend good money on such wrecks? One man did. A camel-dealer. He bought me and clothed me and fed me and gave me back my life. When he saw how skilful was the way I spoke with the beasts, and how they did my bidding, he made me his headman, and after four years he gave me my freedom. Two years ago he gave me his daughter to wife.

'I still work for my master in Attaleia but now I am his son-by-marriage and there is a little one who is the image of his beautiful mother. And so my mother was right to name me Sakoura, was she not? And as the good Kara Kemal says, there is always faith.'

Sakoura's tale ended. No one had spoken throughout and no one spoke now. This was beyond anything they had encountered, anything they had imagined.

At last Hatice asked, 'Is it true? About the female slaves? They are killed and eaten?'

'This is true, mistress. Not by my countrymen, you understand, but by the heathen cannibals whose country borders with ours.'

'That is a terrible fate.'

'Is it any worse than what you have suffered? While they are slaves, they are well cared for and food and clothes are lavished on them.'

'Why are the heathens allowed in your country?'

Sakoura smiled. 'They have precious gold mines and where there is gold there is always trade.'

'Is it true that a slave became a ruler? A king?' asked Asperto.

'Indeed it is true. All I have told you is true.'

'They say there are terrible creatures in your country,' Giles said. 'Creatures that crawl on four legs with their bellies close to the ground but they can swim and live under water as well. Their flesh is armoured and they have daggers for teeth and they eat men.'

Sakoura laughed aloud. 'You speak of the crocodiles that live in the rivers. Yes, they are dangerous flesh-eaters with huge jaws and dagger-sharp teeth but they carry the eggs of their young in their mouths and do not crush a single one.' He looked round the table at their astonished faces. 'We have other creatures that live in the rivers, the hippopotami. They have an enormous body bigger than any horse, and their feet are like the feet of an elephant. They come out of the water to pasture ashore and that is when we spear them with strong ropes passed through the spear end so that the animal can be brought down and killed. It is very good eating.'

'If you have such creatures,' said Giles, 'perhaps it is true that there are men whose heads are beneath their shoulders?'

'Or them as have a great foot that they shade theirselves with?'

'I have not heard of this,' Sakoura said gravely.

'Why do your poets wear the costumes of birds?' asked Kazan. She had been engrossed in the tale, sitting cross-legged and resting her chin on her hand.

'That I do not know, little one, only that it is a very old custom, a custom kept long before we became good Muslims, and so it continues, this reciting of the good deeds of our ancestors. It reminds our Musa that he must try to rule as they did.'

Later, when the fire was burning low, Mehmi picked up his *tanbur*. 'A song for the dead infant,' he said. 'A lullaby to rock him to sleep.' He trembled his hand over the strings, deep and low, a mournful sound. A second sound, a voice, deep and throaty: Hatice. Niko, drowsy and falling back amongst the cushions, recognised the lullaby, a Christian lullaby that sang the boy to sleep night after weary night.

Lullay lullay sleep baby sleep
Lullay lullay sleep baby sleep
With the dawn you will wake
Safe in the arms of your holy mother
Sleep baby sleep
Lullay lullay

'Our babes are asleep,' said Tom, and laughed, but his voice was choked with emotion. Niko and Kazan sprawled together amongst the cushions. 'Better get them to bed, Dafydd.'

Dai and Blue hoisted them up and carried them to mattresses laid ready for sleeping. Neither one stirred though Kazan mumbled something incomprehensible and Niko smiled in his sleep. Dai resisted the urge to smooth the bright hair from her face. Instead, he matter-of-factly tucked covers about them both.

Dreaming. Sleeping. Dreaming while she slept.

That was the long winter of my disgrace and the difficult birth of your mother. The woman who attended me thought we must surely die, mother and child, and for my father it would have been a merciful relief from shame. But we are strong, the women in our family – isn't that so, child? Çiçek's daughter? We are strong and so we survived, both of us. She was welcomed by no one but me. A girl-child. Perhaps she might have found some favour with my father had she been a boy, a grandson, but not a feeble, half-alive girl-child. A foolish man, my father.

❁ 255 ❁

She was beautiful, your mother. Always, to me, from the moment she was torn out of me, crumpled, red-blotched face, tiny as a doll, always she was beautiful to me. Later, it was clear she would be a rare beauty. She had your grandfather's brown eyes and my golden hair. Yes, it was golden in those days. Your grandfather admired my hair very much. Now – well – that's a different story. Brown eyes and golden hair, dimples where we had none, not Will nor I, and a smile to beguile the heart of everyone except my father. Even my dour cousin had a kind word for her. A happy, golden girl, like a flower, and that was my secret name for her, a Welsh name told me by Will. Fflur. You truly are Çiçek's daughter. How I laughed when I knew what those young boys of the tribe called you. Daughter of a flower. She must have cried. All babies cry. But this I do not remember. Only her smiles and dimples. So precious, as all children are precious. Her death was my death. Only you kept me alive, daughter of my daughter. Çiçek's child. My Fflur.

Back by the dying fire, Asperto and Hatice were determined.

'It is not good to stay here,' said Asperto. 'The winter is coming and it is harsh in this place. Besides, Hatice will grieve over the grave. Better for us to come with you to Attaleia and start a new life. There we can find work and make a home for the boy. At least,' a shrug, 'if I can find work, useless as I am.'

'Not useless,' Hatice said, briskly. 'I can work for all of us if you make a home for the boy. He needs a family. If you truly mean to set us free, master?'

'Truly indeed, madam.'

'Then we shall do very well together in Attaleia.'

Sakoura said, 'Perhaps I can help you. There is work for you in my father's house, and a place to live. My wife also needs a woman about her.'

'You are very kind.'

'That is settled, then.'

Later still, and the fire built up because the wind blowing down

❀ 256 ❀

from the mountains carried snow that was, they were told, more than a month early. All were abed apart from Brother Jerome and Giles, Thomas and Dai. They talked in quiet voices that would not disturb the sleepers. Brother Jerome was returning from a visit to a poor friary that tried its best to serve the poor that lived near it. He had taken the opportunity to travel in the footsteps of Paul of blessed memory. 'Such a man,' he said. 'Such a vision, to change a man and his destiny overnight.' He planned to travel down to the coast by way of Seydişeyhir, to stay in Alaiye at a small monastery in the Greek quarter, though it was not Franciscan. He had friends there who had shared part of his journey. 'Then home to Assisi in the spring.' His whole face smiled as he spoke the words. 'Nothing can compare with the holy places of Jerusalem but, for this tired old man, I confess I shall be content to be home.'

Dai flicked a glance at Tom, who nodded. 'That is our road too, Brother,' he said. 'You are welcome to travel with us – isn't it so, Dafydd?' He mimicked the Welshman's lilt.

Dai laughed. 'Well,' he drawled, 'one more now, and a holy man at that. It's very welcome you'd be, Brother, and who knows? You may be needed for nuptials as well as a funeral.'

'Nuptials? Ah, you mean your two angels – the girl with pale gold hair and the boy with golden curls. Yes.' He was smiling, remembering. 'Two innocents together, and the boy all the better for a gentle creature to protect, perhaps?'

'It's not much you miss now, is it, Brother?'

'The target was too large to miss. I would be very grateful for your company. I admit, as well, to being intrigued by you all and would like to know more of you. But before we go to our beds, come Giles, time now to hear what you have to tell me of your brother,' said Brother Jerome. He prodded gently. 'You promised me.'

Giles sighed and shuddered. 'Dai, Thomas, don't go. You should both hear this. I owe it to you both. Especially to you, Thomas.'

'You owe us nothing,' said Dai.

'Then I would like you to know. Brother Jerome has asked it of me. He was a friend to my brother, and a friend to me.' Giles the Marcher, the land of in-between; Giles the laconic, the uncommunicative, the unemotional whose language was measured and whose actions were deliberate but who was always ready for action. Only once had they seen him speak impulsively in praise of the 'bright fiery star', Kazan. Now, his voice was deadened and his face blank as he readied himself to tell his story.

21

Giles' story

'I have four brothers and two sisters, all of them older than me. The brother of whom we speak was nine years older than me. He was not the eldest and so when he begged my father to be allowed to go to London, to Greyfriars, to study theology, my father was content. We had not huge wealth. We were comfortable, that is all – as comfortable as one could be at that time, living as we did in the Marches and threatened by the armies of both Isabella and Edward. My father probably thought Simon, my brother, safe enough at Greyfriars and an uncle – my father's brother – lived nearby. My father was persuaded as well by my brother's account of St Francis' conversion from the sinful rich boy glorying in wild parties and knights and battle to a saintly life of care for the poor.

'I was ten years old when he went away and I missed him. He was a wonderful older brother. He always had time for me, and took my part when my other brothers tormented me. I was the baby of the family, you see, and they never let me forget it. I lived for the times he came home, and so did my mother, though she was careful to hide it from the rest of us.

'But at Greyfriars Simon met with William of Ockham, newly arrived from Oxford and full of philosophies and controversy, and Simon joined in the discussions and disputes. He was a great thinker himself – always had been – but once he had come to a decision he would not be moved. And neither would William of Ockham. Before two years had passed, Ockham was called to the Franciscan chapter meeting to explain himself. It was held in Bristol that year, I remember, not so far from our home and I had hopes that Simon would spend some time with us. But he didn't. His place, he said, was with William of Ockham because he faced a charge of teaching heresy.

'Father was furious. He said he was not wasting good money for his son to turn heretic. He demanded that Simon return home immediately but Simon refused. Worse, when William Ockham was called to Avignon to be investigated, Simon gave up his learning and went with him.

'At first, all seemed well. They stayed at the Franciscan convent and Simon assisted William Ockham in his work – his writings – and the investigation did not condemn his views as heretical. It even seemed as if the breach between my father and my brother might be healed but it was not to be.'

'I remember this time very well,' said Brother Jerome. 'It was when I first met with your brother, when I was visiting our brothers of Avignon. You and your father came that spring, did you not?'

'Yes.'

'I remember there was a quarrel.'

Giles sighed. 'A friend had brought my father news of the controversy raging in Avignon between the Franciscans and Pope John.'

'Ah yes, that vexed question of property.' Brother Jerome smiled at Dai and Thomas. 'There are those of our calling who believe that Jesus and the Apostles owned no property at all, and lived their lives according to this principle. I myself have no money, I own nothing. I live entirely on the generosity of others – such as yourselves, and your gift of tonight's meal. In return, I give what service I can. It was God's will that I arrived in time to perform the rites for the little one. But these others held an absolute belief in the rule of poverty. The Pope would not accept the doctrine and matters became…difficult.'

'My father thought Simon to be in danger and he was right, as it turned out. It came to a head when William of Ockham stated that in his considered view the Pope was himself a heretic. Simon said it took Ockham by surprise, but though he went over and over his findings, each time Ockham came to the same conclusion: Pope John was himself teaching heresy and should abdicate. My father and I visited Simon in spring; when you were visiting the friary, as you say, Brother Jerome. Simon was obdurate. He held by Ockham's views and swore he would stand by him and, if need be, die for the truth. Father raged at him but that had never had any effect on Simon and nor did it this time. I wept, I confess it, and begged him to return home with us. I reminded him of our mother, and her grief, but he said he owed his allegiance to a higher power. He would answer to none other than God himself and his Son, our crucified Christ. Jesus was in his heart and his eyes and his ears and his mouth and his hands. He was wearing the brown robes of the Franciscans but he said he would have otherwise stripped off his clothing, as St Francis did, returning everything to his earthly father and calling only God his father, as the saint had done.

'And I suppose you would have taken money from me as well, as your saint did from his father,' my father said, and his words were bitter.

'Indeed, it is my great regret that I did not do so. You have more than enough. I know a dozen families who have more need of money than you.'

'So we left him. Father said there was no more to be done and he washed his hands of him. He would no longer look on him as his son, and I should no longer look on him as my brother. I was sixteen years old and my brother twenty-five and in the prime of his life.'

'I remember this. Your brother was very cast down by the quarrel but he would not change his mind, though some of us tried to persuade him that he owed his earthly father obedience. I left soon after to return to Assisi. I only heard the news some months later.'

'The news? Ockham's escape?'

'Yes. We heard that Ockham and his friends had escaped from Avignon one night in May.'

'We heard this also and we thought at first that Simon had escaped with him. But this wasn't so. A message was smuggled to us: he had been arrested and was on trial for his life.'

For the first time Giles' voice faltered. He had spoken without emotion, recounting bare facts. Now, his voice was shaking as he continued. 'My father was as obdurate as his son; he would not be moved from his decision. He had renounced his son and he would renounce me if I went to him. He left me with no choice; I had to go to my brother. If I could not persuade him to recant at least I would be with him to the end. It was my poor mother who secretly gave me money and items of jewellery that she said would bring a fair price. I would need money.

'When I arrived in Avignon it was to find that Simon was cast into prison. I was allowed to see him – it was hoped I would change his mind; that he would recant. I knew my brother better than that. He was in a pitiable state. He was not allowed to sleep but was kept always awake, with the continual dripping of water from the ceiling of the prison on to his body. He was subjected to taunts and insults. He suffered. How he suffered. And all for his faith.

'When he was taken before the magistrate he said only, "I will die for truth." Truth! What truth? He said he would die for Christ but what Christ? What is this God that allows such terrible deeds?'

'Hush, my son. You must not say so. That is blasphemy.'

'You have your beliefs, Brother Jerome, let me have mine. He would not choose to recant but went to his death. "I will die for Christ," he said, but does Christ truly demand our suffering and our death? Didn't He suffer and die that we may live? Isn't this what the holy fathers preach, day after day?

'I watched the procession through the meadow and the town. I heard one woman cry out, "Martyr of Christ, you shall receive your crown!" But she was not the one going to the stake.

'And then – ah then – he was taken into the hut where he was to be burned and he was bound to the stake. He sang the *Te Deum*. His voice came to us standing outside. And then the fires were lit and smoke and flames engulfed all. He burned. He burned. And after, we saw his face was towards heaven and his mouth was open, still chanting praise to the Lord.

'After that, I did not return home. I could not bear to look my father in the face without blaming him though, in truth, there was nothing he could have done – except he should never have renounced his son. Never. For that I could not forgive him. They say my brother was a martyr who died a martyr's death and who is now a saint but I have no love for a God who would allow an innocent to die such a death. A terrible death. And Ockham escape to enjoy long life. This God shows no justice.'

'Your brother was indeed a good man, a martyr, God's warrior. His beliefs live on. Believe me, my son, though it is difficult to hear God's word in these times.'

'What did you do?' Dai asked quietly. He thought of the bereft boy Giles had been, too young to be adrift from his family.

'After? I went as a mercenary for some years. I'd always been proficient with sword and bow. It didn't matter to me whose army it was, nor who was in the right of it. As if anyone cared about right! It seems to me that all any of these great men care for is wealth and power and land.'

'There's truth enough in that,' Dai said, drily.

'After that, I met another good man.' Giles gestured towards the dark man sitting silently by him. 'Thomas Archer. He needed a bodyguard, a man-at-arms, a squire, a man-of-all-trade.' The look that flashed between them spoke of long friendship, of trust and loyalty. 'He chose me. And I have been his man since that time.'

'As Sakoura would say, lucky you were in finding a good master. And it has been my good fortune to have you both with me on this journey.' Dai was silent a long moment. 'I am very sorry for your brother. Very sorry. Such an end – and you no more than a boy yourself. No older than Rémi is now.'

'Or Kazan,' Tom added.

'True.' Dai sighed. 'God grant they suffer nothing like this; their lives have been hard enough. God knows.'

'And Pope John has been dead these past five years.' Brother Jerome gazed into the red embers of the fire. 'Only God and his Son know what purgatory he suffers. He has many souls on his conscience. I shall pray for yours, my son.'

Tom said, 'I wonder what our firebrand would say to your story?'

Giles laughed bitterly. 'No doubt share with us the good Nene's wisdom.'

'Perhaps so. I wonder…' Tom was silent again. All these years and he had known nothing of this, only that the young man Giles, who had served him so loyally, was strong and skilful and unwearying. Tom thought of the black moods that dogged him, and how Giles never reproached him, was never impatient. He stirred. 'Perhaps the good Nene would say that to deny Christ is to deny your brother's faith? And to deny your brother's faith is to deny him, and your love for him. "Each to his own," remember?'

'Is that what Kazan told us? I had forgotten.'

'"Find gladness in your living," That is what Kazan said. "It is in gladness that you worship and honour the life God gave you and for which you are intended."'

Brother Jerome raised his eyebrows. 'That was well said. And by the young boy with the golden eyes?'

'There was a wise woman living with his tribe; these are her words.'

Brother Jerome was thoughtful. 'And you remember these words by heart?'

Tom's dark face reddened. 'They are good words to remember, Brother.'

'Indeed they are. You should take comfort from them, Giles.'

Dai had been silent. Now he asked, 'Why did the rest escape that night and not your brother?'

'He was with a poor family who feared their youngest would die. They had asked Simon to pray for the boy.'

'So...he did not know of the escape?'

'He knew but he would not leave the child.'

'Did the child live?'

'Yes.'

'Your brother's choice, then, was to give his life for the little one. As you all chose today to risk your lives for those poor wretches of slaves,' Brother Jerome reminded them.

Giles smiled more easily. He exchanged glances with Tom. 'It's Dai here who would have risked all to rescue them.'

Dai grunted. 'Put you all at risk, you mean?' He sighed. 'It seems to me,' he said, slowly, 'that it's yourself you have to live with. Yourself and your God, if you like. Suppose your brother Simon had recanted? Had been saved from the fire? What then? What would his life have been then?'

'Hell,' Giles responded. 'The burning fires of Hell while still on this earth. He would have betrayed his Christ just as surely as that other Simon did.'

Silence settled on the group by the fire and with it the noises of the huddled shapes of the sleepers sounded louder: snores and mutters; a teeth-grinder; a whistler; one who always farted in his sleep. The girl and the woman lay separately in the furthest corner. Kazan was curled next to Niko, both half hidden in a huddle of quilts.

'Time we were abed ourselves,' Dai said.

22

May earth and sky be my witness,
May mighty God be my witness
Let my life be sacrificed for yours.
(*Book of Dede Korkut, c. 9ᵗʰC*)

The old men of the town were right: by morning, the storm had blown itself out. The lake was flat calm, unruffled, reflecting a sky that was clear, light blue. The air was icy and the mountain tops were white. 'Snow,' they said and shook their heads. It was too early in the year for snow; it was a bad omen.

Certainly, the morning brought unsettling news: messengers had risked all to travel through the savage night to bring word of a landslide in the valleys below Seydişeyhir that had blocked the road. A caravan had turned back, three of its cameleteers killed in the rush of falling earth that swept two camels away. The route was impassible and there was a risk of more slips.

'They are saying the fates are against us, Dafydd.'

'So I have heard. You do not believe such things but maybe, Twm, the fates are pushing us to the Eğridir route. What do you say to this?'

'I say you are playing with me, Dafydd the Welshman.'

'Am I now? Who knows what fate waits for us but Almighty God himself?'

Twm rolled his eyes. 'Almighty God and you – knows it means so many more miles, so much time lost.'

'Careful, Twm, heresy! And the good Brother all but within earshot.'

'The Venetian fleet will surely have sailed by the time we reach Attaleia.'

Dai sighed. 'Maybe so. There is nothing we can do about it, Twm. Our holy man would advise us to leave it all to the good Lord.'

'I thought you, like Giles, had ceased to believe in a good Lord.'

'There's always room for faith.' Dai smiled. 'After your words last night, I thought you had faith enough for all of us.'

Twm's face was stiff. 'Giles needed comfort. It seemed to me the old woman's words might give him that.' He stopped. Dai waited. 'Giles asked me if he had brought shame on himself last night. Shame on himself and, because he is my man, on me. He asked me that!'

Dai waited.

Shame on me, thought Thomas, when I am the one who carries shame with me always. His jaw was clenched.

'What did you tell him?'

'He had brought no shame. His honesty and love for his brother brought only honour.'

Dai nodded. 'That was well said now. Did it satisfy him?'

'I think so. He seemed easier in himself for the telling of his story. And what a story! How could any man hold faith in the face of such a death? I could not. Could you?'

'I think none of us know until we are tested.' Dai watched Twm's brooding face.

'Kazan says you know all our secrets.'

'Kazan is wrong. I know we all have secrets.' Dai's lips twisted. 'By the time we're safe bound for Venezia, maybe he'll have all our secrets out of us.'

Twm grunted. 'Maybe he will at that. Your Kazan has a strange influence on us all.'

'So it seems.'

'Is he to be trusted, do you think, Dafydd?'

'What do you think, Twm?'

'What do I think? Why, what I have said before; he is a strange one.' They were standing by the horses ready to mount and he concentrated on checking his saddle-bag. 'He tells me you know his secrets.'

'Does he now?'

'That is why I ask you; is he to be trusted?'

'Do you expect me to blab his secrets?'

'Of course not but are we all beguiled by pretty manners and a pretty face?'

'I'm sure of it. And a too-ready tongue.' He was laughing suddenly. 'Enough, Twm. A promise is a promise and the boy is well enough. As for time, *wel*, we must take it on trust, isn't it? Three days should see us in Attaleia.'

Blue came alongside them. 'Attaleia and a night wenching, Dai,' he smirked. He passed by them, discordant sounds floating back to them: "*One, two, three, four, five, six, seven – all Dai's men shall go to 'eaven.*"

'May God and His Son and Allah and His Prophet protect us all,' Twm murmured.

'And all the saints of my poverty-stricken little country?'

'All the saints of every country, if that's what Blue has in mind.'

'Will a plodding old friar do instead?' Brother Jerome was philosophical about the changed plans, standing pink-and-grey in the bright morning. 'Leave it in the hands of the good Lord,' he said simply. He didn't see Twm's sudden grin.

It was a slow journey following the causeway that led along the marshy lakeside. After the storm, the land was flooded; impossible to tell, in places, what was solid ground and what was deep and treacherous marsh. Feet and hooves made sucking noises in the mud and the stink of the marsh rose around them. 'Just like back hoöme,' said Blue with satisfaction. 'Squidgy, this is. We'll be spruttled all over wi' muck afore the day's done.' He was as sure-footed as Sakoura, and picked his way with the same instinct for safe ground. He was leading his horse, trusting to his own two feet, but he'd insisted Hatice ride. She'd done enough walking, he said, and Edgar agreed. His own horse could easily carry his weight and that of slender Agathi, if she would trust herself to him.

She would. She darted little glances from under lowered lids, let herself be helped into the saddle, sat demurely behind Edgar with her arms about his waist.

Kazan stared expressionless at the pair then leaned down and hoisted Niko into the saddle behind her, careful of his injured arm. She was still riding Yıldız. Dai had insisted. The mare was used to her now. Let gentle Asperto ride the sure-footed chestnut. She was keen to be in the open air again, true, but she would be safe with him, as he would be safe with her if there was any faintness or falling. Brother Jerome was content to sit astride a mule, his lean legs dangling low each side and his sandalled feet swinging. And so they journeyed through the cold day, through a watery world with the wide arc of pale sky above them. The road left the great lake behind for the firmer ground amongst the foothills of the mountains until it swung back towards another vast lake with the encircling, snow-topped mountains reflected in water that shimmered deepest blue to green and icy air nipped cheeks and noses. Sakoura pointed out the mountains: Barla Dağı and Karakuş Dağı to the west; Davras Dağı to the south and behind them now, in the east, Dedegöl Dağı and Kirişli Dağı. There, down on the lowest slopes, were the remains of the yürük summer camps. There were signs of hasty leaving. This was an early winter.

By sunset they had reached the solid, plain *han* on the banks of the lake, the last before Eğridir, thankful to tumble from mounts to bath to supper to sleep. The next day was their last in the high plain: after Eğridir they would start the long descent down the mountains through the Aksu gorge, down to Attaleia and, God willing, the Venetian fleet.

The road twisted and looped through the mountains alongside the lake; the wildness gave way to cultivated stretches of orchards high above the glittering water, the trees all but bare of leaves now, most ripped away in the storm. In spring, Sakoura said, it was beautiful to see the blossom-laden trees. In autumn, as well, when the fruit was ripe and the branches hung heavy. Dai nodded his agreement; he had been this way before in spring, summer and autumn. He knew when the road would twist around the last outcrop of rock and there would be the walls of Eğridir below them on the lakeside, and the high minaret of the new *cami* that was barely ten years old and the causeway that reached across the lake to two small islands.

He was riding behind Kazan and Niko when they breasted the road and urged the brown horse alongside them though the way was narrow enough. 'There.' He pointed. 'Not long now. Tired, are you?'

'Tired of riding.'

Dai laughed. He shifted in his saddle and eased his shoulders. 'It's been a long two days. We've done well. We'll be comfortable tonight. Eğridir has one of the biggest *hans* I know, as big as the Sultan *hans*.' He meant the *hans* commissioned by the Sultans themselves, not just wealthy individuals. Blue shouted to them. He had been whittling all day at a piece of wood he had begged from the carpenters at the last *han*. Now he held out his handiwork to the small boy clinging one-armed to Kazan's waist: a stick with triangles of cotton fixed like sails horizontally across the top.

'A windmill,' said Dai. 'I made those for my brothers.' Long ago, he thought, in another life, as if it had never been, yet the sight of the simple toy brought all rushing back.

Niko tugged at Kazan's sleeve to be let down. They watched as he stumbled, stiff with the day's journey, hugging his injured arm, then recovered his balance and ran across to Blue to take the toy, uncertain at first of its purpose. Blue's big hand engulfed the boy's and together they held the sails into the gentle wind that was ever-blowing from the mountains. The sails fluttered and moved very slightly. Blue tilted the windmill further into the breeze and the sails whirred round. Niko's mouth opened in surprise and pleasure and at once he seemed like any young boy, a child again delighting in a child's simple toy. Somewhere, there was another child, too young to have been taken from his parents, dead now and newly buried; others also, young brothers long since dead from painful starvation.

'Look Hatice!' they heard him cry and then the miracle: Hatice's gaunt face, watchful and suspicious, half-hidden under the indigo-blue bonnet, breaking into a smile. A cautious smile, it was true, more a grimace, but a smile for all that. Blue grinned back at her. 'Eh, but yer an eyeäble woman,' they heard him say in his broadest dialect, and saw the woman's perplexed expression.

'Let's hope she thinks he's saying something about Niko,' Dai murmured.

'What did he say?'

Dai repeated it in Venetian and watched Kazan's face crease into laughter. She answered in the same language, with more ease than at first. 'It would be very difficult if Blue and Asperto were rivals in love, would it not? Perhaps they will fight for her.'

Dai grinned again. He felt suddenly light-hearted. 'It would save you from that night out Blue's promised you once we get to Attaleia, isn't it now?'

'What do you mean?'

'Seems he's promised you all a night's wenching – said that it would do you and Edgar and Rémi good. Be an education for you.' He watched with interest as the clear red came up into her face. 'He said you blushed. Now, how did he put it? "Thowt as he'd go pop he were that red in the face." That was it.' He laughed out loud at her outraged expression.

'It seems to me,' she said loftily, 'that men have only one thing in

● 271 ●

mind and that is the thing they carry between their legs, and that is nothing much. I have seen it.'

Her words registered slowly. 'What?' She nodded with mischievous satisfaction at his shock.

'Yes. I have seen. Once only, when I was hiding behind the waterfall. In the morning the men brought the beasts down for water and one man, he stood naked under the waterfall. He had nothing but a shrivelled purse and a drooping white finger like this.' She crooked her little finger. 'And you men boast of this?'

'The cold water does that.'

'So when it is warm then their thing grows as big as the men say?'

'Kazan, this is not…you should not say this.'

She laughed at him. '*Your* face is red. I think perhaps *you* will go pop.'

'I begin to suspect, Kazan, that your grandmother did not beat you enough.'

'She never did.'

'A pity. Perhaps I should repair the omission.'

She poked out her tongue. 'You would not. Besides, you spoke of this night of wenching, not I. And who should I ask about these things if not you?'

'Better not ask at all.'

'But they tease me and joke amongst themselves and laugh because I do not understand. They talk about what they would do to a woman.'

He closed his eyes. Of course they would, and it was no fit talk before a maid. If – when – they knew her sex, there would be many faces red enough to pop.

'It is not for you to repeat. It is men's talk and vulgar talk at that. A beating, Kazan, that is what is needed for you.' She only laughed in answer.

The *han* was further from the town, just beyond the walls and close to the lake shore. It was the last *han* on the busy route from

Konya before the mountain road began. There had been a smaller *han* in the town itself but it had become a *medrese* since the town had grown with trade; this new *han* was enormous, as Dai said, with six corner towers and fourteen along the sides. The portal was grandly decorated with braids and stars and blossoms and arching arabesques and led into a huge courtyard bursting with activity.

The news of the landslide had spread quickly and new plans made to change routes. There were the nomad tribes as well, travelling down from the summer pastures. An early winter and the prospect of blocked routes; time to move down to the plains, now, before worse weather. The *han* was full, buzzing with caravans, nomads, travellers, merchants like themselves anxious to reach the coast and the Venetian and Genoan fleets. Late evening, they sat by the fires, and Hatice and Asperto told how they had been captured and taken as slaves. 'We think Vecdet planned to take us to Candia,' said Hatice. 'We are worth more there.'

'My sister is valuable.' Niko's voice was very quiet. 'She is a virgin. She is worth many *akçe*.'

'I think she is safe now,' said Dai, 'if you are happy that she becomes the wife of this Edgar of ours?' He spoke quietly so that the young couple could not hear though they were so deep in a world of their own making it was unlikely they heard anything except their own hearts beating.

Niko's face was ecstatic. 'He is just the man for her,' he said. 'He will know how to look after her.' He grimaced. 'I think I shall not tell him she is very hard work and that she cries too much. He might change his mind about her.'

Dai laughed at that and encouraged the boy to talk. He told the story of how he had rescued Kazan and hidden him behind the waterfall. His dark eyes, long-lashed, mischievous, flickered to Kazan, and met the inscrutable, golden gaze. 'Kazan the invincible,' he said. 'Kazan who escaped from the evil donkey Vecdet.' His eyes opened wide when they all laughed.

'*I am the hero Kazan whose boasting words fly faster than arrows.*'
sang Mehmi.

'Oh Kazan, bright star, hero, warrior!'

And then the tale of her riding and shooting had to be told again,
and Mehmi's song sung though Kazan protested and hung her head.
'Kazan the Great,' she thought. 'Who amongst these men would ever
believe that Kazan is a feeble girl who deceives them all?' *Shame it
is for a warrior to hide his name from another.* Her gaze met Dai's.
Soon she must tell them who she really was and risk their anger. She
owed it to the quiet brown man that some called dangerous and
Thomas would call worse.

The next day they started early along the route that would take
them down through the gorge to the coastal plain and Attaleia. This
was country where travellers had to beware of wolves and bears and
wild boars that lived in the forests of cedar and pine. Early as they
were, the *yürük* were before them, travelling before dawn. Perhaps
they would catch up later in the day. Kazan knew of them, knew their
password. All *yürük* had special passwords and secret signs so that
they could communicate with one another. At first the going was
level and easy, the bubbling river swollen by the heavy rain but giving
no sign as yet that it would become huge and fierce, its dark water
rolling with the rapids that gave it its name of Aksu: white water.

The day travelled on. Feeble sunlight gave way to threatening
clouds that massed over the mountains. The track dropped more
steeply, with limestone outcrops rearing up on one side and on the
other crashing down into the gorge, a dizzying depth below them
where the river rushed in the valley bottom. They passed waterfalls
cascading out over the chasm; they passed a bridge leaping in an arc
across the empty space between the sides of the gorge and Dai
wondered at the miraculous cleverness of those who had built it. An
ancient bridge, Sakoura had said, used from time out of mind. A
bridge built by the Old People. The same who had made the roads
they travelled.

A grey sky and the air silent. They travelled down the track, the gorge on their left, a stone's throw away; to their right, the high crags of the valley walls. Down and down, the camels and mules and their herders; men on horseback and the rushing river, the noise they made unnaturally loud in the silent air. When they stopped to rest Sakoura searched out Dai.

'This silence,' he said, 'it is wrong. No sound. No birds, no animals, nothing.'

'We're making enough noise – and there's the river.'

Sakoura made an impatient gesture with his hand. 'It is not that,' he said, 'but something more. I do not like it. We should go carefully.'

Uneasiness was affecting them all, animals and men alike. Again and again the horses shook their heads and had to be urged on; again and again the mules resisted, shying away from the muleteers; again and again they halted, listened: silence except for the distant roar of the water. Far below them they caught glimpses of the *yürük* flocks, a flash of white, a black goat, a plodding figure, a bright saddle cloth. Sometimes the jink, jink of harness. Above them another caravan was jingling and chinking its way down. Sometimes the voices of the men floated down to them, a quiet call, a whistle, the whine of dog, the bray of a donkey. The wall of rock gave way to overhanging crags, and forested ravines that travelled far back into the mountains. Sakoura paused by an outcrop of rock; there was a symbol crudely drawn on to its surface. 'Look, Master Dai. This is made by the *yürük*. It is one of the signs the boy told us of.'

'Kazan!' They waited until she had ridden down to them. 'What is this?'

She studied it, biting her lip in concentration. 'It tells the traveller to go carefully. There is danger.'

'What danger?'

'It does not say. At least…' She paused, frowning. 'I cannot read this. The earth,' she said. 'I think that is what it says. Perhaps it means the path?'

'Maybe.' Dai debated with himself: too late in the day to turn all around and go back to the *han* at Eğridir; there was no place here to camp safely, and silent the forest may be but in its silence were wild animals. But to travel on into unknown danger? 'What do you think, Twm?'

'The nomads have not turned back.'

Dai nodded. 'Go to the back of the caravan,' he told the girl. 'Tell Asperto and Hatice to go with you. Edgar and the girl as well, and the good Brother. You should be safer there if there is danger.' She nodded, obeyed without word, turned Yıldız, keeping Niko balanced behind her.

It was as she came up to Asperto that it happened. A strange sensation, as if she were falling, as if she were dizzy and faint though she knew she was not. Another tremor, hardly felt at first. 'Earthquake,' someone shouted.

'There's land sliding!'

'Look out!'

Danger it was, and from the earth, as the sign had said, but the danger was not at the front of their caravan. It was above her, where she and Asperto struggled to keep the mares from plunging and rearing in panic, and the earth tremor had shaken loose the rain-swollen earth. Rocks and earth cascaded past them, tumbling and crashing. High above a pine tree creaked and groaned, sliding upright, eerily, slowly slowly towards them before it fell roaring down the mountainside dragging a torrent of mud and scree in its wake. The pebbles hit them, hard and sharp. Rüzgar screamed and flung sideways. Asperto was thrown from her back and rolled away from under her clashing hooves to lie perilously close to the crumbling edge. Kazan felt Niko slip, his one-armed hold precarious. She twisted in the saddle and pulled him up and in front of her. 'Hold tight,' she said, and felt his good arm grasp her round the waist and the other arm – what it must have cost him – he shook free of the sling and twisted that hand around the material of her tunic. It left both her hands free: one to pull on the reins of the frantic animal; the other to reach out to Asperto. She had him by the wrist, desperately trying to pull him high enough to get a firm grip on the saddle and all the while pebbles and earth were skittering away from under him and there was the roar of waterfall booming in her ears. Out of the corner of her eye she saw Rüzgar scramble clear to safety, felt the splattering mud and earth, saw the fall of rock that must surely sweep them over the edge, down into the gorge where the swirling, white-foamed water waited for them unless Yıldız could carry them to safety.

'No good!' gasped Asperto. 'No good. Too much weight. Take care of the boy.'

From the head of the caravan Dai watched helplessly. 'We must keep moving, Dafydd,' Twm yelled. 'There's no room on this path to do anything else. Too narrow. Keep moving.' Keep the animals calm, he thought, keep them moving down the path and away from the falling mountain. He didn't dare look back but Dafydd now, Dafydd was staring back. Sakoura was of Twm's mind, urging the animals and their herders on to safer footing and surer ground. One of the mules slithered and slipped, scrabbling uselessly for a hold. It fell screaming over the edge, its heavy pack breaking loose. The animal bounced once and once again on outcrops of rock before falling into the water with a spurt of white foam. The packs burst open and the bright saddle cloths billowed into sails then collapsed into the water and were tumbled along and out of sight.

He had sent her into danger, Dai thought, she and the boy. All of them. Edgar and Agathi. Where were they? Brother Jerome? Asperto? There was the chestnut mare scrabbling over the rocks, safe on the path but riderless.

'There they are,' Giles pointed. Dai's first rush of relief lasted the seconds it took to see how Niko clung to Kazan while she was pulling on Yıldız's rein and leaning far over towards something unseen on the edge of the road. The edge! They were on the very edge of the road, and earth and rocks were rushing towards them. The world stopped, forever frozen in the moment of earth falling and the girl and the boy on the mare in the path of the murderous fall.

'Why don't they move?' breathed Twm.

'She's trying to hold Asperto as well.' They watched the desperate struggle. 'She can't hold him,' said Dai. The words were jerked out of him. 'He's too heavy for her. She's not strong enough and neither is the mare.'

'She?' Thomas stared at the brown man, the inscrutable. 'She?' he said again. He shifted his gaze back to the girl struggling to hold the boy, the horse, the desperate man.

'My God,' he heard Giles say. 'We must have been blind.'

Even as they watched, Asperto fell away over the edge of the gorge. Down and down. They watched his body fall, arms and legs flung out. Soundless. That spurt of white water and his body swept from view in the tumbling water.

She almost had him safe but he weighed heavy. Too heavy.

'Take care of the boy. Tell Hatice I'm sorry.'

His gaze on hers, his eyes sombre, beseeching under the thick black brows, and then the letting go. His falling. For as long as she lived she would remember his look and his falling. There must have been noise but she remembered no sound. No scream. No rush of rock. No breath of air. No roar of falling water. Only the endless falling…falling…a doll, no more than a rag doll, the doll a mother would give her child, arms and legs splayed, falling falling into the abyss, into the canyon, down into the river, white shock of hair in the white water swirling and splashing far far below.

Nothing after that. A scrabble of hooves and Blue beside her, pulling on the bridle, leading the mare to safety while around them the rocks fell silently, slowly, for ever and ever. Hatice taking Niko from her. Nothing. No sound. The brown man lifting her from the mare, from Yıldız the Star, on to his own brown horse and his arms wrapped around her. There was red splashed across his tunic sleeve. 'Like cherry juice,' she murmured. Hatice's shocked face. Asperto falling falling and herself falling after him falling falling…

Rousing to the roughness of coarse blankets and night quiet and the low muttering of a voice. *Is he safe? Is he safe?* Hearth flames. The dark goats' hair walls of a tent, familiar and safe. For a moment she wondered if she had dreamt all of the last weeks, if she was home and Nene was alive still. Then she remembered and, with remembering, realised it was her own voice that was muttering and mumbling, on and on. She made an effort to still it. She waited a moment until her memory came clearer.

'Asperto. Niko.' Her voice was hoarse, her throat painful. Her head ached and ached.

'Lie still, Kazan. Be at peace.'

'Niko?'

'He is at rest, there, beside you, fast asleep, as I've told you many times now. And so should you be. You must lie still.'

The hearth fire crackled and spat. By its light she saw Hatice sitting quietly by her. She tried to raise herself on one arm and felt the shocking stab of pain. She lay back. Beyond the tent there was a roaring, dull and persistent and never-ending. Vaguely she wondered if the earth was still falling.

'Where are we?'

'On the road to Attaleia. We have made camp here by the river with the *yürük*. It is safe here. Try to sleep, little one.'

The river. It was the river she could hear pounding down the gorge on its way to the sea.

'Asperto?'

A pause. 'He is at rest. And you must rest also.'

'I know he is not,' she whispered. 'I saw him fall. He was too heavy. He let go.' Her own voice, wavering, as if it did not belong to her. 'I could not hold him. He let go.'

Beside her, the little bundle that was Niko stirred restlessly.

'Hatice, tell me…'

'You must rest now. No questions.'

'But you must tell me…'

A hand on her head and a soft exclamation. Hatice moved away quietly towards the entrance of the tent. A travelling tent, she realised now, quick to erect and quick to take down but sound enough for all that. Kazan could see her there, a dark shape, and through the opening she caught a glimpse of fire leaping toward the starry sky, the bellying curve of the bright moon, another shape of a cloaked figure. A man. Whispering.

'Awake at last, Kazan?'

Dai. The Welshman. He would answer her questions. But before she could frame any, his quiet, flattened voice was telling her she shared the tent with others, with Niko sleeping next to her, with women who must rise early in the morning and who must sleep undisturbed. Now was not the time for questions. Yes, Asperto was dead, swept away by the river. She knew that already. Why ask what she already knew? Matter-of-fact, calm, final. She felt fingers touching her cheek, resting on her forehead, her shoulder, felt the tucking-in of blankets. 'Sleep now. Remembering is for later.'

She caught hold of the hand that touched her cheek, held on to it as if it would stop her falling after Asperto into the depths of the gorge.

Sleep. Forgetting. Falling. Forgetting.

Awake again in the dark night. The moment of dreaming herself at home with Nene then the remembering: shaken earth, tumbling rocks. The terrified boy and the falling man. Screaming at him to grab the bridle, her hand, anything, so she could pull them all clear of the falling mountain. The moment of knowing that three were too heavy for Yıldız the Star. They were full in the path of the falling rock, the sliding tree. Asperto's face, that ugly-kind face, calm, resigned, letting go of her hand, his fingers slipping away from hers though she tried to hold tight, hold tight…his falling falling falling into the water far below. Remembering Nene's face, that time she slipped and was slithering away over the edge of the gorge. Grabbing at her arm and her fingers closing round bone as frail as a lark's wing. It was easy to haul the old woman back to safety. Not Asperto. She made herself remember the women who must sleep and the need for quiet and pressed her lips tight close.

Hatice's voice. 'Come, drink this.' A wooden bowl held to her lips. 'Careful – it is a little hot and perhaps a little bitter but it is good for you.' Hatice whose man was dead.

She must have slept again. When she woke the dark night had shifted. Not long till dawn. A fire still burned in the hearth. A small shape curled next to her and a larger one by her side.

'Hatice?' she murmured.

'She is asleep.'

'Dai?'

'Yes.'

'Am I ill?'

'Injured.' Silence. A cool hand on her head. 'We were worried a while about fever but that is gone now. Falling rock it was. On the side of your head, your shoulder.'

'I remember Blue coming. He took Yıldız. And Niko. Hatice was there.'

'Yes.'

'But Asperto...'

'He fell into the gorge.'

'He wanted to save us.'

'And so he did, Kazan.' Silence. The river rushing and a night bird's mournful cry. 'He knew he had not long to live.'

Silence.

'What of Niko?'

'Sleeping. See. He refused to leave you so we kept him by you. He was very frightened but he is not harmed. His broken arm is well enough, thanks be to God. And thanks be to Hatice.'

'Where are we?'

'The *yürük* came back to help us. Some stayed to make camp with us, lower down the mountain. Safer like that. We are on the road to Attaleia.'

Silence. He remembered how he held her in his arms, felt the slightness of her, how fragile she was beneath that show of whistling courage, his fear that she would die before he got her to safety, before he could see how hurt she was. *A Duw caniatáu, mai hi'n dal i fyw. A Duw caniatáu.* God willing, she is still alive. God willing. And there had been nothing else he could do but subdue his rising panic and pray under his breath in the Welsh words that came most readily to his tongue, and trek steadily down the mountain path to a level stretch by the tumbling river where it was safe to make camp. He blessed the nomad tribe who had come to their help without fuss, without caring who these travellers might be. All that mattered was their need.

She was unconscious, and had a dark bruise where the rock had hit her head. A wound in her arm poured blood. Like cherry juice, as she had said before she fell unconscious. She needed to breathe. Nothing but truth would help her now, and he'd already blabbed out her secret to Twm and Giles in those desperate moments when he had feared she would tumble with Asperto into the gorge. 'Take these bandings off her,' he told Hatice. 'She needs your help.'

Hatice had taken one look. 'Of course, master. I shall see to this.'

And she had. She was a remarkable woman, he thought, plain-faced and abrupt but true and honest. She said nothing when she knew Kazan was a girl but tended her as if all was the same to her. Her man was dead, and with his death the plans they had made together, but she laid that aside. She helped Dai clean the wound to the girl's shoulder, put cool bandages round the girl's head, sat by the unconscious girl for long hours while the *yürük* women gave up the warmest part of their tent and kept to the shadows.

'Sleep again and all shall be well…'

'…and all shall be well.' In her head Kazan tried to repeat the mantra but was asleep before she had finished.

Grey dawn seeping into the tent. Stealthy movement. The women working carefully around her, packing ready for travelling. Niko sprawled on his back now, his breath whistling quietly, his long lashes fluttering. He was on the verge of waking, the noises penetrating his sleep. Her head ached but her mind was clear. She cautiously pushed herself upright, rolled off the sleeping mat and up on to her feet. The tent swirled round her but steadied. She was dressed only in her under-tunic and *şalvar*. The constricting cotton binding cloth was gone. She breathed in and out. This was much easier. She had forgotten how easy it was to breathe when there was nothing binding her. Then she remembered: the women around her, Hatice tending to her. They knew, then. Dimly, she remembered Hatice sitting there; every time she roused from her sleep, Hatice was there. And the Welshman.

Shame it is for a warrior to hide his name from another.

She put a hand up to her head, felt bandages and pulled them aside and fingered the swollen lump they had concealed. Blood stained bandages around her arm. She considered them then decided to leave all as it was. She was struggling into her outer tunic when there was a quiet movement at the entrance to the tent and Hatice was there.

'You are dressed,' she said, unnecessarily.

'Yes. Time to move on, isn't it?'

Hatice sucked in her breath. 'Master Dai must have the saying of that.'

She stood upright, swaying. Hatice clicked her teeth. 'You are not well enough, child.'

Kazan steadied herself, said, 'Tell him I am well and ready to travel.'

'Master Dai must have the saying of that,' the woman said again. Her face was haggard with grief and fatigue but she touched the blood stained bandages with gentle fingers and her voice was gentle. 'He will say as I say: you must rest.'

It was the gentleness that stripped away the false calm. Kazan caught her hand and held it pressed to her cheek and then to her mouth. 'I'm sorry, Hatice. So sorry,' she mumbled into it. 'So sorry. I couldn't save him.' She buried her head in the woman's shoulder. The gentle stroking went on.

'He did not want you to. It was his time to die. Do not distress yourself, my daughter; you did all that you could. Lie quietly now.' Hatice pressed the girl back down on to the blankets. 'I must tell Master Dai you are awake and restless.' She left the tent as quietly as she had entered it.

Kazan lay still for a moment, covering her eyes with her good arm. Then she struggled up again and concentrated on pulling the tunic over her head, easing the bandaged arm into the sleeve. Niko stirred, yawned, remembered. His lower lip quivered. 'Kazan? I thought you were dead too!' He clung to her, weeping. She hugged him to her with her good arm. He was wan-faced this morning, heavy-eyed with shock and loss.

'You can see I am not.' She hugged him again. 'Come, we are both of us alive and well enough to travel. Help me with this sleeve.'

She was casting round in search of her soft-skinned boots when Dai came in, frowning, demanding to know what she was about. She didn't answer until she had pulled the tunic straight and fastened her cloak – the new cloak given by Dai – about her shoulders, awkwardly because she had only the use of one hand. A one-handed band of travellers, she thought suddenly; herself, Niko, Thomas only just recovered.

'I am making myself ready to travel,' she told him. She looked at his face, dark-closed, stern. 'Do not be difficult, Welshman,' she said. 'Amir's son travelled and he was badly wounded. I shall do well enough. My head aches, it is true, and this arm is stiff but I have no fever. Besides, these people are making ready to leave.'

'We do not have to. They will leave us the tent. We can return it when we reach Attaleia. They have said so.'

Stubborn, she thought, so stubborn. But so was she. She tilted her head. 'I think they must all know I am not Kazan the boy.' He nodded. 'I do not care to hide in here. I would like to see the men.' *Shame it is for a warrior to hide his name from another.*

'Yes *wel.*' He rubbed the side of his nose in a way that was becoming familiar. Always it boded something unexpected. 'Seems how they want to see you now, isn't it? Had to stop them coming in, didn't I? Wanted to know if you were dead yet.'

She stared at him. 'They are not angry with me?' she asked. 'Kazan the Great Pretender?'

'That they are not. Think you're no end the hero, they do. Kazan the Great...' His eyes held hers, level, impassive. 'I'm the one who's angry. I'm wondering how many more times you're going to risk your life.'

The colour drained from her face. 'Why do you not say what you really mean? Why do you not say I risk the lives of those around me?'

'I say your life and I mean your life.' He spread his hands in an empty, futile gesture that was unlike Dafydd the Welshman. 'You've pulled away the bandaging around your head,' he scolded. 'And what of the bandages round your arm? The sleeve of this tunic is too tight around them. I need to see the bruising on your head and the wound to your arm and then it is I who shall decide if we travel today.'

She caught it then, that note in his voice so like Nene's when the girl had worried her with some foolishness: tumbles when she was a little child unsteady on her feet but rushing from place to place; when she had out-dared the young boys and was thrown from a horse; when she had fallen from a crag on a steep climb searching for birds' eggs; once when weed had trapped her in a river and she had been hauled out half-drowned...Nene scolded. She did not cosset or fuss. She scolded. And wiped away the blood and repaired the damage so that the girl could risk her life another time.

'I am sorry I worried you,' she said quietly, 'but you know I could not leave him. You would not have left him, Welshman.'

He sighed. 'No,' he agreed.

'See – I think this bump is not so serious. My head,' she told him, 'is no softer for being a girl's.' Beside her, she heard Niko's shaky laugh.

He bent over her, inspecting the bruise. He prodded with careful fingers, felt her flinch. 'I'm sorry.' Sorry for more than the pain of his touch.

He helped her remove the tunic, as matter-of-fact as ever; it was she who was suddenly consumed by confusion at his closeness, conscious of the small swellings her breasts made under the cloth. He had insisted that he would tend her, with Hatice's help. He unwound the bandaging around her arm.

No man had ever been so close to her but this was Dafydd and his hands were gentle and careful. It was Dafydd and yet she was conscious of him as she had not been before, not even when she lay next to him at night in the *han*. It made her awkward. She turned her head away so that he could not see her face.

Again the careful scrutiny. 'No infection,' he said. 'It needs to be bathed and fresh salve applied. The skin is torn but there are no deep cuts. As you say, you are well enough to travel and I would be the happier if you saw the physician at the next *han*. There's one condition.' He regarded her gravely.

'And what is that?'

'You travel with Blue today, as Rashid did.'

'If the blue man agrees. I am no longer Kazan.'

'I doubt he'll hold that against you,' Dai said with a wry smile. '*Da fy merch i, cariad.*' She looked at him suspiciously. 'Good girl,' he said. He didn't translate *cariad*. He helped her back into the tunic. 'But not your injured arm,' he said. He looked over his shoulder and called out. 'You can come in now, Blue, see for yourself she's alive and already it's making trouble she is.'

Hazy daylight was blocked as the big man bent to enter and then straighten up. His head almost reached the top of the small travelling yurt. He stood there, crumpling his hood in his huge hands, saying nothing. Nothing. She was unforgiven.

'I am sorry I lied to you all, Blue,' Kazan said sadly. 'It seemed the best thing to do at first but then I did not know how to stop. Forgive me.'

He didn't answer. And then she heard his gaspy breath and a tearing sob deep in his throat.

'Is he crying, Kazan?' Niko whispered.

'Eh boy, A'm blubbing like a bairn. A'm an aimless owd gowk.' He wiped his nose along his brawny forearm. 'A couldn't bear to see yer scathed, lass. Such a great ding i' the eäd as you took an' yer arm all bloodied an' me abless to 'elp yer.' He snorted back tears and snot. 'Yer hair all lunkered wi' blood and yer were that limmuck when Dai took you away A thowt as yer would dwine away.'

His language was broader than ever so that she could scarcely understand a word; but words were not needed. She went straight into his arms and they closed round her in a bear hug.

'Not so tight, Blue!' Dai warned.

'Yer nowt but a little lass,' Blue crooned but he heeded the warning and his hold slackened. 'Eh but yer a rare 'un.'

'You forgive me then?'

'Fergive yer? What's to fergive? We're be'int yer back an' edge, all on us. Eh, sichna shock it were. Sichna shock. The lad an' all. If yer hadn't had wit enough to cling on, she'd nivver 'ave kept yer safe.' He reached out to Niko, kept the two of them safe-close in his arms.

'But not Asperto. I could not keep him safe.'

'His choice, little lass. Would 'ave been my choice an' all.'

'She's well enough to travel, Blue, if you'll carry her.'

'A'll tent the little lass, Dai.'

'Best let the rest see she's well enough.' He was at his most non-committal.

Dai was right; she was a hero. No matter that she had failed to save Asperto. 'He was truly the hero,' she said sadly. 'Asperto. Is it not so, Niko?'

'Asperto,' he agreed, 'and Yıldız the star. She was very brave. But you also Kazan. Do I still call you Kazan now you are a girl?'

They were outside in the fresh morning, breathing in the scent of crushed mint and pine. There was mist on the river mingling with fine spray from the rushing water. Droplets clung to leaves and grass. Their faces were beaded with moisture and the animals' coats gleamed slickly. Pale pink sky edged over the rim of the gorge; pale rays of sunlight struck the opposite rim but below in the gorge they were in shadow and, further back, the way they had come, clouds darkened the sky, stopping abruptly as if a quill had drawn a straight line under them. Her arm was re-bound and supported in a triangle of cotton tied securely behind her neck. The empty sleeve of her tunic was pinned out of the way. An empty sleeve like Rehan, she remembered, though Rehan had lost his arm. It seemed a very long time ago that she had rested in Maria's house that first morning of her journey. Not even a full moon since she had left the camp.

'A can't not call yer Fustilugs no more,' Blue said. He shook his head in wonderment. 'You 'aven't 'alf taken it to do, ent yer lass, and yer done it all by yersen.'

'Not by myself, blue man. I have had all of you to help me.'

'Well,' said Giles, 'I can't think of him – her – as anything other than Kazan.'

'Truly Kazan the Great,' said Edgar. Everything to him was full of wonder: the beautiful pale girl at his side, the boy-girl who had tried so valiantly to save the slave Asperto; the nomad tribe who had risked so much to save them. All was cause for wonder and gratitude even while he mourned the dead man.

'"Shame it is for a warrior to hide his name from another,"' Kazan said. 'Your song was truer than you thought, Mehmi.'

'Indeed it was," he agreed, and sang softly, '*I am the hero Kazan who rides a bright star...* I think my father knew you for who you were, Kazan.' His father, who had sent the girl and the bride-gift of his favourite mare to his friend Dafydd-the-Welshman. A flash of understanding and he knew now why the Welshman had kept the girl so securely with him, was so protective of her. But she...she was unaware of his love, of that Mehmi was sure, and as sure that Dai had made no sign of it, for honour's sake. 'You did well, Kazan,' he said. 'And if you were other than you said – well – we all have our secrets.'

She nodded and should have been content but she was not. She had cheated them with her secrets and now this. If she had been truly a man, young and strong, then she could have saved Asperto. She was desolate.

Dai turned to Niko, saw he had the same shadowed eyes and wan face. 'You ride with Hatice today and both of you must eat before we travel. You must not go hungry, now, with all the way we have to go. Come.'

Eat? Any mouthful would stick in her throat. From Niko's face, she guessed he felt the same. Figs and white goat cheese and flat bread. Dai watched them nibble without appetite and choke and nibble again. He sighed and sat down beside them. 'You know you must eat if you are to travel.' His voice was kind. He saw her shudder, and the boy's face twist in grief. He was not needed to make ready for the journey; his companions would see to all that was necessary. Better to sit with these two sad souls and try what he could to heal their hurt. 'Listen,' he said. 'This death of Asperto, *piti gythgam* it is – a terrible pity – but it was his gift to you, wasn't it now?'

'It was a gift I did not want.'

'Even so, it was his gift to you and you must accept it as such.' He looked down at the ground, his hands resting on his knees, fingers interlocked. 'It is a gift that weighs heavy, I know, but it is a gift.' He stopped, searching for the words to explain how he knew this to be true. *I couldn't save him.* He knew the despair, the hopelessness. Who better than he? *I couldn't save them.* And living because of the gift of another's life. That was a heavy burden. 'Listen,' he said again. The words came awkwardly. 'My *taid* – my grandfather – was a good man. You have heard me say this before.'

Kazan raised her head. 'The grandfather who rescued mine from drowning?'

'Yes.' He stopped, head still bent, hands knotted together. 'You should know also that he gave his life to save mine.' He glanced briefly at Niko. 'I was about your age.' He stopped again. He had never told a single soul of that time.

'What happened?'

He sighed. They needed to know, and now, while they were secure in this *yürük* camp high above the teeming river.

23

Dai's Story

'This was in the time of the Great Hunger. It started one summer."

The summer before simmering discontent became open revolt, he remembered.

'The early summer of 1315,' he said. 'It rained. Rained heavy, it did, all summer long. Still falling in autumn, it was. There were rivers where there should have been roads. Fields were flooded and crops and pasture were under water. The seed beds were sodden. Grain stood rotting under water. The harvest was late, where there was any harvest. No hay – meadows too wet to cut hay, see – so the animals were starving. Land too wet to plough in autumn or the next spring and there was still the rain.

Blue halted by them. He'd been tethering the animals but he stopped now. Time enough before they started down the mountain track. 'Knew yer'd remember that time, Dai. Evil, it were. Foälk were warned of it, like. That comet that was in the sky that year. Remember that? Blood red. A warning, that was. Famine and death. And the moon blotted out in the autumn. Another warning.'

Giles abandoned his checking of the baggage. 'There were earthquakes in France those years. My brother told me so.'

'See? Warnings, innit? Wickedness about. Should have knoöwn it weren't going to be just that one summer. No. That summer were only the first of it. Nowt to yetten fer year on year. Round our way, fish traäps were wrecked and dykes were washed awaäy. Couldn't not make much salt, neither – too cold and wet and not fuel enough.

Any theer was, prices were aboon what poor foälks could paäy. Besides, no food to keep with salt, was theer? Sheep diseased. Beasts dying with murain. God saäve us, they stank to heaven. Stuff cooming out of their eyes and mouths and noses. Remember that, Dai? Made yer boäk to see 'em.

'I remember.'

'The shits, poor beästs, brusting out of 'em. Or they'd be trying to when theer weren't not nowt left for them to shit. Died where they stood.'

'The winters were long and cold. Bitter cold. No let up then. One year the land was frozen from the Feast of St Andrew right till Easter.'

He stopped again. Around him, the men were packing the animals ready to move on. Sakoura was keeping a careful eye. No need to him to be watchful. Giles came up to them, glanced down at the two wide-eyed young ones. He had heard Dai's words. 'End of November is St Andrew's Feast.'

Twm as well; Dai hadn't expected an audience.

'The northern seas were frozen over as well – Heinrijc Mertens said so, didn't he Dafydd?' Twm dropped down beside them. 'The Great Famine, that's what you're talking about? So no ships sailed. Snow everywhere. It wouldn't melt. Heinrijc Mertens remembers that well. Remember he said so? The north lands were as bad as our poor country. And France. And all this when it seemed the whole world was at war. England against Scotland; England against itself, when the second Edward and his she-wolf Queen fought for right to rule.' His face closed up, remembering, remembering. 'Why this talk about a hellish time?'

'Dai's story about his grandfather.'

Twm raised an eyebrow. Dai telling a tale? First time for everything, but even so...

'It started the year Llewelyn Bren and the Welsh fought against the harshness of English rule,' said Dai. 'My father was with him.

Heinrijc Mertens told me the Flanders' fight against the French was as desperate.'

Armies must be fed, he thought. King Louis of France diverted grain to his own troops, away from Flanders and England. In wars and famine, the rich got richer and armies had their bellies filled, especially armies on the winning side. It was the little people who suffered. How they suffered.

'My father was a fighting man. He said the roads were quagmires and even the court horses were trapped up to their knees. Getting supplies was almost impossible.' Twm snorted impatiently, picking up Dai's thought, had he but known. 'But there were supplies to be had. Famine in the land and still armies were fed,' he said, bitterness colouring his words.

'It was the grain that was the worst,' said Dai. 'Where there was any to be had, it was mildewed and mouldy.'

'That bread,' said Giles. 'My brother told of bakers who sold bread filled with disgusting things – dregs of wine, pig droppings, stuff like that. He said in Paris they were punished – set on wheels with their hands raised and holding their own tainted loaves.'

'Eating it drove men mad. *Taid* – grandfather – made us swear never to eat rotten grain. He said how it would kill us. We promised, of course, but he knew sharp hunger and how a child's empty belly forgets promises made. He showed us what happened to those poor souls desperate enough to stuff their craws with rotten grain.' He was silent, remembering. Kazan edged closer to him, put her hand over his – tight-knotted on his knees.

'What happened to them?' she asked.

'Hm?' He had all but forgotten where he was, remembering, seeing, telling what he saw and remembered. 'What happened to them? Great swollen blisters over all their bodies. Screaming out they were, on fire, they were burning. Retching and heaving, poor devils, and writhing with the agony of it all. Some ran mad in the streets. And their fingers and toes and hands and feet...' He stopped,

❀ 293 ❀

his gaze fixed still on his hands, seeing again the horror of it all. 'They dropped off their bodies. Just dropped off. And then they died. A terrible death.' He breathed in deeply. 'After I'd seen that, I took care never to eat mouldy grain. But it was hard when there was nothing to eat but grass in the meadows and we grazed that like cattle. Or plants, bark, leather, cloth, dirt, grubs...' He was silent again. 'My youngest brother couldn't help himself. Only a *dwt*, see, and crying with hunger.'

'Did he die that death?'

'Yes.'

'A heärd as theer were some as et their own bairns.'

Blue, unheard, settling in beside them.

'I heard it said there were those who ate dead men's flesh. They said prisoners – Scots men – were killed and eaten by their captors. In Ulster, that was, in the Carrickfergus siege.'

'Maybe so, Giles.' There was some rumour of that years later, when Dai was in Hereford. Could be true. Desperate times and who could say what men would do when they were starving. 'I know there were some who gnawed raw-dead bodies of cattle, just like dogs.' Dai sighed. 'We try to look out for each other in my country. Villagers and monks alike. Our abbey of Cymer has always been a poor House but the monks did their best, even though they were pressed to give money to the King's bridge building plans. Stone bridges every ten miles. A worthy cause, at any other time, but not in times of famine.'

'But do you not have stone bridges in your country?'

Dai laughed at her innocent question. 'Not like here, Kazan, where you have bridges built by the old people, and bridges of great beauty and strength built by the last rulers, and good roads, and pure water carried in pipes and over bridges for mile after mile.'

'But how do you travel in your country without good roads and bridges?'

'With difficulty. There are the old ways, if you know of them, and the monks have built roads and that helps but often the ways are potholed or flooded or thick with mud.' Not like here, he thought, not for the first time, with staging posts with free accommodation and baths and food and physicians and those who care for animals and everything a traveller needs for comfort. And yet, he thought, I long to see my own wretched, poverty-stricken little country. The Mawddach and Cadair Idris and all the lands in between the mountains and the rolling sea.'

'But your *taid*. How did he give you his life?'

'What food there was, *Taid* gave me his share. Said he wasn't hungry. He made me eat and, God forgive me, I was hungry enough to believe what he said. Said it would give me strength to forage for the rest – my brothers and sisters and mother and others of our family. So I did.' Too young to be a provider for so many, to know such hopelessness when there was nothing – nothing – nothing to be found, and only pebbles to suck to fool empty stomachs into believing there was food to fill them. *Taro'r gwaelod*, the pit of despair. *Have courage, have faith, boy bach. Cwyd dy galon. There is always a way.* Ask, and it shall be given? Knock, and it shall be opened? Where were the five loaves and two fishes to fill this groaning, suffering multitude?

'What did you find to eat, Welshman?'

'Pigeons. Doves. Starlings. Anything I could get. The doves I hated. They came to eat what corn we had and it was forbidden by law to kill them. They were the Lord's fowls. But I killed them anyway. And we ate them. Sometimes a pig. Not affected by the times, pigs weren't, and even a scrawny pig can feed many people for a good long time. Not ours to kill so we had to steal them away and that was a risky business. One time even a lap dog of the Mistress, plump enough though her people were not. She wept more for the loss of her pet than she ever did for the poor families who died. But there was never enough. Seabirds' eggs. Needed a head for heights to get those. Rich men's pantries.' A quick smile. 'Needed a head for danger to get pickings from those.' He sighed. 'I watched my family die, slowly. Not a quick death, starvation. *Taid* was the first. Didn't eat, see. Wasted away to skin and bone.' *Dim ond croen ac asgwyrn*. Just skin and bones. The night when he knew death would come.

I've had my life, boy bach. It's been a good life but your turn now. Stay alive. Keep them alive. Do what you must but stay alive. No one should go hungry. Remember that, bachgen.

'Where was your father?'

'Away fighting with Llewelyn Bren. Then news came they were defeated and my father was one of the dead. My mother was with child but the child died inside her, and she died with it.' I couldn't keep them alive, he thought. I couldn't keep my promise to *Taid*. He remembered his mother's sweet, high voice singing an old song: *Peis Dinogat*. The song a mother sings to her son about the father, the fallen hero.

Pan elei dy dad ty e helya,
llath ar ei ysgwyd llory en y law,
ef gelwi gwn gogyhwc,
Giff, Gaff, dhaly, dhaly, dhwc, dhwc...

When your father used to go to hunt
with his shaft on his shoulder and his club in his hand,
he would call his speedy dogs,
Giff, Gaff, catch, catch, fetch, fetch...

'What happened then?'

Dai shrugged. 'I was caught red-handed robbing the manor kitchens. No Heinrijc Mertens to bail me out – this was years before I met him. One of the men-at-arms owed *Taid* a past favour. So many owed *Taid* favours.'

'Like my grandfather?'

'Like your grandfather. This man, this Gascon guard, turned a blind eye so I could escape. They were cutting off the hands of those they caught stealing, see.'

'Where did you go?'

'There's wild land in the Welsh mountains. Wet land, see, that strangers can't travel. Deserters and desperate men had made a home for themselves in one of the valleys of Mawddwy. *Ar herw*. The outlawed.' He looked up at their shocked faces. 'I joined them. I was a *dwt* but desperate enough after all, wasn't I now? And there you go... Like I say, my grandfather, your Asperto, they made a gift of their lives. That's not a gift you can refuse but one you must honour by living as well as you can.'

'A choice made, like my brother's,' said Giles. 'Death and eternal salvation.''

'There you go.' Dai nodded to where streaks of sunlight were lighting up the gorge. 'Day's getting on. Best make tracks if we're to reach the *han* before night. One good thing, better weather down the mountain.'

She didn't move immediately. 'What happened to your family?'

'Most died. There was a younger brother and sister – twins, they were – the White Brothers took them and promised to care for them.' Once he was gone there was no going back. He had to trust to the White Brothers to take care of the two who were left alive.

And he was going back to find out, Tom thought. You and your conscience, Dafydd. No wonder you feel you have to save the world and those who suffer in it. No wonder your mind is so often on your stomach, and the stomachs of those you take into your care. *No one should go hungry.* For the first time he felt a great pity for the quiet brown man who owed his life to a starving, dying man. *A promise is a promise.* 'You knew Kazan to be a girl?' Tom had demanded angrily. He felt cheated, somehow; not trustworthy after all. 'How long have you known? Since she arrived? You recognised her from the camp but you said nothing?' *A promise is a promise.* How many promises? To his grandfather, to Heinrijc Mertens, to Rémi, to this boy-girl. How many others? The man was shackled by promises, by duty and honour that he would never shirk. Tom had no anger or resentment left in him.

Brother Jerome had quietly joined them to listen. 'You save souls, Brother,' Dai said. 'Me now, I reckon if you save a body God will help the soul find its own salvation. No body, no soul, is there now?'

'Perhaps that is so.' The little gray-and-pink man didn't commit himself.

24

Mi lemman me haues bihot of louue trewe
(My beloved has vowed true love to me)
(Anon, c. 1300)

The road tilted steeply down the mountain pass. They were away now from the edge of the tumbling river and the chaos of rocks and ravines, following the old road that had been repaired and strengthened more than once in its long life-time. One stretch was edged with big stones and had been surfaced with the lids of tombs so long ago that they were already grooved and furrowed with the coming and going of so many travellers. The roadside was littered with columns and shards of gleaming carved marble and ruined walls and mile after mile of tombs, the old Greek style, like stone coffins.

'We are travelling through the land of the dead,' Kazan thought. 'I wonder if they feel our passing.' She remembered Nene's grave, and how she had made them lift the weighty slab of carved stone with its beaded edge and the cross enclosed in its circle; lift it and cover her grandmother's grave. She remembered the carved angel with the broken wing. *The grave is but a veil before the gathering in Paradise.* Where were they now, Nene and Asperto and the nameless child? All these unknowns whose last resting places they passed by and trampled underfoot?

She must have drifted into sleep for a while. She was comfortable enough pillowed against Blue's bulk. They had fallen into the way of talking in a mixture of languages: Blue's halting Turkish; scraps of Fenland words that Kazan had memorised; shared struggles with Italian. More than anything, the bonding that came with Edgar's sharing of his story, and Blue's own story, and now the great debt she owed him for rescuing her from the edge of the ravine. 'You are truly a good pillow,' she told him.

He was shy of her at first, careful for her comfort. 'Are yer right, lass?' he asked, again and again. Later, falling into the rhythm of the horses, he was as caring in his actions, less careful in his speech. 'Yer going good, little'un? Eh but yer were shockened.'

Yes, she thought, but not only because of the earth falling and Asperto's death. The reverberations of Dai's story were with her still. Such a burden, such sadness, almost more than any man could bear. Her own loss was slight, compared with this. And perhaps, at journey's end, there would be the grandfather who had been saved by Dai's *taid*. But for Hatice, with Asperto's death, what did the future hold for her? And for Niko? The mare Yıldız was just ahead of them, strong and steady for Hatice, who rode her, with Niko cradled protectively in her arms, the only one left to her now.

'What will happen to Hatice and Niko?'

'A doän't know. She's had a bad do and now her man's deäd and gone. She wanted to make a hoäme for the boy but a woman aloäne? Well now, that's hard.'

'Sakoura says she is certain of work in his household. And you could help her, blue man.'

'Me? How could A help her? Besides, doän't seem doäble, Asperto just gone an' all.'

'But he would want you to take care of them. It is true what Dai said, though very hard to bear; he gave his life to save Niko. To save me, who he didn't know.'

'She'd nivver not have me.'

She remembered the windmill and Niko's delight and the woman's rare smile. 'I think she would. You are a good man.'

'Oh aye? A drunk and a nowter and only tuts and coins to find my waäy?'

'You are not a drunk unless you wish it so and you are no nowter.' She spoke the word as he did but though it sounded quaint coming from her mouth, neither of them smiled. 'You have money enough and can easily earn more. You are skilled in many crafts. You have travelled far enough, I think, and would like a family to love and be loved by them in return. You would be a good husband and father.'

'She's an eyeäble woman, right enough – and the bairn's a brave soul. Bairn! He's not had no chance to be a bairn, poor mite.' She felt Blue's chest heave against her in a deep sigh. 'A thowt as A'd want nowt no more but to goä hoäme. Back to the Fens. Been thinking on it all the time we've been travelling. Hoäme to the Fens. Yer get weary for yer own plaäce. Different from here, Fustilugs.' The old name came easily. 'Not so grand as here but it's hoäme. It's where A coome from. A miss the big skies and the smell of the rain where it comes down straight from heaven. Pyewipes calling in the marshes and the crows scrawking ahind the plough and partridge wings skirring and owd heronsews crying and a snide wind biting through the reeds. Howry and dark some days but other times yer'd see the sun coome straight up ovver the land in the morning and straight down at night with the whole sky lit up and blaäzing. A wanted nowt so much but to see it agaan. but now… A wonder if A should stay, see her and the boy right.'

'You would do this for them, blue man?'

'A reckon so.' He pulled a face. 'But it doän't mean she'd have me, do it, little blue brother.'

'Listen to me, blue man. I am sure she would be glad if you stayed with her.' She twisted in his hold and pulled gently on the straggly, blue-streaked beard. 'But you must make yourself handsome for her first. You must,' she searched her memory, 'remble yersen. And no more drunkenness. And ask Dai to speak for you. He is the chief man of this tribe of ours and so it is fitting that you go to him first.'

''Appen yer right, Fustilugs. A moänt have no more aäle.' He sighed and scratched thoughtfully at his beard. 'Short, yer reckon, or wench-faäced like yersen?'

'Short.'

'Yer made a good boy.'

'I liked being a boy,' she said, wistfully. 'I liked being with you all just as myself. Do you truly forgive me, blue man?'

'Nowt to fergive,' he said simply. 'Plenty to be graäteful fer. Eh, all that talk of wenching and you red-faäced and ready to pop...'

And they laughed together, at ease with each other and nothing more to say about her deception.

They reached the *han* that was a day's journey from Attaleia and where they were warmly welcomed and anxiously questioned about the road and their journey.

She was glad to rest. Her head ached and her shoulder felt wrenched out of its socket, despite Blue's care, but when Dai came stern-faced asking how she did she put up her chin and swore she was well enough after the long day's ride. 'Blue wishes to speak with you,' she hurried on, ignoring Dai's disbelieving frown. 'It is of great importance.'

'Oh aye? Been meddling again, Kazan?' His smile was fleeting and warm. 'Let's get you to the *han* physician and after that Blue can tell me whatever he has on his mind.'

Whatever they spoke of, Kazan never knew, nor what words passed between Dai and Hatice, but Blue whistled his way to the *hamam* and returned spruce and clean in fresh clothes and stroking a neatly trimmed beard, still wiry but with a surprising amount of red in it now the blue-black woad was cut away. He beamed at Tom's raised eyebrow and Giles' knowing grin and ruffled Edgar's curls and hoisted Niko on to his broad shoulders so that the boy shrieked with alarm and excitement. Rémi grinned with pleasure. Rémi who had not been at all surprised by her change from boy to girl. Rémi who would not speak of what he knew, even if he could. Blue winked at Kazan but she saw under the swagger the bashfulness of a modest man who couldn't believe his good fortune. She reached up and hugged him and kissed his new-smooth cheek and stroked his fine tunic. 'Well rembled, blue man,' she said. 'Now we must call you by your true name.'

'Eh, that yer mun't.'

'But you are Oswald,' she said simply.

He wriggled his big shoulders and rubbed his nose. 'It's like this,' he said. 'If yer were to call me Oswald it puts me in mind of my fayther's wife and thoöse troublous times and now them time's is paäst. A'm a different man now from what A was then. A like to be called Blue. Like the woad magic, see? And the indigo.'

'I see,' she said, gravely.

'A marriage broker, Dafydd? That's unexpected of you. First Edgar and Agathi, now the Fen man and the slave woman.' Tom pulled a face at Dai's frown. 'Blue and Hatice,' he amended. Dai nodded.

'Not what I had in mind when we set out, Twm, that's for sure.'

'He's set on it then? I thought he was after going back to his own country.' The Fen lands, he thought, waste and desolate, but the pull of a homeland – any homeland – was strong.

'Seems he'll give it up for the woman and the boy.'

Tom laughed. 'Don't tell me it's a love match?'

'Why not?'

'Well, she's not comely nor of child-bearing years. He'll harness himself to a barren woman and a boy neither his own nor the woman's son.'

'Yes.'

'Ah, again your disapproval, Dafydd.' Tom sighed. 'You are right,' he said, 'and I am very much in the wrong. If they can make a family out of these – shards – then that can only be good. I wish them well.'

'That is more worthy of you, Thomas Archer.'

Tom said nothing. There was nothing to be said. Much to be thought but nothing to be said.

The girl, too, thought a long time about Hatice and Blue; about Edgar and Agathi. The two younger ones, children when they were thrust into lives neither wanted – both held captive, she thought, though one was in slavery, the other within the confines of a monastery – living with hopelessness and dread. Now they were free, and with freedom came the longing to spread their wings and fly like the birds in springtime but they had met and, with meeting, loved. *Our eyes met. Just once, fleetingly, but it was enough.* Nene's words came back to her. That was how it had been with Edgar and Agathi, both.

Hatice and Blue? That was a different story, a different love. There was affection and gratitude and an end to loneliness and who was to say that was a lesser love? She thought ruefully about herself and her foolish dreams and the dark handsome man with grey eyes smoky like hearth fires, and lashes thick and long like a girl's. Beautiful eyes. But they had not met hers, not even fleetingly. Once, she could hardly bear to look at his beauty and now…now, it was different. When it had become different, she did not know, could not tell, could not remember. She only knew he was not Bamsi Beyrek of the Grey Horse. How could he be? Bamsi Beyrek was a dream-hero from the old stories, and she knew now heroes came in many forms. Like Edgar and Blue and Rémi; like Sakoura and Niko. Thomas Archer was a flesh-and-blood man. Just that: a good man, a brave man, a sad man with much on his mind and she wondered what his story might be. He was so very handsome, and his eyes were very beautiful, but they did not tear her heart and soul. What was it Nene had said? *What was it, then, that tore my heart and soul? Who can tell, girl? When you feel this, then you will feel love and you will give your heart and soul and life for your beloved.* But she had not and would not. She did not feel love like that for Thomas Archer, as he had no such love for her.

Her thoughts drifted to the quiet brown man who had seemed dull and plain though his voice was soft as the threads of silk carpets, and had music wefted through it, though it could be cold and sharp as winter winds if he was displeased. Kara Kemal had sent Yıldız to him as a bride-gift. She wondered who the bride was. She wondered if their eyes had met, just for a fleeting moment that was long enough to feel the love that would give heart and soul and life for the beloved. Would there ever be such a moment for her? There was a great weight where her heart should be; the cold stone of envy for those who loved and who knew themselves loved in return. Such envy was a sin. There should be only gladness. She sank the stone deep inside her.

It was unexpectedly a festive evening, this last before they reached Attaleia. There was a remembering of Asperto, and the child too young to know his name and who should never have been taken into slavery; but a well-wishing also for the couples whose futures were bound together, and Mehmi's soft songs of love, and other songs that brought colour to the women's cheeks and laughter to the men.

'I shall take Agathi to England,' Edgar said, a bold Edgar who was sure now of what was owed him. 'First to my older brother and then to my father to ask his blessing. And if he does not give me his blessing – well, then…' He shrugged, held his hands out in acceptance of what might be. 'I shall have done my duty,' he said. 'But Brother Jerome, Agathi and I wish to make our betrothal promises to each other before you. If we are to travel together, it should be as man and wife.'

'A handfasting?'

'Yes, a handfasting.'

'What about you, Blue? Are you for wedding and bedding?' Giles grinned.

'Nivver drempt as A should ever be.' His look lingered on Hatice: a woman who had never been beautiful; a woman with a strong face and thick black brows and angular jaw. He was learning to read that face better than he could speak her tongue, knew that she was content to take him as husband and the boy as her own. 'We'er not of the saäme faäith but it seems to me thaäy saäy the saäme, when all's said an' done.'

'Love and tolerance,' Tom said.

'Always room for faith,' murmured Mehmi.

'If that's what yer like to caäll it. It's enough fer us.'

'Satisfied?' Dai asked Kazan later that evening.

'Very.' She smiled. 'All shall be well…'

'"…and all shall be well." Maybe so, Kazan, maybe so. You'll miss the boy when we leave Attaleia?'

'Of course, but it is better for him to have a true family. They will take good care of him, those two, and find joy in each other. All of them have a great need of being loved.'

'And you, Kazan?'

'I was loved. Nene loved me and cared for me as did our tribe who took us in and made us one of them. To be unloved all your life,' she shivered, 'that is truly a great evil.' She looked up at him, serious and intent. 'You as well were much loved. Your *taid* loved you and, I think, your family. You suffered much, Welshman, but it seems to me it was all for love. The blue man has never been loved. Edgar had his brothers but he has forgotten how it is to be loved. Hatice and Agathi, it is the same for them. This is very good.'

'Wise Kazan,' he said. 'As wise as your grandmother. There – is that better?' He was adjusting the bandage. She sighed with relief.

'Much better.' She waited a moment. 'Will you truly travel with me to the cold lands and help me to find my grandfather?'

'I have said so.' He tilted her head towards the light, examined the dark bruising. 'Good. The swelling's gone. No redness but bruising worthy of a warrior. Still painful?'

'A little. Not so bad.'

He smoothed a soothing salve on to the bruised temple. 'We must travel first by ship to Venezia then overland to Ieper.'

'Mm. That feels good. Health to your hands. To Heinrijc Mertens?'

'That's it. All that travelling will take a while, now, and then there's the winter to come. Best wait out the winter with the old man, if you're willing to wait, and I owe him some time. Travel on to England in the spring.' She nodded. He thought of Edgar's words: *if we are to travel together, it should be as man and wife.* He asked suddenly, 'How do you like your women's quarters?'

'All rooms are prisons,' she said. 'I am *yürük*, after all.' She chuckled. 'It seems to me that women sleep more quietly than men. Men are noisy and smelly in their sleep with their snoring and farting and belching and mumbling.'

'You alarm me. Am I like this?'

'No. You lie very quiet, very still.' But like an animal, ready to wake at the least threat of danger, she thought.

'I'm relieved to hear it.' He was smiling. 'You curl up like a small cat.'

'Do I snore?'

'Not even a purr. Now away with you to bed, Kazan.'

'*Nos da*, Welshman. See? I do know some of your strange language.'

'So you do. *Nos da, cariad.*'

Quarters full of the noisiness and smelliness of sleeping men, but she had grown used to it. It was the women's quarters and company that seemed strange to her. Strange, as well, to have emptiness where there used to be the brown man stretched out close to her in his quiet, tense sleep.

25

*We have journeyed safely across
these mountains and woods,
these vineyards in our sight, glory to the Lord.*
(*Yunus Emre, 14ᵗʰC*)

The air grew warmer as they wound through the low steep hills and
into the coastal plain. Now they were back into late summer. The
ground was dusty. No rain here though clouds were building up over
the sea and the far mountains beyond the sweeping bay. A thin haze
divided one range from another. This was a world away from the
high plateau and bitter wind and sleet over the lakes and mountains
that lay behind them. Here were the gardens and gazebos of the Bey
who governed Attaleia and its lands; here were the cherished,
cultivated fields and fruit orchards, vineyards and olive groves; hives
for the honey bees; wheat and pulses and sugar crops; all being
harvested now. Precious water was channelled miles and all was
carefully guarded all along the road to Attaleia. Men and women
laboured in the afternoon sunshine, incurious about the travellers.
So many came and went along these roads.

'A paradise,' Giles said irritably, 'if it were not for these evil
mosquitoes. Surely they are cousins of Edgar's demons?' He slapped
again and again at his neck, his hand, his cheek.

Tom grinned. 'Nothing should go hungry,' he pronounced then
swore quietly and slapped at his own neck.

Long before they arrived they could see the dust haze of other caravans, and the long smudged line that was the walls and towers. Attaleia was at last within reach, and the long caravan journey almost done. For the muleteers and cameleteers, they would be home at day's end. Their employers had a sea journey yet to make to the strange sea-city of Venezia. Would the Venetian fleet still be at anchor in the harbour?

Excitement and apprehension rippled through the caravan. One of the check-points was ahead, a round-domed stone building where all caravans must register on their way into and out of the city. As always, there was a queue and a tedious wait for slow-moving officials. Their own caravan was greeted with interest and more anxious questions about the mountain road to Eğridir. Was it true that there had been an earth tremor, a landslide, as the nomads who travelled through earlier claimed? That was calamity indeed! They were lucky to escape with so little damage though a life had been lost…and no caravan had followed after them?

All the same, caravans passed them heading towards the mountains, a last journey to the north before winter closed the routes. Earth tremors, landslides? Such things happened, especially on that route. No doubt the road was already cleared. Business was business and the roads must be kept open.

The Venetian fleet? Ah, they were lucky, though the captains wouldn't say so. They had met with the *meltem* on their way here, and that had delayed them. They had been forced to take shelter for many days until the wind had blown itself out. And now it was the turn of the *lodos;* it had blown too strong for safe sea journeys and had kept the fleet at anchor for days now.

'Fettle oursens and yer can still maäke it,' Blue said with satisfaction.

'"No matter how strong the wood, the sea can smash the ship,"' Mehmi crooned. He grinned at them. 'That's Yunus Emre's words, not mine. He visited my father once and played and sang for us.' His dark eyes glittered with excitement. Yunus Emre, never to be forgotten, the poet who travelled from village to village and whose songs were in Turkish, not Persian, so that ordinary men could better understand. Yunus Emre, who had fired him with the desire to play and sing and travel, and now Attaleia! He had never dreamed he would ever see this place. His heart yearned to tell his father of his travels; to thank him again and again for setting him free to fly. *Let the white horse come. Let it go free. Let go of your grief. Set that free as well.* Tonight, he would play and sing in honour of his father. And who knew? Perhaps there would be a rich merchant or landowner who would hear him and take him into his household? Perhaps – his mind reeled at the thought – he would be paid well, and the money he would take back to his father so that there would be no more hunger. His father could eat *aruzza* every night to the end of his life if he wished.

The last stretch of straight, flat road to Attaleia, hooves and feet clopping over one of the slender, high-pointed bridges of this country; past more orchards and gardens kept and farmed despite the wars, and then they were in the shadow of the city walls, huge high walls, long and thick with battlemented tower after tower after tower. City walls that had been there for many years, more years than anyone could remember. But wasn't that the way of it in this country? Build and rebuild. Use the cut stone of the older buildings to replenish and renew; waste nothing, especially well-cut, well-shaped stone. The lower stones of the city wall were so enormous they'd been shaped by giants, some said, but Dai knew it was ancient building. He had seen the like before. Impressive these might be but he'd a Welshman's dislike of cities. Once inside these walls and lodged in the Merchants' Quarter, come the curfew, the gates would be locked for the night; they'd be prisoners till morning, though that was never said. Jews, Greeks, Turks, merchants, the Bey and his court, together and separate in their own high-walled, heavy-gated sections of the city. The rest of the Muslims lived in the main city.

'What do you think, then?' he asked the girl beside him. She had insisted on freeing her arm from the sling, insisted on riding Yıldız, and he had been equally insistent that she keep close by him, surprised by her docile agreement. More tired and uncomfortable than she'd say, most like. He saw her shiver.

'It is big. Very big.' Her voice was doubtful. 'Do you have such cities in your country?'

'Not as big as this but something like,' he said, 'built by the *Sais* for the *Sais*. We *Cymry* aren't ones for cities and towns. Never have been.'

She thought about this. 'You are like the *yürük*?'

'Not exactly. Maybe. In some ways.'

'Same but different,' she said. 'That was what my grandfather used to say. Nene told me so.'

'Same but different.' He mouthed the words carefully. 'Seems to me that's what we all are, isn't it? Same but different. Us lot here, the whole heaving mass in there,' he nodded at the city gate, 'all the whole wud world. Same but different.'

She smiled. 'Different but the same is better.'

'Well now, wise woman, let's be in so you can see for yourself the "different".'

It was their turn to pass through the heavy, fortified gateway and into the busy street.

Always after the solitude and emptiness of the high plateau he was confused by the noise and busyness of these streets thronged with the clatter of heavy-wheeled carts pulled by straining oxen; over-laden mules and donkeys and men, too, brisk about someone's business, wearing padded hats on which were balanced copper trays piled with merchandise or mysterious bundles wrapped in cloth and bound with rope. Others were street-sellers with trays laden with sweet pastries dripping in sugar syrup and honey and nuts; the just-ripened apricots with the sweet almond kernel for which Attaleia was famous and which would be dried and exported to Egypt; nuts and fruit and figs and olives and flat bread smeared with soft white cheese and sprinkled with pungent herbs...no one in this place would ever go hungry, he thought. This was a man's world; there were few women to be seen on the streets and those few were accompanied by older women or the men and servants of the family. Obediently, they walked with lowered gaze and guarded modesty, their bodies and ornaments covered from common sight. It was, as well, the custom for the rich and well-to-do to veil themselves. He glanced at Kazan's proud, tilted head, her uncovered hair once again gleaming gold-copper-bronze; it was a custom unknown to the women of the *yürük*. He thought of the equally regulated western world and wondered how she would take to being female again after her boyish freedom. Stormy times ahead, he forecast.

Everywhere, it seemed, was the clamour of buying and selling. And everything was there to be bought and sold, at a price, and all was taxed, imports and exports. Caravans unloaded at one end of the city and transport to the harbour had to be paid for – fixed rates, no haggling here. As well, thought Dai; haggling took time and time was against them.

Time to unload and pay off the muleteers and cameleteers. Time to store their goods in a warehouse that included transportation to the harbour in its charge. Time to find a berth. Time to find lodgings for the night. Time, if any, to scour the markets for the spun gold and silver that were specialities of Attaleia. The fleet was sailing next day. All being well, and if the weather signs were right, out of the bay before noon. How to cram in all they had to do before then? Lucky for him he knew the place, knew the best places, best men to deal with. All the same...Dai pulled at his lower lip. 'Best like this,' he said. 'Twm; you, Giles, Blue to the harbour. Find us a ship. How many of us?' He counted them off in his head. 'Seven. No – eight – Brother Jerome comes with us. Baggage space? Horses? Can you sort all that? Good man.'

Kazan tugged at his arm. 'The chestnut,' she said. 'Rüzgâr. She is not mine. I took her without permission.'

'Can't turn her lose, Kazan, and you won't be wanting to sell her.'

Sakoura was standing patiently waiting ready to dismiss his men. 'I can return the mare,' he said. 'Next summer, the next time we pass that way. Amir will know where to find the *Karakeçili*.'

Amir! Dai had forgotten so easily the promise made to take news to Amir's wife patiently waiting in Alaiya.

'Do not disturb yourself, master,' Sakoura said in his quiet, measured way. 'It is an easy matter for me to visit his wife, take news of Amir and Raschid.'

'You are a marvel, Sakoura.' Everything quietly and efficiently dealt with, including the homing of Blue and Hatice and Niko. A message had been sent to his home telling his wife to expect three extra in her household. A marvel of a wife, Dai thought. 'Rémi, come with me. We need to sort what dues we owe the *muhtesib*.' The official in charge of the market, for its law and order, for the customs charges levied on exports, would expect them. 'Edgar, take the women and find lodgings for the night. Brother Jerome, best go with them.'

'No need, master. We have one of the courtyard houses. There is plenty of room for all of you, and we shall be honoured if you would share your supper with us. I am sure I shall be given permission to take you as my guests. The Merchants' Quarter is already full to bursting. If I can be spared for a little while, I shall go myself to make the arrangements. Niko and Kazan, these little ones with wounded wings, are tired, I think, though they pretend otherwise.' Sakoura hesitated. 'You will all be our guests but please to remember, master, the hour of the curfew.'

And non-believers must not be in the streets of the Turkish quarter, Dai thought, though Sakoura was too polite to say so. 'That is very generous of you, Sakoura.' Dai felt a great wave of relief sweep over him. He rubbed his forehead, tried to get his thoughts in order.

It was not long before sunset and the curfew and locked gates. 'Rémi, we're for the *bedestan*.' It was where all business was done.

Tom, Giles and Blue made their way through the narrow crowded streets to the broad flight of stone steps that led down and down to the quayside and the harbour. They could see the Venetian fleet below, with its huge round boats and smaller cogs safely at anchor under the protecting battlemented walls and towers. Single-masted, two-masted alike, all with sails furled, whether lateen or square rigged, all jiggling and jostling together with the smaller ships of the Egyptians and Cretans and Turks, all penned in together for a whole seven days by the gusting *lodos*. Small fishing boats with old-fashioned trailing steering oars were lashed side by side, and despondent fishermen sat whittling pegs and mending nets, waiting for the break in the weather. Tomorrow, they told each other, tomorrow the sea would be calm and the harbour would empty. Already, the round ships were loading, their hulls open and ramps down. Later, when all was loaded, the openings would be sealed and caulked against the seawater. Water butts, fodder for the animals, came first. Provisions for sailors and passengers would come later. The horses would be cajoled on board in the morning to be stabled in threes in canvas slings for the voyage. Room enough on these huge ships for more than sixty horses; better stabling than the smaller boats. Double decks and better stabling for humans but all berths were full, they were told.

'Been here days,' a sailor grumbled. 'Bad enough on the journey coming here but now waiting and waiting for that cursed wind to fall. Every day for days and days without number. Time enough for every pirate ship between here and Venezia to ready themselves for raiding.' He chewed on his lip, as camels did, then sucked in weather-beaten cheeks and spat noisily into the harbour water. He rubbed his nose. 'How many did you say? How much baggage? How many animals?' More chewing and hawking and nose rubbing followed by a quick-voiced exchange with a fellow seaman. 'There's the one you want. He's the one who can help you.'

He pointed to an important-seeming burly man striding along the quayside towards them, holding his cloak tight about him. He was impatient when they stopped him, glaring at the three men. He was tired and anxious; how much longer would they be held here? The fleet should have been well underway on its journey home. Every day of delay meant a loss of profit and worsening weather. And now, when all seemed settled, a new group of merchants demanding berths and baggage space and stabling as if there was never-ending space.

But it seemed there was room after all for a small number such as they were, if they could get their goods on board before evening. The horses? 'Bring them early in the morning. One of the cogs – you'll have to make do,' they were warned. 'Tight squeeze in the berths.' Short, sharp speech. No time to waste on words.

'As long as we sail, and arrive safe, we'll be content.' Tom was shaking hands on the deal when he heard his name shouted across the harbour. 'Thomas! Thomas d'Eyncourt! It is you!' A lithe young man leaped down the last of the harbour steps, clearing three together. He pushed his way past the quayside crowd towards them. 'I can't believe my eyes! You vanish in the night, not a whisper of your whereabouts, and now all these years later I find you in this heathen place.'

Giles was conscious of the way his friend had frozen into stillness. His dark face was tense, his speech clipped as if he spoke through clenched teeth.

'Roger de Comfrey.'

'What are you doing here of all places, Thomas? Hey?'

'Like all the rest here, securing a berth for tomorrow's sailing.'

'Merchant man are you now, then? Pilgrim?'

'Neither exactly.'

'Neither exactly?' the young man echoed. 'You're as spare of speech as ever, Thomas. Tell me, what *exactly*? Heaven and all the saints, man, you appear out of the air as suddenly as you vanished into it. Can you blame me for curiosity?'

Thomas eyed the smiling, carefree face in front of him, a face not seen for many years and little changed. A thatch of brown hair, clear grey eyes, a wide mouth that curled into smiles and dimples that any woman would envy. The years had been good to Roger de Comfrey, that was clear. A beloved only son, he'd been a squire in the same manor as Thomas in the old days. 'Not quite sure what I do. Man-of-all work, that's me. And you? What are you doing here?'

Roger de Comfrey pulled a comical face. 'Shackled to my mother. She's always been one for iffing and butting and last minute journeys, more so since my father died five winters ago. First of all it was a journey to Winifred's shrine at Shrewsbury. That was not so far from our home but three years ago nothing would do but to make a pilgrimage to the shrine of Our Lady at Walsingham, and she insisted I travel with her. Now she's taken it into her head to go to Jerusalem. A long pilgrimage! At her age! As for waiting for the spring when most folk would set off on such a journey, oh no. Not mother. *I might not live through another winter to see the spring.*' He wickedly imitated his mother's high-pitched, breathless voice. 'So here we are, on our way to Antioch, when this cursed wind makes up its mind to let us travel.' He looked at the two men with Thomas, liking the look of the soldier-like younger man. He looked a second time at Blue, taking in the big man's size and broad shoulders. 'You're a mite on the short side, aren't you, little feller?' He grinned amiably, his dimples flashing, sure no offence would be taken, because none ever had been taken. He had always had that easy way with him, Thomas remembered. Take nothing seriously and nothing serious will take you. That had been his motto.

'Cursed wind maybe, for you, but a blessed wind for us. It's been a slow journey. We've just this hour arrived, and lucky to catch the fleet. Look Roger, we've much to do if we're to sail tomorrow.

Perhaps we could meet this evening?' He hoped not; the old life was dead and gone and he feared Roger would want to breathe new life into it. But Roger would no doubt be seething with curiosity. Thomas d'Eyncourt, the squire who vanished in the night without trace and who was standing in front of him, solid flesh and blood. There would be a story here for sure.

'For certain,' Roger said. 'My mother is with friends tonight and has already said she doesn't want her son there "*reminding me of what I should and shouldn't eat and drink.*"' Again the good-humoured mimicry. 'Your friends as well?'

'Perhaps. There are more of us and a parting of the ways tonight for some of us.'

Giles listened to the conversation, evasion on one part and keen curiosity on the other. He was amused and curious enough himself. 'I'm sure Sakoura would wish your friend to join us,' he murmured helpfully. He swallowed a grin at the expression on Thomas' face.

'What about the curfew?'

'Another one to bed down for the night?' Giles shrugged. 'The house is in the Turkish quarter,' he told Roger.

'Is it so? That would be an adventure. We've kept only to the merchant's quarter while we've been here – apart from church-going, that is.' His face was bright. 'Never had a meal in a Turk's home before. It would be something to tell them back home.'

An adventure, thought Tom. Something so simple, so harmless, so everyday yet this carefree boy-man saw it as an adventure. What would he think by the time he reached Jerusalem? What would he think of their tumultuous journey? He caught Giles' eye, saw Blue turn his face away to hide his mirth, caught back his own laughter. No, not a hope of putting him off. *Wel*, as Dai would say, so be it.

'I'm sure Giles is right and Sakoura would be delighted to welcome one more. His father-in-law is the Turk,' he added. 'It is his house where we shall stay. Sakoura is from Mali.'

'Mali,' breathed Roger. 'Where the city is paved with gold?'

'You'd best ask Sakoura if that is so.'

'I shall. I'd be honoured to join you.'

'Meet us by these steps. Best not be late. Remember the curfew. Better tell your mother you won't be back till morning.' Thomas couldn't resist the advice. He hoped Roger's mother had more seasoned companions than this one.

As they parted company, Blue caught a glimpse of two figures he recognised. A big-bellied, shrill-voiced creature strutting like a peacock on the further side of the harbour wall. With him a mountain of a man. If Blue had been close enough he knew he would have seen a thin seamed ridge stretching from the corner of the man's left eye down to his jawline. 'They're here,' he breathed. 'Vecdet and that great oäf he keeps with him.'

'Stay out of trouble, Blue,' Thomas warned. 'No time for it – and you've a family to look out for now.'

'Aye, A have that,' he agreed. All the same, it was with a regretful shake of his new-trimmed head.

26

In the blink of an eye he was swallowed by fate
As a speck of straw on to a lump of amber flies
(Shanameh of Ferdowsi, 10/11thC)

The merchant remembered them. He would make a good deal for them, he promised. Dai smiled and nodded and mentally subtracted half the amount the man demanded, knew Rémi, shrewd boy, did the same. Trouble was, little time they had for haggling. They agreed on a price for the spun gold that was more than Dai knew he should pay but he knew as well there'd be as good a price in Venezia. Better. He hesitated over a bracelet cunningly worked in twists of gold and silver and copper; beautiful it was, the kind the women of this town kept close covered in the public street and admired in the privacy of their home.

'Fine craftsmanship,' the merchant said. 'You will not find its like in all Attaleia. You wish to buy?'

'Too costly for me,' Dai said but he knew he would buy it all the same. He caught Rémi's understanding smile and felt the heat rise up his throat.

He and Rémi negotiated the fees due to the city state and headed for the house of Sakoura's father-in-law. The street next to the mosque that had been a church, Sakoura had told him, an ancient church until the Selçuk Muslims had made it a mosque. They'd taken down the Christian bells and fashioned them into lamps to use inside the mosque and so the two religions were still there, one inside the other, much as the sacred books shared the same prophets. And what, Dai thought, would the Pope-in-Avignon make of that? It was as Sakoura said: they couldn't miss the way. They reached the cross roads where one street led to a *hamam* but they were to keep straight on and there ahead of them was a huge building with stone carving that was clearly Greek, not Muslim.

It was late in the day. Not long till curfew. He hoped Twm had secured berths for them. If not – well – needed rethinking, didn't it? Meanwhile, a last night in this strange and beautiful land then the long voyage back to Venezia then overland to Ieper, God and winter permitting, and Heinrijc Mertens. After that? *Wel, amser a ddengys*, isn't it now? Wait and see. Happen the old grandfather was dead. If so, he couldn't leave her alone and friendless in a strange land. Honest now, Dai, you couldn't leave her if you wanted, could you? Head over heels, you are, *dros ei phen a'i chlustiau mewn cariad,* and helpless with it.

'There it is now,' he said to Rémi as the huge church-mosque came into view.

Kazan and Niko were restless. True, they were tired but it was a once-given chance to explore this coast city where so many mingled. The house of Sakoura's father-by-marriage was comfortable, very comfortable, with its cool buildings ranged around a courtyard and pool and fountain; two storeys, the lower one of good stone, the upper wood-framed, and all carpeted with beautiful rugs. 'It is one of the old houses,' Sakoura's wife told them. Neither she nor her father had shown any surprise when Sakoura arrived with a large party of foreign guests. It had happened before; it would happen again. That was Sakoura, and they loved him for it. Besides, they had so much it was a sin not to share.

'This house, it was falling into ruin after so many years but it was still sound so after the wars my father claimed it and re-built it.' She was proud of the garden. 'Orange trees,' she said, 'such as the Bey has in his own gardens. They are very pretty with these dark green leaves and white blossom in spring that has such fragrance it makes your head spin. We did not know we could eat the fruit until Sakoura showed us how.' She showed them the fruit hanging like small green moons, some blushed with pale orange. 'It is too bitter now but in one – maybe two – months more they will be bright like the full moon and then they are ready to eat. They are sweet and tart at the same time.' She smiled at Hatice. 'Then you shall taste them,' she promised. Already she liked this gaunt, stern woman with the scarred forehead and cautious smile who was, Sakoura had informed her, a new addition to her household.

Sakoura's face glowed with pride and amusement at the way his pretty wife showed off her knowledge. He reached up and pulled at one of the green balls and dug his thumbs into its surface. Juice sprayed into the air and with it a sharp, nose-tingling scent. 'See,' he said, 'there is a bitter skin and pith but the fruit inside is as my wife says, sweet and tart. Why grow such trees for decoration only when they can be useful?' He breathed in the smell of the fruit. 'This is winter to me,' he said, 'when so many little moons hang in the trees and light up the dark days.'

It was clear that Sakoura was more than a cameleteer, more than the son-by-marriage of a favoured daughter who was as slightly built as her husband, with lustrous eyes and dark hair dimly seen through her gauzy veil. She was a prize-bride for any man yet her father had given her to Sakoura, his freed slave. The father was an elderly man, frail now, and kept to his quarters. He had come to welcome them but his daughter had soon taken him back to his own rooms. Sakoura was the head of the household. Whatever quirk caused him to act as a hired man was for Sakoura to know. In Attaleia, his good name was known. They were made welcome for Sakoura's sake and then for their own. Rest, they were told, and later there would be a meal to celebrate Sakoura's return and the wonder of two betrothals made on the journey – and it was their last night, all of them together.

But Kazan and Niko did not want to rest. The restless city called to them. Niko wanted to taste the sweet mouthfuls that were theirs for a few *akçe*. Kazan wanted to see this great place, bigger and grander than their closest walled town. And the harbour where they would go in the early morning and from where she would leave the country that was home. Only a peep, they would not be missed, not if they went now and took care to be back well before the curfew call. It could do no harm, surely?

At first, there was excitement. The chaotic streets, the people of all races and creeds, the traffic, the bazaars, the noise…in the section for metal workers they saw Dai and Rémi deep in bargaining with a tradesman whose hands and arms waved in the air like branches and twigs of a wind-swept tree. They caught a glimpse of Blue, taller than all the rest, at the head of the steep flight of stairs leading down to the harbour, his gaze fixed on something that had caught his eye. Guiltily, the truants slid away down the next street sloping down to the harbour, threading their way through the crowd rushing to complete the day's work before the gates were closed, before the evening call to prayer halted all activity.

They saw him a stone's throw away, a solid, square, swarthy man. Not tall but wide and plump, with a thick fleshy neck like an ox and buttocks like an ox. They knew that when he spoke it would be with a high piping voice, like a gelding. Niko went white as winter mountains. He slipped his hand in hers.

'Let us go back, Kazan.'

They turned but it was too late. The man had seen them. A moment of recognition then that loose-lipped, sensual mouth stretched into a smile. He nodded. At first they thought it was at them. Realisation came too late. Aziz was behind them, smiling his awful, one-sided smile, his heavy hands hoisting them up, one under each arm. Flailing arms were no defence. A heavy slap was all that was needed. 'Blue!' Kazan shrieked. 'Thomas!' A huge hand clamped her mouth and nose, cutting off all air but Niko took up the yell, screaming: 'Thomas!' high-pitched and desperate. The trio at the head of the steps were too far away to hear the cries; there was too much noise and bustle. What was one more cry amongst all these?

Roger de Comfrey heard the shrilled name. Thomas, he thought. How many Thomases were here today? He was pleased he had bumped into this aloof fellow-squire from so many years ago. Life had been adventurous then, holding out so much promise when they were training together. Now, he led a plodding existence at home, the man of the house since his father had died though, in truth, his mother ruled the household. It was his mother who had arranged a bride for him, an amiable, sensible girl made desirable by her father's lands. When he returned from this pilgrimage, it would be to marriage and the serious business of begetting sons. He sighed. A little adventure in his life before domesticity, that was all he asked, but little hope of that, tied as he was to his mother by their mutual affection as much as her leading-rein. He had a suspicion she was taking him away from England before the rumours of war with France became a reality. Thomas. The shrilled name echoed in the air. Wasn't there some never-spoken-aloud story about him that he should remember?

Curfew almost on them. 'All done?' Dai asked. It needed no answer. Baggage loaded, berths secured, all dues paid and the men laid off… early morning they would be aboard, away before noon on the long journey to Venezia. God willing, it would be a smooth voyage. Tonight? *Wel*, a farewell for them, these chance-met folk who had become a part of his life. A chance-met friend of Twm's, too, though not by Twm's choosing from the look on his face, and Giles grinning as he was. He hoped it was not an ill-chance meeting for Twm. The past was past, after all. But now here was Hatice alarmed and protesting that the two were missing. No Kazan to be found, nor the boy Niko. She was sure they had gone into the streets.

'It is not certain,' said Sakoura. He was unhappy. A young boy and a boy-girl, his guests, alone in this city and strange to it? And at curfew? 'They are not in the garden?'

'No,' said Hatice firmly. She and Blue had searched the garden from end-to-end. Sakoura's wife had had the whole house scoured. They were nowhere to be found. To leave without a word, without permission, that was badly done and discourteous to their hosts. Perhaps they had hoped to creep back quietly, their absence undiscovered.

'Sir.' A servant, discreet, waiting.

'Yes?'

'It seems the young people left the courtyard together.'

'Yes? Go on, Mehmet. Tell us what you know.'

'That is all, sir. One of the young serving boys saw them leave.' A wistful young boy, envying them their holiday while he scrubbed pans and ewers.

'What time was this?'

'An hour ago, maybe less.'

'They know they must return before the curfew,' Twm said. 'They have sense, those two.' But his voice carried his doubts.

'Not sense enough to stay where they were safe, is it now?' Dai bit out. 'Who knows what might happen here? Strange to city ways they are, the pair of them.'

'Maybe they are lost,' said Mehmi. 'If so, surely someone will help them, perhaps bring them back. This house is easy to find.'

'These two,' said Twm's friend, 'they are young?' He stopped, feeling foolish.

'Yes.' Dai was curt. 'Too young to be out alone.'

'I'm not sure if this is of any use but…' He stopped again, thinking what a far-fetched chance it would be, how foolish he would sound, but the brown-faced man with the dark, fierce eyes was staring at him.

'Well?'

'I just wondered…a strange thing…maybe nothing…'

'For the sake of all the saints in my country, say what you have to say, boyo. Don't be huffing and puffing any nonsense here, now.'

Roger's face crimsoned. 'Not long after you left me, Thomas, I heard your name called. The voice was shrill and sharp, like a young boy's.' They were all staring at him now. 'I thought nothing of it at the time, you not being the only Thomas, you see, though I did think it was a coincidence, at the time.' Now he sounded more foolish than ever. His face was on fire.

'A sharp, shrill voice, you say?'

'Shouting Twm's name, was it?'

'It was more of a screech, really. And then – yes – it stopped suddenly.' Cut off, perhaps.

'Where was this?'

'I was still down in the harbour.'

'But you saw nothing?'

Roger shook his head.

'Think, now, think. Did you look to where the cry came from?'

'Well, yes, of course.'

'Then what did you see?' Dai was barely containing his anger and impatience.

Roger frowned in concentration, seeing again the teeming harbour, the fishermen making ready, hoping the sea would be safe tonight; labourers heaving bundles on board the ships; shackled slaves not sold at market returning to the place where they would be kept for the night then loaded on board the Candia-bound ship early in the morning. Slaves. The fat man and the huge, black servant with the scarred face. He was carrying bundles, wasn't he? A bundle under each arm. The bundles were moving.

'Aziz.' Dai was certain. 'Is the merchant Vecdet here in Attaleia?' he wondered.

It was Sakoura's wife who answered. 'Why yes. He is often here for the slave market.'

'Where does he keep his slaves?'

'In an old warehouse by the harbour – but there is a house he uses when he is here. It is close by the warehouse in the Merchants' Quarter.'

A small, dark room full of shadows and filthy, clinging cobwebs. There was a musty smell, as if the room were rarely used, and a faint whispering and hissing of invisible cockroaches. 'I am frightened, Kazan,' he breathed, and she hugged him to her and felt him cringe away from her. His arm, the bruised arm, was hanging uselessly. 'He will come for us,' she said. 'All will be well, Niko. All will be well. He will come.'

They were cold with fear and the clamminess of the stone-built room with its vaulted ceiling vanished into blackness. A narrow grille was high above them. Through it gleamed the smallest sliver of light. They instinctively moved towards it, saw each other's pale faces swim into view. Shadowy shapes were nearby; storage jars and crates and barrels. She clambered up one of the crates to peer through the narrow slit of the grille, but it was still high above her head. She thought she could see a corridor, dimly lit and rank with neglect and foul water but it was too dark to be sure.

She dropped back down to the ground and heard the crack and crunch of cockroaches underfoot. Her body ached with bruises from her struggles with the big man's crushing hold on her. The wound in her arm had broken open. It was throbbing painfully and, if she touched it there was thick, sticky blood under her fingers. She remembered little of how they were brought here and imprisoned in this chill, damp chamber, only the smothering hand and lurching and jolting and the agonising grip of strong fingers digging into her flesh.

'But you shall have fresh sea air tomorrow,' Vecdet had promised, smirking, his features distorted by the lamplight. 'We sail for Candia.'

'We are not slaves,' she had protested. She struggled to remember what she had been taught, to be still, an empty vessel, but it was very hard. 'The Welshman gave us our freedom. You have no right to do this.'

'It gives me great pleasure to cheat him of you,' Vecdet assured them, 'free or not free, wretched maimed creatures. And the Welshman dared accuse me of ill treatment.'

'He is a better man than you could ever be, than you could know how to be. We would have died if it had not been for the Welshman and his friends.'

'Yes?' Vecdet seemed entertained by this bedraggled, bright-haired young boy who dared defy him. 'A pity to bring down such a fearless creature as you, boy, but, life is full of such pities. And such pleasures.'

'The avalanche would have taken us.'

'Oh-ho. So it was his caravan that was caught. A pity he didn't break his neck. One dead only, we heard.'

'Asperto,' she said, reluctantly.

'Asperto?' Vecdet opened his eyes wide. He giggled, high pitched, shrill as his gelding's voice. 'Now that is deliciously entertaining. The Welshman saves him from death at my hands, and then plunges him into another death. Intriguing.' He smiled at the two in front of him. 'If you are good and well behaved, you will be sold. If you are troublesome, well then, I will have the greatest pleasure in killing you.' He was polite, his high-pitched voice even.

They did not doubt him.

Aziz stood ready. These two problems? He could deal with them. See how only a simple lash from his fist had silenced them? Let him work on them and then see. But they were two pretty boys who would bring a good profit in Candia, and so he had told his master. Give them a night of hunger in the dark and the cold; that would lower their high spirits.

'Be thankful I am keeping you alive. It would give me such great pleasure to kill you but, as Aziz says, despite your blighted flesh, you will bring a good price in Candia.' He smiled. 'Sleep well, pretty boys.' The heavy wooden door closed on them, shutting out light. They heard the bar thrust into place.

Sakoura knew the officer in charge of the city guards who insisted they lay their case before the consul in charge of the Merchants' Quarter. 'There has been an abduction,' Sakoura said in his calm, careful way. 'Two young boys.' Better not reveal the girl's identity; it would be seen as grave immodesty, were she Muslim or Christian. 'They are both in our care. The older is on his way to his grandfather, escorted by my friend here, and they must sail with the fleet tomorrow. We must enter the Merchants' Quarter tonight. It is the curfew, I know, but by morning it will be too late.'

It took a long time to persuade the reluctant consul. He was a Genoese stationed here in the Merchants' Quarter and not sympathetic to any who had dealings with the hated Venetian rivals. Besides, he had established a good understanding with the man who was accused, an understanding that included regular bribes to sweeten deals. Why should he spoil that because of these wild accusations? What proof was there? A boy's cry? A name called? Nothing more than this? The man Aziz carrying bundles? And this was their evidence? How could he demand entry and accuse Vecdet-bey of kidnap, and he a respected trader? He sighed. A heavy sigh. Very well. If Sakoura insisted, he would question the merchant. The men with him must not follow. He would not allow it. They must return to their own quarter. They were not the law.

It was a group of men, because Sakoura had many friends. Besides, this was Vecdet the Slave Trader and though the citizens of Attaleia relied on slave labour they expected the best. Sakoura's household had no slaves but that was to be expected from a freed slave. Not that they ever thought of Sakoura as a slave, especially now he was the old man's heir and married to the daughter. And such a good man who did much for the city and its poor. 'If you choose to have slaves, at least keep them healthy,' he said, and it made good sense. Vecdet's slaves were weak and feeble, half starved and lice-ridden yet he expected a good price for them. He gave Attaleia a bad name. And now he had stolen two boys who were the guests of Sakoura, the man from Mali! No matter that these guests were non-believers; they were guests and so honour was owed to them. The foreign consul was here to oversee the Merchants' Quarter; he should do something.

A slow march with an armed guard to accompany them along the street to the gated entrance of the house and a demand for entry... There was denial at Vecdet's house, of course. What boys? The *bey efendi* had no idea of what they were saying. He had slaves, yes; this was part of his trade, but boys taken in the town? Of course not. That was against the law. It was the Welshman who wanted to cause trouble. This Welshman swore he kept no slaves but now he was searching for two slave boys? There was a long history of the Welshman's anger against him. If he had bought worthless slaves, and one had died, that was his misfortune. He had insisted on buying them. If two had escaped, that happened. He, Vecdet, had no quarrel with the Welshman but for this gross intrusion on his privacy. There were no slaves here. The consul knew that Vecdet housed his slaves by the harbour, ready for loading in the morning. Look there, if he wished to waste his time. All was in order, all taxes paid, all accounted for. Now, it was late and he had a very early start, if they would excuse him. He was on the early morning sailing for Candia.

The consul shrugged and exchanged glances with his second-in-command. There was nothing they could do here. Vecdet Bey was within his rights. If they searched the cellars, as the foreigner was insisting, there could be problems with the Genoese and Venetian authorities who wanted to maintain a peaceable relationship with their Muslim neighbours – and profitable trading, of course. The foreigner would leave tomorrow; the merchant would be here next month and the month after, and the month after that. The foreigner refused to deal in slaves but the slave market brought wealth to Attaleia. He had great respect for Sakoura and had done what he could but more he could not do. Meanwhile, the gates would soon be closed for the night and Sakoura and his friends should go home for the evening Call. They considered the dark, angry face of the foreigner and advised Sakoura to take him away before there was trouble and his guest was the one under arrest.

Rémi-the-street-child slithered past them silently and as silently returned, his hands making small signs to Dai; *a room, a dark room underground*. They were there. Dai stealthily gestured thumbs up. He looked around them all, at the outraged Vecdet, the obdurate consul, the flustered officer, watchful Aziz. If he told them of Rémi's discovery, what then? By the time all was explained and a search authorised – if it were authorised – it would be too late. They would find only an empty room. Vecdet was too clever to be caught that way. Only one way to go, wasn't there now?

He apologised to Vecdet, to the consul, the officer of the guards and, later, to Sakoura's armed and determined friends. He was sorry to have disturbed them all. It was worry for the two young people, that was all. He was wrong to accuse Vecdet without positive proof. He had embarrassed his friend and host, Sakoura. Perhaps the two absentees had already returned before the gates were locked for the night. He was grateful they had been granted permission to stay with their friend in the Muslim quarter and would most certainly stay within doors. They retreated.

Soon after, the muezzins' *Akşam Ezanı* rang out and resonated over the city rooftops, echoing from one minaret to another, Come to prayer. Come to prayer. Allah is Most Great. *Allahu Akbar.* Mosques that had once been churches with bells ringing out to believers to come and worship; now, tall minarets pieced the sky and muezzins' cries pierced the air and carried out over the harbour to the sea and the distant mountains and the sky above. Allah is Most

Great. *Allahu Akbar*. Same but different: different but the same. In his own country it would be Vespers and it would be bells ringing come and worship. Dai muttered his own prayers to both the Muslim Allah and the Christian God. *Let her be safe. Let her be safe.* Contrite, he changed it. *Let them be safe. God willing. Inşallah.*

At first they didn't believe it. A low-pitched whistling. Nothing more. It came from the grille high in the wall. 'Let's look, Niko.' She hoped she sounded hopeful. She climbed back on to the crate and would have hoisted Niko up beside her, but he was white faced and trying not to shout with the pain of his arm. If he held it like so…he craned his head upwards and saw a shape against the dark cross-lines of the grille.

It was Rémi, lying flat on the filthy ground, his face pressed sideways against the grille and one eye glinting at them, and then his hand just visible against the fading light gesturing and signing. 'Wait,' it said. 'Wait and we shall come for you.' Then he was gone, without a sound, and only empty space where he had been so that she wondered if she had dreamed it all but if she had dreamed so had Niko. They hugged each other, carefully this time. They were not forgotten. He had come for them. He had come. Soon after, the evening call to prayer echoed around the city and into the shadowy cellar where they were imprisoned. *Let him find us. Let him save us.*

'Sakoura, you should go home now before there is trouble.'

'I shall not, Dai bey. These two young people are my guests and so I must take care of them.' He grimaced. 'This consul, it seems he is very friendly with Vecdet. He is not well-liked by my people. They say he takes too many bribes but he is clever. There is nothing to take to the Bey of Attaleia.' He shrugged, his hands in the air. 'But I have friends on the gates and they will let us through into the Merchants' Quarter.'

Dai nodded and closed his eyes. Kazan and Niko, kept in an

underground room and no way to reach them except through the house. He couldn't think. At least Rémi had reached them; let them know that help was on its way. Help! He breathed hard. How best to help them? Get them safe out of there?

'Dai, listen, this might work.' Twm's face was more intent and fine-drawn than ever. A desperate plan. How could it work?

A knocking on the door and a demand for entry: three men, one very drunk. Vecdet raised his eyebrows at the intrusion.

'You have left Dafydd the Welshman?' he asked. He was disbelieving. 'On the night before you sail for your grey sorry country, you leave him? All your profit you throw away like this? And you ask me to believe you?'

'It was today that did it,' Tom slurred. 'Those two boys. Runaways but he won't have it.' He winked. 'Likes pretty boys, does Dafydd.' He smirked at Vecdet. 'Nothing wrong wi' that but likes to pre… pretend otherways. Hypocrite. Accused you. Shpite! Enough, I shaid, and sho did my man Giles here. Enough. Pay me what you owe me. Not shtay – shtayin' to be inshulted by a thieving Welshman. Never should have travelled wi' him. Knew it. Knew it from the shtart. Never should 'ave…'

'Indeed? And this other? This third friend?'

'Roger de Comfrey, sir. I haven't seen Thomas for years and then there he was on the quayside. What a chance meeting! We were squires together back in the twenties. I was so pleased to see him again – he invited me to join him at his friend's house. I thought it would make a pleasant evening but…' He shook his head sadly. 'I was shocked when he told me of his troubles with this Welshman and then this intrusion into your own house. I would have left but it was impossible without giving offence to my host. And it was almost curfew.'

'But you changed your mind?'

Roger grimaced. 'It was changed for me.' He indicated the man slumped against the cushions, smiling foolishly. 'I hadn't realised how much he'd had to drink until he was deep in a fierce quarrel with the Welshman. Dagger at his throat. You know that sort of quarrel – it can only end badly. I thought it best to leave them to it but his man here begged me to take Thomas with me, out of harm's way. He said maybe you would give us shelter for the night.' Roger's smile was a blend of embarrassment and entreaty. 'So here we are, rather late in the evening. We were lucky to beat the curfew and the closing of the gates.'

Vecdet watched them suspiciously from pouchy-lidded eyes. His loose-lipped mouth pursed. 'Why are you here in this city?'

'Me? I'm accompanying my mother on her pilgrimage to Jerusalem. We hope to be on our way in the morning now the wind has dropped. As I say, this was chance-met and now I'm wondering if it were well-met or not. He's a good enough man but,' a shrug, 'truth to tell, he's quarrelsome when he's had more than he should to drink. I don't remember him like this but we knew each other long ago. I couldn't take him to my mother in this state. Besides, he wanted to come to you. Wouldn't be told no.'

'He wanted to come to me?' Vecdet's brows rose high in his head. 'Not his man's idea, then, as you told me?'

'Giles' idea first but Thomas took it up.' Roger smiled, helplessly. 'You know how it is with men in his state. He was insistent. To tell you the truth, sir, I didn't know what else to do, what with the curfew and all.' He sighed. 'It seemed a small thing to do for an old friend but now…' he sighed again. 'I am afraid we have inconvenienced you.'

'Not at all. I am just wondering why he was so – er – insistent.'

'More profit to be made from slaves than silk, he said. He seems to have some idea of offering you his services but I think he should go home.' He scratched his neck, more embarrassed than ever. 'Maybe not home – there's war brewing between England and France. Best out of it. I could perhaps persuade my mother to let him accompany us on pilgrimage. There's always a place for a man handy with a sword.' He sighed. 'Not a hope if she sees him like this. Very particular, my mother.'

'I see.' Vecdet was silent, stroking the wisps of beard that clung to his jowls. 'I am flattered you came to me. And his man?' A quick glance towards Giles standing aloof and expressionless.

'Oh, Giles goes with his master. Knows which side is best served.' Roger's eyes opened wide. 'You do not know? Thomas is the son of a wealthy man. He has been amusing himself, travelling like this, but this is enough. Giles agrees with me.' He hesitated. 'I truly think it would be best if he came with me tomorrow. Perhaps, once he is sober, he may agree. Perhaps,' he eyed the broad bulk of the man, 'you could persuade him so? His father would be relieved and – er – generous.'

Vecdet's small eyes bored into Roger. 'You think so?'

'I am certain of it.'

'You give me much to think on.' Vecdet was silent again, lost in thought. 'Much. Meanwhile, you must have sleeping quarters for the night. Aziz!' he called, sharply, 'have our guests taken to a bedchamber.' He turned back to them. 'Perhaps you have not eaten? You will join me?'

Roger smiled and smiled. 'You are very kind. We left before the evening meal. We would be grateful for your hospitality.' Giles hoisted Thomas upright, steadying him as he lurched badly. Roger sighed again. 'I would be grateful,' he amended. 'Nothing for my friend, I think, except a bed. Giles will stay with him, of course – perhaps some food and drink could be sent in to him?'

'Of course.'

'Sir, I cannot tell you how grateful I am for your hospitality and forbearance. This is a great embarrassment for me. If I'd had any idea the evening would end this way...' He let his words tail off, a strictly brought-up young man mortified by the company he was keeping. 'My mother must not hear of this,' he said worriedly.

Vecdet sneered quietly:. 'She shall not hear of it from me,' he promised. 'Now, about that supper?'

It was quiet in the streets after the curfew. Every now and then dogs howled in the darkness. Small waves lapped the harbour shore. A man laughed in the house across the street and a second later a woman's softer laugh echoed his. Giles could hear it all clearly through the window of the small chamber they were to sleep in. It was a barred window with a straight, steep drop down to the street below, but that was nothing unusual in these houses. It was a comfortable enough room with, unexpectedly, a sleeping platform piled high with quilts and cushions. A servant brought a tray of food and drink. 'That's a welcome sight,' Giles told him. He gestured towards the huddle in the bed. 'Asleep, thanks be to your God and mine. He's not an easy master.' He pulled a face at the unresponsive servant. 'All the same, he is my master and I am bound to him. No,' as the man betrayed his surprise, 'I'm no slave but it is the custom in our land to swear an oath of fealty. I am sworn to serve him.'

'I understand. We have this also.' The man struggled between his orders and sympathy because he also was bound to a difficult master. 'Goodnight, sir,' he said.

'Wait a moment.' Giles stopped him. 'I need to ease myself.'

The man smiled. 'Of course sir. If you would follow me.' He paused outside the thick wooden door elaborately carved with scrolls and flowers. A key in the lock, Giles noted.

'We are to be locked in?'

'Master's orders, sir.' He looked uncomfortable. 'He doesn't trust strangers.'

'And why should he? We may be cut-throats, for all he knows. Though I don't see why you're bothering with it now – he's going nowhere.' He jerked a thumb towards the bed.

'True,' the servant said, and left the key unturned in a sudden gesture of goodwill towards the man who, like him, served a difficult master. No one need know.

Outside the room a wooden balcony stretched around three sides of the upper floor; wooden steps led down to a small courtyard. It was similar in layout to Sakoura's house but smaller, with no pool or dancing fountain, and an air of neglect lay over all. Some of the wood, Giles noted, was rotten and some of the stair treads creaked, the second and fifth in particular. The servant had relaxed, was becoming talkative.

'It's a good house but he doesn't look after it as he should. He's a better house in Alaiye. It's a pity to let this one fall into ruin. There's many would be glad of such a house. There are so many of you merchants and travellers needing lodgings that there aren't places enough for you all. That house of Sakoura the Slave's, I've been told that's like a palace.'

'It's very comfortable,' Giles said. 'Fine carpets, a pool and a fountain and a well-tended garden.' They both looked at the one great mulberry tree that grew in a corner of the unkempt courtyard. In the light of the rising half-moon, and the flickering glass lamps hanging from hooks under the arcaded roof, the spreading branches cast intricate shadows over walls and mosaic-paved floor and the barely visible side-gate that led into a narrow access street.

'It still gives good fruit,' the servant said at last. 'Come, this way.'

Giles blessed the Turks for their love of hygiene, even in small, run-down houses like this one. He'd grown fastidious since he'd been in this country and wrinkled his nose in disgust as he thought of the evil stink and stench of the world he was returning to. As he expected, the servant had waited and accompanied him back to the bedchamber and opened the door. Thomas was still motionless, lost in his drunken stupor. 'Hasn't moved,' Giles said, 'and I pray he doesn't till dawn. Me, I'm so weary I could sleep through the night and all next day but we must both be awake before dawn. Where is the delicate Roger to sleep?'

'There is another small chamber next to this, sir.'

'If someone could wake us before the dawn Call, I'd be grateful.'

'Of course, sir.' The man hesitated. 'I think, sir, the young man will be late to bed. My master keeps late hours.'

'Oh yes?' Giles snorted. 'I can't see our Roger keeping them with him. Pity. It would do the boy good. Too tied to his mother's strings, that one, from what I can see.'

'Yes sir.' The servant's face was wooden.

'No need to look like that. I only met the man today. Man! He's a mother's boy, more like, running away from his country when it's on the brink of war. I suppose I owe him thanks for helping get that one here safely – and speaking for him.' He stretched. 'Lock us in, then. Remember to wake us early.'

He sat down on a wooden bench under the window and waited. An old fashioned clay lamp flickered and guttered. The half moon was well risen; he could see it beyond the window bars where the street lay in darkness with darker shadows in corners and gateways. It had risen to the height of the window bars when he heard the steps creaking and two sets of footsteps pausing outside the room next to him. Lamplight glimmered under the door. A loud yawn and a sleepy 'goodnight' and a higher pitched 'sleep well' in answer. A long, listening pause and soft breathing outside the door. A key stealthily, soundlessly turned. One set of footsteps. Giles counted: one step – creak – three, four – creak – continuing down to the courtyard. 'Aziz!' The piping voice carrying clearly in the night air. Giles held his breath, waiting for the sound of heavier footsteps climbing the stairs but there was nothing. No sound. No sound either from the sleeper in the bed. That didn't surprise him. He waited until the moon had journeyed past the window, waited for faint sounds from outside the door: a whisper of a footstep; the muffled, scraping sound of a turning key. He watched the outline of the door shift, move slowly inwards. A dark shape slid silently round the door and into the room.

'All well?' murmured Tom.

He waited, hidden by the wall under the shadow of the great mulberry tree. He was in a narrow side street running alongside the massive wall dividing the Merchants' Quarter from the Christian Greek. Easy to see, so close up, how the wall had been repaired again and again, old stones making good the damage done by time and war: the round ends of one-time pillars; old door lintels wedged between massive stones; a square inscribed with a circle and the sign of a cross carved diagonally into it. The elegant curves of Arabic script, holy words carved in stone. Like the church-mosque all over again, this was a city that lived side-by-side with other times, other rulers, going back and back until he was dizzy with the hugeness of it all.

He waited. One by one, lamps went out in windows and gateways. At the end of the narrow side street he could see light flickering from the street lamps kept alight throughout the night on the main streets. A dirty black-and-white cat rubbed itself against his legs then vanished through an invisible opening into the courtyard. If only it were that easy for him. He heard the cat yowl, and another answer.

He waited. The half moon was high in the night sky before he heard the sounds he had been waiting for. They came from the small side door set in the courtyard wall and almost under the mulberry tree. Muted sounds but loud for all that in the night quiet. They ceased and silence fell once more. Nothing stirred. More soft sounds and the door was open. Dai ducked under the low lintel and into the courtyard where a trio waited for him in the shadow of the branching mulberry tree: Twm, Giles and the reluctant pilgrim, Roger de Comfrey, eyes gleaming with the thrill of danger. Dai looked at Twm who nodded. All well, then. Everything quiet, everyone to bed. He moved silently back into the street; they'd agreed an owl's call and he'd made those calls often enough in the bandit days. Soft, fluting, carrying down the length of the narrow street. A pause and an answering call. Silence then shadows became substance, became men who crept noiselessly closer in the deep shadow of the wall. They halted outside the half-open door. Blue, Sakoura, Mehmi, Edgar, three of Sakoura's own men who had been eager to join this desperate venture. There they would stay unless or until they were needed. No noise, see. That was their best weapon.

Dai and Twm edged noiselessly along the courtyard wall hugging the shadow of the mulberry tree for as long as they could. The lamps hanging from under the courtyard arch would burn all night. At the further end of the courtyard they showed a night guard but he was dozing, certain that the house was secure. His master would not have it otherwise. Besides, who would want to break into this rotting, mouldering place? A small corridor, Rémi had signed. Beware dry leaves, pools of stagnant water, sherds of broken jugs. They could see the black opening but to get there they had to break away from the shadows of the tree. Their clothes were dark but they knew it was movement that would give them away, a shifting of shadows within the shadows. That, and if Vecdet had kept any of his mastiffs here at this house. No sign of them, no sound. The marauding dirty white cat stalked boldly across the courtyard; from somewhere unseen its mate yowled softly. They looked at each other. Nodded. No dogs here, for certain. They crept out of the shadow of the tree along the inside of the courtyard arches, keeping away from the revealing lamp light, until they came to the dark mouth of the corridor.

The grille was low down, at ground level, barely an opening at all and hard to spot. Dai would have stooped to it but Twm nudged his arm and shook his head. No noise – best weapon. Better not risk a low call. They crept along the rank corridor, feeling their way now in the deepening dark. A door was at the further end, a small door, very low, not head height. It was not locked but steep steps went down into an underground corridor. Stone steps but crumbling, Rémi had said, as far as he could tell. After that, he didn't know. It was dark and he dare not risk taking the time to look further.

'You've done well enough as it is, Rémi,' Dai had told him. 'We'd have no chance it it wasn't for you.'

Rémi gave a ghost grin. It was street-life learning. However long ago, however young he'd been, you never forgot lessons learnt on the streets. It meant the difference between life and death.

The door was still unlocked. The reason was clear as soon as Dai grasped the wood and felt it crumble beneath his hands. They felt for the low lintel, slid under and edged down the treacherous stone steps, finger-tipping the rough walls, toe-ing for the next step, the next, down to the black corridor, their eyes in their finger tips and toes. A scutter behind him and Twm moved too hastily. Rats. Only to be expected but unexpected, all the same. Small stones rattled down the last of the steps. They froze into stillness. Nothing. Silence. They were in the corridor, the ground firm earth under their feet, but it was pitch black, and not even a rancid smoky sheep-fat candle to guide them. They felt their way along the corridor, their quiet breathing abnormally loud in their ears. A door, this wood half rotten as well. Another door, hanging crazily half open. An empty doorway. All opened into empty blackness that stank of damp and decay. Then a solid door, new most like, with a wooden bar pushed firmly into its socket in the stone wall. Dai eased it back. Plenty of practice, see, breaking into pantries and kitchens and storerooms. However long ago, however young he'd been, he'd never forgotten lessons learnt on the run. It meant the difference between life and death, didn't it now?

The door opened on to blackness. 'Kazan?' he said in the soft, flat tones that wouldn't carry as whispers did.

'He will come, Niko,' she said again and again. 'I know he will. Have faith.' *There is always room for faith.* But so much time had passed and they were so cold and so frightened and still there was no sign from him. *There is always room for faith.*

She had grown used to the rustlings and squeakings and hissings around them. Let the creeping, crawling, scuttering creatures go about their business. They were not the enemy. They meant no harm. A rustle outside the grille. She stiffened, listened, intent. Nothing. Only a cat's call. An owl she'd heard earlier, soft fluting in the night; another cat's call. Both out hunting little defenceless creatures. Niko was uneasily asleep, pillowed against her, muttering and restless. She stroked his curly hair, kissed his forehead. Poor child. He was so young, too young to live through such troubled times. She saw again the crudely made windmill with its sails turning in the wind and the laughing boy held in Blue's strong arms. That was how it should be, she thought. Hatice and Blue and Niko, safe and happy. Not this. It should not be like this. *There is always room for faith.* He would come, she told herself, but her whole body ached with despair. At first she didn't hear the slight sounds at the door, her name spoken in a soft, flat voice.

'There they are,' Giles murmured. Four figures emerging from the deep shadows of the corridor: Dai half-carrying Kazan; Tom with Niko slung over his shoulder. Only the courtyard to edge round, then they were in the shadow of the mulberry tree, the wonderful, unexpected, life-giving door to freedom just beyond.

Giles stumbled, clutched tight to the boy, cursed silently as loose tiles rattled. The guard jerked awake.

'Who's there?'

He saw across the courtyard shadowy shapes. Not his master's men. He was wide awake now, yelling the alarm, his shouts sharpened by dread of Vecdet's fury.

Men roused suddenly from sleep in alarm and confusion, grabbing weapons and bursting into the courtyard. Tom dropped Niko on to his feet and pushed him towards the mulberry tree and the open door as Giles and Roger ducked through, Blue close behind them. Tom drew his sword free from its scabbard and knew Dai already had that lethal falchion in his hands.

Blue breathed deeply. This was more like it. Brusting for a fight, he was. And that big bastard with the squashed nose and scarred face? That cruel bully who'd hurt those two young uns? He'd a reckoning to make with that one.

And there he was, towering over the rest, huge and hard and heavy fisted. No sword. He'd charged out without it, trusting to his bare hands. Good enough, Blue grunted, for he had little skill with a sword. Weapons God gave a man, now that was different; bare hands and fists and feet – teeth and nails, if needs be. Blue charged towards him. And then recoiled feeling as if he'd smashed his fists into the stone wall behind him. He shook his head to recover himself and clenched his fists again, smashing blow after blow after blow, forcing the huge man back a step, and another. Then, out of nowhere, a massive fist landed a blow that sent him reeling. He felt blood in his mouth, blood pouring down his face and blinding him. He swiped it away, somehow twisting and dodging the next murderous blow but it landed on his shoulder with paralysing force. He staggered backwards into two who were close-fighting and the clashing of their swords rang in his head. Big Aziz was towering over him, his booted foot poised ready to stamp into the shamefully soft flesh of his belly and groin. Blue flung himself sideways and rolled and rolled again. He lumbered to his feet but his timing was wrong. The man's foot swung hard into his ribs. He felt a crack and realised he was wrong: this man was more than his match. This man was hardened by cruelty while he, Blue, was softened by drink and quiet living. Out of the corner of his eye he saw the boy he would have taken as son, and the boy who was a girl and full of courage. He shook himself clear-headed again. He could not lose. These two were dear to him, trusted him, loved him. Hatice whose poor ravaged forehead told him of brutality and suffering. Dai who had taken him in. Edgar-the-altar-boy who had won a fair, pale bride. All these. He could not let them down. He gathered his strength. He must square up and fight and win.

Edgar staggered with the impact of Blue's fall. He felt the clash of the guard's sword against the flat of his own, felt pain in the palm of his hand and vibration travel up his arm and jar his whole body. He was no fighting man but he'd insisted on his share in the rescue and here he was helpless, confused, his back against the wall. His opponent swung his sword up and over his head and lunged in for the killing stroke. Somehow, Edgar shifted sideways, heard the singing blade travel past him and hit the stone wall, the singing reverberating on and on and on like the struck bells of the monastery. The guard followed the strike and fell against the pommel, the wind knocked out of him, and in that moment Edgar brought his sword edge up and across the man's body, but the blow was too feeble to do more than rock him off balance. The man stumbled sideways and took a fresh hold on his sword but Edgar had already shifted his grip, raised the pommel and smashed it up under the man's jaw. Once, and again. A third blow caught the side of his head with a sickening sound of bone crunching. The man fell to the ground.

Dodge back, knee up and boot kicking hard into the man's groin, sending him staggering back, arms flailing; a stride forward, blade up and arrowing towards the man's body and in between his ribs; twist and pull. Dai felt movement behind him and whirled round, deftly side-stepping, falchion lifted and sweeping down, slashing deep into the man's leg and cutting through, the force of the thrust keeping it going, almost severing the leg, and the man howling and clutching at the spurting blood. Dai ignored him, focused on the next attacker, launching himself at the man's knees and pulling up, sending the man backwards and across the sword-swing of Giles' opponent. The swing caught him full across the face. Giles jabbed under his opponent's raised arm and into the exposed armpit. He spared a glance at Dai's intent, expressionless face streaming blood from a slash wound. His body was balanced, tensed, his hands in their leathered gauntlets grasping the pommel of the falchion, crunching upwards into the under jaw of a guard who had launched himself forward. One glimpse, then Giles saw no more as he parried a thrust and tangled the man's arms, bringing his own blade against the man's neck, forcing it into his flesh, cutting off air. He was hardly aware of the man behind him until Tom was there, his free arm grabbing and trapping the man's sword arm by the elbow, his own sword sweeping down into the flesh and bone of the trapped elbow. Metal struck against metal, ringing and echoing in the confines of the courtyard. Grunts and cries of pain and heavy panting breaths. The din of men desperately doing each other down to death. From beyond the wall came the first cries of alarm and the pounding feet of the night watch.

Vecdet looked down on the chaos from the balcony. How had it happened? How had the Welshman and his man found a way in? And his men, his own fighting men, taken by surprise, forced back, on the edge of defeat? That night guard, that useless, woman-hearted creature; that blow-fly-ridden turd; blind-eyes he had been, and blind-eyed he would be before the night was done. And those three, betraying his hospitality, traitors all, fighting alongside the Welshman. How could he, Vecdet, the wily one, be so taken in? His beady, pouchy eyes blazed like kindling. That boy, that slippery creature who had escaped him once before. He was the one. Let him be destroyed now as he should have been destroyed then, like the vermin he was. Vecdet eased his bulk down the steps, his back against the wall. There he was, the wretch, at the foot of the steps, a thin-bladed dagger glinting in his grasp. Well then. He pounced, grabbed the boy, dashed his wrist against the sharp edge of the stone wall and heard with satisfaction a gasp of pain. Good. He grabbed the dagger as it slipped out of the boy's grasp and hauled the wretch upright by the hair on his head, twisting his podgy hands tight into the strands and up the steps backwards, one by one, yanking remorselessly when the creature stumbled and cried out with pain, up the steps, one by one to the top. He stood on the balcony with the boy pressed against his fleshy body, pinioned by one engulfing arm so that the sour stench of sweat rose to the boy's nostrils. The boy's own knife, sharp-pointed, fine-honed, he held under the boy's ear, its tip just pressing into the flesh. 'Dafydd the Welshman,' he shrieked in his gelding voice. It carried over the courtyard. 'Look here.' It was enough. Chaos ended and silence began. 'Stop now or the boy dies.' He imagined sliding the point into that neck, lusted for the feel of the flesh giving way under the blade, sliding up and into the eye sockets and reaching into the head space. He shivered with pleasure. But he must not. Not yet. That was to end his own escape. 'Put down your weapons.' The Welshman's sword was the first to clatter to the ground.

'Let him go free.'

'Tell me, Welshman, why should I do that?' He smiled, sure of himself again. He had the boy, his sure shield; the fool of a Welshman would do anything to keep the boy safe. And that commotion at the gates, the night guard demanding entrance, let that be to his advantage as well. 'Let them in,' he shouted. 'Let them see how this murdering Welshmen breaks his word as easily as he breaks the peace of the curfew.' Then there was searing pain in his wrist and he screamed. The wretched boy had bitten him to the bone. In the moment he relaxed his hold the boy twisted and wrenched himself out and away and fell flat against the balcony railing, gasping and panting. The rotten wood cracked under the force of his fall. Vecdet lunged towards him, the thin point of the dagger raised. He crashed against the broken balcony railing. Crashed through rotten wood. Crashed through and down to the courtyard below. His huge body smacked dully on to its surface. His head cracked sharply on the tiles. Blood seeped in a dark pool.

Kazan could never quite remember the afterwards. The guards

arriving, yes; the consul roused from his bed and loud in disapproval until it was clear the two young boys had indeed been stolen. This was not something that could be explained away. Vecdet was dead but there was no one to blame. A rotten balcony, and the man threatening death to the guest of an honoured citizen, in front of witnesses, Sakoura's friends, who would demand justice of the Bey. The consul saw the way the wind was blowing. He was already regretting his refusal to search the property. Best let these travellers leave in the morning, keep the events of this night from the Bey, if that was possible. At least keep it from Genoa. And there was Vecdet's man to deal with, the huge, hulking Aziz, battered and bruised, one eye swollen and closing up, confused at his own defeat and loudly grieving over his dead master. That other big man looked in no better shape.

Blue had never felt so beaten. His whole body hurt. He had lost one tooth at least and his mouth was full of blood. There was blood in his eyes. He had a broken rib. But he had won through.

Tom watched Dafydd's rush up the stairs to the girl. She was dazed and shaking, clinging to the fragile railings. He watched as Dafydd pulled her away from them and to safety close against him, cradling her. 'Safe now. Safe.' His hand was stroking her hair, smoothing away fear, because that was what he did, this one-time pot-boy. He brought comfort in the dark to terrified creatures, man or woman, boy or girl. His conscience, that terrible conscience, bound him to care for any strays who came across his path, even the coward son of a knight-at-arms, sobbing in terror in the blackest night. *Safe now. Safe.* And in the caring he found some comfort himself, and relief from the guilt of being alive when those he loved were dead. I thought myself dishonoured, Welshman, but I was wrong. I was wrong. *Safe now. Safe.*

Roger was bright-eyed still but his boyishness was gone. There had been so much at stake. This was no game. *Take nothing seriously and nothing serious will take you. That had been his motto.* And now? It was life and death. No game. Sword piercing flesh. Life ended on a sword thrust. A dagger's blade. A pommel smashing into a man's brains or his jaw or smashing the teeth from his head. A fall from a balcony on to the hard stone below. He thought he would for ever remember the sickening crack of skull on stone.

'I would rather be a pilgrim,' he confided to a miraculously unscathed Edgar and a torn and bleeding Thomas. They were standing in the dark shadowed secrecy of the mulberry tree waiting for the consul to make his decision. Edgar opened his mouth to agree but it was Thomas who spoke.

'And so would I,' said the dark man.

Roger paused the moment it took for his heart beat to pulse and pulse again. 'You had no pleasure in warfare even when we were squires,' he remembered. 'Not even the pig-hunts.'

'Never. To kill. Be killed. What life is that? To torture, maim, crucify your enemy. What victory is that? Christ was crucified for our sins and our redemption and yet we fight on and on spilling more and more blood.'

'You should have been the monk,' said Edgar. 'Not me.'

'Yes, I think so too, Edgar, I think so too.' Thomas was surprised at his own words.

27

Let's go, we two, my lovely girl.
O white-bright face, my maid whose eye's
a glowing ember, if we'll go, let's go now
(Dafydd ap Gwilym, 14thC)

Later. Sakoura's home. His wife and Agathi and Hatice there to welcome them with caresses and soft exclamations of distress. The wounded were tended and eased though it would take time for ragged cuts and gouged flesh to heal. Niko was asleep pillowed between Hatice and Blue, with Agathi never far away. She was leaving him at daybreak, this brave young brother of hers, and what had seemed right yesterday was no longer so but she was promised now to this young man with the golden curls and very blue eyes who she loved with all her heart. Yet she owed her brother her love and loyalty as well. She felt as if she had awoken at last from the nightmare that had kept her in its thrall for so long now. Edgar felt her distress. He didn't know what to do or say.

Blue gritted his teeth against groans. He was wrapped in salves and bandaging and Hatice's care. Already they were a family, intent on each other, careful for each other. He thanked God and Allah for his good fortune. Maybe, sometime, they would journey to his own country and she could see for herself the broad, flat land of his birth but somehow he doubted it. His life was here, with this woman and the boy. Life moved on. He had seen indigo-blue on the stalls in the bazaar on their way through to the harbour.

There was firelight and lamplight though it was close to dawn.

Roger sprawled against cushions, exhausted. 'Is it always like this with you?' he asked Giles.

'Only since Kazan joined us.'

'That is not true. Do not listen to him, pilgrim.' Her voice was sleepy. She was nestled against the Welshman, safe, her face burrowed against his sleeve. She had confessed her shame to Sakoura. She should never have left the safety of his home, never should have taken Niko with her. It was against the laws of hospitality and, worse, had taken them into danger and others with them. Dai had told her of this fault in her but she was guilty of the same fault yet again, and this time it was beyond forgiveness. Sakoura shook his head. 'Enough, child. There is no need to chastise yourself like this. You are young, and the young do such things.' He saw she was still agonised, her bright soul daunted. He smiled at her. 'You will find this hard to believe but what I tell you is true. This wife of mine, I never dreamt she could be mine. After her mother died she became a spoilt and wilful girl. Her father doted on her and despaired of her both at the same time.'

'As bad as me?'

'Worse. Far worse.' He shook his head, remembering, but he was smiling in remembering. 'I was the one who rescued her again and again from her own folly, and I chided her as a slave should not chide his master's daughter, but she heeded me, because she was as full of goodness as she was full of spirit. That was when my master gave me my freedom. He saw that love flowered between us. And now she is my beloved wife and we laugh together at her past follies.'

She hardly remembered the moment when she was free, when Vecdet had crashed through the balcony to the ground below. She remembered the rancid taste of his flesh in her mouth, and the metal taste of blood and knew she had bitten him deep. Then there was Dai pulling her away from the railing and she had clung to him. 'You came. You came.' And his grunted, matter-of-fact, '*Wrth gwrs*,' as if it were the most normal thing in the world and she had laughed wildly. 'Safe now,' she heard him breathe. 'Safe.' And his hand stroked her hair and smoothed away fear. Now she was *cwtched* against him, unwilling to leave his side. She scrabbled closer, sleepy and trying not to sleep because too many nightmares lay in wait for her.

'My honour,' Roger groaned. 'You realise, Thomas, I lost my honour, spinning all those tales for that fat slave trader?'

'In a worthy cause, Roger. What an actor!' Tom laughed. 'It was better than the Feast of Fools.' He regarded the young man's down-turned mouth. 'You were magnificent,' he said. 'Without you, we could not have carried out our plan.'

'Without Rémi,' Roger said austerely, 'there would have been no plan.'

Tom drew a sharp breath. 'You are right, my friend. If and if and if. We are all part of one great whole. This is the miracle, the mystery.' His dark, handsome, austere face creased into laughter. 'And Blue deserves credit – oh, of course, for his great battle against the mighty Aziz, and you must sing of that, Mehmi. But I never thought I'd thank him for his drunkenness. I only had to think of Blue's drunken warblings and I knew exactly how to fool the fat donkey.' There was general laughter though Hatice's smile was stiff.

Sitting all together before the crackling fire before daybreak, and none of it as they had imagined this last night together.

Roger said. 'My life has been so dull I have longed for excitement to break the monotony. Now, in one night, so much is changed. So much.' He laughed, shook his head. 'I do not think I want your lives. I hate to admit this, but my mother is right; I want a settled, secure life. I do not want to go to war with France. What has France to do with me and mine? I do not want a battlefield and the groaning wounded and sorry dead. I want my promised wife and my home and the children to come, and their children after them. I want fertile fields and secure harvest.' He looked round at them all defiantly. 'I do not count this as cowardice.'

Brother Jerome sat with them. He was exhausted by anxiety, exulted in their victory but he was, after all, a man of peace. 'To keep God's holy laws, keep a happy home for your family and dependants; cherish your lands and make all fertile.' He smiled. 'That is a good ambition. And necessary if, as you say, England and France are to be at war. There must be those who keep the peace.'

'You are right, of course, Brother Jerome,' said Dai, 'but Vecdet was not a peace-keeping sort of man.' His arm tightened about the girl, hardly believing she was safe, even now.

'He was an evil man who brought evil down on too many,' she said in a low voice. 'It is better that he is dead.'

'Little fire-eater, I cannot grieve over his death,' Giles said, wryly. 'Not a man like that.'

'What will happen to those wretched slaves now?' Tom wondered.

'I shall see that they are taken care of,' Sakoura promised.

'Aziz?' asked Blue. 'What of him?'

Sakoura hesitated. 'That I do not know.'

Tom raised his eyebrow. 'You are surely not concerned for this man, Blue?'

'He's a man like me, fighting for a life, and a good fighter at that. He had a bad master. A wonder how he would be if he had a good man to serve.'

'Who knows? Tom shrugged. 'Maybe he has learnt to enjoy cruelty too much.' He paused. 'But a man's life can change in a moment. A sweetmeat seller may happen along, or you may be travelling along a road to Damascus.'

'Or it may be a voice in a vision telling you to serve the Master rather than the man,' Brother Jerome said, 'and to turn away from a life of luxury and warfare, like St Francis.'

'Or revelations from the Angel Gabriel to a man who was once a merchant,' said Sakoura, 'like our own great Prophet.'

'Or,' said Tom, 'it may only be a boy voicing comfort in the darkness, and a hand smoothing away fear and distress.' His eyes fixed on Dafydd's, saw them widen, saw the slow smile on the brown man's face.

Later still, and dawn rising.

'There was a song I wanted to sing for you on this last night, Kazan.'

'If it is the same song I would rather you did not.'

'The same but different. This is not the night I had imagined for us all but I would like to sing for you, even so. Listen now, little blue brother.'

> '*Warrior on the prancing Arab horse*
> '*What warrior are you?*
> '*Shame it is for a warrior to hide his name from another.*
> '*What is your name, warrior? Tell me!*
>
> '*I am Çiçek, granddaughter of Sophia-the-Wise*
> '*I am Çiçek, granddaughter of Will-the-Wordmaker*
> '*I am Çiçek who rides a bright star*
> '*I am Çiçek who shines brighter than a thousands suns*
> '*A weaver of words is Mehmi the Minstrel.*'

The strings quivered into long silence. A sigh rippled round the room. Yes, the boy-girl who shone brighter than a thousand suns, who cozened their stories from their hearts and whose telling made peace amongst them all.

Daybreak, and leave-taking between those who stayed behind and those who travelled on. Roger had hoped to persuade Thomas to join the pilgrimage but he was adamant he could not. 'I have to see Dafydd safely to Venezia,' he said. 'I made my promise to Heinrijc Mertens. After that? Who knows? Perhaps my own road to Damascus.'

'I shall say a prayer for you when I arrive in Jerusalem.'

Kazan had a wedding-gift for Hatice. She held out to her the little gold ring with the carved amethyst stone she had found so long ago in the ruins of the monastery of Alahan. 'Something of my own finding to give to you for your own keeping,' she said.

'I shall treasure it always, my daughter.'

'He is a good man, this blue man,' the girl said. 'He will be a good husband and a good father, as you will be a good wife and mother.'

'As you will be to the Welshman, and he to you.'

The girl blushed poppy-red. 'You are mistaken,' she said, quietly. 'He is my very good friend, none better, but there is not the love of husband and wife between us. Besides, he is promised to a girl in his own country. The piebald is Kara Kemal's bride-gift to him. I am only Kazan who he has promised to help.'

Hatice smiled but said nothing. Time enough for the girl to discover her own heart. Of the man's she had no doubt; she had eyes in her head, and she, for one, did not believe he was promised to any other. Time enough, and a long journey ahead.

Niko was crying without shame. His sister Agathi and his great friend Kazan, both leaving him. For a moment, he longed to be going with them; for a moment, Agathi longed to stay behind with him, but the moment passed. This was what was best for them all. He stood contentedly between Hatice and Blue on the harbour side watching the last of the ships making ready.

The girl stood on the swaying deck of the cog watching the last of the ships making ready. There had been early mist on the waters of the bay, but already the sun was breaking through and patches of sunlight lit the harbour in dazzling glinting flashes of silver and blue and green. This was how she was leaving her country of seventeen summers in search of the grandfather she had never known, only stories of him. She fingered the pouch that hung from its thong about her neck and that contained the tiny axe of polished jade. A token of love so skilfully worked, so ancient, so carefully kept. 'I promised, Nene,' she murmured. 'I keep my promises.' She remembered the night she had left the camp, secretly, silently, not daring to take her leave of anyone. *Leaving, what is that? It means nothing. While the heart remembers there is no leaving.* She glanced at the man by her side, a quiet brown man with a sword cut down his face that would always be there, always remind her of a night of terror, always tear at her heart and soul. *I caused this, I who would give my heart and soul and life for you.* Now, she was not alone.

Glossary

Impossible here to give a complete and thorough account of the alphabets and pronunciation of Turkish and Welsh.

What might be useful is the following:

Turkish

ç	– 'ch'	–	softens the c, as in *çiçek* (flower)
ğ	– is silent	–	*oğlu* (son) pronounced 'o-lu'
Ş ş	– 'sh'	–	as in *Inşallah, şehir* (city)
ı	– short 'i'	–	pronounced 'uh'
i	– long 'i'	–	pronounced 'ee'

Welsh
much simpler to read than English, once the letter values are known!

c	–	always hard, as in 'k' – *cariad*
dd	–	'th', as in *Dafydd* (Davith)
ff	–	equivalent to English 'f'
f	–	equivalent to English 'v'
w	–	used as a vowel 'oo' as in *cwm* (valley)

Select bibliography

Cooking and Dining in Medieval England by Peter Brears, Prospect Books, 2008

European & Islamic Trade in the Early Ottoman Empire by Kate Flett, CUP, 1999

History of the Countryside by Oliver Rackham, Dent & Sons, 1986

History of Turkey, Vol I edited by Kate Flett, CUP, 2009

Nomads in Archaeology by Roger Cribb, CUP, 1991

The Surgery of Jehan Yperman by Dr. A de Mets (trans. L.D. Roseman MD), Xlibris Corp., 2003

Author's note

The Book of Dede Korkut is an Islamified collection of oral legends of the Oğuz Turks of Central Asia. Oral stories of shamanistic nomads may have been first written in the 14th century.

More from Honno

Short stories; Classics; Autobiography; Fiction

"Hooray for Honno" Sarah Waters

"a leading light for the writing of women." Mslexia

*"Honno's record of publishing women works not just because
they are by women, but because they are good."*
Steve Dube, Western Mail

Vibrant new fiction, autobiography, short story
anthologies, and Classics from a publisher of great
Welsh women writers.

All Honno titles can be ordered online at
www.honno.co.uk
twitter.com/honno
facebook.com/honnopress

ABOUT HONNO

Honno Welsh Women's Press was set up in 1986 by a group of women who felt strongly that women in Wales needed wider opportunities to see their writing in print and to become involved in the publishing process. Our aim is to develop the writing talents of women in Wales, give them new and exciting opportunities to see their work published and often to give them their first 'break' as a writer. Honno is registered as a community co-operative. Any profit that Honno makes is invested in the publishing programme. Women from Wales and around the world have expressed their support for Honno. Each supporter has a vote at the Annual General Meeting. For more information and to buy our publications, please write to Honno at the address below, or visit our website: www.honno.co.uk

Honno, 14 Creative Units, Aberystwyth Arts Centre, Aberystwyth, Ceredigion SY23 3GL

Honno Friends
We are very grateful for the support of the Honno Friends: Jane Aaron, Annette Ecuyere, Audrey Jones, Gwyneth Tyson Roberts, Beryl Roberts, Jenny Sabine.

For more information on how you can become a Honno Friend, see: http://www.honno.co.uk/friends.php